WICK AND ARROW

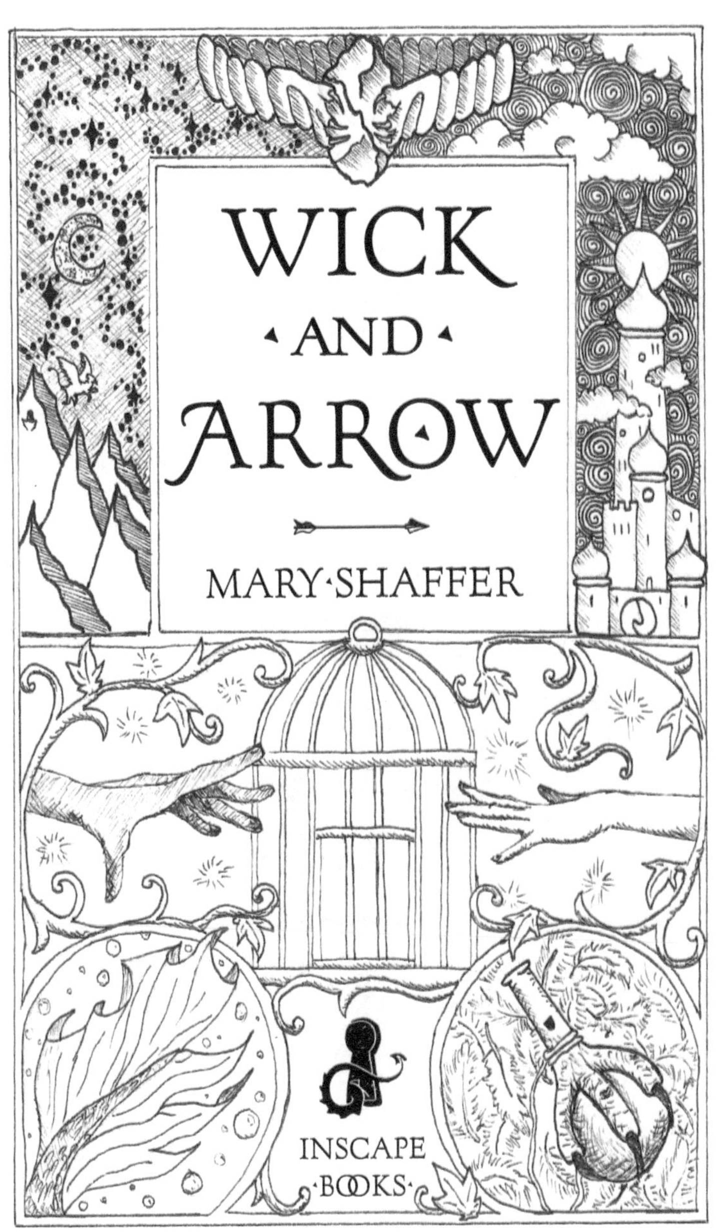
WICK
AND
ARROW
MARY·SHAFFER
INSCAPE
·BOOKS·

First hardcover edition, February 2026

ISBN 979-8-9986136-2-3
Library of Congress Control Number: 2025909290

Cover design by Hannah Reller, Daniel Brechting, and Megan Pilcher
Interior art by Daniel Brechting

This book was typeset in CalifornianFB Text.

Inscape Books
New Richmond, WI, USA

wickandarrow.com

For Erika Zabinski

Contents

PART I

THE PARADOX

"That which is in motion must arrive at the halfway point before it arrives at the goal."

—Zeno of Elea

I

Someone tried to teach Arrow a paradox, once.

A visiting wizard, with yellow smoke for a beard and eyebrows like two pine branches sagging under wet snow.

Between all things, he said, *is a space we can never cross over.*

He put her hand thus, palm facing his. Then he showed how his hand travelled half the distance toward hers, and again half, and half again, and so on, until his palm met her palm and his rooty fingers bent hers slightly back.

Even now, we do not touch. It is mere illusion. Between your hand and mine stands an infinite sliver of space. A half of a half of a half of uncountable halves. Do you understand this, child?

Arrow closed her eyes. She pushed each of her fingertips—one, two, three, four, five—against the wizard's. Her hand was hot; his was dry and cool as a crust of bread.

Wizards, as everyone knows, are born with only two fingers and a thumb. A wizard grows new fingers—one on each hand—each time he does a truly impossible thing. The handprint of a wizard shows his rank. A newborn is called a Wizard of Three; he remains an apprentice until he becomes a Wizard of Five.

The hand that pressed against Arrow's had as many fingers as hers, plus two more sticking out like crooked twigs. A Wizard of Seven. He had done four impossible things.

Yes, she said. *I feel it. I feel the space between us.*

Her other hand stretched toward Wick's hand. Wick put out his palm as she reached for it, mirroring the wizard with round-eyed solemnity. Arrow closed her eyes again. She shook her head.

But not between me and Wick. All the space is gone. Someone must have taken it away.

Arrow could not remember a time when she had not known Wick. That is, she could not remember a time when she had known any human other than Wick. That is, she could not remember a time when she and Wick had not lived together in the cage that hung in the southeast window of the boudoir of the Queen of the Giants.

She must have had parents. How else would she have gotten the name Arrow? Names did not drop out of the sky. Perhaps she had the kind of mother who baked apple dumplings, laughing while Arrow's father stole kisses.

Arrow had never seen anyone bake apple dumplings. She had never been outside the boudoir of the Queen of the Giants, where the cook brought a platter of apple dumplings—already baked, each as large as a human girl—every Tuesday afternoon for the meeting of the Highborn Ladies Concerned for Culture.

Arrow had seen many people steal kisses. That is what a boudoir is for.

The Queen's boudoir stood between her public parlor and her bedchamber. Only certain types of giants were allowed to enter it. Arrow could tell which type they were from the way the Queen said from the parlor, "Ah, but *that* is in my *boudoir*." Either a firm apology, or a suggestive invitation. The boudoir contained many curiosities: two stuffed dragons who served as bookends, a globe of swirling liquid in which was preserved the remains of a silver-colored sea-serpent, a rug made of the pelts of several hundred bears, and a cage with two live human children, who danced and sang at the Queen's command.

The cage had formerly housed one of the dragons, before it was stuffed. Because the habits of humans were closer to those of giants than dragons, a few fitting comforts had been added. A silk handkerchief strung from the bars formed a curtain around the bed, which had formerly served as a nurse's pin-cushion. A thimble functioned as a chamber-pot, a porcelain teacup for a bathtub.

The humans' clothes were stitched by the Queen's own tailor. Arrow's gowns were miniature copies of the Queen's latest costumes. Wick wore a variation of the same, with pantaloons.

Whenever the Queen introduced a new guest to her boudoir, she would show first the dragons, then the sea-serpent, and save the humans for last.

"Ah, here they are!" the guest would cry. "I've heard them much talked about, of course. They're even smaller than I imagined. How many years have you had them now?"

"At least ten. They were babies when I got them, no bigger than my thumbnail, each!"

"I'm told they sing and dance in the most amusing way."

The Queen would smile. Lifting the cage from its hook by the window (Wick and Arrow had to grip the bars of the cage to keep from tumbling over), she would set it on a round, three-legged table that stood in the middle of the bear-pelt rug.

Taller than three trees, the table was used exclusively for this purpose. When the Queen unlocked Wick and Arrow's cage, they had to grip each other's hands—tight, tighter!—to find the courage to creep from their familiar prison into this new one with its walls of air.

"They invent the songs themselves, and the dances, too," the Queen would boast. "Guests from faraway places—wizards and such, who stumble across humans from time to time—say they have uncommon talent for children their age."

The Queen would bring her face so close Arrow could no longer see it. She could only see one slick black pupil snapping out from under an eyelid, or the deep holes of pores pocking a nose, each big enough to stick a finger in. The wet heat of the Queen's breath would blow back Arrow's hair as the giantess hissed, "Sing."

Sometimes the Queen did not like the song or the dancing. She was especially testy on Tuesday afternoons when they performed for the Highborn Ladies Concerned for Culture. Several of the ladies had highly nuanced tastes, and they made comments the Queen, not understanding, inevitably took to be criticisms.

After the guests left, the Queen would take the cage and hold it next to the fireplace, which was built in the shape of a wide, grinning mouth, with a chimney for a nose and a stone mantel carved to resemble a moustache of curling smoke. The Queen would bring the cage closer to the greedy mouth until Wick and Arrow pressed against the back of the cage, screaming.

"If you don't sing better next time, I will throw you in the fire," she would say.

They begged and pleaded (all the time, the metal of the cage was getting hotter) until the giantess relented, hanging the cage back on its hook near the window. Sometimes the children's skin turned red and puffy, or their eyebrows singed off. But even then, they could not write sad songs; the Queen did not like them.

Every two years, the Queen of the Giants bore a son. She currently had eight; the eldest was fifteen, and the baby had just passed his first birthday. All but the two youngest were allowed to come into her boudoir whenever it was unoccupied. The Queen had no daughters, which might explain why each of the giant princes, in his own way, had a special fascination with Arrow.

The eldest and third-eldest liked to take Arrow out of the cage and tease her. The fifteen-year-old, Prince Dob, would set her down near the edge of the three-legged table. Making a wall out of his hand, he would slowly push her until she teetered off the edge. The eleven-year-old, Prince Fob, would hide under the table waiting to catch her, so that she never dropped more than twenty feet. They laughed until they cried over Arrow's shrieks of terror. Gob, Lob, and Nob, the littlest princes (except Mob and Sob, not yet allowed in the boudoir), were sometimes permitted to witness this game, but Dob and Fob never let them attempt it. If Arrow were killed by some accident, they might never recover from the beating their mother would give them.

After a time, Arrow found ways to spite their teasing. She jumped off the table before Dob could push her, and Fob had to dive to catch her in time. When they snatched her by one of her ankles and dipped her head in the brine that pickled the sea-serpent, she drank it, which made her so ill the princes dropped her back in her bed and slunk away, lest their mother find them holding a dead human girl.

"You shouldn't, Arrow," Wick murmured, holding her hair in one hand and the giant thimble in the other while she vomited. "What if you really get hurt one day?"

"It's worth it."

But Wick shook his head in the slow, mournful way that made him look eighty rather than ten. "No, Arrow. Not for them. They're not worth dying for."

"How would you know?" she snapped, pushing herself up on one elbow. Wick flinched away from the diamond-sharpness of her eyes. "They've never done it to you."

Though Wick often begged the giants to tease him rather than Arrow, they only laughed and pinched his arms and legs.

She buried her face in the pincushion bed. They both wept.

"I know what I know," he said fiercely, wiping his tears off her shoulder.

It was the Queen's thirteen-year-old son, Prince Cob, who gave Arrow the most trouble. He never pushed her off the table or dangled her over the sea-serpent tank. He unlocked the cage door and laid his palm like a drawbridge across the doorway.

"Come out, Arrow," he called softly. "Come dance for me."

If she didn't climb into his hand, Cob would reach in and pluck her out. Wick used to stand in the way, but the giant flicked Wick's legs with his finger. This caused bruises so severe the boy couldn't walk for two days afterward. So Arrow always let the prince catch her before Wick got between them.

Sometimes Prince Cob would just hold her—once for nearly an hour. Arrow thought he had fallen asleep with his eyes open, so she lay down in his palm and slept, too. But when she woke up he was stroking her hair.

Mostly, he wanted her to dance. For some reason, this was worse than getting dipped in the sea-serpent brine. Arrow would dance as stupidly as she could. Holding her arms and legs stiff, she'd hop like a cricket or teeter back and forth like a rocking chair.

"No," Cob would whisper. "Dance like a human girl. Or I'll throw you in the fire."

"You can't throw me in the fire," said Arrow, putting her hands on her hips. "Your mother would beat you."

"Dance like a human girl, or I'll flick the boy's legs."

So Arrow would dance.

Once, when a Wizard of Five came, Prince Cob asked if he knew a spell that caused human girls to grow to the size of giants. He offered to pay the wizard three life-sized golden wolves and a flowerpot that grew miniature shooting stars. In short, everything of value he possessed.

The wizard looked dubiously at the wolves, which were of rather crude design. Wick and Arrow stood silently with arms linked, blinking down at him through the bars of the cage. He shook his head. "I'm sorry, my prince. There is only one wizard with the power to change things into other things, and I hope that he may never cross your path."

One night, Wick refused to sleep in the pincushion bed next to Arrow. They were getting too big, he said; it was too crowded. But they only had one blanket, and in the middle of the night Arrow heard his teeth chattering.

"Wick, come under the blanket this instant. What's the matter with you?"

His face turned red and he mumbled. Arrow prodded until the real answer came out.

"Prince Dob said it's not right for us to sleep in the same bed, since we're not brother and sister. He said something awful, but I can't explain it."

"Since when do you listen to a word Prince Slob says? Come to bed before you freeze to death!"

Wick really was very cold, and he didn't need to be asked twice.

"Anyhow," said Arrow as she put her arms around his shivering body, "I'm sure we must *be* brother and sister. Don't you think so?"

"I don't think we can be," said Wick. He held up his arm next to Arrow's. "See here, your skin is the color of cold butter, and mine is the color of rye bread."

Arrow snorted. "Oh Wick, that's got nothing to do with it at all. What matters is, we're the same height. I think we must be twins."

"If we're twins," he said meekly, "I don't think we can get married when we grow up."

Arrow shoved him and rolled over in the bed, facing the wall. "You've got every piece of it wrong, Wick. That's got nothing to do with it at all."

Neither of them could remember when they decided to get married. They didn't associate marriage with kissing and its accoutrements, for the exchange of such niceties in the Queen's boudoir had little to do with that institution. Nor did they associate it with the stuporous attentions of Prince Cob and his willingness to surrender his dearest possessions for the hope of transforming Arrow into a giantess. Nor did they associate it with Prince Dob's baffling suggestions regarding the purpose of certain anatomical differences between Wick and Arrow.

All they understood of marriage was the fact that the Queen, being married to the King, had a child every two years, and that this child was referred to as belonging to both the King and the Queen. They understood that the Queen named these children, called for them, coddled them, and that even after their issuance from her person she could have them about her whenever she wished. If Wick and Arrow got married, they could have children, and then they would no longer be the only two humans who lived in the boudoir of the Queen of the Giants.

They had already chosen the names of their future children and decided what qualities each would have. Whenever they got bored, they thought up a new one. So far, they planned to have twenty-seven.

"Boy or girl?" Arrow would say.

"Girl," said Wick. "Her name will be Bluebella Rainbow, and she will have blue hair and rainbow eyes."

"That's a stupid name," said Arrow. "But blue hair is nice. We could call her Sky Rainbow."

"Rainbow Sky. She will play the bagpipes and she will be able to fly."

"Humans can't fly, Wick."

"How do you know?"

"Well... because *we* can't fly."

"Maybe other humans can. Maybe nobody taught us."

Arrow thought for a long time. "How can we teach Rainbow Sky, if we don't know ourselves?"

Wick put on his worried old man face. Arrow felt worried, too. Sometimes it fell on them like the weight of a giant's pocket watch—how little they actually knew about being human.

A Song of Wick and Arrow

Pop-a hiss! Kiss kiss
Thus do the flames go
Dance swirl and sway low
Low, below and leap up high
Now, sky now! Singe, spark.
Spit more stars
Into the dark.

This is a flame song.
Speak me your name song.

Black and white, bleeding light
Charcoal and ash see
Glow, glim and flash we
Blink, it winks, and red goes cold
Now, old now. Sink, fade.
What a dazzle
You have made!

PART I · CHAPTER 1

Each morning began this way:

Wick slipped out of the bed so cautiously the blanket hardly moved at all. He tiptoed to the side of the cage that faced the window and looked out.

Arrow always woke up, no matter how quiet he was. She buried her face in the pincushion (they had no pillow) and thought three things: My name is Arrow. I am hungry. There is Wick standing at the window.

Rolling over to squint at him, she called in a sticky, crackled voice, "Wick, what do you see?"

He never saw the same thing. Never, in all the days Arrow had asked this question. Though it was always the same window and always the same mountains and always the same gatehouse and always the same sky.

"I see two sparrows fighting over a piece of grass. They must be building nests. They seem to be poking their beaks into each other's ears, except I don't think sparrows have ears."

"What else?" said Arrow.

"I see rays of orange light spreading over the tip of the first mountain like a knife smearing apricot jam on bread."

"What else?" said Arrow.

"I see the new day pounding on the door of the clouds. They haven't decided if they'll let her in. Ah, Arrow! What will happen if she can't break through?"

"Make her come, Wick. Sing to her. Pull her through."

So he did, and day came.

A Letter of Dame Pugla, Duchess
to one Lady Farpp

My dear Farpp,

How we missed you Tuesday afternoon at the meeting of Highborn Ladies Concerned for Culture! Such an edifying discussion of the architectural innovations of Lumbb, as demonstrated in the corbels of the new bridge between Buf and Pog.

As usual, we enjoyed a remarkable performance from the two humans. It is a pity the Queen, simply because she is queen, must preside over our attempts to stimulate greater cultural sensibility throughout the Kingdom, when she has no cognizance of artistic values such as those present in the song and dance of these miniscule marvels.

The boy, certainly, is the best singer. How true yet how inadequate to call him Wick, as if the flicker of a candle could best resemble the sound which emanates from his tiny throat. Nay, his strains carry some essence distilled beyond the sea. My dear, when I hear him, I feel as though a hole is cut in the firmament itself, and through it pierces a shaft of that light the refulgence of which the stars drop only a threadbare hint.

Yet in the poetry of movement, I mean to say the art of dance, the girl prevails. It is her very smallness which brings tears of wonder when one observes the intensity of her gestures, compact as a finger of lightning—this way her hand, that way her head, and such an arch of her back! Ah, me! We giants are but boulders rolling down hills, and she is the very wind.

Knowing your own interest in enigmatic manifestations of culture, I must share a fascinating anecdote. As others made comment on the minutiae of the performance, I happened to bend close to the cage as the humans retired inside. I observed them speaking in a language I had never heard and inquired as to its origin, knowing that the Queen acquired these specimens before they had any command of the language of their forebears. With much reluctance, the humans at last revealed that they were the authors of this language. It seems to have sprung up naturally between them; when alone they speak it almost exclusively. I enjoined them to continue conversing for my observation. They showed inexpressible reluctance, which only increased my interest. At last, when the Queen laid a hand atop the cage with a suggestive countenance, they agreed to speak.

I brought forth a small notebook which I keep on my person at all times for the purpose of recording noteworthy illustrations of culture or eccentricities of nature. I began to ask the translations of individual words, jotting their approximate spellings in my book. Certain words they spoke easily—he, she, cage, food—but I noticed a significant increase in distress as I prodded them to divulge words more redolent with poetic emotion, such as "sky," "outside," or "someday." Is this not fascinating?

And then, my dear Farpp, they grew mute. I do not say, "They stopped speaking," for it seems to me the poor things had no choice in the matter. They simply could not bring themselves to reveal another word. The Queen threatened and stormed, and finally brought their cage so near the fireplace I saw blisters raise on the boy's arms (he shielded the girl, though she protested). Yet they spoke not another syllable. It was I who intervened, begging clemency, for I saw that they deemed it more desirable to feel the heat of the flames than whatever it is they felt when asked to uncloak the linguistic symbols which had formed such a bond of intimacy between them.

As I think of it now, the incident brings tears to my eyes. What a strange world it is, Farpp. How much the feral excrescences of culture can reveal to us, if only we take care to perceive their epiphanies. If I were the Queen, I would not keep these humans locked away in a private collection. I should hang their cage in the center of the courtyard, and all should have free access to this "school of nature," presenting as it does a miniature pageant of the cosmos for our enlightenment.

I nearly forgot one other detail. When I asked the humans if they had written songs in this language, they replied that they had, but that they did not perform them for the Queen. As I tried to ascertain the reason for this, it became apparent that a peculiar feature of this language is that it lends itself chiefly to sad songs.

With all good wishes for your quick recovery, I remain
Your devoted friend,
Pugla

"Wick," said Arrow, "what if we are the only two humans left in the world?"

They had no mirror. It was only gradually, over a number of years, that Arrow realized she did not look the same as Wick.

What she first noticed was their hair. Hers grew down, like a river. His grew up, like a cloud. This led to the further realization that her hair was the color of dust, and his the color of soot. This led to the further realization that her skin was light, and his was dark.

But she would never have guessed their eyes were not the same. Never, until the day Wick asked, with a tone of extreme urgency, "Arrow, what color are my eyes?"

"Brown, of course."

"Brown, and what else?"

"White around the edges, with a black dot in the middle."

"And... nothing more?"

Arrow looked as carefully as she could. She shook her head. Wick's disappointment prompted her to ask, "What color are my eyes?"

"Oh, Arrow—so many colors. A dark blue center... no, let me start with the outside. A ring of gray, like the sky deciding to storm, and inside it a ring of ice—that's a blue, I mean, very light. Ah, I'm saying it all wrong, terribly wrong. And then twilight, but on top of that is a golden sun; the rays reach out through all the rest, and some of them flicker green sometimes but not always."

The hushed and trembling tone in which Wick issued this description, combined with Arrow's utter astonishment at not having brown eyes, the only kind of human eyes she had ever seen, led to only one possible conclusion. Her eyes had seen magic.

It must have happened this way: Arrow was a baby, sleeping in her cradle, and a kind fairy slipped in at the window.

"Sweet child," whispered the fairy, "won't you know me? I have watched you sleeping now seventeen nights, and you have become my cherished one. I am not allowed to wake you, but if you wake on your own and see me, the fairy law will oblige me to give you my true and only grace."

At that moment, Arrow awoke. The fairy was right in front of her nose, standing on the blanket tucked in around her. "She sees me!" the fairy cried in delight. "I must give her the grace. I have only one to give, and how I wished it would belong to her, my cherished one."

Then the fairy gave Arrow her true and only grace. Anyone who receives a fairy grace, as is well known, will grow up to be very beautiful, live in a castle made of moonlight, eat nothing but apple dumplings, and be loved and adored by all who lay eyes on her all her life long.

At the moment the fairy gave the grace, such a bright magic burned from the center of her that it dazzled Arrow's eyes, and they turned all the colors of the fairy.

"If we really were twins," Wick pointed out, "wouldn't I have been in the cradle next to you? Why didn't I wake and see the light? Why weren't my eyes dazzled, too?"

Arrow had to think about this a long time. "You had already woken. The nurse carried you away to change you. That's when the fairy came. Because I think the fairy liked girls better than boys, just a little bit."

Arrow loved to ponder that unremembered night. Everything would be alright for her and Wick, in the end. Her eyes proved it.

It became rather a habit with Arrow, after a visit from Dob and Fob, to ask, "Wick, what color are my eyes, again?"

He elaborated each time on his description until he might have been describing the jumble of silk and gems that lay beneath the lid of the Queen's jewelry box, or the largest treasure chest in the hall of the King of the Giants.

So that possession of hers which allowed Arrow to see all that she could see—the western faces of three snow-covered mountains, the army of dark pines charging up the nearest slope but never capturing its peak, the castle gatehouse and the stone wall weaving through the sinews of the mountain—Arrow saw only through the eyes of Wick.

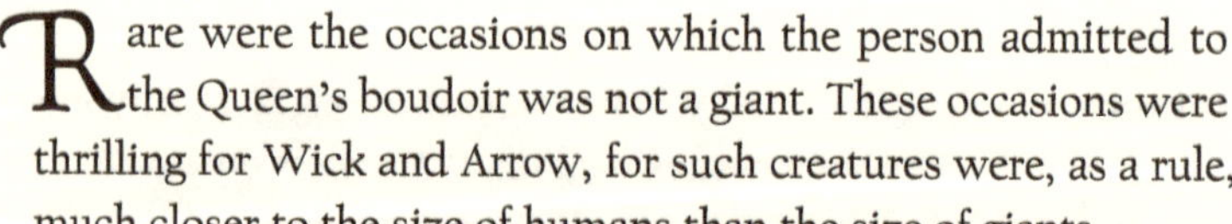

Rare were the occasions on which the person admitted to the Queen's boudoir was not a giant. These occasions were thrilling for Wick and Arrow, for such creatures were, as a rule, much closer to the size of humans than the size of giants.

Once a centaur came. The centaurs shared the mountain forests with the giants. But their shabby peace was threatened when a new, daring sport gripped the passions of the giant youth. According to giant law it was strictly forbidden to kill a centaur. (The centaurs provided medicines on which the giants depended.) Thus was the thrill of the hunt increased tenfold. Soon the only real way to prove oneself as a young giant was to take one's comrades to a secret cave and proudly reveal the carcass hidden inside. Then, to hold a furtive victory feast lest the crime be discovered.

The King apologized profusely to the centaur ambassador, unable to imagine how the thing had gotten so out of hand. He made several hastily-scribbled treaties promising a serious punishment for any giant convicted of harming a centaur. As a token of the sincerity of the giants' repentance and their genuine goodwill toward the centaurs, the Queen offered the ambassador a tour of her private boudoir.

When Arrow saw the centaur, a soaring feeling, all wings and feathers, shot up inside her chest. The centaur's human skin was darker than hers but lighter than Wick's. Its black hair grew like hers—down like a river—but was smooth and shiny as a sheet of ice.

"Wick! See! It's half a human. Half a human buried in a horse."

"Oh, Arrow," he whispered. "See how beautiful we are when we grow up."

The centaur glanced first at the stuffed dragons, then at the bearskin rug, then at the caged humans.

"I've seen enough," he said in a voice of stone and flame. Whirling, he fled. Arrow heard his hooves clatter down the long corridor she had never seen and out the gate and through the gatehouse. Then he veered from the cobblestone path and the earth must have been softer there, for he made no sound as he vanished into the forest.

They never saw a centaur again.

They saw a few griffins, with their eagle wings and shaggy manes. They saw the King of the Bears, who was later added to the rug. They saw a water nymph, who had to be transported in a sloshing wheelbarrow. They saw many wizards.

Wizards are the type of creature who must see all there is to see in the world. This is mainly due to their need to accomplish impossible things. Each time a wizard does an impossible thing, it ceases to be impossible. Therefore, each generation of wizards must search wider and deeper than the generation before it.

In the Kingdom of the Giants, great excitement accompanied wizards' visits due to the magical gifts they presented. Some of them used staffs to work spells; others merely muttered words. No giant would have harmed a wizard, but neither was a giant afraid of any wizard.

Except one.

A wizard with yellow smoke for a beard and eyebrows like two pine branches sagging under wet snow.

It was impossible for wizards to grow more than seven fingers on a hand. At least, none ever had. Only one wizard alive had achieved this highest rank. All the giants felt dread in the presence of the Wizard of Seven, for they said, "This is the wizard who changes things into other things."

He it was who tried to teach Arrow a paradox.

"If everything when it occupies an equal space is at rest,
and if that which is in motion is always occupying such a space at any moment,
the flying arrow is therefore motionless."

—Zeno of Elea

2

The Queen wrung her hands as she ushered the wizard into her boudoir. Mumbling, she made a vague gesture in the direction of the stuffed dragons and the sea-serpent, but she stood in front of the humans' cage and made no reference to it.

"I would like to speak with the humans," said the wizard.

The Queen winced. Without a word, she banged the cage down on the table and unlocked it. Bending to the floor, she offered her hand to the wizard so he could step into it. But he declined.

"I will ascend on my own."

To see what happened next, Arrow lay on her stomach and peered over the edge of the table. Wick did the same.

Approaching one of the table legs, the wizard began to climb it. Not with his claws, the way a squirrel climbs a tree; he walked on air, as if an invisible spiral staircase wound around the table leg from bottom to top. The Queen gasped and whimpered.

Arrow was not afraid. She felt something darker than fear, a swarm of shadowy sensations mingled in a solemn flutter. The world seemed to tilt on its hinges, and she was caught in the crack of a door about to swing open.

"Tell me your names," said the wizard once he reached the top.

They did. They stared at his seven-fingered hands.

"Are those your real names?"

"Yes," said Arrow.

But Wick said, "Is there something wrong with them, sir?"

Even standing next to the wizard, Arrow couldn't tell whether his beard was actually made of smoke or of yellow fuzz so light it floated. His eyes were pale gray.

"They are not proper human names at all, but words signifying objects. Humans have names like Ezekiel, Hatshepsut, or Pliny the Younger, generally denoting qualities or relations."

Wick and Arrow looked at each other, unsure whether they should bow their heads in shame.

"Oh," said Arrow. "We didn't know."

"What is your name, sir?" asked Wick.

The wizard smiled. His teeth were brown and some of them sharp. "Names do not exist."

They didn't know what to say after that.

Wick stood in his usual shy way, with his chin tucked down and one hand grasping his other elbow. He glanced from the wizard's hands to his face a few times before he found the courage to venture, "Other wizards can't climb table legs. Is it because you're a Wizard of Seven? Was that one of your impossible things?"

"It is because I am not a wizard only, but a philosopher."

"So... how did you climb it?"

"I didn't. The table is an illusion."

"Then what is the cage sitting on?" said Arrow. She stood in her usual way, with her chin thrust up and her head tilted to one side.

"The cage is an illusion too."

"It can't be." Wick shook his head solemnly. "Maybe to a wizard, or a philosopher, but not to us."

"Either it is an illusion, or it is not. Things cannot be real to some people and unreal to others. But, in fact, things are not real. Only ideas are real. If you came to understand that, you could walk off this table and out of this castle forever."

"Please," broke in the Queen, quivering with distress. "Dear sir! What are you saying? The children are very impressionable, and if one of them were to—"

The wizard looked at her and frowned. "I wish to speak with the humans *privately*."

Staggering back the Queen slumped on the divan.

Arrow swallowed. Clearly they were in the presence of a wise and learned person. She and Wick had never been taught a single principle of grammar or mathematics. They didn't know how to print their own names. She'd never felt ashamed of this before, because no one had ever asked them to do anything but sing and dance. But from the way the wizard stared at her, it seemed as if he expected her to carry on the kind of conversation exchanged by the Highborn Ladies Concerned for Culture. Her face grew hot under his gaze, and all words fled out of her mind.

"Could you carry us off the table?" asked Wick, still on the same tack. "The way you climbed up, could you carry us down on your back?"

"That is not the point." The wizard again showed his brown, pointed teeth in a patient smile. "To speak precisely, since the table does not exist, I can do no such thing. Further, since all motion is an illusion, none of us are, in reality, capable of going up or down."

The wizard tried to explain a paradox about an arrow, which, at each instant of its flight, is standing still, and therefore motionless the entire time it appears to move.

"But it will still hit," said Arrow. "If..." (she tried very hard to sound learned) "...for example, if someone drops an arrow off a table, the arrow will hit the floor, even if very wise people say otherwise. It will not be an illusion for the arrow that gets dropped on the floor. So what does it matter?"

The wizard squinted at her. "Let us try another paradox. I think this one 'strikes too close to the mark'. Ha ha. But here, put your hand thus, facing mine..."

And he tried to teach Arrow that it was impossible for their hands to touch, because of the infinite sliver of space between them. This made more sense. She could feel it, that sliver of space. Indeed, more than a sliver—there seemed an uncrossable chasm between her and the wizard, growing wider every minute.

But when she put her palm next to Wick's, the space was not there.

"You are mistaken," said the wizard. "It is impossible for two things to touch."

"I thought you said..." Wick broke in. He lost his courage for a moment, but caught it and blurted, "I thought you said things weren't real at all."

"Exactly. That's why it's impossible for them to touch."

"But I tell you, I'm touching Wick right now." Arrow was growing impatient.

"Wick doesn't exist."

Now Arrow was angry. She put her hands on her hips. The more she tried to think of a wise and learned reply, the more her words melted away. The space between her and the wizard grew wider and wider, a wall of menacing mountains.

This seemed to please the wizard. Smiling, he patted the top of her head. "There, now. What is Wick? Skin and blood and bones, made of smaller particles, made of smaller particles yet, in the end specks and dust and nothing. But what is the idea of Wick? Comfort, solace, sympathy, tenderness, cheerfulness, trust, protection, innocence, belonging, song, laughter, light, warmth, spring and summer, home, family, the end of loneliness. Love, if you will."

"Everything," said Arrow. "Wick is everything."

"The *idea* of Wick is everything."

"There's no difference." Arrow clenched and unclenched her fist.

"Are you sure?" An unpleasant look flashed over the wizard's face. It was like a hunger, like the tongues of flame that flicked out from the grinning mouth of the fireplace. "Are you quite sure?"

Arrow forgot that the Queen was afraid of the wizard. She forgot that all the giants were afraid of him. She forgot that he was the wizard who changes things into other things. She forgot that he was a Wizard of Seven, of which rank there were only three known in the history of the world. He had begun to remind her of Prince Dob.

She put her hands on her hips. "Are you quite sure you're not a coal scuttle?"

"No," said Wick. "We're not sure."

Arrow shot him a look. His face startled her.

The black pupils had swallowed up the brown parts of his eyes. He stood stock-still as the stuffed dragons on the bookshelf, but she could see his heart pounding as he stared at the wizard. Why was he afraid? Should she be afraid? She took his hand, and he gripped hers so hard she winced.

"Oh Arrow," he whispered in their own language. "Don't let go."

A Letter of Gemff, Queen of the Giants to one Lady Pugla, Duchess

My dear Pugla,

Something terrible has happened. I'm so vexed I've beaten all the servants twice since this morning. I write knowing you will understand, being so Concerned for Culture and all that. Forgive the scrawl, as I'm quite agitated.

Who do you think has done it? That wizard. The One Who Changes Things into Other Things. May a street-wench step on him this very day! What do you think he has done?

He has taken one of my humans.

The boy. Oh, he sang so sweetly, and I shall never hear it again!

This is how it happened: he found out a secret. The wizard, I mean, not the boy. I shan't tell you, of course. ~~But it had to do with someone you know whose name starts with H and a little exchange in my boudoir.~~ I suppose the humans knew all about it but it wasn't them told the wizard. They never tell. He must have read it in the very walls.

Do you know, he had the impertinence to claim I was no bigger than he was? That size was an illusion, or some such nonsense? He said it to my face! My first instinct was to thrust him down the front of my corset and squash the life out of him by simply breathing. But I didn't. He terrifies me.

Well, anyway, the wizard started talking with my humans and afterward declared he wanted the boy. I absolutely refused. So he threatened to tell the King unless I gave him up! He said the boy was needed for a philosophical experiment proving the nonreality of Things. Of course that was a naked lie, since we all know philosophy is a great joke amongst wizards. The truth was he came here determined to take one of my humans—to become a Wizard of Eight, I heard him muttering. A Wizard of Eight! What can anyone do with so many fingers? Play the harp I suppose, but I've never met a wizard who did.

I don't quite understand how he means to do it. There was nothing impossible about taking the boy, seeing as I caved right in. It must be what comes later—what he's going to do with the boy, you see—that's the impossible thing.

It was gruesome when we had to separate them. They simply wouldn't let go of one another. I tried to pry them, but if I had pulled any harder I would have broken them. You know how fragile they are—their ribs are like my fingernail parings. Eventually the wizard put a sleeping spell on them, and we got them apart.

I was with the girl when she woke up. "He's gone, Arrow," said I, "and likely forever. You know that wizard is the one who turns things into other things. The boy may be a badger now, or a hairpin." Said she, "No. Wick could never be anything but Wick." Said I, "Call him what you like, my girl, but if he's an eel, you'll dance with him no more." She crumbled then. I should have kept my mouth shut. Now she won't eat. She won't move, just lies on her bed. I'm not sure she's alive except I see her blink.

This morning I held the cage over the fireplace and told her if she didn't eat I would throw her in. Suddenly she sprang to life. You must have noticed how if I ever bring the cage near the fire, they huddle in the very farthest corner, trying to escape it. But this time, she ran <u>toward</u> the fire, threw herself against the bars, screamed and sobbed, begged it to take her. Well the heat was such she fainted away, but I pulled back the cage before she burnt up.

She won't last long now. I try to dip water into her mouth on the tip of my finger, but she won't take it. I scold and tell her it's naughty to try to die. But I wonder—is it? For a human, anyway? I can't imagine what she'll do without the boy. All their songs were duets. Now that the cage will be empty, I wonder if I could get myself a water nymph. Or would it need a pool to swim in?

Your very distressed friend,
Queen Gemff

Whenever Arrow woke up, she thought three things: My name is Arrow. I am hungry. Wick is not standing at the window.

Then the pain came. It was like this: like the mountain swallowed her. In its bowels, all was black and close and grinding. Sometimes the pain pressed on her, wedging her deeper and deeper into a dark crack until she couldn't breathe. Or it scraped her between two slabs of stone as the earth shifted its weight. The mountain let go then, and she fell into nothingness.

The nothingness was better than the pain. In it, Arrow did not know where she was, or what she was, or whether the shadows that loomed and receded around her still inhabited moments crowding past. In the nothingness there was no time. There was no hunger or thirst. There was no need for anything. There was no Wick, and no Arrow.

"Arrow."

In truth, there was one need in the nothingness. Once she had fallen into this state, Arrow had a need to remain there as long as possible. She didn't know how she clung to this need, because she didn't know anything at all. But if anyone attempted to wrench her back into the place of knowing, the place of pain, she fought him in the nameless dark that lay behind the nothingness.

"Please, Arrow. Please eat something."

A splash of warm water poured over her face. Water would not have been enough to bring Arrow out of her refuge, but when it ran into her mouth, she tasted salt. This sharpness on her tongue tore a rift in the nothingness, and a dim shaft of knowing poked through.

Arrow lay cupped in a giant's hands. She knew the hands: Prince Cob's. Another splash of saltwater followed the first, and her mind cleared still further. Soon she understood that he was weeping with his head bent close to hers, his tears falling on her face.

Then came the dreaded thing:

Wick. Wick's eyes, and Wick's mouth, and tears running in sheets down Wick's smooth brown cheeks. How he said, *Arrow, don't let go*. How they clung to each other, and even the Queen of the Giants could not pull them apart. Then—the waking, and him gone. The mountain swallowed Arrow. She gasped and shuddered her way through the pain back into nothingness.

It might have been, but she wasn't sure, that a hand reached into Arrow's cage and drew her out. It might have been that the hand let go, dropping her into a dark, soft place that was like a sack or blanket, but may have been a giant's pocket. It might have been that the giant began to walk, and Arrow bumped against his leg with each quick, nervous step.

He walked across the room. He walked through the doorway Arrow had never passed, leading out of the boudoir of the Queen of the Giants, and out of the castle, and through the gatehouse that Arrow saw every day from her window. He walked away down the side of the mountain to a place no one would guess, where the river ran swift and wide and bore straight on to the sea.

But Arrow understood nothing of this, not only because she had passed so thoroughly into the realm of nothingness, but because she was at the bottom of a giant pocket, where it was quite dark. Only when the giant drew her out and held her in the sunlight, only when her ears filled with the noisy, unfamiliar music of the river, did she realize: I am outside.

"Will you promise me," said Prince Cob, "that you will not die?"

She stared at his one green eye, which filled her plane of vision.

"I am setting you free, Arrow. This is my toy boat Uncle gave me. It's actually a real human boat. He found it in the sea and shook out all the humans. He brought it back for me to play with in my bath, but I'm too old for that now. I'm going to put you in it and send you down the river to the sea."

The giant laid Arrow on the smooth wooden deck of a boat with one square sail. The boat was not wider than her cage, but nearly twice as long. Reaching into his other pocket, Prince Cob pulled out a loaf of bread four times as big as Arrow, which filled a third of the boat. He brought out a porcelain teacup, one of the Queen's favorites, and dipped it in the river, filling it with fresh water. This, too, he set on the deck of the ship; it filled another third.

Arrow was not strong enough to stand. She lay on the deck of the ship and breathed. Her chest pressed into the wooden planks, and their roughness proved with each breath that they were real.

"Will you promise to eat?" said Prince Cob. "Will you promise to live, Arrow?"

She said something, but he could not hear. Bending down, he plucked the boat out of the water and held it close to his ear.

"Help me," she said. "I will try."

He broke off a crumb of bread and put it in her hand. Finding what he thought was a small wooden thimble in a corner of the ship (it was actually a human bucket), he scooped water from the teacup for her to drink. She drank. She drank and drank.

"Where will it take me?" said Arrow. "What comes after the sea?"

"I don't know. But it will be very far. I will never see you again."

Trembling, Prince Cob set the boat back down upon the river. He held it there with his hand. "Will you never forget me, Arrow? Even if you come to a place where humans are, and they are all the right size to kiss you?"

She shook her head. "No, I will never forget you. But I will never come back."

With a sob that shook him so hard the whole ground rumbled, the giant let go.

3

The water nymphs had never seen a boat. When giants came to the river, they stepped over or waded across. None of the furry animals used boats. Centaurs also swam, and wizards walked on water. When the nymphs rose out of the water to peek into the strange vessel, they saw a human girl lying on the deck, staring at the sky.

"Who are you?" one of them asked her. "Where are you going?"

"I am Arrow. I am going to the sea."

"Why?"

"I don't know. Because I promised him."

"Promised who?"

"Wick."

The nymphs did not understand the girl, but she was theirs; the river had given her to them. Each time the boat caught in the trees along the shore, or ran aground in the shallows, they pushed it onward.

On the first day, Arrow ate and drank and slept. The more she satisfied her body's demands, the more they awoke, demanding more. The more they awoke, the more the nothingness receded. But the mountain of pain did not swallow her as before. She had a task now, the task of living; as long as she engaged in it, the mountain stood aside, waiting its turn in the proper unfolding of a sorrow.

On the second day, Arrow lay in the bottom of the boat and stared at the sky, saying over and over: I am outside. Each time she said it, terror flooded her. Behind the terror lay many other things, and one of them was joy. But for now, each blink and reopening of her eyes brought a stab of fear more terrible than what she used to feel the moment Prince Dob pushed her heels off the edge of the table in the Queen's boudoir.

All around her was space. She couldn't escape it by shrinking down against the deck so the boat's sides hid the tangled riverbanks and the valley with its trees, mosses, and lichen-fuzzed rocks. Even with all that hid, she could not escape the wideness of the sky. What frightened her most was that it must have always been this huge, her whole life, and she had not known.

On the third day, she listened to the rumble of the river, the crick-crack of trees in the wind, the chatter of birds and the rush of flapping wings as her boat startled them. She smelled the aliveness of the water, the tangy sweetness of wet, green, growing things, the dank, earthen banks where claws were digging. By now, the sounds and smells were familiar. The silvery-blue nymphs, too, with their weedy hair and reedy voices, had proven to be friends.

This is the world, Arrow told herself. This is my world. I must learn it.

On the fourth day, she sat up and gazed around. This was her world; she would look upon each of its things and tell them—yes. But even as she greeted them, they changed. The green slope of the valley yielded to towering walls of black rock. The sky narrowed to a blue ribbon overhead. The water rushed faster and faster, corralled by the close-pressing walls.

Toward evening, the sounds changed. New, shrill bird cries swarmed and faded in the breeze. The river hushed, yet hinted at a deep tremor somewhere in the distance. The smells changed, too: sweet turned salt, fresh turned ancient, growth turned decay. Fear slipped back into Arrow's heart.

All at once, the walls of stone gave way. The earth gave way. Green things gave way, and solid things, and things with legs. Only vastness remained.

She had reached the sea.

For the first time in her life, Arrow saw the setting sun. There at the sea's far edge, a flower of blood and flame bloomed defiantly as it died. To her amazement, the red-gold path it shot across the liquid mirror ended precisely at her boat.

It knew her.

"Yes," she called. "I am coming."

Arrow felt no seasickness, because the dip and swell of the waves was like the swing of her cage on its hook when a strong wind blew through the southeast window, or when the youngest princes batted at the cage to watch the humans tumble to and fro.

She was concerned, though, for her giant teacup and loaf of bread, which slid back and forth with every great swell. If they flew overboard, all would be lost. Using ropes she found coiled in the slimy place under the deck, Arrow tied the cup and bread in place. Also under the deck were pieces of canvas to patch the sails. These she tied over the top of the teacup and around the loaf, to keep the saltwater from drenching them. It would have been nice if there was a third piece of canvas to keep the water from drenching Arrow. But there wasn't.

More than anything, sailing reminded her of standing on the three-legged table in the Queen's boudoir. There were no metal bars surrounding her, no locked door. But just as the table guarded her with walls of air, so the sea drummed a warning against the sides of her boat: this far and no farther. You will fall off the edge of the sky.

As Wick and Arrow had clung to each other, in the time before the wizard touched them and they went limp with sleep, they said many things. They spoke their own language, which not even the wizard could comprehend. They must have said a hundred things each. The things poured out like silver beads, one after the other, so thick and fast Arrow hadn't been able to seize a single one.

But later, as the boat rolled up and down the great blue empty and Arrow burrowed in a cave she carved out of the loaf of bread to escape the relentless sun, she began to remember them. They dripped out of the air into the bowl of her mind. She did not snatch at them; they came.

These are some of the things Wick said:

It's true, Arrow—we must be brother and sister. I understand now.

Where will he take me? I'm afraid I'm so afraid.

This morning it was just the same.

I'm sorry.

And we can always sing the songs.

I know. I know. I know.

Arrow, Arrow! Will it hurt? Will it hurt, Arrow?

These are some of the things Arrow said:

Tell me, Wick. My eyes. Tell me what color they are.

I will find you. I will come find you, Wick.

Do you hear me? I will find you.

I promise.

PART I · CHAPTER 3

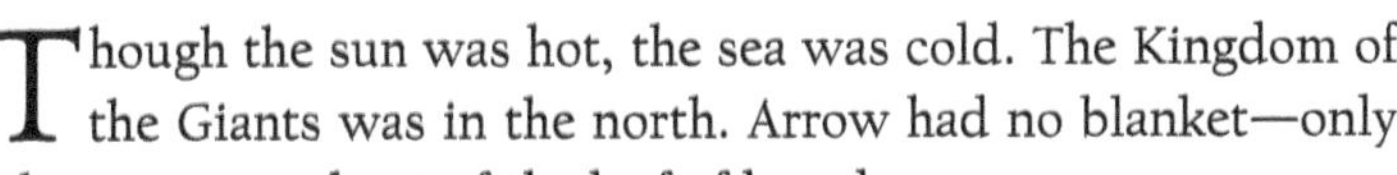

Though the sun was hot, the sea was cold. The Kingdom of the Giants was in the north. Arrow had no blanket—only the cave carved out of the loaf of bread.

Soon the bread began to crawl with white, eyeless things. She could no longer eat it without growing ill, yet she had no choice but to use it for shelter. In the morning she shook off all the white things clinging to her.

There was also a net in the slimy place below the deck. Arrow learned to use it, but for a long time she did not have the heart to kill the fish she caught. For a long time after that, she did not have the heart to bite into the fish she killed. But she learned.

The fish's skin could be torn off with her teeth, and the scales spit out.

Then, the flesh eaten.

There were many bones.

Eating took the greater part of each day.

Once, Arrow caught a fish too fierce for her. She could not haul it in, but if she let go of her net she would lose her only means of obtaining food. Setting her jaw and planting her foot on the side of the boat, Arrow wrestled the slippery monster. Two times, she thought she would go overboard. Whenever a voice said, *Let go*, she said, *I promised*. At last the fish, in a grandiose gesture of surrender, leapt into the boat, bringing the net with it.

As she ate the fish, Arrow felt strong. Stronger than a giant.

She thought of the wizard telling the Queen that size was an illusion.

She thought of the wizard.

She thought of Wick.

This, too, was one of the things Wick said:

Don't forget them. Never forget them.

Who?

Our children, Arrow.

There were also birds, sometimes. White birds with yellow beaks and gray wings. If Arrow left the remnants of a fish on the deck, the white birds would come and peck at them. The net could be thrown over a bird, and the bird's neck wrung. It had many feathers, but not so many bones as a fish. Its flesh was warm, for a little while.

As she ate, Arrow began to wonder—what if all humans ate this way? What if roasting meat and sipping wine were customs peculiar to giants? What if human consumption was all tearing with teeth, and groping with fingers, and licking the blood off one's hands?

Maybe Wick was not a human anymore. Maybe the wizard had changed him into something else. There was no way to know. The list of things Wick could have become was endless.

He could be a dog.

Or a donkey.

Or a sparrow.

Or a cricket.

Or a pinecone.

Or a smooth stone.

Or a piece of water, held in a bowl.

Or a button on the wizard's cloak.

Or a strand of his own hair.

Or an eyelash, resting on someone's cheek.

Another terrible idea took hold in Arrow's mind: perhaps at the center of the sea was a place where the water went round and round. Its path might be wide enough that a sailor would not know he had been circling around the same place for days, and months, and years, until he grew old and perished without ever reaching the shore.

Stars' Song

How many nights have we
seen her, sheen of her
carving a path through
dark water?

Earth small, sea smaller,
she smallest of all
seems scarce to move
night follow night.

What are miles of men to us?
What seas of dark water?
What tears of children,
brine and salt and sorrow?

Still.
Each night we spread
a blanket of light
over her fear of dawn.

How many nights
have we seen her?
Children do not live
as long as stars.

Sea's Song

Hush my sweet, my small, my lone
Rise and fall, rise and fall
Weary blood and weary bone
Rise and fall, rise and fall.

This the way, the way your mother
Rocked you, rocked you, rise and fall
None's alone beside another
Watched you, watched you rise and fall.

Where is she, and where are we
Child so small, rise and fall?
Does she wait across the sea
Does she call, rise and fall?

I will be the one to hold you
Hush you, shush you, rise and fall
Tell you all your mother told you
Swing you, sing you rise and fall.

Hush my heart, my love, my light
Rise and fall, rise and fall
Dawn and day and dusk and night
Rise and fall, rise and fall.

If there was a place where the sea went round and round and a boat could not escape, Arrow must not have reached it. She must have arrived somewhere new, because in this part of the sea there were no fish. Hour after hour, day after day, she waited with her net, but none came.

It was not cold anymore, but very hot.

In this new place, there were no birds either.

Arrow tried to eat the bread, which was now black and slimier than the place below the deck. She grew ill.

She remembered that her shoes were made of leather, and that leather had once been the skin of an animal. It took a very long time to chew a piece of leather, until it grew soft enough that edge-bits began tearing off and could be swallowed.

But what else did she have to do? The days were longer in this part of the sea.

Or a starfish.

Or a star.

Or a pocket watch.

Or a silk stocking.

Or a lady's perfume bottle.

Or a wick, encased in wax and slowly burning.

In the end, the choice was always between pain and nothingness. Nothingness itself was a kind of pain. She hadn't understood this before. It was the pain of saying: it wasn't enough, all the fish I caught, all the birds whose eyes looked so surprised after I wrung their necks. It wasn't enough, all the gazing at the sky and thinking that perhaps the stars were in a different place tonight, perhaps I was nearer land. It wasn't enough, all the wrestling out from the mouth of the mountain and telling it no, you will not swallow me today. It wasn't enough, all the mornings I woke and said aloud, my name is Arrow.

But it only hurt at first, the nothingness. Later it became a warm, white, comforting blanket. Warm and white, because when the sun beat down Arrow did not crawl away into her cave. The sun knew her. It had laid a path for her when she first saw it set across the sea. Why would she try to escape it?

As before, when Arrow had fallen into this state, she had a need to remain there as long as possible. And as before, if anyone attempted to wrench her back into the place of knowing, she fought him in the nameless dark that lay behind the nothingness.

This time, the intruder was a shadow.

There had been no true shadow in all the time Arrow had been on the sea. Only the flicker of the sail and the tomb-like cave of bread. But suddenly, as she lay in the center of the salt-sticky, sunbaked deck, a solid shadow spread over her whole body, tearing off the warm, white, comforting blanket of nothingness.

Now she felt something more—the boat jolting and shuddering. She heard sounds that were like voices calling, feet stamping on wooden planks. Fear waved a bright flag, trying to shake her back into the world of thoughts. No, said the nothingness, don't listen. What can fear say to you now? Walk one step further with me, and have done with fear forever.

Arrow was being picked up and carried.

Had the sea brought her back to the Kingdom of the Giants? Was all to be reversed? Was she in Prince Cob's pocket, bumping against his leg as he rushed back to the castle? Would she waken in the old, familiar cage?

Would Wick be there, standing at the window?

Water poured into Arrow's mouth. Noisy shouts crowded against her ears. Soft, warm things touched her arms and legs and face. Fear triumphed over nothingness, and she opened her eyes.

All around her, a crowd of humans.

PART II

THE WAGER

"Someone, I tell you, will remember us, even in another time."

—Sappho

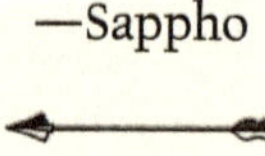

4

Tomás de Rueda
2nd Pilot of the Silver Egret
Written at Lipa
3 June, in the Year of Sails

It is now certain that a week from tomorrow, on Saint Bernabé Day, we sail to take the Isle of the Firebirds for His Majesty's Crown. Not our fleet from Lipa only, but fleets from all the Sorry Islands. One might as well write, it is now certain that on Saint Bernabé Day, all the able-bodied seamen of the Sorry Islands depart to their deaths, and Governor de la Concha must answer for our blood to those we leave behind. I can see them now—our widows marching, our orphans with their torches and stones. His palace burning.

But what will it matter to us? We will be dead. We will be corpses stretched along a lonely shore, our roasted flesh picked bite by bite from our bones by the victor's beaks.

We will be dead.

We will be bodies, parts of bodies.

When I first heard of the campaign, when the Admiral spoke of it as a definite course and not a mad crime, it seemed to me I could not die. If all others perished, I alone would be swept up in a saving current, or carried on the backs of dolphins, or dragged by serpents down to the Buried Isle beneath the sea, because I alone know the story of Arrow and her wager.

But as articles were signed, weapons commissioned, commands given, it grew clearer in my mind that I am a man only. My flesh, like that of other men, when struck with flames or slashed with talons will burn and bleed.

So I set out to write of Arrow before I die. I leave this chronicle with Brother Agostin, who knows more than any other and soon will know all I have to tell.

When I met her, I had not yet joined the Egret but was serving my apprenticeship on the Tailcatcher. A boy of thirteen or fourteen, serious, speaking as little as needed. Full of my own dreams. To be a pilot—that was everything to me. I was learning to read, calculate, chart positions, and master the stars. It seemed to me I was born to master them.

The Tailcatcher had been sent to the Far Deeps because a prophecy came to an old nun that on Holy Cross Day of that year—it was the Year of Olives—the Buried Isle would rise from the center of the sea beneath the constellation Barba Dei, offering mountains of gold and beaches glittering with gems to the conqueror who sought her in God's name.

Each night, I looked through the astrolabe with my master, watching Barba Dei rise as we approached the Deeps. My master charted our course so skillfully we arrived beneath the constellation two days before the feast. But all the time, he grumbled. *A fool's errand*, he scoffed.

Was it? Was it a fool's errand? Then God bless the fool who sent us, bless him and keep him and make him prosper and give him a high place among the angels of heaven.

God bless that fool, and bless him, and bless him.
God bless that worthy fool.
When I am dead, God bless him.

Holy Cross Day came and went, and the Buried Isle did not rise. Not, at least, beneath the stars of Barba Dei. Next morning, as we turned the Tailcatcher homeward, up came a speck on the northern horizon. Men shouted—*the Isle! See, she rises!*—and we sped toward her, hearts lusting for gold.

We found no island, but a decrepit vessel with sail in rags. A longboat of the Norsemen, its oars missing.

On the ship's deck lay three things: a curious water cask fashioned like an overgrown teacup, a stinking mound of black, spongy filth with a piece of canvas roped over it, and a girl, withered from starvation, on the point of death.

Thus, for the first time, I saw Arrow.

She was ugly. Not in the ordinary way of ugly girls, but in a truly repulsive, hardly human way. My chest tightened with the same sinister awe I felt at the sight of a scrabbling beetle, a scorpion, or a corpse. The more she horrified me, the more I stared.

Her skin sucked tight around the bones of her arms and legs so they were not really limbs at all but bundles of twigs roped together. When the men first carried her onto the ship, she wore nothing but a few tattered scraps. I saw her rows of sharp ribs, the hollow where her stomach should have been. Her face like an old, shriveled skull—but with eyes still in it.

Her hair was matted in ropes and crawling with vermin, so the barber-surgeon shore it off close to her head. She didn't protest. Nothing mattered to her: not when they cut off her hair, not when they stripped her clothes and bathed her reeking body, not when they laid her in the officers' cabin in a bunk with pillow and blanket (something I greatly envied). She made no sound, never spoke but in her sleep. When she opened her eyes for a little while, they grew wider and wider until she squeezed them shut as if she would shatter to pieces if she saw one more thing.

She only came to life when someone held food close to her mouth. That was what horrified and captivated me most of all: to see her eat.

Mundo Albares, the barber-surgeon, often ordered me to bring her food because she seemed less afraid of me than of the grown men. I held out the biscuit or salt pork or what we had. She snatched it from my hands, tearing into it with a ferocity I had only ever seen in dogs. Sometimes, as I watched her, the blood came to my cheeks; I felt the shame she was unable to feel for her wretchedness.

The sailors said she may have been on the boat a month or more. They said she caught fish and seagulls, and ate them raw without even a knife to prize into their flesh. They said she had begun to eat one of her shoes.

I lay awake some nights, imagining the girl in her battered boat. The putrid, rotting mound at one end, the teacup-cask at the other, and her in the middle. Thus had she passed each day, alone. Why alone? Why was she on the sea, alone?

The sailors spoke of her in hushed tones, as one speaks of miracles.

I imagined myself in the boat. If it were me, I would not have become like the girl. I would not have become a skull with eyes, a frail, spidery, no-better-than-beast. I would have been strong. When I reached the Deeps, and the fish came no more, I would have—

I would have—

And here my imagination failed.

Each time I saw her, I was more in awe of her, and more afraid.

The first word she learned was *food*. She learned it from Mundo, not me; I never spoke to her. One day, when I came in with her dinner plate, she looked up at me, pointed, and said, "Food."

A new frustration struck me with sudden force, like a gust snapping a sail leeways. Without thinking, I lifted the plate beyond the reach of her grasping hands. She drew back, confused.

"Food?" she whispered, her face reddening. Her voice was unnaturally low for a child's.

I shook my head and tapped a finger on my chest. "Tomás."

She only stared, biting her lip.

"Tomás," I insisted. "Tomás."

The strangest thing was, I didn't know why I was doing this.

"Food." I pointed to the plate. "Tomás." I pointed to myself. An infant could have understood.

Her face brightened. "Food," she repeated proudly, pointing to the plate. Her eyes fixed on it as she licked her lips.

Sighing, I handed her the plate. She began to eat and did not look at me again.

The next day, something changed.

As I entered, she sprang from beneath her blanket and knelt up on the bunk. Hands trembling, eyes searching. My heart beat fast. She had never been like this before; she had always leaned quietly against the wall, propped up by her pillow.

One of Mundo's linen shirts covered her like a nightdress, sagging off her gaunt shoulders. Her ugliness was more shocking now that her body was exposed. Alarm flooded me. Was she ill? I licked my lips to ask, but they twitched in a strange way and no words came out.

"Tomás," she cried. "Tomás!" She was on the point of tears, like a guilty child facing its mother. Lunging forward, she threw her arms around me and kissed my cheek.

I stiffened. With one jerk of my arms and shoulders, I flung her backward. The mug of water I held sloshed over the blanket. The girl gave no more resistance than a doll. As she fell, her head banged against the back of the bunk with a sharp crack.

She made no sound. Only stared at me with a look so terrible I couldn't absorb all it emanated: remorse, fear, shame, confusion, sadness, sadness, sadness.

My face and neck warmed. "I'm sorry," I mumbled. "Sorry. You scared me."

Setting down the mug and plate, I blotted at the blanket with my sleeve. The girl shrank from me, drawing her knees to her chest.

I tried to hand her the plate. She shook her head, burying her face in her knees.

As I stood there, holding the plate, my face grew hotter and hotter until I could feel the flames curling up into the roots of the hair around my temples. I slid the plate onto a shelf and hurried to go, but the girl looked up. Though her face was cold and iron-hard, her eyes burned me.

I swallowed, clearing my throat. "I'm sorry," I repeated, though she couldn't understand. "Did you hurt your head? Let me see."

Reaching out, I felt the back of her head. A lump swelled beneath her shorn hair. I blushed again.

"It'll be better soon." I talked because it was better than staring stupidly at her. "There's no use telling Mundo; he can't do anything for a bump like that. But you scared me, see. You were never like that before. You only wanted the food."

"Tomás?" she whispered.

There was a tiny quiver in her nostrils, like a frightened rabbit. She had freckles on her cheeks and nose. She was so sad, sadder than anyone I had ever met.

I nodded. "Yes. My name is Tomás."

Taking the plate from the shelf, I handed it to her. She took it, but not as on previous days. She set it on the blanket beside her, picked up the biscuit, and broke off a small bite. Trying to eat normally, trying not to be a starving person, trying to show me she wasn't so different from other girls I knew.

"What's your name?" I asked after a pause.

She shrugged, not understanding.

I put my hand on my chest as I had the day before. "My name is *Tomás*. Your name is...?"

Her eyes flashed. With an eagerness that was almost a smile, she made a terrible, guttural sound. Like a deep moan combined with the smacking sounds men make while sloppily chewing. I know now she was speaking the language of the giants. But at the time, I only knew that this awful sound—her name, apparently—confirmed all my initial horror of her.

The girl saw my aversion. She looked down, a pink flush rising in her cheeks. She thought hard.

Kneeling up on the bunk, she put one of her arms straight forward, making a fist. The other arm she pulled back at the elbow, a perfect gesture of an archer drawing his bow. Her movements were graceful, deliberate, strong.

"I don't understand." I shook my head. "Are you... was your father an archer? A fletcher? But what's your *name*?"

Her finger traced an arc in the air. She again made the motion of a bow pulling back, then three times quick traced the arc of an arrow in flight.

There was no mistaking her meaning. "Arrow. Is that your name?"

Say it again, her eyes commanded me. *Say it again*.

"Arrow." I mimicked her gestures to show I understood.

She nodded, pressing one hand solemnly against her chest. "Arrow." She pointed to me. "Tomás."

I had never met any girl or woman with such a name. I never have since.

When we returned to Lipa, we didn't know what to do with her. Was she princess, peasant, or pirate? Her fawn-colored hair and blue eyes hinted of a northern origin, as did the Norse-fashion boat, but this told us nothing of her parentage and dignity.

Mundo decided to take her home with him. His wife Ona would fatten her up, and his three daughters would teach her to speak until she could explain how she should be treated.

As we landed in Lipa Harbor, Mundo's girls came running along the quay, barefoot and shrieking and waving.

The oldest, Noemi, was my same age. Noemi was nothing but handfuls of happiness thrown into the air. Dark spilling curls and red lips always twisting up. Though we had been childhood friends, her breasts had grown between us like two torches; I couldn't look at her without sweat running everywhere. The worst of it was, I knew she saw it all—the sweating and the confusion and the determination not to bolt. She laughed at me. She was always laughing.

Loida, the middle sister, was about Arrow's age, a frank and sympathetic girl whom I thought of only as a kind of ornament to Noemi, therefore scarcely at all.

Irma was just old enough to follow her sisters everywhere, yet young enough to weep each time she was made to feel the misfortune of short, chubby legs and a near-incomprehensible lisp.

Mundo came down the plank with Arrow in his arms. He'd tied a kerchief round her head to hide her shorn hair and a piece of rope round her waist to suggest the shape of a dress. Gripping Mundo tightly, Arrow took in our island city's white plastered walls and monastery-crowned hill with a solemn, unblinking stare.

Noemi gasped and clutched her sisters by the shoulders. "Oh, Father, how horrid! What is it?" Then she burst out laughing.

"Is it from the Buried Isle?" cried Loida. "Oh, Father, is it a *mermaid*?"

Irma jammed two fingers into her mouth and wrapped herself in Noemi's skirt until only her eyes peered out.

Arrow made a kind of choking noise. We all stared at her.

It was the first time I'd seen her smile. Cries of wonder burst from her, followed by a spurt of awful words in the language I now know to belong to the giants. Her deep voice sounded deeper now, alongside other girls' voices.

The girls screamed. Noemi's screams were both fear and laughter, and tears began to stream down her face.

Arrow looked at me urgently, as if knowing her name gave me the ability to translate the rest of her demonic chatter. She clutched at her chest, then pointed to Mundo's daughters. The strangest thing was—I understood.

"I think...." In those days it cost me great effort to speak when Noemi was near. "I think she has never seen another girl before."

Arrow beamed at me. I shrank from her gaze, humiliated by this moment of apparent kinship.

"We found her on the sea, my daughters," Mundo explained. "All alone in a shabby boat, almost starved. She speaks a strange language. But we're going to take her home, and feed her, and find out her story."

"Must we?" Noemi trembled, running her hands through Irma's sweet curls. "She's so frightening and ugly. And we can't fit a fourth girl in our bed; it was only made for one."

"She can sleep under the table with Pipo," said Loida. Pipo was a three-legged dog with both ears chewed down to stubs. "Poor thing! We can nurse her, as we nursed our pup."

"Why doesn't she know any girls?" chirped Irma's high, lisping voice.

"I don't know," replied her father. "You'll have to teach her to answer, if you want to ask."

And they did.

I can't tell you firsthand what it was like for Ona and her daughters to uncover Arrow's history fragment by fragment, piecing together gestures, figures drawn with sticks in dirt, and finally words cobbled into patchy phrases. Mundo and I set out again almost immediately on a cargo run, leaving Arrow on a mat under the table beside Pipo the dog. Irma stood over her with a bowl of soup, feeding her the way she fed her dolls. That was the memory I took to sea: Irma brandishing her spoon, Arrow obedient as Pipo.

I can tell you that Arrow's fame on our island came in waves. Her shoddy longboat was moored in Lipa Harbor for public exhibition. The teacup-cask found anchorage in a library of the governor's palace, where scholars blustered theories as to its origin. At first, visitors packed into Mundo and Ona's one-room dwelling, but as Arrow could speak little and was unpleasant to behold, the crowds quickly dissipated.

Then came the discovery that she hailed from the Kingdom of the Giants, where she had dwelt as a captive since infancy. The city erupted in a frenzy of pilgrimage, as if she had been a saint.

But the biggest hurly-burly arose when Arrow began to display her strange dances, which bore no resemblance to the steps of Lipa or any other lands we knew. Noemi and Loida would bring her to the nearest square, where a ring of spectators gathered. Carts rolled in, selling sweet nuts and roast meat. Other freaks came, and clowns and acrobats. Arrow became her own festival.

But Ona grew tired of this and forbade it, giving Arrow chores alongside the other girls. The grumbling crowds dissipated, the clowns went home. By the time the Tailcatcher returned, Arrow had come to be regarded as simply a member of our city, albeit an interesting one. Our crew members were the last to hear her tale, and our astonishment formed her last bubble of notoriety for seven years.

The lives of Mundo's daughters now centered around the task of teaching Arrow the language, geography, and fashions of Lipa, as well as the customary behavior of human girls in the civilized world. At Noemi's insistence, I often joined them during my furloughs. Not, of course, to teach the ways of human girls. To show Arrow the best places for curious children to explore. I was an expert in that.

Arrow had to touch everything. Trees. Caterpillars. Each of the blacksmith's tools. Each stone and each gap in the city wall. She had to hoist the bucket from each well. Pet every dog.

She preferred to run instead of walking. Sometimes, if we found ourselves on some high point on the island, she would look down at the water and suddenly—off like a shot! In as straight a line as she could, until she reached the water's edge. Or she ran along the shore, far out of sight (we never bothered to follow) until she reached a cliff or cape, then turned and ran the whole way back.

We laughed at it, then. Later, when I understood her better, it tore my heart.

Almost as soon as Arrow learned the word "boy," she began to speak of Wick, as a monk might speak of his God.

It was all what Wick would have thought, or something Wick said once. Everything she saw brought her back to this boy, her twin brother, the sole human companion of her childhood. We knew that Wick's favorite month was June. We knew that Wick liked rabbit stewed with cabbage, and hated fennel. We knew how Wick had been taken by a Wizard of Seven, who climbed table legs and put Arrow to sleep with a touch of his hand.

At first we listened eagerly, because everything Arrow shared about the giants fascinated us. But soon we realized—all the stories were the same. All in the cage, all with Wick, all the Queen and the Queen's sons and the giant fireplace shaped like a greedy mouth. There was nothing else. I began to feel stifled every time Arrow told a story, as if her words were the metal bars of the cage she described. My stomach tightened at the boy's name, and I tried to distract her by showing her more new things.

I wasn't the only one who felt this way. Noemi's irritation with Wick-talk grew day by day, expressing itself in little snaps and barks.

One day, we decided to show Arrow the ruins of the great watchtower that crowns South Hill. From its top, you can see the whole island and the sea in all directions. Arrow ran up the crumbling stairs, too quick for us. When we reached the top, she was standing in the middle of the ruined parapet, perfectly still, hugging herself.

"This like the table," she said. "The table I danced with Wick, and we sang. We always afraid, stand in the middle—here. Wizard climbs up table, takes Wick."

"But it's *not* the table, is it?" Noemi snapped, out of breath from her climb. "It's not the table, and there are no giants here. Wick is gone, isn't he?"

The expressiveness of Arrow's eyes faded by degrees during what followed, as the tide smooths away a footprint in sand.

"My God, I'm so *sick* of hearing about Wick I could tear my hair out! I'm glad the wizard took him and good riddance."

"Noemi!" Loida cried. "Don't be cruel."

I have said that Noemi was always laughing. It's not true. I had seen her get angry before—at Loida, usually, or her mother. When her dark eyes and red lips turned to storm, she couldn't stop until she'd let all her thunderbolts fly.

"I hope the wizard turned him into a feather and blew him into the wind. And I wish you'd stood by to see it, so we'd never have to hear of him again. I hate Wick, do you hear? I *hate* him. I hope he's dead."

"Me too," said Irma, who hated boys in general.

"Stop it, Noemi," I mumbled, heat flashing up my neck at the fear of placing myself in the storm's path. "She can't help it."

"She can. And she will now, won't you, Arrow?"

We none of us breathed.

"No," said Arrow, in a voice that struggled up from the hidden center of her. "Not a boy. Never a boy with me. Just... a doll. I pretend he my brother. A doll named Wick."

You will not understand how terrible this moment was, because you have not met Arrow. You don't know the light that came into her eyes when she spoke of Wick. You don't know the way his name turned her mouth soft, how this one word was different than all other words to her. You don't understand that there was also a flash of pain in each utterance, like a shard of glass twisted under a bare foot.

"What do you mean?" Loida staggered back. "You mean... it was all make-believe? About your brother. All this time?"

Arrow paused. "Yes."

Noemi stared. The storm had not yet spent itself. "Wick was a doll?"

"Yes."

"And all this time," Noemi spat, "we've been beaten over the head with stories you made up about your damned *doll*?"

"My damned doll."

"That's a bad word, Arrow," warned Irma.

Tears started to fall from Loida's eyes. "Oh, Arrow! How lonely you must have been. All alone, in that cage. But you pretended—"

"Yes," said Arrow. "Never a boy. Only a doll."

5

I didn't believe her, then.

I remembered how she tried to kiss my cheek, the first time she said my name. She had assumed I would be like this other boy. Instead I shoved her away and banged her head against the wall. But the way she looked at me then, the way she cried out my name and embraced me—that must have been how she looked at Wick. He couldn't have been a doll. Whenever I thought of that moment, I didn't believe her. But Arrow never spoke of Wick again. Never so much as said his name.

Except once.

I used to bring her presents each time I returned from a voyage. She was so much easier to please than Noemi. A bit of broken shell, or a mermaid's scale, or an empty wine bottle in an unusual shape. Once I found a little hand mirror in some debris washed against a dock. Arrow was not at all ugly then; her hair had grown in fine soft waves, her limbs were healthy and her freckled cheeks round, resting on high cheekbones. It occurred to me she might not know what she looked like, and she had every reason to be happy in the knowledge.

But when I gave her the little mirror, she held it close to her eyes, staring and staring. She looked the saddest I had seen her since those early months of our acquaintance.

"There's not nothing special in them," she said. "Not one bit."

Referring, it seemed, to her eyes.

"They're blue," I encouraged. "Not many blue-eyed girls in Lipa."

"But he saw them different," she replied. "I thought they seen magic, but they are just eyes."

"Who saw them different, Arrow?"

"Wick." Then she stopped. She turned to me slowly. "Nothing. I make it up, you see? My old doll, that doll I have before... I pretend the doll saw magic in my eyes. But it wasn't real."

So I began to believe her.

Fool that I was, I believed her.

PART II · CHAPTER 5

A Song of Wick and Arrow
(Little Lady Linden)

Little lady sitting in the linden tree,
please come down, won't you marry me?
Won't you marry me?

We'll have a house with a roof and a floor
a well full of wishes and a big blue door
a grandfather clock that doesn't tock anymore
tock anymore
big blue door
roof and a floor (breath)
Little Lady Linden won't you marry me?

Little lady sitting in the linden tree,
please come down, won't you marry me?
Won't you marry me?

We'll have a house with a spoon and a cup
a wicker baby cradle and a tame wolf pup
a pond full of fishes that will never dry up
never dry up
tame wolf pup
spoon and a cup
tock anymore
big blue door
roof and a floor (breath)
Little Lady Linden won't you marry me?

Little lady sitting in the linden tree,
please come down, won't you marry me?
Won't you marry me?

We'll have a house with a table and a chair
a window wearing curtains and an up-down stair
a song we always sing that never goes anywhere
goes anywhere
up-down stair
table and a chair
never dry up
tame wolf pup
spoon and a cup
tock anymore
big blue door
roof and a floor (breath)
Little Lady Linden won't you marry me?
Won't you marry me?

PART II · CHAPTER 5

From the beginning, Noemi took advantage of Arrow. She meant no cruelty—at first. As I have said, Noemi was always laughing. It was a game to her.

Most of the pranks were purely for Noemi's enjoyment, such as when she told Arrow that the word for muffins was *shitcakes*, or that fine ladies wore veils of seaweed whenever they entered the cathedral. Others were less innocent. She taught Arrow to greet the governor's retinue in the street with a backwards curtsy, her bottom in the air. Dancer that she was, Arrow executed this move with brilliant precision. Thus was she perfectly poised for a kick from a guard's metal-plated boot.

Even more serious was the time Noemi took Arrow into the forest and told her that the imps who lived there were good fairies who would grant a wish if you followed them to their burrows. Without Loida running breathless to secure Mundo's aid, Arrow might have been lured to her death.

This was one of the first times Noemi had been caught at her games, and she took her father's beating with great resentment. Having received a whipping from Mundo several times in the course of my apprenticeship, I understood its potency. But I felt guilt for my sins and took the punishment as impetus to avoid future transgressions. Noemi felt only the need for revenge.

I should mention that Noemi and I were, by this time, about fifteen. She had begun to let me kiss her. Noemi understood the power of her kisses: either to be granted as reward or withheld as punishment. It pains me to say that each time she took advantage of Arrow, I was required to laugh so as to receive my reward. If I failed to find the appropriate level of humor in Noemi's prank, I would be punished.

Be that as it may, I felt much sympathy for Arrow. As an apprentice seaman, I felt kinship with any small or weak creature beset by strong ones, which gradually drew me to her despite my initial repugnance.

In addition to her ignorance of both the general way of humans and the customs of Lipa, Arrow had a chronic, perilous naivety which made it nearly impossible for her to believe that Noemi didn't have her best interests in mind. Though Loida sat her down each time and explained that she had been tricked, Arrow simply couldn't understand.

"But Noemi is a human."

"Yes, and she tricked you," Loida would reply. "She meant it as a joke, but it was mean and foul."

"Giant jokes are like this. She behaved like a giant, not a human."

"Alright, if that's how you want to put it."

Eventually Loida simplified her explanations: "Noemi was acting like a giant again."

Arrow's eyes would grow large and sad. "But why, Loidita? Why would she act like a giant with me?"

"I don't know. Because she's the oldest, maybe."

After much quiet plotting, Noemi at last embarked on her revenge. I was desperate for a kiss, having endured a lengthy period of punishment, and determined I should laugh, whatever happened. Noemi and I took Arrow up to the monastery gate. Hiding in the nearby foliage, we watched the gray-robed monks come in and out. Old men and orphans rang the bell begging for alms, which the bearded porter gave with words of blessing.

"Arrow," said Noemi, "do you remember the dance you showed us last week, that you called the serpent dance?"

It was a peculiar dance indeed. Arrow seemed oblivious to its sensuality, for she performed its undulations with wholehearted abandon.

"It would honor the porter very much if you performed that dance for him."

"Really?" said the ever-eager Arrow. "Why that one, Noemi? Why not the bear dance, or the centaur? I like those much better."

"Because serpents are sacred to the monks. The holy brother will see it as a sign of reverence."

Noemi meant to have blood for blood; Arrow would be severely beaten by the monks, the way they beat the harlots who hung by the gate to tempt the novices.

I was thrown into agony, because for a moment Arrow doubted. Glancing at me, she tried to read in my countenance whether to believe Noemi. My jaw clenched hard; I had no stomach for the joke and felt furious at myself for coming along. But Noemi, crouching beside me, slid her fingers through mine and squeezed—a promise of the reward to come. Looking back at Arrow, I wrenched forth a smile and a perfidious nod.

She beamed at me, saying without words, *oh trustworthy Tomás, my first human friend, you would never lie to me.* My conscience seared me. Arrow sprang up quick as a deer and ran toward the monastery gate.

"Noemi, why must you do this?" I whispered.

"It's only a joke. I'll never forgive you if you spoil it. Please be good, Tomás."

Lifting her smooth round cheek, she reached out her lips to tug the corner of mine. Now I was seared by a different heat than that of my conscience. Noemi giggled as she watched me struggle to breathe.

Arrow rang the bell. Came the porter, younger than most monks—between one and two score years—with short black hair and a wild nest of black beard with one bright streak of rust-gold. His gray tunic was held together with darker gray patches that looked as if Irma had sewn them in with fishing cord. From a face browned like a sailor's, his teeth flashed white as he looked down at Arrow with an amused smile. "*Deo gratias*! God's blessing on you, child. What need has brought you to beg the brothers' assistance?"

"I am Arrow, sir. I have no need. I came because my friends told me to dance for you." Her voice was still unnaturally deep and had a roguish-sounding accent. She might have been a pirate's daughter.

"Where are your friends, who told you to dance?"

"They are hiding in the bushes, there."

"Why? Are they afraid?"

Arrow stopped. She looked back as we shrank further behind the foliage. Clearly it had not occurred to her to wonder why we were hiding. "I don't know. Shall I ask them to come?"

"If they lack the fortitude to meet Brother Agostin, they must suffer the privation according to their merits. But I see you have no fears. I like that, little Arrow. May I see your dance, then?"

With her flash-quick smile, she nodded and struck a pose. Arms twisted above her head, neck stretched back, one leg raised in a hook-like curve.

When the day of my judgment comes and I stand in the halls of heaven with the all-seeing angels as my witnesses, I will be able to declare: have mercy on my soul, for I did not prove false Arrow's trust in me.

I burst from the bushes.

"Wait, Arrow!" I called. "Don't do it. Stop."

"But Tomás—"

"No, Arrow. The holy brother doesn't want to see your dance. It's not right for him... will make him angry. Noemi was acting like a giant again. She tricked you."

How blue and how wide her eyes. "But Tomás, you—"

"I... I didn't mean to. I..."

"But Tomás!"

"He is sorry," came the monk's soft voice through my stammers. "You made a mistake and now you are sorry, Tomás. Yes?"

I nodded, too miserable to speak. I heard Noemi thrash backward through the bushes and bolt toward the town. She would never kiss me again. In those days there was no greater devastation I could suffer, except if my apprenticeship had been lost. But the torture of my conscience cleared.

Arrow dropped her dancer's pose like a puppet gone slack.

"Arrow," said Brother Agostin, "you must forgive Tomás."

"I don't know that word, sir. No one has taught me it yet." Her hand darted to wipe a tear as it fell. She wouldn't look at me.

"It means in your heart, you hold no debt of bitterness toward him. You will never try to hurt him because of the wrong he has done. And you wish that every good thing in the world may come to him."

"Why must I forgive Tomás?"

I knew the best answer and how to say it, so I did: "Because otherwise you'll start to act like a giant with me."

The monk continued, "We must forgive everyone who has done wrong to us, little Arrow, if our souls are not to become crippled."

For a moment she grew so still I wondered if she was about to be sick. Then— "Not everyone. Not wizards, I'm sure. To wizards we should be always cruel, and never forgive."

Brother Agostin looked down at her in astonishment. "Who has taught you this, child? What do you know of wizards, that you wish cruelty on them?"

She paused a long time before she answered. "If a wizard took something that belonged to a girl. Something very precious, the most precious in the world, that she loved more than anything.

A doll, maybe, that was all she had. She had nothing else in the world. And he changed the doll into something else—something magic—into a spoon, maybe. She would never wish for the wizard to be happy. She would hate him always. If ever, for one day, she did not hate the wizard, or hated him less, it would mean she didn't love the doll. Enough. Didn't love him enough."

Brother Agostin looked at me in bafflement.

"She is the girl found on the sea by the Tailcatcher," I explained. "She grew up in the Kingdom of the Giants. Wizards came there. I think one of them has done her ill."

Arrow added nothing to my speech, incomplete as it was.

"Ah! I have heard much of you, Arrow. I longed to meet you, for I've been compiling a work on the History of Giants. And now God has brought you to me."

Arrow didn't reply, still laboring under dark thoughts. Brother Agostin watched her carefully, seriously. Bending his knees, he leveled his head with hers, so that when he spoke his eyes looked straight into hers. I felt instinctively that he was a holy man.

"She could still love the doll, and forgive the wizard."

"You are wrong," Arrow replied. "You have never known a wizard."

"I have known only one wizard," Brother Agostin admitted, "who was wise and did me no ill."

"Are there many wizards in the world, Brother?" I asked.

"Not many. Perhaps seventy? They live five hundred years, but the birth of a wizard is a rare thing. Only once in my lifetime has our map shown someone new."

"What map?" I was always interested in maps.

"Our Map of Wizards. A precious thing in our library. Very ancient—made by the wizard who was the first inhabitant of Lipa. The map shows every wizard in the world and where they are wandering in their journeys. Sometimes the wizards themselves come to survey it when they lose track of one of their own."

Though Arrow made no outward change, I felt tension rise in her like a beast facing its rival, whose hair stands all on end.

"A map," she repeated. "That shows the wizards. All?"

"Would you like to see it?" said Brother Agostin.

I answered for her. "I would like to see it, sir." I was not about to pass up this chance.

Opening the gate, the monk bade us enter. I had never been inside the monastery, nor had my father or anyone I knew; my life was spent among sailors who had no use for monks. Two aged brothers tending a flower-dazzled courtyard glared as we passed, but Brother Agostin pretended not to notice. We threaded through several passageways, their stones still cool in the midday heat, until we reached a room the size of a forecastle, packed floor-to-ceiling with books, manuscripts, and artifacts. I could have spent days there.

Brother Agostin brought out a ring of keys from his belt. Unlocking a wooden chest near the window, he drew out a piece of parchment in a leather case.

As he unrolled the parchment on a table and smoothed its edges, he said, "Now children, you may truthfully boast to whom you will that you have seen the Map of Wizards."

The map showed the world in a very different fashion than I had seen it laid out in any pilot's chart. The center was not Iberia, nor even the Sorry Islands, but a place called Gnoze. From it, the known lands of the world—even those known only in legend—stretched out like legs of a spider, not in any form a ship could navigate with longitude and latitude, but as so many beads or knobs along the spider's legs.

Scattered across the map were small flags or pennants, not drawn with ink but truly standing out from the parchment, tiny poles of twig bearing bits of ribbon. On each pennant was written a name. Next to the name was the mark of a hand, each with a different number of fingers—some three, four, or five. A few had six. They were of different colors: all the threes were blue, the fours green, and so on.

"Yes, it's magic," Brother Agostin whispered. "Each time we look at the map, it has changed, for wizards are always on the move. So also we know when a wizard changes rank—the map shows it. Here is the wizard I mentioned, a venerable Wizard of Five. He is in India now, living in a den with leopards. No one knows why, but if wizards have reasons that mean naught to us, that does not make them poor reasons."

Arrow stared at each little flag, though she couldn't read.

"Are you looking for a name?" I asked, proud to display my skill before the learned brother. "Tell me it, Arrow, and I'll find it for you."

"What rank is he?" said Brother Agostin. "That will be easier to start with."

"He is a Wizard of Seven," said Arrow.

I knew next to nothing about wizards and had no idea what this meant.

"Impossible," said Brother Agostin. "There has been no Wizard of Seven since Quodvolo in the fifth century."

"I know he is a Wizard of Seven. I touched his hand."

"What is his name?"

"He hasn't a name."

"What are you saying, child?"

"The Wizard of Seven. He has no name. He says names do not exist."

The monk stared at the map, wrinkling his sun-weathered brow.

"What can it mean, Brother?" I pressed.

"I don't understand. You see, the names of wizards are not like ours. Our names may change: my mother named me Lorenzo, I was Renzo to my friends, and became Brother Agostin on my clothing day. But no one gives a wizard his name. Their names are born with them, discovered not bestowed. I have always been taught that a wizard and his name are one."

"He has done with names, I think." Arrow's voice was very low and very quiet. "Since he became a philosopher."

"It is impossible for a wizard to remove his name," said Brother Agostin.

Arrow looked at him as a master will look at a stupid pupil. "How do you think he became a Wizard of Seven, except by doing impossible things?"

"My God," whispered the monk.

"But what does it mean?" I persisted. "How can we find Arrow's wizard?"

"The map's magic is tied to a wizard's name. The name appears with its pennant the moment he is born, even before the Namers in Gnoze have descried it. It disappears only at his death."

"You mean, sir," said Arrow, "that I can never find him. That no one can find him, if he has no name."

"I didn't say no one can find him, but the Map of Wizards will never show him. I'm not certain he can be what you say he is, Arrow. A Wizard of Seven—with no name. There must be some mistake."

"No. There is no mistake."

Arrow sat in a chair near the table. Drawing up her knees, she put her head in her hands and wept. I had never seen anyone weep like this, except once a widow whose husband had been lost at sea. Being a boy of fifteen who no longer admitted I had cried since infancy, I felt great unease. But Brother Agostin bent down and drew her in his arms, until they were sitting in the chair together with her head resting against his chest, soaking his patched tunic in salty grief. He looked up at me, but neither of us spoke. What could we say?

Thus, from the first day, Brother Agostin understood that Arrow was not like other girls.

As I had.

PART II · CHAPTER 5

A Song of Wick and Arrow
in their own language

I am here.
I am here.
I am here.
I am here.
I know. But don't let go my hand.

For some reason, that day's events signaled the end of Noemi's feud with Arrow. Perhaps it was because Noemi didn't want to follow through with her threat never to kiss me again and saw that making peace with Arrow was the best way to preserve goodwill in our little kingdom. Or perhaps she truly was struck with compunction and resolved to do better. I'd like to think it was the latter, especially given an incident that took place several weeks later.

By that time, the three girls—especially Loida and Irma—had begun to refer to Arrow as their sister. Mundo, being possessed of a warm heart that would've adopted every stray in the Sorry Islands if his wife let him, saw no reason he shouldn't call her his daughter. Only Ona seemed to retain a sense of the girl's strangeness and called her "my Arrow-child," but never "my daughter."

One day, Noemi pointed out, "If Arrow is our sister, it's not right for her to sleep under the table with Pipo. She should share the bed with us."

"But she can't fit!" Irma rightly protested.

"We should take turns," said Loida. "Each night, one of us can sleep with Pipo, and the rest take the bed."

Noemi nodded and the thing was settled. "It's only right."

Eyes wide, Arrow shook her head with characteristic quickness. "Oh no, no, that would not be right. No, you see... I have always slept alone. Just with my old doll. I couldn't sleep with another human. I am very happy with darling Pipo. I will be your sister who sleeps with the dog. That is just right for me."

Arrow developed an odd form of greeting other people. She would run eagerly to meet them, then stop close up. Uncomfortably close, I used to think. After a short pause, she would place her hand, palm first, then each of her fingers, on the center of one's breastbone. Looking up with a smile, she would take her hand away. As brief as a handshake. She did this to men and women alike, without the slightest embarrassment. It was so natural to her, she hardly knew she did it.

At first, in my boyish way, I didn't like it. Strange, alarming. My heart beat faster—had she heard it speed up? But I got used to it. After a time, I felt fondness for it. I came to associate it with coming home after a sea voyage. Like an anchor, assuring safety and rest. Like the blessing of a priest.

Once, a noblewoman, Lady Isabel de la Costana, approached Arrow as she and I were on our way to visit Brother Agostin. How old were we then? I was sixteen, maybe, and Arrow thirteen or fourteen. The lady addressed her in the condescending tone some adults, especially the wealthy, will use with children.

"Well, dear waif of the North! Do you remember me? I came to visit you when you first arrived, poor wretched thing! I brought a pot of honey, you must remember. How fine and healthy you look now, with your dainty hands—"

And Lady Isabel stopped mid-sentence as Arrow drew uncomfortably close to her, placing a dainty hand in the middle of that lady's prominent chest.

I felt my usual urge to apologize for anything odd Arrow did. But a second urge pulled in the opposite direction. This is Arrow, I thought. If the lady doesn't understand, she's not worth anything.

Lady Isabel's face changed, only a flicker, the way light washes over a stone wall as the clouds lift. Arrow smiled as she let her hand drop. Not a warm or eager smile, just one that seemed to say, *here we are, you and I, on this earth together*.

The lady remained speechless as Arrow and I walked on. But she watched us go, bringing her own hand to her bosom. The change in her face—the wash of light—remained.

I felt proud of Arrow then. Proud simply of who she was, and proud that it was I, Tomás de Rueda, apprentice pilot, walking with her up the monastery hill, while a great lady remained awestruck in our wake.

Our friendship with Brother Agostin continued. Arrow saw him more than I, for I was mostly at sea. He taught her to read. Some others complained of this, including Ona. Brother Agostin reminded Ona that young noblewomen brought up in monasteries often learned to read, and that for all we knew Arrow might be a noblewoman.

"Yes," replied Ona, "and she might be a swineherd's daughter."

But there was no way to know, so Ona let Brother Agostin win out, just in case.

Once, while I was away, he taught Arrow the stars. How surprised I was on my return when she started naming each of the constellations! Delighted, I explained how ships used the stars to navigate; she gobbled up my teaching as greedily as she had gobbled food when we first met. Noemi had never asked me the name of a single star.

Arrow had to know everything. As soon as she discovered the existence of some branch of science—astronomy, alchemy, geometry—she had to learn it. If Brother Agostin couldn't teach her, she found an apothecary, or a shipwright, or whoever it was who could explain to her the way this set of things worked, and what they meant.

She read poetry. Her favorite poets wrote in Greek, so she made Brother Agostin teach her that language, which not two other souls in Lipa could read. I remember one line she told me, from the poet she loved best: *Time passes, and I lie here alone.*

When Arrow read, she pressed both hands down on the pages, as if her fingers were the roots of trees sucking knowledge from the inky fibers, from everything she touched.

Her hands were always dirty.

Arrow and Loida grew closer as Noemi and I became more and more preoccupied with each other. We weren't a pack of children anymore. Though Arrow and I always planned a visit to Brother Agostin on my furloughs, and though I still brought her a present after each voyage, she receded into the background the way a younger sister does when one's sweetheart fills all his plane of vision. I planned to marry Noemi as soon as I finished my apprenticeship at age twenty. I would have married her sooner if I could.

Knowing my death is imminent, I am driven to lay everything bare in this chronicle, which is not Arrow's tale only but my own confession. Thus I record the reason Noemi and I would have married sooner, and why I never thought of marrying anyone else. That is to say, Noemi was afraid to marry anyone but me, as I was the only prospective husband who would not be surprised to discover he had not married a virgin.

It only happened once, when we were eighteen. Rather, it happened only for one passion-drunk week in which we sought each other every night and sometimes during the day. We thought of nothing but the bright burning that swept over us. Then, as it happens with all lovers: the terror of being found out, the fear of a child, the impossibility of marrying for two more years. When at last Noemi bled, we both wept for relief.

We never lay together after that. This was chiefly my doing; I knew if Mundo found out he would do me violence from which I would never recover. I sometimes ran from Noemi, unable to overcome myself by any other means.

I'm sure I made some promise to marry her. Why wouldn't I have, if I dreamed of it every hour? But it was never a formal betrothal. That had to wait until after my apprenticeship. Everyone knew it was coming, all my family, all hers. Arrow knew it too; she never doubted it. No one doubted it. I never doubted it.

Weeks before my twentieth birthday, I returned from my final voyage on the Tailcatcher. I had already secured the position of second pilot on the Silver Egret, and there was nothing to prevent my immediate betrothal. But some domestic duty kept Noemi from being there to meet me at the quay. Instead, as I heaved my sea-chest down the plank—for the last time as an apprentice!—I turned and saw Arrow.

She had become a woman. That's all I can say.

For the past few years, she'd been a girl struggling in the weeds of womanhood. Lanky-armed and large-footed. I never looked at her but with teasing pity. Perhaps it was because of Arrow's freckles (none of our island girls have them) that I vaguely felt she would never make it out the other side of girlhood. Or perhaps it was because she still slept under the table with Pipo the three-legged dog.

But there she was.

Oh glory and heaven and fallen earth, there she was.

None of it might have happened if it wasn't just there that I saw her, with the sky and water painting her eyes a blaze of blue. My heart stopped. My knees grew so weak I had to set down my chest. She told me where Noemi was, why she hadn't come to meet me, but I didn't hear. Sweetness poured over me as I watched her mouth form the words. The wind whipped her hair around her face; she kept catching it back with one hand, then the other. When I reached out and held it back for her, she laughed and snatched my hand away. So simply. She wasn't playing any game; she didn't know how. Arrow did whatever came to her each moment, without calculation. That was her way.

"Do you know you've grown up?" I asked her.

"I think so." Her deep voice grew serious and confiding. "Everyone's always looking at me, and they never did before. Not since I first came. Do you think Mundo will notice?"

"Yes. He will."

"I've been learning Aristotle. Perhaps that's what has caused it."

"I think it might be a different reason."

Even then she didn't blush. She looked at me, curious, with those clear, perfectly frank eyes. Then, reaching out, she put her hand on my chest in her familiar gesture of greeting.

Every other moment I had known Arrow came crowding into that one. The moment I had first seen her, starving in her little boat. The moment I taught her my name. The moment we met Mundo's daughters, and she looked at me as if I were the only person on earth who could break through the barrier of incomprehensibility surrounding her. I saw her running along the shore; standing on the watchtower of South Hill; naming off constellations. I saw her dancing. As all those moments burst into the present, *this* Arrow flooded backward to fill them. Not the ugly girl on the boat, not the hapless waif trying so desperately to be a human. *This* glorious creature: she was the one I had known, secretly, in every moment of Arrow.

If I had not been lost before, now I was utterly lost. I felt almost angry. How could everything I wanted, my whole life, be taken from me in an instant? I stepped backward, grabbed her hand, and pushed it away.

"Don't do that, Arrow. Not anymore." I sounded angry, even angrier than I felt. "You're not a child anymore."

Her eyes widened as she pulled her hand back, cradling it in her other hand. "Tomás. I..." She hesitated. Her gaze ricocheted three times between the water and my face, unwittingly dealing me three deft blows. "Did it wake you up? My hand. Did it wake you?"

I said nothing. Everything I knew, everything I wanted, everything real and necessary was slipping away from me, and in the back of my mind a warning bell threatened consequences terrible and severe. I felt so angry, so helpless.

In a whisper, she added, "It woke me up, too."

Then she fled.

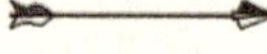

6

The worst evening of my life followed. Mundo had invited me to supper, expecting, of course, the celebration of a long-awaited announcement. When I arrived, Arrow wasn't there.

"She thinks Nazo is sick," Noemi explained. Nazo was Mundo's ancient donkey. "She wants to stay in the barn to nurse him. As if Nazo's more important than *you*!" Laughing, she threw her arms around my neck.

I let out a ridiculously hollow laugh, returning my beloved's embrace with a peck on the cheek. I felt an utter fool, disgusted with myself.

"She's probably speaking Greek to the donkey," Noemi added, pursing her lips into a smirk.

Loida glanced over, not hiding her annoyance. (She and her elder sister had not grown closer with age.) "She *does* speak Greek to the donkey. It's more than you can do."

It flashed through my mind that I wished I was Nazo, nibbling straw while Arrow whispered poetry in my woolly ear. This deepened the fear that my case was serious. My stomach tightened; dread settled over me.

All through the meal, the family laughed and chattered. They were in the highest spirits, sparkling with anticipation. I was distant and distracted, foolish and mumbling. They thought they knew why, and this drove their spirits higher. Even Irma understood what was supposed to happen; she kept looking at me and dissolving into giggles, covering her face with her hands.

I could think only of Arrow. I had to see her. Mostly (I told myself) to assure myself that nothing had really happened, that it was a mischance of ocean in her eyes, of too-long-at-sea, that I had mistaken her for the one expected.

As the night drew to a close, a whiff of frustration began to drift off of Noemi. The whiff swelled into a gale. Her eyes became like augers, boring into me with the hope that my declaration would come pouring out the holes. My dread increased to the point I couldn't look at her. At last I stood, my chair screeching on the stone floor.

"I'm sorry, but... I must go. Greet my mother and father. Sisters. Brothers. Haven't seen me. Thank you so much for having me."

"Tomás!" cried Noemi, propelled to her feet. "You're going? Without—?"

There was nothing to do but play the fool. I knew she wouldn't have the courage to say it aloud. How I hated myself in that moment.

"Without—what?"

Her face grew pale, then deep, raging red. "Nothing. Never mind."

"It's alright, love," said Mundo, patting her shoulder. "Let him go. He's had a weary journey, and so much to tell his family, eh? Second pilot on the Silver Egret! That's a son anyone'd be proud to call his own." He winked at me. "But a lot for a young man to shoulder. From boy to man, apprentice to pilot. One thing at a time, eh? One thing at a time." All the time he kept patting his daughter's shoulder, until the patting became pushing and he forced her back into her chair.

"I'm sorry." My voice so pathetic it cracked like a boy's. I looked at her once, hard. "I'm sorry, Noemi. I'll come back tomorrow."

I turned quickly and left, knowing she would burst into tears. She did, loudly; I shut the door on her wailing. Then I made my way to the barn.

Arrow didn't see me enter. She lay against Nazo's gray-bristled back as he slept, facing the wall. Pipo cuddled beside her, his one front paw draped over her stomach. When he saw me, he thumped his tail, and Arrow looked up.

She sprang to her feet with such panic that Nazo awoke and lumbered upright. Pipo, barking, stumble-dashed toward me on his three legs. I shushed him by giving him my hand to lick as my other hand closed the door behind me.

"Why are you here?" Arrow positioned the donkey between us. Her trembling hands ran along Nazo's neck, soothing him. He nibbled the end of her braid.

"It's alright," I assured her. For some reason, the sight of her alarm made me utterly calm. I felt more in command of myself than I had since I first saw her in the harbor. "I just wanted to make sure you're alright."

"Of course I am," she said too loudly, picking at a piece of straw stuck in Nazo's mane.

"I'm sorry about what happened on the quay." My voice sounded so tender and brotherly, I almost convinced myself of my own indifference.

"I am, too. So very sorry. I'll never do it again. I didn't know." She only looked up once; the piece of straw was stubbornly stuck in Nazo's mane.

"Arrow, please don't feel badly about it." I took a step forward. Nazo shifted, and Arrow darted back to ensure he remained between us. “Things happen sometimes. They’ll happen to you now that you’ve grown up. It’s just—part of it all.”

“Thank you. I think I understand. Will you please go now? Nazo is sick. See how upset he is? You’re upsetting him.”

“Arrow—”

“Are you betrothed? To Noemi? Did you tell them at dinner?”

Poor, brave girl. Her voice shook, but she asked it anyway.

“No.”

At last, she looked up. I knew, then, that what happened on the quay was not some passing disturbance. It was the homeward wind filling the sails.

I stepped closer until nothing but the beast of burden stood between us. Somehow I kept my shell of calmness, stroking Nazo from one side as she stroked him from the other. Our hands didn’t touch and I didn’t try to make them. It was so new for her; the newness flooded out of her. It was new for me too, in a different way. I still felt the rush of *this* Arrow flooding backward and changing every other moment of her into something that glittered. As we stood there, petting the fuzzy old donkey, looking down at his white-frosted fur instead of each other, I simply gave in—let myself love her.

It felt like being a king, when one had only ever dared to dream of being a pilot.

“Why?”

“Why what?”

“Why didn’t you ask for Noemi’s hand?”

Our fingers touched, then. She thought it was an accident; I knew it was not.

“Because I need time to think.”

“You are a pilot now?”

We touched again. This time it was her doing, not mine.

“Yes.”

"Will you go now, Tomás?"

"Yes."

I stepped back. Before I left, I filled myself with the sight of her. Her high cheekbones and little trim nose, her slim throat and simple curves, the graceful strength of her. Her dancing and astronomy and Greek poets. Her donkey and dog.

"Arrow—"

"Please go, Tomás, please!"

Her urgency told me all I needed to know.

I left. I walked home through Lipa's darkened streets feeling as if each of my steps could shake the island to its roots, as if my breaths were puffs of eternity, as if I were a giant in one of Arrow's stories, squeezed into the body of a man.

I knew—truly knew—that great misery would come from loving Arrow. I knew that Noemi was a storm no man could weather. I knew we had gone too deep, tied too many knots, to simply cut anchor. But I couldn't *feel* those things that night.

I could only feel that I was a king.

Not just a pilot, a king.

I didn't see Arrow for three days after that. She avoided me. Because I also wished to avoid Noemi, the situation was difficult. I found myself sneaking like a thief, hiding in the shadows of buildings.

I did see Noemi, once. I told her, "Give me until my twentieth birthday. I'm still an apprentice. Anything could happen before then."

Anything could happen.

Those were my exact words.

On the fourth day, I had the happy idea to look for Arrow in the harbor. At last I spotted her surveying the shipyard, where a huge carrack slumbered, half-built, its fresh pine gleaming like the sun-brightened bones of a whale. The master shipwright, Eloi Fernandes, was showing Arrow the mixture of pitch, tar, and grease used to caulk the hull's seams. I slipped alongside her and listened; the shipwright saw nothing strange in this, for Arrow and I had come many times to see the ship together.

She took a quick breath, not letting it out for a long time. Though splashes of red colored her cheeks, she took no other notice of me. Her fingers ran along the side of the hull. I put out my hand and let it trail the beams in her wake.

The carrack had been nearly two years in the making, the biggest ship ever built in Lipa Harbor. Noemi and I had once climbed up into its hollow frame at night and kissed under the stars. We used to dream I would be its pilot someday. Now, my hand on its hull brought a strange sympathy with the vessel, as if it had been a living thing; we understood each other, that ship and I. Both of us huge and empty and waiting for something to happen.

A caulker came with a question, calling Eloi Fernandes away. Left to ourselves, Arrow and I stood looking past the shipyard toward the quay where another ship was docking.

"It's the Silver Egret," I said. "In two weeks' time, I'll be her pilot."

A pause. "Second pilot," she corrected.

I laughed. "Second pilot, then. Still, it's what I've worked my whole life for."

She nodded.

"Shall we go and greet her?"

She nodded.

As we walked, I was determined to draw her out of her silence. "I haven't seen you, Arrow. Not since the night I arrived."

This line of attack had no effect. I tried another.

"How is Nazo? Is he better?"

I should have known better than to ask questions that could be answered by a nod. My next question demanded at least a sentence.

"What was wrong with him?"

She stopped abruptly, staring at the ground. "Nothing. Nothing was wrong with him. You know that, Tomás." Then she hid her face in her hands.

I felt truly sorry for her. I had never met anyone so incapable of concealing her feelings. No wonder she had avoided me.

"It's alright." I put my hand on her shoulder, but she shrugged it away.

Wrapping her arms around herself, she quickened her steps until she was a few paces in front of me. A swarm of seagulls shrieked into the air as she disrupted their meal of seaweed and fish offal.

"Arrow," I called. "Can't you tell me what's wrong?"

But I already knew. She knew I knew, and she was frustrated at my pretending we didn't both know. All at once I saw my course forward. With Arrow, the only way was the straight channel, the open sea.

"Arrow, I think I might be in love with you."

She kept walking, didn't stop or turn around. "But how do you know? You thought you loved Noemi, all these years."

"I don't know. I said I *think*."

"Then what? What do you do when you think you're in love with someone?"

"You have to find out."

"How?"

"You have to talk to them. You have to face them. You have to look at me, Arrow. How else are you supposed to know?"

She stopped. She turned. Her nose and cheeks were burned by the sun, her eyes ice by contrast. "Me?"

"Yes. If you think you're in love with me, you have to find out." I took her hands, so soft and warm and trembling.

"I'm scared, Tomás."

"Me too." I pulled her in, not tight to my body, but enough so I could wrap my arms around her waist. She folded herself into me without a thought, as if it were the only thing to be done.

"Someone will see us. They'll tell Noemi."

"I know."

"But you said you didn't know. You said you *think*."

"I lied, Arrow." This I whispered, leaning down until our foreheads touched. "I *know*."

She closed her eyes. Her breathing shuddered. "But how do I know if I know?"

"I found you, Arrow. I found you in the Far Deeps. A whole sea, and I came right to you. Doesn't that mean something?"

"I don't know," she whispered. She was falling into me. Without trying, without resisting. Sliding and falling into me.

"I think I loved you even then, Arrow. That's why I was so afraid of you. Remember the first time you said my name? You tried to kiss me."

But here I miscalculated.

I felt her tense. Lifting her head, she searched my eyes as if she were trying to see behind them. Then she reached down and plucked one of my hands from around her waist. Holding it up, she pressed her palm flat against my palm and held it there. Closed her eyes, furrowed her brow, and held it there. Listening for something, it seemed, listening through our hands. I held my breath.

It felt like a test, whatever it was.

She dropped her hand. A deep, sweet sadness bloomed on her face: love and sorrow and regret. I felt alarmed, sure I had failed the test. But she didn't pull away from me. She laid her sad face on my chest and let my poor silent hand steal back around her waist.

"Between all things," she murmured, "is a space we can never cross over."

"I want to marry you, Arrow." It came pouring out of me, there was no stopping it. "I want to marry you and not Noemi, in two weeks when my apprenticeship is over."

"And then—what?"

"You'll sail away with me, on the Egret. We'll go to live on another island, where no one knows us."

This, I thought, would be necessary in case Noemi told her father our secret and Mundo sought my death. It didn't seem like the right moment to explain this to Arrow.

"And?"

"I'll be a pilot, and you'll be my wife. We'll be so happy people will say, 'There go the happiest man and woman in the world.'"

"And?"

"We'll have children. They'll have eyes like the sea. You'll teach them alchemy and Aristotle."

I felt her sigh. She turned around, still in my arms, until she was facing the quay. Closing my eyes, I breathed in the scent of her hair. Her arms folded across mine; she threaded her fingers through mine. We breathed together. The seagulls cried. I was lost in her.

Then she screamed. "Wick!"

My eyes flew open. Tearing herself from my arms, Arrow bolted toward the quay where the Egret had docked. A crowd had gathered. I started running before I understood what was happening. Arrow fought through the crowd, and I fought after her.

Huddled near the dock, stooping over each other or sprawled with exhaustion, was a cargo of black Africans. Their ankles were shackled and chained. There must have been forty or so in all.

To the best of my knowledge, the Egret had never carried a cargo of slaves before. There had certainly never been Africans in Lipa. I had seen them on other islands where they grew sugar, but we were all fishermen and sailors. Though I was intent only on Arrow, the crowd's chatter sifted through my brain until I pieced together that these slaves were bound for Mirda, but Governor de la Concha, having decided to keep a few for himself, had asked that they all be brought out for his men to inspect.

Arrow ran from one slave to the next, crying out over and over, "Wick! Wick!"

"What's that girl doing?"

"She acts as if she knows one of them."

"Look, it's the girl rescued by the Tailcatcher!"

"The girl from the giants."

"The girl from the sea."

I finally caught up with Arrow. Any time I tried to grab her elbow, she tore away from me. She was sobbing by then. I saw a sailor coming with a whip, one of the slaves' guards, a mountain of a man. Putting myself between him and Arrow, I urged, "Arrow, come away, you must come away!" She heard nothing.

Some of the Africans looked at her with surprise, some with hope, some with pity. Some did not look at her at all, locked in their despair. After she reached the last one she whirled at the guard bearing down on us. She didn't see me at all, looked past me as if I were invisible.

"Why are they chained?" she demanded, her grief turning to sudden rage. "What are you doing to them? Let them go!"

And she attacked the guard. There was no reason in it, no clear goal; it was pure wrath unleashed. She tried to wrest the whip out of his hands. She scratched his face and kicked him. It was like watching a fox attack a bear. He flung her aside with one arm. Then, dragging her up by the hair, he began to shower blow after blow on her face.

I leapt at him, plowing into his waist. Though my full strength was hardly enough to set him off balance, he let go of Arrow and turned on me. We fell to the ground, wrestling and striking with fists. Some in the crowd shrieked in fear, some cheered for one of us or the other. Two other guards came and dragged us apart.

But the moment we were separated, Arrow attacked him again.

"Stop, Arrow!" I broke free and this time rushed for her, grasping her around the waist with both arms and dragging her away, staggering back into the crowd as a way to protect her.

She fought me like a snarling animal. When I wouldn't let go, she bit my arm. At last, when the pain was too much to bear, I released her, gasping and clutching the wound.

"She's mad!" some cried.

"She's possessed by demons!"

"The Africans have bewitched her!"

Arrow started running. I ran after her. The crowd followed like a swarm of angry bees.

Dizzy from her blows, she stumbled as she reached the shipyard.

"Arrow!" I begged. "Please!"

I picked her up off the ground. My arm was bleeding where her teeth had torn it. She had fallen close to one of the firepits where they were melting pitch to caulk the ship, so I half-shoved, half-dragged her a few steps away.

"Why, Tomás?" Her voice was not a cry now, but a quiet plea. "Why?"

"They are slaves, Arrow. The traders are bringing them to work in the sugar fields."

"I don't understand."

"They grow sugar, Arrow." I yelled it because I didn't know how to make her listen, and because the crowd was surging toward us. "Sugar! The sugar you eat."

I once met a sailor from Hibernia who told me of a creature which haunts that island, a female spirit called a banshee. The banshee utters a shrieking howl of blackest agony, a harbinger of death filling its hearers with maddening terror. This sailor had heard a banshee once; he could only speak of it in a whisper, his face paling at the memory.

The cry Arrow gave then—no banshee could have held a candle to it.

The crowd halted, a mass of bodies thrown back as if by an invisible wall. I, too, staggered from her, terrified.

Arrow turned. In one swift motion, she slammed her body into the side of a barrel full of pitch, overturning it. The pitch flowed through the coals, igniting into a lake of fire. The crowd screamed. In the span of a few seconds, the lake reached the half-built carrack's hull. At the same moment, sparks sputtered up into the cauldron of pitch that had been heating over the coals. The cauldron exploded, sending up a ball of orange flame. Flames streaked along the hull in bright ribbons as the ship began to burn.

It is so impossible to write truly of a moment like that. In the midst of it, one has no thoughts. One is only actions: leaping out of the fire's path, tearing off one's shirt to beat out the flames, throwing buckets of water as they are passed, choking on smoke, staggering back, gasping for air, grabbing more buckets, rushing back into the blaze, until at last, someone grabbing me, pulling me back, saying, "She's lost, Tomás, she's lost." Understanding: *the ship, he means the ship*.

Remembering Arrow.

Remembering her standing back, staring at what she had done.

Remembering her running away.

"The moon has set, and the Pleiades.
It is the middle of the night.
Time passes on and on, but I lie here alone."

—Sappho

7

My father came and took me home. He led me by the hand, like a little child. My mother washed me, tended my wounds, and put me to bed. They spoke to me in soft voices. I didn't speak at all. It happened around me as things happen in dreams.

The next morning, a soldier brought me to the prison to be questioned. I was not accused of starting the fire, for at least fifty people had witnessed Arrow's fit of madness. They mostly asked me questions about her. I answered them in perfect truth.

We were walking along the harbor.

When she saw the Africans, she cried out.

She seemed to be looking for someone she couldn't find.

She attacked the guard.

She attacked me.

I ran after her.

She started a fire.

Did it seem that she started the fire on purpose?

Yes.

Do you know why?

No.

It cost me nothing to answer their questions. I was a thousand miles distant from myself—the same dreamlike feeling as the night before. They examined the bite on my arm, bringing in a petty sorcerer to determine whether there was any witchcraft in it, a curse or enchantment. The sorcerer said it was an ordinary human bite. The soldiers thanked me for my attempts to save the ship, commending my courage and lamenting what it had cost me, for my body had many burns. Then they let me go.

I went home and slept. My mother rubbed salve on my burns. My brothers and sisters peeked into my room with frightened faces. I began to feel pain gradually as the numbness wore off. So passed the night.

The next morning, I woke up and knew where Arrow was.

It wasn't a vision; it was the certainty that comes from knowing a person. I knew where she was and I knew she had been there since the night of the fire, so I brought a loaf of bread and a skin of water.

I climbed to the top of the old watchtower on South Hill. There she was, huddled in a corner of one of the battlements, watching the last shreds of smoke rising from the ashes of the ship. The whole left side of her face was bruised and swollen from the guard's blows.

Without speaking, I handed her the water. She stared at it, as if doubting whether she deserved my aid.

"Take it, Arrow."

She drank, but wouldn't eat the food.

She tried to touch one of my burns. I winced and pulled away, for they were quite painful.

We sat together in silence along the wall.

Then I asked, my voice still hoarse from the smoke, "Did you mean to do it, Arrow?"

"Tomás," she whispered, eyes fixed on the paving-stones before her, "how can I explain? I wanted to burn down the whole world."

Something broke in me, some gate that had been holding back everything I couldn't feel. Stuttering sobs burst out, then a volley of tears. I curled on the ground, weeping like a child. Arrow took my head in her lap.

"I was sorry, Tomás," she tried to soothe me. "A moment after I did it, I was sorry. But... I wanted to burn down the whole world."

After my tears were all spent, I lay in her lap feeling empty. She stroked my hair. It could have been minutes or hours. I'm not sure whether I fell asleep. I was so empty.

Finally I asked her, "Why?"

She took a deep breath. "Do you remember when I told you about my doll, Tomás? My doll named Wick?"

But I already knew this. I had always known it, deep down, and the knowledge fought to the surface as she screamed his name on the shore. I rolled over, my head still in her lap, until I could look up into her face. "He wasn't a doll," I said.

She shook her head.

"He was an African?"

"He looked like them."

"I thought he was your brother. Your twin, you used to say."

"I thought so, too. I didn't understand how it worked—brothers and sisters."

"Where is he now?"

"The wizard took him. That part was real. The Wizard of Seven."

"So when you saw the slaves—"

"Of course it wouldn't have been him. Not without the wizard. But oh, Tomás, just for a moment... You can't know what I felt when I thought, one of them might be Wick."

All through this, fear rose in my heart and I tried to push it down. I could hardly bring myself to ask her, "What are you going to do?"

Instead of answering, she touched my face. Avoiding my bruises and burns, she traced along my hairline, then around my jaw to my cheekbones, my nose. She felt the curve of my lips. A few stray tears leaked out the corners of my eyes, and she wiped them away.

"I can't stay here," she said.

"I know."

She seemed surprised. "You do?"

I sat up. "Arrow, you committed a terrible crime. Everyone is looking for you. If they find you, you will be hanged, or burnt at the stake."

"Oh."

Her eyebrows furrowed. I waited, praying it would sink in.

"But... the men who trapped those other humans... they will not be hanged?"

"No."

She looked out over the sea. "I can't stay here, Tomás."

"We have to find a way to get you off the island. The Egret sails in less than two weeks for Mirda. I'll find a way to hide you on board. When we get to Mirda, we'll run away somewhere until the ship sails on without us. We'll take false names. After a time, I'll join a crew where no one knows me, on a ship bound for the mainland. From Iberia, we'll go north. Perhaps we'll come to the land of your birth, wherever that may be. You'll look the same as everyone else, and no one from Lipa will ever find you. You'll be safe."

"It won't work, Tomás."

"It will. The hardest part will be in Mirda, where you could be so easily recognized by your northern features, but we'll find a way. I promise."

"No, I mean—I can't be with you."

"I don't understand."

"I can't marry you, Tomás. You can't come with me. I have to go alone."

"What are you saying?"

"I have to find Wick."

The blood came pounding into my ears until they rang. Heat and coldness washed over me in waves. It was a fear I had never felt even in storms at sea. "I'll come with you. We'll find him together."

"You can't."

"Why?"

"Because I can't marry you."

"Why? Why, Arrow?" For some reason, every terrible thing she said made the pain of my burns stronger, as if she were scratching them with a fingernail.

"Because Wick and I are one person. I can't explain it to you because you don't know what that's like."

"You *were*. You *were* one person. But you were children. Noemi and I—we were like that, once. Now we've grown up. Things change, Arrow."

She shook her head. "I won't change. I'll grow up, but I won't change."

"You already have changed!" I cried. "You speak a new language. You read and write and calculate. You started that fire. Didn't that change you?"

"I will unchange."

"You can't, Arrow. You can't unchange. It's the one thing you can't do."

"Wizards do impossible things."

"But we're human. Humans change, all, always."

This troubled her, yet she thrust her chin up defiantly as if to say, *See my armor; I am safe; your truth cannot reach me.*

I looked hard into her eyes. She started by meeting my gaze, but lost her courage. "Arrow," I asked in a low voice, "do you love me?"

She flinched. "You know I do, Tomás."

"That is change. Don't you see?" I took her in my arms.

"Not yet," she said. "It's not change yet."

But she laid her head on my shoulder. As on the shore, I could feel her sliding and falling into me. I slipped my hand around the side of her face and tilted it toward my own. She didn't pull away.

"This changes you, Arrow."

And I kissed her.

It was like this: when the sea touches the sun, and the sun floods it with gold.

"Oh," she said. "Oh, Tomás, Tomás."

We kissed again. It was as if an anchor had been buried in each of us, in each other's hearts, and we were winching them in crank by crank.

I laid her on the paving stones, my arm cradling her head. I ignored the pain of my burns because I wanted all of my skin to touch all of hers, no matter how it hurt. I kissed her neck and her collarbones. I pulled down her bodice to kiss the place between her breasts.

Then I realized she was saying something, her eyes tight shut, in a language I had never heard in all my travels. It wasn't Greek, nor Latin, nor even Giantish. The words rolled and sighed like the tongue of the barbarous Celts, half music, half prayer. The beauty of the sound somehow invaded my vision, each word bursting behind my eyes like a succession of suns tearing through cloud. Fear shrank my innards. I pulled away, gasping, as the thought flashed through me that she was a witch after all.

Her eyes flew open, their blue weirdly bright against the dark bruises surrounding them. Her gaze burned into me, down to a depth I didn't know I possessed until that moment. She blinked, once. In that blink I felt the certain knowledge that I had failed a second test, as I had first failed on the shore when she pressed my palm against hers. Tears poured down her face. She shook her head.

"Please," I choked. Witch or no, she was my heart's blood.

Turning away, she pushed and squirmed from out my arms.

I whimpered, both from the pain of my burns, suddenly returning, and from the pain of desiring her. Gripped the ground, gripped loose stones, closed my eyes, not trusting myself to look at her. Her footsteps clattered as she stumbled further from me, dragging herself up.

"I must find Wick," she said, her voice cold, hard, flat. "I promised him."

Hoarse and pitiful, I flung her name out like a net. "Arrow. Arrow. O God!"

"I know, Tomás. I feel what you feel."

How could she know, and feel, and answer in a voice so cold, hard, flat?

"It's like… it's like a desperate gambler," she said, "who risks everything on a great wager. Everything—his whole happiness. Love, even. If he loses the wager, he loses all. But there is no other way to win."

I thought of hurling myself off the battlement, but I was still too much in the grip of desire to move. Breathing into the dust, I tried to focus on my body's pain. At last I calmed enough to drag myself to the bottle of water and drink. I sensed where she was standing and kept my face turned in the other direction.

"I must leave now, Arrow. Otherwise—I'll touch you."

"Go, Tomás." The same terrible voice. "Tomorrow, will you bring Brother Agostin?"

"It's too dangerous. I'll bring him tonight, when it's dark."

"Don't come without him. Don't come alone."

Making no answer, I fled.

I told Brother Agostin everything. Except the part about kissing Arrow and the fey language that, when she spoke it, drove us apart.

He said, "I will come. Meet me after sunset at the base of the stairs."

We met as planned and ascended. The monk brought a leather pack I assumed held food.

She stood waiting for us. One of her fists clenched and unclenched; otherwise she was still. Ignoring me, she fixed her gaze on Brother Agostin. "Has Tomás told you?"

"He has."

"I forgot about Wick. I *tried* to forget him. Ever since the day I first climbed this tower and made him into a doll. But he's real, Brother. Not just real; he's everything. I promised him I would find him. Don't you see? If I were to be burnt at the stake, it should not be for starting that fire, but for breaking my promise to Wick."

I strode forward, arms crossed tight over my chest. "You were a child. What is a child's promise? Just words. Like wishing on a star."

But the monk put a hand on my quivering shoulder. "True, Tomás, in themselves promises have little strength. But promises are like poems, flares set off to brighten for one instant some dark mountain of mystery behind them. The strength of the promise is in the size of the mountain."

When he said that, *some dark mountain of mystery*, I thought, for some reason, of the fey language she had spoken. I thought, too, of how she had pressed her palm against mine on the shore. What depth was she sounding in me, and what was my lack? A cold despair beat down on me as Brother Agostin continued.

"The truth behind your promise, Arrow, is this: Wick is your task. He belongs to you and none other. Whether you promised him or no, you must find him. And the task that he is requires all that you are."

Arrow inhaled sharply, mouth pressed shut, as one might when a doctor probes a wound. "Yes, that is true. It's the truest thing in all the world. But... how do you know, Brother? How can you possibly know, when you don't know Wick?"

His smile creased all that could be seen of his face above his beard as he put a calloused hand on her cheek. "My child, for seven years I've taught you, sat beside you, walked with you. Do you think I've learned nothing of your heart save what you meant to reveal? I do know Wick. I know him in you."

She grasped both his hands and kissed them. "Thank you, Brother. Oh, thank you for knowing him. Then you will understand my wager. Tomás doesn't understand."

"I don't," I spat. "I defy your wager."

She ignored me as a mother ignores a child flinging itself on the ground in a fit of wailing.

Brother Agostin folded her hands between his. "The mystery of Wick and Arrow may grow darker still, the more you shed light on it. My child, I have learned something about the Wizard of Seven. Something that may guide you in your task. I didn't tell you before because I was waiting for the day you yourself chose, without coercion, to speak the full truth of your past. That day has come."

Arrow jerked her hands free and took a step backward, a step toward me. I moved in behind her, noticing for the first time that she still smelled like burning. Though her whole body trembled, I dared not even put my hand on her shoulder.

"It began five years ago," said the monk, "the day I showed you the Map of Wizards. You told me of a Wizard of Seven who had no name. Though I knew nothing of Wick, I knew this wizard had committed some crime against you much worse than taking your doll.

"You may remember that a few weeks later I tried to question you about the wizard. But you wouldn't talk about him—*couldn't*, I realized, because the pain of his mention was too acute. One thing, though: you told me that other wizards who came to the Kingdom of the Giants knew of him. I consulted the map for wizards in the northern regions. One of them, a Wizard of Five named Merkum, was known to me. I hadn't met him, but the wizard acquaintance of whom I have spoken described him as a worthy wizard.

"I wrote to him relating all I knew of your story, asking in particular about the Wizard of Seven. I sent the letter to the mainland, its only address being *To the Wizard Merkum, in Hibernia*. Well, as you can imagine, it took three years to reach him. It was another year before I received his reply."

Opening his pack, he pulled out a letter.

PART II · CHAPTER 7

The Wizard Merkum, to one Brother Agostin, in Lipa of the Sorry Islands

Dear Brother Agostin,

Terribly sorry for the delay. I left Hibernia six months ago and have been sailing around the coast of Albion with a crew of pirates. Not, to be sure, as a pirate myself, but as a kind of scientific observer. The customs, codes, and superstitions of these particular ruffians are most amusing, and on some occasions edifying. Not to mention they have taught me to dance! After three hundred years you'd think someone else would have attempted it, but no. Only barbarian corsairs had the courage to take me in hand.

Now, to your question about a Wizard of Seven with no name. The girl is telling the truth, as far as she knows it. Here is my contribution to the tale, as far as I know it.

Any wizard over a hundred years old will remember the name Falcius. He was a Councilor in Gnoze for some thirty years until he suddenly died, or rather disappeared, about a century ago. Well, time went on. The disappearance of wizards is by no means unusual. But the reason we thought he died was, as you yourself have mentioned, the Map of Wizards in the Sorry Islands. It no longer showed him. In all previous instances, the disappearance of a wizard from the Map of Wizards indicated his disappearance from this mortal plane.

Then came rumors of a Wizard of Seven. They came from far-flung places; from isles beyond the Far Deeps, from the Virgin Shores, and, yes, from the Kingdom of the Giants. In these rumors, the Wizard of Seven never had a name. He has been called "The Wizard Who Changes Things into Other Things," a morbidly unwieldy appellation.

No one connected him with Falcius until a certain, jocular wizard, known for his inobtrusive wisdom and eccentric choice of acquaintance, noted some similarities between reports of TWWCTiOT and the aforementioned. In particular, a lust for power, flagrant disregard of the natural rights of creatures, a veneer of philosophical language confounding the ignorant, and very bad teeth.

Well, this got some of us wondering—what would happen if a wizard removed his name? The first objection brought forward was that it was impossible. You can imagine how this set a room of wizard-scholars roaring with laughter. We like a good joke about impossible things. Then we wiggle our fingers. So, if a Wizard of Six named Falcius removed his name, he would be a Wizard of Seven with no name, strongly resembling TWWCTiOT.

We then discussed the implications of having no name. We conceived it like this: a human with no soul. That is to say, a human having some kind of animating principle, but not one that illuminates—quite the opposite. Like a vacuous hole inside the body of a wizard, animating that body from obscurity and emptiness instead of his starborn light.

Have I made you shiver yet? Well, put this letter away, wrap a blanket around your fusty monk's robe and drink some hot tea. I suppose I've spent too long with pirates, and have begun to revel in contemplating the world's nasty underbelly!

But here's one more thing. At least twice now have I heard this rumor: that he intends to become a Wizard of Eight. What would this mean? A power unprecedented in the history of wizardry, but hinted at in some of our least popular legends. In these legends, the Wizard of Eight and the ending of the Race of Wizards always coincide.

My advice is, find out what he did to the girl. Anything we understand about his motives could be a step toward preventing such unpleasant business as the rise of a tyrannical demi-god and the annihilation of our race.

And eat a biscuit into the bargain. With your tea and your blanket. Merciful day, what a gruesome letter! If you weren't a monk I'd suggest a nip of brandy.

If you have need of me, the ship I'm on is called the Lusty Badger. Don't ask me—I didn't name it.

Ever at your service,

M

Without knowing it, Arrow took hold of my hand as she read. I pressed in close behind her, reading over her shoulder. The further we read, the tighter she gripped my fingers. I folded my arms around her, intending comfort, not possession. I don't think any of it was quite real to me until I read that letter. A terrible, relentless peace settled over me, like a fog wrapping a harbor in white stillness.

When she finished reading, Arrow ceased crushing my fingers but remained in my arms. "What does it mean?" she asked.

"It means you were right," said Brother Agostin. "There is a Wizard of Seven who has no name, and he is wicked."

"What about Wick? Where is he, and how can I find him?"

"I don't know, but your best hope lies in this: you must go to the Wizard Merkum. Find this ship, the Lusty Badger, and tell Merkum everything you remember about the Wizard of Seven. Wizards are notoriously selfish. Neither he nor any other wizard will care much about your search for Wick unless you offer something in return. What you have to offer is every word the Wizard of Seven said to you, everything he did in your presence. If this nameless wizard is as great a threat as Merkum describes, your information may be valuable indeed."

She pushed free of my arms, clenching her fists at her sides. "Yes. That is what I will do. The pirate wizard will help me. I will make him help me."

"How will she get off the island?" I asked.

Brother Agostin put his hand on my shoulder. "She will need the help of her friends."

This is how we did it.

The Tailcatcher left for the mainland a few days later. I was not on it, as my apprenticeship had ended. But I bribed a sailor whom I knew to be deep in gambling debt to hide Arrow in the cargo deck. We offered a bribe greater than the reward for her capture; though I at first proposed to pay it from my savings, Brother Agostin preferred to take it from the monastery's alms, over which he had charge as porter and almoner. We smuggled Arrow in a cart from the old watchtower to Lipa Harbor, and in a wine cask onto the ship.

The ship sailed.

Since then, seven months have passed. I have had no news of Arrow except my accomplice's assurance, when he came to collect his bribe, that she made it safely to the mainland.

Just before she left, Arrow hugged me very tight. She traced the lines of my face, the way she had as I lay in her lap atop the watchtower. "When I find Wick, I will tell him everything about you. The way it was between us. It will make more sense to him than it does to me."

I'm not sure how or why she thought this would comfort me.

"I will never forget you, Tomás. But I will never come back. Don't wait for me. You mustn't wait for me. Promise me you won't."

"I make no promise. Even if you never come back, you can't stop me waiting."

This troubled her, and I wanted it to trouble her. I imagined that she took these words with her into the empty wine cask, into the belly of the ship, that they echoed around her as she huddled in the dark for days on end.

But more likely, they did not.

More likely, she thought only of Wick.

And yet—

Brother Agostin told me of a dream he had some weeks ago. In his dream, Arrow carried a small silken pouch, finely embroidered. Something valuable was hidden inside, but Brother Agostin didn't know what it was. At night, she stole out to sea in a coracle which brought her to the Far Deeps, beneath the constellation Barba Dei. The Buried Isle rose from the sea, with its glittering cities and gem-strewn beaches.

A mermaid sat on a rock amidst this golden glory, combing pearls out of her hair. Arrow held out her little pouch, and the mermaid opened it. A tiny piece of amber sea glass, shaped roughly like the head of an arrow, spilled into her hand.

That bit of glass was the first of the gifts I ever gave Arrow, when she was still an ugly child who couldn't speak and I was a boy who knew nothing, nothing, oh nothing at all.

"This is it?" asked the mermaid.

"This is everything," said Arrow.

"It is enough."

The mermaid swallowed the bit of glass. The Buried Isle broke apart. Its cities crumbled, its beaches caved, and it collapsed into the sea. Arrow's coracle spun in the swirling foam.

Then Arrow sailed on. She sailed on and on.

That was the end of the dream.

"It reminded me of something," Brother Agostin told me. "That night, on the tower, Arrow said something about a wager. What did she mean?"

I didn't answer him. I didn't want to. But now our fleet sails in four days. The ship is waiting. The firebirds are waiting. Noemi is waiting. Only Arrow is not waiting, will never wait for me. Yet I've written all this—for what purpose?

Because someone should know.

It is right that someone should know.

—Tomás de Rueda

Addendum by Brother Agostin
Written at Lipa Monastery
17 July, in the Year of Sails

On 11 June, Tomás de Rueda departed on the Silver Egret with a fleet of twelve ships from the Sorry Islands to take the Isle of the Firebirds for His Majesty's Crown. No word of his end has come back to us, for the Battle of the Firebirds—that unspeakable catastrophe—had no known survivors.

Two days before he sailed, on 9 June, Tomás de Rueda suddenly married Noemi Albares, daughter of Edmundo Albares, barber-surgeon of the Tailcatcher. (N.B. Edmundo Albares also perished in the Battle of the Firebirds.)

More than eight months have passed since the burning of the ship. I have heard nothing of Arrow.

—B.A.

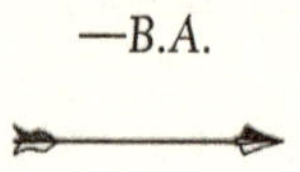

PART III

THE CAVEAT

"So have I, burdened with sorrow, bereft of my home, far from dear kin, bound up with fetters my heart's hidden thoughts."

—The Wanderer

8

The city will be big, Tomás had said. *So much bigger than Lipa. Think of twenty Lipas crushed together.*

But it was nothing like that. Lipa was a sleepy turtle whose back slouched up from the sea, settlements dotting its hills like barnacles. The city was a whale. Its yawning mouth of a harbor could have swallowed twenty Lipas in its sleep. Its ancient slab of flesh, sheathed in a pitted, growth-encrusted skin of teeming streets and weary buildings, stretched out to the horizon, and still Arrow could see no flicker of its tail.

Get out of the city as quick as you can, Tomás had said. *Seek places without sailors or merchants, places with farmers and craftsmen who will have heard no news from Lipa.* But here was quay after quay, market after market. A tumult of unknown languages piling thick in the air, mixed with the common Iberian tongue, which was close enough to the dialect of Lipa for Arrow to understand. Wares of all kinds flashed by their sellers: brilliant cloth, rioting spices, ornaments, tools, gold and silver, wood and steel, fur and feathers. The noise of it pressed Arrow backward, clung like smoke as she passed.

Don't touch anything.

That was what Tomás had said most. At least ten times.

Why? Is it wrong?

It's different. It's not everybody's way. It draws attention.

So Arrow wrapped her arms around herself as she fought her way out of the city. At first, she was too afraid to lift her eyes past the level of carts, dogs, and small children. The feeling seized her that *burner of ships* was blazoned into her black pupils, and anyone who met her eyes would see her crime beaming out. The mark of one small burn on her left collarbone had ripened into a scar, where pitch from the exploding cauldron had splashed. When people saw her, did they see anything but that scar?

Soon enough she realized: no one saw her at all. It was like a magic in the city's air. For the first time in her life, Arrow felt invisible. It frightened her more than being seen.

After the city will come a road, Tomás had said. *Wake before dawn, start your travel early. Always stop well before nightfall, before evening if you can.*

Can I run?

Run?

Along the road.

No, Arrow. Only thieves run. Only those who are afraid. Never let anyone think you are afraid.

Still, when a stretch of road came with no one on it, only sheep nodding in the fields, Arrow ran. She couldn't help it. Those were the best times.

Whenever a wagon passed her, she begged for a ride. More often than not, the driver agreed. But if he asked for payment, Arrow shook her head and waved him on. The purse of coins hidden around her neck was for food only, too precious to spend sparing her feet.

Tomás had given her all he saved during his apprenticeship. Though he dropped the purse casually into her palm with his chin jutted skyward, feigning interest in seabirds, she knew what it was. He would have used it to furnish a home for Noemi, if...

If.

Always find a shelter to sleep in. Sometimes Arrow had no choice but to pay for lodging. But whenever possible, she crept into dark corners of barns, empty shepherd's huts, mills gone silent at the day's end.

Tomás had given her a knife in a sheath. *Wear it outside your clothing, where everyone can see it. If ever you feel threatened, put your hand on the hilt. Try to look manly, as if you've used it before.* Arrow was surprised how often she needed to do this. The Knife Dance, she called it. She felt false and stupid, like a rabbit wearing a fox's tail. But it was enough; the strange men walked on, laughing that she wasn't worth the effort.

The more Arrow danced the Knife Dance, the less she felt like a rabbit in a fox's tail and the more she felt like a fox.

As she walked, rode, and ran, Arrow thought. She thought of Mundo swinging her around when she ran to greet him after a sea voyage, just the way he swung his own daughters. She thought of Ona teaching her to wash clothes and card wool. She thought of Loida, dear Loidita, of braiding each other's hair and giggling secrets. Of Irma's sticky kisses smelling of goat's milk and figs.

She thought of Tomás.

She thought and thought of Tomás.

Tomás-thoughts were like seashells, each one a different shape, size, and hue. All beautiful. Arrow arranged them in her mind the way she and Loida arranged shells on the beach. The shape was like a starfish or a spoked wheel; in the center was the kiss. Everything, all the other beautiful things, led back to that, always.

Why had she not kissed him again? Why not every time she saw him, from that first night on the watchtower until she said goodbye and crawled into the wine cask?

Sometimes she remembered the kiss just the way it happened. Sometimes other ways it could have happened.

She never asked herself, why didn't I marry Tomás? Why didn't I let him come with me?

Only—why didn't I kiss him more, when I had the chance?

She thought, too, of Wick.

At first, Wick-thoughts were so painful that Arrow didn't consider them in the same vein as other thoughts. They were more like a surgery performed on her mind, one of those gruesome operations aboard ship Mundo found a strange pleasure in describing. First, to bind the tourniquet tight, tighter, tighter. Then, to give the patient strong brandy and set a piece of wood between his teeth. Then, to start the careful, relentless sawing until one felt the bone give way and the limb fall. The difference was that Arrow's operation was an un-amputation; each grind of the blade opened up the bloody stump where she had cut Wick away, grafting him back into his rightful place.

This is one of the first things Arrow remembered, while still crouched in her barrel-prison in the stifling hold of the Tailcatcher:

It was November, bleak and bare. She had awakened to Wick standing at the window and asked as she always asked, "Wick, what do you see?"

"I see the trees waving at us, waving so hard, afraid we're not looking. They're calling something, Arrow! Do you know what they're saying?"

"No," she grunted into her pillow.

"They're calling, 'Happy birthday! Happy birthday!'"

Arrow struggled upright. "What do you mean?"

"It's our birthday, Arrow!"

"But… how do you know? We don't have a birthday."

"You're not listening to the trees! They're *telling* us—that's how we know."

"Well, how old are we, then?"

Wick waved the question away. "We must give each other presents, Arrow. Secret presents! All day, we'll work on them; when evening comes we'll give them."

Arrow worked on Wick's present crouched in the top corner of the bed, while Wick hid behind the bathtub. She decided to make him a little toy reindeer; he loved to watch reindeer leap across the foothills.

To make the reindeer, Arrow tore a strip off the edge of their blanket. She folded, twisted, and tied the strip until it made four legs and a body. Then she wrapped thread (also stolen from the poor blanket) around the end of the strip to bunch it into a snout and ears. That was the hardest part. She couldn't get the ears the same size. Once, in frustration, she snarled at the reindeer and hurled it across the floor. Then she hollered, "Close your eyes, Wick! Tight!" as she dove to snatch it before it skidded through the bars of the cage.

Under the bed was hidden a crumb of soot from the fireplace that the children used to draw pictures on the floor, rubbing them out before anyone could see. With it, Arrow drew two black dots and a line for the reindeer's eyes and mouth.

Now for antlers. She and Wick had a cache of leaves and twigs that had blown in through the window. Arrow found two twigs with five sprigs each, peeled off the bark, and rubbed them silky smooth. Biting two tiny holes in the top of the reindeer's head, she worked the twigs down into the cloth. Then she secured them with string.

At the last minute she added a tail—a braided loop of her own hair.

"Our birthday feast," whispered Wick when the maid brought their dinner.

They laughed until they fell over. The maid shook her head, muttering that there was nothing funny about stewed goat and parsnips.

After the feast, it was time for presents.

"I'll go first," said Arrow, because she always did. She handed Wick a package that was her silk petticoat tied with a sash. They tried to be solemn as he opened it, but they kept erupting into guffaws of laughter. Until Wick saw the reindeer.

He gasped. "Arrow! You—you made it? It's so beautiful! I've never seen anything so beautiful in all my life."

"Well... its ears aren't the same size quite."

Wick kissed and kissed the reindeer, smudging off most of its charcoal mouth, then charged around the cage trying to make it gallop as fast as a real reindeer.

Every night, Wick slept with the reindeer in the crook of his arm. When he woke in the morning, the first thing he did was bury it deep in the clothes chest, inside an old pair of underwear, so Prince Dob and Prince Fob would never find it.

One day, about a year later, the tailor came without warning and took away the clothes chest to discard their oldest clothes and make them new ones in the Queen's favorite styles. When the chest came back full of dazzling new clothes, the reindeer was gone.

Wick cried every night for a week, while Arrow threaded her arms through his and hushed, "It's alright, Wick, it's alright. I'll make you another."

"But it was our birthday," he sobbed. "Our only birthday."

And it was. They never had another.

Wick's gift to Arrow fared better than hers to him. "It's only a song." He dipped his chin and half-shut his eyes the way he always did when he was nervous. "It's not nearly so nice as a reindeer."

"I'd rather have a song," Arrow said, not stopping to consider whether this was true.

"Here it is," said Wick.

And he sang.

The beautiful thing about a song is that it can never be dropped through the bars of a cage, or stolen by giant princes, or whisked away by a self-important tailor. It can stay with you for years and years. After it has been forgotten, it can come again, suddenly, while you fold yourself into the dark in a ship's groaning belly. Even when you are hiding in peril of your life and must be silent, you can roll the song over in your heart until your heart beats loud with it.

Arrow's Birthday Song

Turn my pockets inside out
Hang me from a star
Burrow me beneath the hedges
Where the rabbits are.

Call, then call, now call me out me—
Echo-shout the hill.
I'll scurry out and shimmy down
And up my pockets fill.

We haven't got a silver thread
We haven't got a flare.
We've only got a paper fish
That swims across the air.

But it's your birthday all the same
You're older than before
So catch his tail and take my hand
And swing me out the door.

Oh swing me out the door.
Swing, then swing, oh swing me out me,
Swing me out the door.

Arrow remembered all twenty-seven of her and Wick's children. The oldest was called Rina. She was a wolf. They imagined her before they understood that each species gave birth only to its own kind. When they got older, they tried to change her into a human, but Rina always retained her furry, pointed ears, her silver plume of a tail, and her sharp teeth.

Next came twin boys, Lanky and Spanky. They were not nice and teased Rina until she bit them. A very nice boy followed, Manky. But because Manky was so nice and so seldom bitten by Rina, they tended to forget about him.

Chew-Chew loved to eat. Werpa loved to belch. Blappy loved both to fart and make farting noises, so one only knew the truth of the matter by the smell.

Greenie, Bluey, and Reddie looked exactly the same except the color of their lips. Tippen-Toppen could walk on the ceiling. Flicker could breathe fire like a dragon. Spy-Face had eyes in the back of her head. Windy was a prankster; Cloudy was irritable; Rainy was always crying. Sunny had a pet reindeer and she was Wick's favorite, though he would never admit it.

Jewel was so beautiful everyone who saw her felt irresistibly moved to give her money and jewelry. Her dress was covered with diamonds, rubies, and emeralds; each strand of her hair was gold-plated. Her wealth enabled her to purchase several exotic pets, including a unicorn and a baby moon.

Pellow was as tall as two humans but as skinny as one. Nika was only half as tall as a human, so she was always riding on Pellow's shoulders.

Remmy wasn't afraid of anything. He fought giants by chopping off their toes until they tripped and fell into mountain chasms. He was Arrow's favorite, though she would never admit it.

Pearlie Ribbon was a fairy-graced dancer whose frolics could make wishes come true. Hero Glorious could tame wolves, bears, and wizards by stunning them with his poetic brilliance. Hero Dashing could rip wolves, bears, and wizards in half with his bare hands. Magnificook was exactly what his name suggested. Frizzle Lips could swallow lightning. Rainbow Sky could play the bagpipes, and she could fly.

When Prince Cob set Arrow free, as she drifted toward the Far Deeps, she had only imagined what object the wizard had turned Wick into. A thimble. A potpourri canister. A ring. She had never imagined Wick remaining a human, getting older, becoming a man. That was what she tried to imagine now, as she trudged along the road through Iberia toward Gallia.

Wick as a young man. Taller than her. No longer her twin.

His voice fully deepened. How deep? Did his chest rumble when he sang?

His shoulders broadened. Somehow Arrow pictured them very broad, broader even than Tomás's. The muscles in his arms thickened. Round and bold-veined as a sailor's? Or sleek and slack as a nobleman's?

His eyes—the same, but wiser.

His mouth—the same, but harder.

His hands—the same, but stronger.

Though Arrow could manage to transform each of Wick's features, one at a time, she could never grow up the whole Wick at once. Whenever she imagined standing in front of him, looking into his eyes, he ended up a sort of boy-man. Tall and sinewed, with a boy's face and a boy's smile. A boy's eyes, speaking boy's thoughts.

Grow up, Wick, she would tell him. *You must. I have.*

But he never would.

It frustrated Arrow so much that she sometimes found relief in imagining him as a shoehorn, or a quill pen resting in an ink pot. That was easier than imagining him a man.

One night, as Arrow lay half-buried in straw in a barn loft, she tried to imagine kissing Wick the way she had kissed Tomás.

She pictured herself back on the watchtower, putting Wick in Tomás's place. She imagined laying her head on Wick's shoulder. Wick slipping his hand around the side of her face as Tomás had done, slowly tilting it toward his mouth.

And Arrow pulled away.

Every time. She couldn't make it happen, unless she changed Wick back into Tomás at the last second. Once she tried imagining Tomás almost the whole way, not swapping him out for Wick until their lips were already together.

But this time Wick pulled away! Hurt and sadness filled his boy-man eyes.

"I'm sorry, Wick," she told him. "But we're grown now. We said we would get married."

He only shook his head.

Arrow felt angry. She turned him back into Tomás and kissed him harder than ever.

Then she lay in the dark, listening to the muffled shifting of sleepy goats and horses.

This changes you, Tomás had said.

You can't unchange, Arrow, Tomás had said. *It's the one thing you can't do.*

The straw grew stifling. Arrow pushed her way out onto the hard wooden planks, where the air was cool.

Somewhere in the middle of Gallia, Arrow's shoes went out. They fell off her feet in little heaps of crumbled leather, first one and then the other. Counting what remained in Tomás' purse, Arrow estimated enough for eight days' food at most. Nothing to spare for shoes.

The cuts on her feet became infected and swollen. Arrow limped slower and slower. To make matters worse, it was getting cold. Each morning brought a deeper chill, until one morning the ground was frozen solid.

Ten steps on the frost-glazed road told Arrow she couldn't go on without covering her feet. Wincing, she sat down on a stile. The only article of clothing she could spare was her shawl. Ripping it into thick strips, she bound her feet as snugly as she could.

Within half a day, the strips were reduced to tatters. Arrow had nothing left to replace them, and without her shawl the cold bit deep into her bones. Her hands went numb. She began to shake, first her arms, then all over.

Finally, Arrow stopped.

She didn't decide to stop; the motion of her legs dwindled to a halt like a millwheel without water. Her feet wouldn't lift from the ground.

"I haven't made a mistake," she said to a sparrow pecking at the stiff, glittering grass. "I must be so close now to the Cold Seas, where the Lusty Badger is. I was right to come, and come alone."

But she couldn't convince her feet to take another step. Sliding to the ground, Arrow bundled her feet up in her skirt and wrapped her arms around her knees. She tried and tried to think what she must do next, but her shivering rattled all the thoughts out of her head.

"Mademoiselle! Please, are you hurt?" cried a voice in the Gallic tongue.

Arrow looked up. A young man on a horse approached.

"No, I'm alright. Please, go on," she said in Iberian, trying not to use the dialect of Lipa. She tugged at the neck of her bodice to make sure the scar on her collarbone was hid.

"You are hurt," insisted the man, swinging down from his horse. "Your poor feet!"

He rushed forward, but Arrow struggled to her feet, putting a hand on the hilt of her knife.

The man retreated, holding out his arms in a gesture of peace. "Won't you let me help you? You are in distress, mademoiselle. You cannot convince me otherwise. And with this terrible cold spell—please." Then he repeated himself in Iberian, to make sure she understood.

The man was simply dressed: not a nobleman, but obviously not a peasant. A merchant, most likely. He was handsome, perhaps ten years older than Tomás, with hair smooth and glistening as his horse's black flank. If she was back in Lipa, the old Arrow in her old life, she would have reached out and touched it. A softness in his seal-gray eyes spoke true concern. His face held no hint of the look men sometimes had, like animals, that signaled danger.

"Please sir," she chanced, "do you have anything I could use to bind my feet? My shoes are—lost."

"I would give you my riding boots," he said, continuing to speak in her language, "but they would fall right off your little feet. Can you mount my horse? We can go to the next village and I will find you new shoes there."

The man flashed such a wide, earnest smile that Arrow's frozen cheeks grew momentarily warm.

"You don't know me, sir. I couldn't accept such a gift from a stranger. But if you have a sturdy cloth of some kind, I will pay you for—"

"Please, I beg you to let me help you. Will you permit me to lift you onto my horse? He's very gentle."

Arrow shook her head. "I've never ridden a horse." She had never even ridden Nazo the donkey, for he was sway-backed. "And... I'm alone, and a woman, and..."

"I see, yes, of course. A thousand pardons." All the man's actions were quick and eager, as Arrow's were under normal circumstances. "But surely there must be something—"

Turning to his horse, he rummaged through his saddle-pack, at last pulling out a pair of thick wool stockings. "See here! They're not fit for a dance, but they'll last you to the next town."

Arrow tried to give him a coin, but he refused with another easy smile. Too numb to argue, she thanked him. Moving a few yards away, she sat in the road and pulled the stockings over her swollen, frozen feet. The man remained politely at a distance.

When she stood, he was looking at her.

"You are so small," he said.

Arrow said nothing, but she thought: *so are you*. No one understood that who had never seen giants. Waving him farewell, she tried not to limp as she continued along the road. The man didn't seem likely to leave her unless she could prove she wasn't going to perish before sunset.

He was not convinced. Instead of remounting, he began to walk beside her, leading his animal by its reins.

"My name is Marc," said the man. "You are—?"

"Loida." She gave this name whenever asked, each time with a pang of longing for her foster-sister.

"You are from Iberia?"

"Yes."

"But you don't look Iberian."

"No."

"You come from the far south, I think. Your accent is strange."

Arrow made no reply.

"Where are you traveling, Loida?"

"North."

"Obviously," he laughed, a deep, rich laugh. "But—how far?"

"To the Cold Seas. I am seeking a ship."

"Name of ship?"

"I prefer not to tell. Forgive me."

"No, forgive my prying," he said with a bow of repentance. "I only thought to help you, if I happened to know the ship."

Arrow couldn't hide a small smile. "In all my travels, sir, no one has been so keen to help me as you."

"Has anyone else come upon you huddled and shivering, with bleeding feet?"

Arrow laughed outright. With a start, she realized it was the first time she had laughed since she left Lipa. "No."

"I would have needed a heart of stone to ride past you." This, with another of his wide-sweeping smiles.

Arrow wondered just how wretched she looked. She hadn't bathed or washed her clothes since winter set in. For a week at least, she'd been sleeping in haystacks. Smoothing her hair a little, she realized it was full of straw.

"I'm returning home after a long journey," Marc explained. "My wife and children have not seen me these three months."

It was most unaccountable that a pinch of disappointment should crimp Arrow's heart at this revelation of family ties. Yet there it was.

"How many children do you have, sir?"

"Three. Colette, Emmelot, and little Robin."

"Robin is the baby?"

"And the firstborn son."

"Spoiled, of course."

"Terribly. He has a horse already and cannot yet walk."

"His sisters must be jealous."

"Only a little. They get to break in the horse for him, until he's ready to ride."

Arrow hardly noticed the pain in her feet as they walked along. It had been so long since she talked to anyone like this. She felt giddy with the joy of it. At the same time, she missed everyone so much more: Tomás, Brother Agostin, Loida, Irma, even Noemi.

"Have you family, Loida?" Marc asked.

She nodded.

"Back in the Sorry Islands?"

She looked at him.

"You're an islander, I've decided. By your way of speaking."

"I have three sisters."

"And a sweetheart? Such a beautiful girl must have left many broken hearts back on the island."

Marc said it with a twinkle in his eye, but pain hooked into Arrow's heart.

"Yes. Just one broken heart."

"You can write to him," he coaxed in the same gently teasing voice.

"No. I can't. Please—don't talk about it anymore."

"I'm terribly sorry. Please forgive me, I didn't mean to pain you."

Marc reached out and touched Arrow's shoulder. No one had touched her, except to shove her out of the way, since she hugged Tomás goodbye. The gesture flooded her with warmth from the crown of her head to her frozen feet. It made her feel a little wild, a little drunk almost. If, in that moment, Marc had put his warm, strong arms around her, Arrow would have received his embrace. Never mind Tomás. Never mind Colette, Emmelot, and Robin. Never mind his wife, whose name he failed to mention.

But that is not what happened.

Instead, they reached a long, narrow bridge. There was not room for Marc with his horse to continue across it at Arrow's side, so he dropped behind with a gesture for her to cross first. The river below was fast and deep, churning with frigid water. Flecks sprayed Arrow as she stepped onto the bridge, making her shiver. She had just reached the center of the bridge when she heard Marc call from behind.

"Arrow."

She froze. Everything in her field of vision wavered: the riverbanks, the naked trees, the hard, clean winter sky.

"That's your name, isn't it?" he said. "Arrow. The girl from the Kingdom of the Giants."

Slowly she turned to look at him, heart battering the walls of her chest like a blacksmith at his anvil.

Marc had tied the reins of his horse to a post of the bridge. He drew a knife from his jacket.

"Please," gasped Arrow. "I can explain. About the fire."

"I don't know anything about a fire. There's nothing to explain. Please don't try. I don't want to hear."

It was impossible to outrun a rider, especially with her injured feet. Arrow had no strength or skill to fight; she had never actually used her knife.

"I didn't mean to do it," she pleaded. "Not really. Please don't take me back to Lipa! Not yet. I need to find someone first. I NEED TO FIND SOMEONE."

"I'm not going to take you back to Lipa." His seal-gray eyes were still soft, but his mouth grew grim and hard.

"You weren't sent from Lipa?"

He shook his head. "I know nothing of Lipa."

"What do you mean? I don't understand."

"I have no choice, mademoiselle. My family— he will hurt my children, unless I do what he demands."

"Who is he? What does he demand?"

"The wizard. He demands me to kill you. Forgive me. I don't want to. You are so small."

9

The most important thing to do was scream, which Arrow did without delay. Ragged echoes tore up and down the river's rocky banks. Marc lunged at her, his knife a white streak of reflected sunlight. She dodged, hurtling herself against the railing of the bridge. He sprang again, and without thinking Arrow slipped under the railing and swung herself off the side of the bridge deck. Marc yelped in surprise.

The bridge's beams jutted out past its deck; Arrow dangled from one of these. Beneath the bridge was space to crawl between the beams and deck, if she could somehow pull herself up. Marc dropped to his belly on the deck and reached out to slash her grip loose. Arrow swung under the bridge where he couldn't reach, still hanging from the beam. The noise of the water crushed upward. Cross-supports slanted between the piles. If Arrow could find a foothold on one of these, she might be able to scramble on top of the beam. Hand over hand, she inched toward the nearest pile.

But her fingers grew numb. The water snapped at her feet with teeth of white foam. Her pack's weight pulled her down, but she had no way to cast it off. Gritting her teeth, Arrow tried to hook one of her feet up onto the nearest cross-support. She missed. Her body jerked back heavily. One hand lost its grip.

With a short scream, she tightened her other hand's fingers and fought to regain her hold on the beam.

Before she could do so, Marc swung off the side of the bridge, lowering his body with precision and strength, his knife between his teeth. As soon as he gained his balance, he let go with one hand and reached to take his knife in it.

With her free hand, Arrow pulled her own knife from its sheath and hurled it with all her strength.

It struck Marc in the middle of his abdomen. Amazed, he dropped his weapon. Looking down, he closed his hand over the hilt of Arrow's knife; bright red stained his fingers.

"No," he whispered. "Please, no. Robin. My boy."

His gaze locked with Arrow's. She froze, her face white. A fire flashed out from Marc's seal-gray eyes—terror, disbelief, anger, regret. As his grip loosened and his body began to fall, his pawing hands grasped one of Arrow's feet, still clad in his wool stockings. Her fingers slipped.

They plunged together through the water's angry surface to its black depths.

River's Song

I don't ask who comes.
I take them.
They come.
They want me to take
and I take them.
They don't want me to know
and I don't ask.
They want to be taken
and not known.
Don't they?

A man came once, blooded and dead.
My rocks didn't kill him; no,
his lungs never drew my water.
His bane was the girl that followed,
half his size, without shoes.
She, I am sorry to say,
did break upon my rocks.
But wasn't she, after all, a thrower
of knives? Who else she was
I never asked.

Arrow was trapped in a cold, dark place that pressed so closely on all sides she could hardly breathe. Each breath brought a sharp, stabbing pain. Eventually she realized why: the Wizard of Seven had turned her into a knife, and she was trapped inside a sheath. The pain when she breathed was the edges of her blade pressing into the sides of the sheath.

Then she heard Wick calling out to her.

"I'm here, Arrow, I'm here! See, I promised you I would come find you."

He bent forward to free her from the sheath, but Arrow cried, "No, Wick, stop! I'm a knife now. My blade is wicked sharp. I will hurt you if you touch me."

Wick laughed—the best sound in all the world. Pulling Arrow free of the sheath, he held her in his hands.

Then Arrow saw that Wick was no longer a boy, but a man. She could see him so clearly, fully grown, as she could never imagine him before. He was beautiful! The joy of it made her want to laugh and cry and dance and sing all together, but because she was a knife she could do none of those things. How proud she felt of his tall stature, his broad shoulders and his strong chin.

"Wick, you're alive! You're still human! Why hasn't the wizard changed you into something else?"

Wick smiled. "You know why, Arrow."

Arrow agreed, though she didn't really know. She felt so happy, nothing mattered.

Then Arrow reached out to put her hand on Wick's heart. But she forgot she had been changed into a knife. The point of her blade drove deep between his ribs. He looked down at her with amazement, fear, and pain. Red blood spread across his chest.

Arrow tried to scream, but Wick's blood flowed over her, filling her mouth and nose and eyes, until she drowned in it.

Arrow opened her eyes. Before she could focus them, a piercing shriek filled her ears.

"Mamaaaaaaaan! She's awake!"

A little girl, seven or so years old, stood over her as she lay under piles of heavy blankets. As the girl scurried away, Arrow peered at her surroundings. She was in some kind of one-room traveler's lodge, with a row of beds along a wall and a fireplace and tables opposite.

"Ah, poor tiny one!" cried a woman—Maman, presumably. The girl dragged her into the room by a corner of her apron. Pouring out a long spout of sympathy in a rustic dialect Arrow couldn't understand, Maman sat heavily on the side of the bed and began to mash joyous kisses into all parts of Arrow's face.

She was a huge peasant with forearms like fenceposts and round, looming breasts. Sweat plastered frizzles of fair hair around her red face. She smelled of ale and herbs.

"Where am I?" asked Arrow in a pause between kisses.

Then she remembered.

The bridge. The knife. Bright red spreading across Marc's hand.

Robin. My boy.

"Is he dead?" Arrow struggled to sit up, then gasped at the pain in her side and fell back down.

"Dead? Yes, thanks be to God!" Maman let fire another volley in her dialect, its tone suggesting a tirade against the perished villain.

"Someone told him to kill me," said Arrow. "A wizard. He didn't want to."

But Maman shook her head, not understanding, and prattled on.

"Oh!" cried Arrow. "My pack! Is my pack here? Did you find my pack?"

This time she succeeded in sitting up, grimacing and clutching her ribs. Her pack, which contained the Wizard Merkum's letter and an answering letter from Brother Agostin, was nowhere to be seen. Neither, for that matter, were her clothes. She wore a nightgown that, judging from its size, belonged to Maman.

Maman screeched in alarm, gesturing to Arrow's side. Planting a beefy red hand on the girl's face, she squashed her back down against the pillow. A long, severe, unintelligible admonition followed. Her daughter joined in with equal enthusiasm and verbosity.

"I've got to find my pack," interjected Arrow at intervals. "Someone told that man to kill me. Someone still wants to kill me."

Until—

"Mother of tripe!" burst a voice from the other side of the room. "I can't take a moment more of this."

Arrow looked. Sprawled in the bed nearest the window was a lanky figure with a battered, wide-brimmed hat covering his face. His legs were too long for the bed and splayed at odd angles. One arm flopped toward the floor while the other pressed the hat down over his eyes.

Without removing his hat, the man said in a perfect pronunciation of the Sorry Islands' dialect: "A farmer heard you scream. He saw you being attacked and fished you from the river. You've lain here for two days while this worthy hen cackled and peeped over you like a drowned chick. You have three broken ribs, two infected feet, and one case of near-drowning. The doctor says you must lie still. Kindly shut up and do so."

"My pack?" Arrow insisted.

He translated the question into Maman's dialect. She

replied with an emphatic speech lasting several minutes. At its conclusion, the man sighed, swiped the hat from his face, swung down his trunk-like legs, and sat up, looking at Arrow.

"She says you had no pack. The river must have taken it."

Arrow's mouth dropped open. He was a boy. An enormous, stretched-out boy well over six feet tall. His tempest of hair was a shocking, brilliant rust color, his skin pale as moonlight. With only the faintest trace of a red beard, he looked no more than fifteen years old.

On each hand, he had only one finger and a thumb.

"You're a wizard," said Arrow.

"I can tell you received high marks in Creature Identification."

"A Wizard of Two? There is no such thing."

"But not in Logic, unfortunately."

Before she left Lipa, Brother Agostin had given Arrow a scrap of paper containing the names, ranks, and locations of all the wizards shown on his magical map. Hidden in the hold of the ship, Arrow had passed the time memorizing this list, then destroyed it.

There had never been a Wizard of Two on the Map of Wizards.

Just as there had never been a Wizard of Seven.

Despite Maman's yelps of protest, Arrow bolted upright, gripping her side. Her eyes cast around the room for a weapon, but the fire poker on the opposite wall was her nearest option. If she needed to, it might be safer to spring for the kitchen and hope for a butcher knife lying on a table.

"Tell me your name," she demanded.

"And as to Etiquette—"

"Tell me your name this instant!"

The wizard's face screwed up in disgust. "It is my practice never to respond to indelicately-phrased demands made by humans who smell like decomposing fish."

"Is it you?" Arrow continued. "Are you the wizard who sent that man to kill me? Are you with *him*?"

"She just killed someone herself, and while refusing to acknowledge my existence, accuses me of having murderous intentions toward her. Shall I tell our good hostess to call the asylum?"

"Just tell me if you *have* a name."

"She doesn't believe in Wizards of Two, yet she believes in wizards without names?"

"TELL ME YOUR NAME."

Silence. They stared at each other.

"Dan."

"Dan?"

"Is it not good enough for you?"

"Your name is Dan."

"The Wizard Dan, to be precise."

"Why do you have only two fingers?"

"I beg your pardon!" At this, the wizard propelled his spindle-shanked body from the bed and strode forward until he stood at the foot of Arrow's. Running his hand backward through his flame-colored hair revealed eyes like green sea-glass and a blistering scowl. "Might I inquire as to your name, now that the niceties of introduction have been executed on my end?"

Arrow hesitated. "It's Loida. My name is Loida."

"You're a terrible liar."

"Sir, a wizard wants to kill me. I thought I knew who, because somehow this assassin—Marc—knew my name. My real name. Which means whoever is plotting to kill me knows my name."

"That is generally the case, I have found."

"Can you understand why I would be reluctant to reveal myself?"

"What I can't understand is why a human would demand to know a wizard's name in such an abrasive manner while refusing to reveal her own." The way he said the words *human* and *wizard* made it clear how far above the first he considered the second.

Arrow tried to slow her breath and rein in her thoughts. It was like trying to furl a sail in the midst of a storm. Yet, though she would never have dared to reach out and put her hand on the wizard's heart, she could see this much in his face: whatever he was, he was not cruel. No, not even so cruel as Noemi, much less the Wizard of Seven.

"The truth is," said Arrow, "if you don't know why I'm asking your name, sir, I don't think you're the one trying to kill me."

Dan plopped down on the bed closest to her with a mock sigh of relief. "Well! Glad we've got *that* little matter cleared up."

Here, Maman interrupted with a series of pleading wails which she addressed to the wizard while aiming desperate gestures at Arrow.

"She wants you to lie down," Dan interpreted, "and remain quiet. She's not sure how you went from being such a good, sweet, almost-dead girl to such a loud, angry wench."

"I can't stay here," said Arrow. "I already told you, a wizard—"

"—is trying to kill you. Yes, I've learned that refrain quite well."

"He is a Wizard of Seven—"

"There is no Wizard of Seven."

"—who has no name."

"There is no such thing as a wizard without a name. My dear girl, I hate to disenchant you, but someone has been pulling your leg rather obnoxiously. Or your fever dreams have cooked up a good batch of—"

"The Wizard Merkum knows of him," Arrow insisted.

Dan gave a start at the name but quickly recovered, flicking back his hair. "Merkum! So that's who pulled your leg? Not a bit surprising."

"I had a letter from him in my pack, which I have lost. He's on a ship called the Lusty Badger. I need to find him, to prevent the rise of a tyrannical demi-god and the annihilation of the Race of Wizards."

At this, Dan threw back his head and howled with laughter. "Did Merkum tell you that? Oh, that's rich! It's just too rich!"

"Stop." Arrow used this same tone of voice with Pipo the dog. "You *must* listen to me, sir. Merkum spoke of the disappearance of the Wizard Falcius and the rise of a nameless Wizard of Seven, whom I have seen with my own eyes."

"Forgive me, but who *are* you? Why should I give a damn what you've seen with your own eyes or anyone else's?"

"My name is Arrow. I was held captive in the Kingdom of the Giants until age eleven when I escaped in a longboat and was rescued in the Far Deeps by sailors of the Sorry Islands."

Dan held up a two-fingered hand. "Yes, thank you, that's quite enough. I thought you might say something witty like, 'I'm the long-lost daughter of an exiled king who was spirited away at birth by a jealous uncle.' But this—please, I'll die of boredom."

"You don't believe me."

"I'm not sure the thought ever occurred to me."

Arrow clenched her fist. The pain in her ribs grew almost unbearable as her chest seemed to swell with frustration. She closed her eyes and gritted her teeth, but it was no use; she turned and vomited over the side of the bed.

Maman exploded into a level of concern that approached rage. Chasing the Wizard of Two from Arrow's bedside with physical as well as verbal threats, she eased Arrow back down into the bed, wiped her mouth with a rag that smelled of leeks, and put a cool wet cloth over her forehead.

Maman's little daughter returned, slipping her hand into Arrow's. Without the girl telling her as much, Arrow understood that she was to squeeze this hand as hard as she could until the pain lessened. No matter how hard she squeezed, the girl never drew her hand away until Arrow was fast asleep.

When Arrow awoke, the Wizard of Two was sitting beside her, scribbling in a small black book with a stub of broken quill pinched between thumb and finger. A lock of his vermillion hair quivered on his forehead as he wrote. Neither Maman nor her daughter were in sight. When he looked at her, Arrow turned her head away toward the wall.

"Will you tell me what language that was?" Dan said.

"What language?"

"The language you spoke in your sleep. I've been observing it for hours."

Arrow gave a tiny shrug, trying not to disturb her ribcage. "Wasn't it the tongue of the Sorry Islands?"

Dan snorted. "Do you take me for a fool?"

"It may have been the language of the giants." She looked at him. "But you didn't believe me when I told you that is where I'm from."

"While it would be terribly amusing to hear *you* try to speak Giantish," said the wizard, "I can elocute in that tongue more freely than the giants' own poets. In addition, I can converse with just about any sentient being in the known world. (A few sea-serpent dialects I've never caught onto. Can't properly distinguish the inflections in roars that deep.) The language you were speaking is one I have never heard. I must know what it is."

Arrow stared at him a moment. Then she turned back toward the wall.

After a pause, the wizard sighed. "Clearly you need money.

I'm happy to provide more than you have ever seen in your life. I repeat—I must know what language you spoke."

Arrow said nothing.

"Might I point out that you don't even own a pair of shoes?" Dan's voice grew tight with impatience. "Would you like to wed a duke? You can have your pick with the dowry I'll provide."

"I will never tell you," she whispered. Only she whispered it in the language of the giants because it sounded more hostile.

Dan whistled. "Alright, you do speak Giantish. And rather well, too."

Arrow's response was a foul word the giant princes only said when neither their mother nor their nurse were in hearing.

The wizard cleared his throat. "I admit I may have been a bit disagreeable yesterday. Nauseatingly so, it would appear. Suppose I believe that you did grow up in the Kingdom of the Giants and were rescued by pirates or whatever it is you said. And suppose I also believe that a nameless (yet extant) Wizard of Seven sent an assassin to murder you on the Pont des Loutres instead of killing you himself—which would have been far easier and more reliably successful—for reasons I will not attempt to extrapolate. Assuming I believe all those things, and assuming I will give you a sum of money larger than you can be expected to spend in a lifetime, I pray you tell me at once what language you spoke in sleep and where you learned it."

"No," said Arrow.

Though she still did not look at him, she heard sounds suggesting that Dan stood in anger and kicked his chair several times.

A few moments of silence followed. Then the wizard sat. Leaning close to her, he whispered in a language she had only ever heard Wick speak, "*You've grown up.*"

Arrow's body stiffened like a corpse. She bit her lips to keep from crying out.

"That's what you said in your sleep," said the wizard. "One of the things. Won't you tell me what it means?"

Wick! She had dreamed of Wick! Images flooded her mind, wavery and shadowed, but one thing stood out in sharp relief: Wick's face. His grown-up face, manly and warm and beautiful. Oh, he was alive. She knew it. Every particle of her being sang it.

But there was something more she couldn't remember. Blood. Danger. Fear in Wick's eyes.

"What else did I say?" she whispered, turning to face the Wizard Dan.

He flicked his hair out of his eyes. "If I tell you, will you tell me what it means?"

She shook her head. "I can't, sir. Even if I wanted to—it would tear me in two."

"Please." This single word was the most sincere thing she had heard him say. "I've never heard anything like it. The structure is baffling. I should have been able to decipher every word based on my knowledge of related tongues, but this language stands utterly apart. Can't you at least tell me where you learned it, and by what manner of creature it is spoken?"

Arrow sank against the pillow and closed her eyes. Wick's face—his grown-up face from her dreams—shone in her mind so brightly it dazzled.

I will come find you, Wick.

Do you hear me? I will find you.

I promise.

Opening her eyes, she fixed them on the glittering green eyes of the Wizard of Two. "I will tell you everything I know about this language—everything *except* its translation—if you will take me to the Wizard Merkum."

He grimaced. "Money? Jewels? Gold? I'm sure you can hire swift passage through the Cold Seas with what I can offer you.

It's not that I mind the journey. Heaven knows I've got nothing better to do at this time of year. It's the idea of carting around a human like a sack of rubbish." He shuddered.

"You must take me. The Wizard of Seven is trying to kill me, and only a wizard may know how to protect me from him."

"Hmm." Dan leaned backward in his chair, stretching his long arms and folding them behind his head. "If these are your only terms, I'll consider them. But before I do, I would at least like to know who you are, why you seek Merkum, and why you claim to be hunted by a nameless Wizard of Seven. This request seems not unreasonable if we're to be companions for any length of time beyond our stay at this inn. It seems entirely obligatory if I'm expected to protect you from future assassination attempts."

"I will tell you if you will believe me."

"I will believe whatever does not offend my intellect," said Dan. "Beyond that I make no promises."

So Arrow told the Wizard Dan about the cage in the boudoir of the Queen of the Giants, the Wizard of Seven, and Wick. She told him about Brother Agostin's letter to Merkum, Merkum's reply, and why she was now traveling north in search of the Lusty Badger. Though Merkum's letter had been lost in the river, she had memorized it along with Brother Agostin's list of wizards, so she was able to recite it to Dan word for word.

She did not mention Tomás or the burning of the ship. These details had no direct relevance to her task, and they felt like a blue-black bruise she was reluctant to touch.

Dan's intellect did not seem to be offended, but neither was he wholly convinced. "Merkum's a bit of a fool. Dancing with pirates while he tells himself scary stories about the end of the world. Why seek him out? Why not go straight to the

Councilors in Gnoze, if there's really such a plot on?"

"Because Merkum has heard of the Wizard of Seven and believes him evil. What if the same is not true for others? Merkum can tell me rumors of where the Wizard of Seven has been seen."

"Arrow, the quickest way to learn the whereabouts of a nameless wizard is to set a room of wizard-scholars debating about the implications of his existence. They'll devolve almost instantly into tangential theories regarding his motives, military tactics, physiognomy, and favorite foods. And they'll deduce his location with almost as much certainty as if it were plotted on the Map of Wizards."

"But," Arrow protested, "Merkum—"

"Let me speak more pointedly," Dan broke in. "Now that your assassin has failed, whatever motive this Nameless Wizard has for ending your life will drive him either to send a more powerful assassin to finish the job, or to finish it himself. Gnoze is the only place you'll be safe; he couldn't possibly harm you under the protection of the Council. You certainly won't be safe on the Lusty Badger. And if you're dead, you can't teach me your language."

"But there's no more hope for me to reach Gnoze than there would be for me to reach the Cold Seas. I'll be attacked on the road as before."

"Mother of tripe!" Dan shook his head. "What do you take me for, a tin peddler? We won't be taking the road."

"What do you mean?"

"We'll be taking the sky."

Arrow gasped. She remembered how the Wizard of Seven climbed the air like a staircase. "Do you fly, sir?"

"Me? No. I don't do a damned thing—except speak several thousand languages. But my griffin flies."

10

Anyone who has ever beheld the blade-bright beak of a griffin and looked into its yellow eyes knows that griffins cannot be ridden. That is precisely why the Wizard Dan first attempted to ride one; he hoped it might be an impossible thing, therefore earning him the rank of a Wizard of Three. Unfortunately, someone had succeeded before him. Yet, as he explained to Arrow, the endeavor wasn't a complete loss, for the griffin Halla had been his mount ever since.

Some score or so of years earlier (the Wizard of Two was now ninety-four, though in terms of physical maturity he appeared somewhat younger than Arrow), Dan had travelled through Dragon Country to its south-eastern border, where the mountains are twice as high. The Highest Mountains are the domain of the griffins, who prefer higher altitudes than dragons. For several years, the wizard observed a family in secret until he learned their language. Then he spoke with them, offering knowledge of hidden gold, which draws griffins as blood draws sharks.

The gold was in a labyrinth deep within a dragonish mountain. With Dan as their guide, the griffins found the hoard, but two dragon sentries discovered them as they escaped with the plunder. The griffins were five—mother, father, two sons and a daughter—and though they lost some of the gold they were a match for two dragons. Dan, on the other hand, was quite helpless. When a dragon turned toward him, spewing a river of flame down the gully where he hid, he gave himself up for lost.

But Halla, the youngest of the griffins, swooped down and snatched the wizard up in her claw. As she flew, she swung him on her back, leaving her talons free for battle.

This, of course, was Dan's goal all along. Knowing the fierce loyalty of griffins, he hoped to put himself in a state of danger from which the only escape would be on a griffin's back. Yet when the danger had passed (without, alas, any anatomical addition to the wizard's hands) Halla decided she liked having Dan as her rider. He knew the languages of the birds and other creatures they passed, and he told her fascinating things about both her own land and many lands she had never seen.

Because Halla was an unusually curious griffin—more cat than eagle in her, despite her fine bronze talons—she wished to accompany Dan on his ventures and see the wonders he described. The wizard agreed to this as long as she would bear him wherever he wished. They hadn't tired of each other since. It was because of Halla Dan had been able to learn the languages of sea-serpents and firebirds, which otherwise would have been too dangerous to attempt.

"How beautiful," said Arrow, "to have a griffin for a friend."

Dan snorted. "Wizards don't have friends."

"Whyever not?"

"Because friendship requires equality, as your human philosophers have explained with unnecessary verbosity. And wizards are superior to all other creatures."

"Well, aren't you friends with each other, then?"

"Decidedly not. Friendship also requires love, which is a weakness beneath our ontological structures."

"So you'll never be my friend, though you're going to such great lengths to help me?"

Dan flicked back his hair. "I am helping you because you speak an extremely fascinating language. By gaining your trust I hope to gradually coerce you into unveiling its secrets. Pray never mistake that for friendship, or you'll be morbidly disappointed. It is impossible for a wizard to act from unselfish motives."

"It seems a hard thing to be a wizard."

"It also seems a hard thing to ride a griffin to Gnoze in winter without any clothing. Before you meet Halla, we've got to get you some shoes and whatever else it is female humans wear."

After Dan made a few stops in the village shops, Arrow found herself so bundled she resembled a shaggy mountain goat. A thick knitted shawl crisscrossed her body, while a woolen cloak draped her in protecting warmth. She wore woolen hose and stockings under several layers of petticoats, and her sore feet were cradled in a pair of sheepskin boots.

"I lost my purse in the river," she apologized. "If only I had some way to repay you. Would you like me to dance for you? In Lipa, crowds gathered to see me dance."

"Lord, no," said Dan. "I would as soon pay you *not* to dance for me. As I said, I'm conspiring to earn your trust until you agree to teach me your language. So simply store this up along with my future good deeds and gradually succumb to a sense of obligation to my wishes."

They left the village at sunset, and Dan led Arrow through a wood to the top of a hill.

"We travel at night," Dan explained.

"Won't the Wizard of Seven find us just as easily in the dark?"

"Oh, certainly. There's no avoiding him if he has it in for you.

But Halla prefers the night sky for low flights. Her pride is still somewhat pricked at being seen with a rider."

Then he pulled out an intricate object hanging from a leather thong around his neck, holding it up for Arrow to see. A dark green stone flecked with red the color of the wizard's hair, it was carved in the shape of a talon gripping an egg, with several holes along it.

"Bloodstone," he said. "I had it fashioned for me in Gnoze."

"Is it magical?" Arrow couldn't resist reaching out and touching it. It was smooth as the inside of an oyster. Warmth from the wizard's skin made it feel alive.

"No, but it's the only thing in the world that can make this sound."

Lifting it to his lips, he blew through one of the holes. A sweet, piercing note seemed to quiver in the air before racing down the hill in all directions. As the wizard tapped other holes, the note transformed into a simple, melodious call. Sounds bounced off each other and intertwined until new notes emerged, then the whole song died suddenly away.

Arrow was too astonished to speak.

Dan grinned, replacing the whistle within his shirt. "Now stand very still. When she comes, don't move until I explain everything."

For several minutes they waited in silence, hearing nothing but the dull clack of twigs in the wood and their own muffled sniffs against the cold.

"There! Do you hear that?" whispered Dan, his breath billowing in white clouds.

A distant sound came like an echo of the bloodstone whistle, just as piercing but less sweet. Fierce, noble, achingly wild—as if it contained the strength of stars. Each time the call repeated, it grew louder.

Then the griffin Halla burst through the low-hanging clouds. Each of her wings was as long as a warhorse, her shaggy body nearly the size of the longship in which Arrow had departed the Kingdom of the Giants. Though her back legs and tail resembled a heavily-sinewed lion, her front legs curved into bronze talons. The dark gold fur of her back and neck gave way to the ivory-feathered head of a great, bronze-beaked eagle. Her yellow eyes flashed like slices of sun.

Arrow had never seen anything she wanted so much to touch. Despite her awe, she sprang forward with her arms outstretched.

Halla screamed.

The sound alone threw Arrow to the ground, hands clapped over her ringing ears. Dan leapt in front of her, waving his arms and screeching as he communicated with the griffin in its own language.

At last Halla lowered her talons. Sitting back on her haunches, she curled her tail around her feet. Then she stared at Arrow, the yellow slices of her eyes snapping steadily shut, then open again, as she blinked.

Dan turned and glared. "I told you stand still until I explained! Was that too difficult for a human to grasp?"

Arrow didn't respond because she was too terrified to move. Dan continued screeching and squawking until Halla made a low chirring sound. Imitating this chirr, the wizard approached her and put his hand on her right front flank, stroking her shaggy fur. The griffin began to purr; the deep rumble shook the ground beneath Arrow.

"Alright," called Dan. "I've explained who you are. But she hasn't decided whether she will let a human ride her. It's a humiliating deed, and she owes you nothing."

Arrow nodded, rising slowly to her feet. "Would she let me put my hand on her? The way you are?"

Dan chirped and screeched. Halla only blinked, narrowing her eyes and stretching out her neck toward Arrow. Then she let out a low hiss, displaying a very red tongue.

Arrow swallowed, taking a step backward.

"No, no," said Dan. "That's a good sound. She says yes, you can touch her. Just move very slowly. If you alarm her, she'll bite off your arm and eat it before your eyes."

Arrow put one foot in front of the other until she stood right between Halla's front legs with their shining claws. Then, slowly, she lifted her hand and showed it to the griffin, who remained motionless except for her blinking eyes and a few restive twitches of her tail. Pressing her hand against the griffin's heart, Arrow whispered, "Hello, Halla. I am Arrow."

Oh, it was a magnificent heart! Each thump rocked like the waves of the Far Deeps. The strength of mountains rang in it. Unshakeable courage. Untamable freedom. Unrelenting loyalty. Alongside all of this, a great ache of longing—a seeking, without knowing what is sought.

Her hand still on Halla's breast, Arrow looked up into the terrible yellow eyes. She stared and blinked as Halla stared and blinked. *I am seeking, too*, said Arrow's eyes. *Please help me find what I seek.*

Halla lowered her head and nudged Arrow a few steps back, as if to say, *that's enough now*. Then she made the low chirring sound, swinging her great head around toward Dan.

"Well," breathed Dan, "she says she'll take you to Gnoze."

Arrow nodded, smiling at Halla.

The wizard looked at Arrow, scratching his nose. "That was—unexpected. It wasn't sorcery, was it? You didn't mention any art in charming wild beasts."

"No. It's just the way I am."

To mount the griffin was no easy feat. Halla lay down while Arrow scrambled up her like a haystack, with Dan pushing from below. The pain in Arrow's ribs wrenched from her several sharp cries, but Halla didn't flinch.

Dan's long limbs allowed him to climb with greater agility. "I'll sit in back to keep an eye on you, but do your best not to fall off. If I have to haul you up every five minutes, I may tire of it without warning."

Arrow sat just below the griffin's shoulder blades and the base of her wings, with Dan snugly behind her. Each time Halla took a step, one shoulder blade went up and the other down with an alarming shift. Then the wings unfurled. Halla sank toward the earth as all her muscles tightened.

"Hold tight now," warned Dan.

Arrow grabbed hold of the base of the griffin's wings, where her fur turned to feathers. Suddenly all her weight thrust downward and her chin smacked against the griffin's back as Halla gave one mighty spring and launched into the air. The wings surged on either side of Arrow, pushing down the air as the earth dropped away beneath them.

Catching her balance, Arrow shoved herself upright, colliding with Dan who was leaning forward.

"Perhaps," said the wizard, "you've not yet had the opportunity to learn that wizards hate to be touched. Don't worry; I will remind you of this fact as frequently as necessary. It's bad enough we're squeezed on this beast's back like breasts in a corset, but kindly refrain from draping yourself on me."

"Sorry, sir. I'll try."

Skimming just above the treetops, the griffin sometimes batted the tallest trees with her hind paws as she passed, as if she liked the feeling of having something to push against. The moon, appearing and disappearing through ribbons of low cloud, felt right on top of them. But the clouds grew thicker until they blanketed all light. Halla flew on, undaunted by the utter dark. The wind lashed so bitingly Arrow had to bury her face in Halla's fur for warmth.

"Now," said Dan, "I will teach you to speak in Wizardish, so you can communicate effectively by the time we reach Gnoze."

"But... you said we would reach Gnoze in four or five days, sir. I can't learn a new language by then!"

"You can learn Wizardish. If I speak it to you straight for the remainder of this night, by morning you'll be able to understand what I'm saying. The day after, you'll be able to speak it yourself. By the time we reach Gnoze, you'll be able to converse as freely as though your mother spoke Wizardish over your cradle."

"Is it a magical language?"

"Not what we would call magic, no. The language of the Starborn is the ancient grandsire of all tongues now spoken by bipeds, however various they may seem. Wizardish is simply more perfect than its derivatives, rendering its meaning so effectively the mind can grasp it without effort. You may call it magic if you like, but it's pure semiotics."

"I will call it magic," said Arrow.

Then Dan began speaking in a tongue Arrow had never heard, high and distant yet clear and stinging. He spoke unwearyingly for the next several hours. By the time the sun rose, she found that she could understand him. He was speaking of his great fondness for cheese, presumably having exhausted all other topics.

Shortly after dawn, they landed in a place similar to the one from which they had departed, a remote clearing on a wooded hill. Halla left them, and they walked to the nearest inn to sleep.

Because the wizard was so free with his gold, Arrow was surprised he only asked the innkeeper for one room. To be sure, Dan used his pack and coat to create a barrier down the center of the bed. Then he explained, "My daily wage for carting you around is to observe you talking in your sleep. I'll feel rather cheated if you don't. Is there anything you can drink to loosen your tongue?"

Arrow scowled. "I wish you wouldn't talk about it like that."

"Like what?"

"Like it's just a language."

Dan sighed as he removed his boots. "Well perhaps if you told me more, I could grasp why you're so testy about it. Here's what I understand so far: this language was created by you and one other human for exclusive communication between yourselves. Yet the only other tongue you knew was that of the giants. From what I've heard, this tongue bears no resemblance to Giantish, either in structure or phonation."

"We wanted it to be different," said Arrow. "We were trying to speak as we imagined humans should speak. We thought humans were different than giants."

"Are they?"

"No. Not different, only smaller."

"So you tried to create a language expressing the essence of human nature. But in the end, it was only expressive of the two of you." Dan snapped two long fingers. "That's why you guard it as dragons guard gold. It *is* more than just a language. It's like the songs of the fairies. When a fairy-woman is with child, she sings to herself in secret and this song shapes the child within her. But if anyone should overhear, this places the fairy-child's life in peril, for the song contains the child's essence. He who knows a fairy's essence gains power over it and may ensnare it using the secrets of its own song."

Arrow crawled under the blankets and pulled them up to her chin. Dan did the same on the other side of his barrier. For awhile, neither of them moved but both could tell the other was awake.

Then Arrow asked, "Have you ever heard it, Dan? The song of a fairy-mother?"

"Many times. But I've never used the knowledge for anyone's harm. I'm merely a scientific observer. It's the most astonishing sound I have encountered in all my study of the sentient world. Until I heard your language, that is."

"All the same," said Arrow, "I think I would stop my ears rather than hear."

A Song of Wick and Arrow
in their own language

I know.
I have always known.
I know.
I have always known.
I know.
I have always, always, always—

When Arrow woke, Dan was sitting up beside her, scribbling in his black book with his stub of quill.

"Did I speak, sir?"

"Speak is one word for it. You were so distressed I almost woke you. But I was too engrossed—I told you wizards are incurably selfish. Tell me whether I have hit upon a discovery: do you have different sets of words for the same things, depending on your mood? So that happiness has its own vocabulary, sadness another, and so on?"

"No. Maybe. I don't know. I've never thought about it before."

"But now I've promised to bring you to Gnoze, and I demand you to think about it."

Arrow thought, fighting her reluctance. "I suppose we do, yes."

"And each of these moods has a unique set of grammatical rules?"

"It doesn't have any rules at all."

"Oh, but it does. The most intricate syntactical systems I've ever encountered. Like worlds opening inside of worlds. But how two human children could have possibly created something so complex with no formal education is a riddle to stump a sphinx."

"You're looking at it all wrong. It's not complex at all. It's simpler than Wizardish, much simpler. As simple as breathing."

Dan's brows bent together. "Yet what is breathing," he muttered to himself, "but the most intricate system of physiological processes, beyond the capacity of machinery, artistry, or wizardry to replicate—"

"All I know is, you'll never learn it by picking it apart."

That night, as they flew along a ribbon of river threading together the roots of two green mountains, Arrow asked, "Dan, why doesn't the Map of Wizards show you?" She asked it in Wizardish without realizing it, for whether magic or no, her companion's language had fully opened its secrets to her.

Dan shrugged and stretched his long arms. "Because the map's maker didn't chart for any Wizards of Two, I suppose. Why would he? There was only one other recorded in history, some two millennia ago, and they killed him shortly after birth as unfit to live. (Those were less forgiving times.) The Manual doesn't mention us either."

"The Manual, sir?"

"The Manual of Wizards. It's... a manual of wizards. It explains the science of our race, its propagation, growth, ranks, powers, limitations, tendencies, et cetera."

"Can I read it?"

"Ha! Not likely. The only human translation is in Greek."

"I read Greek."

Dan lurched backward, then righted himself. "Arrow, you upend my expectations more frequently than any other human I've met. I admit it makes you a comparatively enjoyable companion. Unfortunately I don't lug translations of the Manual on casual adventures, but I've had it memorized since I was thirty-five. What would you like to know?"

"I want to know about the ranks of wizards, what they mean. And what it means to become a Wizard of Eight."

"Well, the Manual doesn't mention Wizards of Eight any more than it mentions Wizards of Two. But if you like, I'll recite Section Eleven Alpha Crimson. In Greek—just to make sure you're not bluffing."

PART III · CHAPTER 10

Eleven Alpha Crimson: Concerning the Ranks and their Powers from the Manual of Wizards

The Wizard of Three is as the chrysalis or pollywog. His powers exist in potency only. Though in intelligence he ranks with dragons, sphinxes, angels, and titans, in respect to magic his state resembles the squalor of humans, who have no strength but steel, no art but song, and no recourse but prayer. His first impossible feat shall break his potency into act, forming the shining bud of that power which is to be his glory henceforth.

The Wizard of Four bears the first degree of power, which is to aid the striving of creatures toward their perfections. Each wizard's power is not boundless, but is expressed in accord with what is written in his name. Thus, some develop power to cure wounds and illnesses. Others, to cultivate gardens, banish blight, and restore woodlands. Others, to teach. Others, to heal diseases of the mind and broken hearts. Others, to increase the efficacy of tools and weapons.

The Wizard of Five bears the second degree of power, which is to transcend nature. Some expressions of the second degree are more or less universal, such as the power to invest objects with magical qualities. Other expressions are exhibited by a few, or by one only, such as the power to exist in multiple places at once, to make oneself invisible, or to act in defiance of gravity and other principles of the physical world. Few wizards seek a power beyond the second degree, which constitutes their perfection. Yet some have superabundance written into their names, and these are not satisfied with common glory.

The Wizard of Six bears the third degree of power, which is to control nature. Expressions of the third degree include the power to cause storms, droughts, et cetera, to manipulate objects through intellection, and to command the actions of weaker beings (but not their wills). To become a Councilor of Gnoze, one must attain the rank of six. Some may desire the rank for that reason alone. But woe to the one who seeks what is not written in his name.

The Wizard of Seven bears the fourth and final degree of power, which is to alter nature. That is, to change things into other things. This power is as rare as it is unsettling. For the alteration of nature appears opposed to the first degree of power, which is to aid creatures toward their perfection. If a giant, for example, is changed into a chestnut, she can no longer reach perfection as a giant. And what consolation is it to the giant to tell her she may reach perfection as a chestnut? Will she not weep more bitterly yet? As I say, this power is unsettling. Few have wielded it well. Woe to the one who seeks what is not written in his name.

The Limitation of Power. This example of the giant and the chestnut points to a subtle limitation in the final degree of power. By changing a giant into a chestnut, a Wizard of Seven may for all intents and purposes annihilate that individual's free will. But the wizard cannot destroy her powers of volition as a giant. That is, he cannot remove free will from any creature inherently possessing it. Even though a weak will may be betimes enslaved by a strong one, it cannot be destroyed. This limitation is insurmountable due to the fact that rational volition is the kernel underpinning the order of the universe, which no created being, even the Starborn, has the power to overthrow. Woe to the one who seeks what is not written in his name.

"What does it mean?" asked Arrow. "*Woe to the one who seeks what is not written in his name?*"

"Our names tell us what powers we are born to wield. It's a bit like what some call fate, except we aren't bound by it. We can either accept our powers or not. Things tend to end messily when we don't."

"So, the Wizard of Seven removed his name because he sought a power that was not written in it."

"Or he got tired of signing his papers, one of the two."

"What are your powers, sir? Were you born a Wizard of Two?

Can't you do something impossible and become a Wizard of Three?"

"It seems I have no powers. My star wasn't hot enough. Wizards are born when a shooting star lands in soft mud. Mine was fizzling, they say, as it landed. I spent the first fifty years of my life trying to do something impossible. But a Wizard of Three is born with magical potential, not yet actualized. A Wizard of Two, on the other hand, appears to have the magical potential of a piece of cheese. So I learned languages."

"Oh," said Arrow. "I'm—"

"*Don't* say you're sorry for me. Nothing sets me off more than a human's pity. Do you think I give a damn about fingers?"

"It's not that. I'm sorry that wizards have no parents, no families."

Dan snorted. "That is *such* a human thing to say."

"I suppose that's why you're all male."

"We have no need of brute copulation, if that's what you mean. But we're not really male, you know. We just wear beards to keep our faces warm."

"What do you mean, you're not really male?"

"We don't have any balls, Arrow."

"Oh. I'm s—"

"Stop pitying me! Mother of tripe! Or I'll toss you in the river and let you swim to Gnoze."

As they settled down to sleep after their second night's ride, Dan asked Arrow, "Why did you do that?"

"Do what?"

"All those things you just did: put my boots by the fire, brushed the griffin fur off my coat, turned back my blankets."

"Oh," said Arrow. "I didn't notice I did them."

"Well I wish you wouldn't. Wizards don't have servants, you know."

"As if I fancied myself your servant! I suppose I did them as a friend."

"Wizards don't have friends either. Please stop. It makes me feel feeble and ridiculous."

Arrow put her hands on her hips. "Maybe it's good for you to feel feeble sometimes. Maybe that's what's wrong with wizards, in the end."

"*Wrong* with us?" Dan spluttered. "What makes you think there's something *wrong* with us?"

"You are no one's task. And no one is your task."

Dan snorted as he climbed into the bed. "If that's what you mean by friendship, you can keep it." He snapped the blankets over his head.

The next night they flew over fields where snow-dusted haystacks stood silent sentry. Dan ignored Arrow for the first half of the ride as punishment for her insolence. But around midnight, she asked him a question about Gnoze and he simply forgot not to answer. Being too proud to admit his mistake, he continued to converse with her until morning.

As they spoke—about fairies, imps, ice-bears, and librarians—Arrow noticed that something had changed in the wizard's manner. Several times, when Arrow made a point he hadn't considered, Dan conceded that she might be right. More surprisingly, he made no supercilious remarks while doing so. One other thing: Dan asked Arrow fewer and fewer questions about her language, and more and more questions about herself.

At daybreak they sought lodging in the manor of a farmer well-known to Dan. When Arrow awoke after a fitful sleep, the

Wizard of Two was looming over her with his quill and book, green eyes glittering.

"I've got it," he said. "One of the moods, anyway—the most distressed one."

Arrow tried not to move her sore ribs as she sat up. "Another nightmare?"

He nodded.

"And... you understood it?"

He nodded triumphantly, flicking back his hair.

"Wick was in it?"

"Until you killed him."

"I—what?"

"You always kill him, in all your dreams. That constant became the key to unraveling the rest. Usually with a knife, but not always."

Arrow's face flashed white, then red, then white again. A black shadow rushed over her, nearly choking her with horror of herself, then devouring fear, then a sliding, sliding, sliding toward inescapable darkness.

"Arrow!" Dan was snapping two long fingers in front of her eyes. "Mother of tripe, it was just a dream. Your worst fears. That's what dreams are."

"Some dreams are truer than waking life. So they said in Lipa. Who am I to claim the truth of myself, if my dreams give me the lie?"

"Yes, well, you said a good many things *before* you killed him, and these would suggest you suffer from an excess of affection coupled with loss, sometimes called heartsickness—"

"I killed Wick," whispered Arrow. "I always kill him, in all my dreams."

"In all my dreams," said Dan, "an octopus is clinging to me with every sucker of its tentacles. Or a cloud of spiders is crawling up under my clothes. Or a human is kissing me. My worst fears, you see? Remember, you just killed your first man. You're a poor soldier, Arrow, and your dreams are making too much of it."

"How would you know?" Blood snapped back into Arrow's cheeks, and her eyes blazed. "You know nothing about it. Dreams—love—death—not any of it."

The wizard started back, inhaling sharply. For Arrow had not spoken in Wizardish as she meant to, but in her anger had slipped into the language Dan had only heard her speak in dreams. Now he found that this language had an awful potency when hurled directly at him; indeed, his hand clutched at his breast as if he had been struck by a weapon. He seemed to himself to be falling backward, and tearing open, and coming unmade. Yet the terror flooding him was not so great as the thing causing the terror: a longing for something he did not know and could not know.

Arrow's eyes fixed on him, kindled with a kind of fierce gladness as she beheld the chaos riving him.

"You know nothing," she said again.

Unable to speak, close to panic, the Wizard Dan stumbled from the room.

"Heavier then, the wounds of the heart, sore for the beloved."

—The Wanderer

11

Dan avoided Arrow until they climbed onto Halla's back at sunset. Even then, he wouldn't look at her.

So Arrow said, "I'm sorry, Dan."

"What?"

"I'm sorry."

"For what, exactly?"

"For getting angry at you. For making you upset."

"I'm not sure what you're referring to. Having little grasp of the subtleties of human passions, I took no notice of yours. Whatever you may have interpreted as some form of displeasure on my end was nothing more than the call of nature. I had an upset stomach, likely due to the atrocities served at that trough of a table. Please don't mention it again, lest my illness return."

Arrow said nothing, though she thought a great many things. Dan, too, was silent, until the next morning when the sun rose crimson over a vast water, its edges silver with ice.

"The Bay of Teeth," said Dan. "Let's keep flying; Gnoze lies on the eastern side of the bay. We'll reach it by noon."

The landscape was flat and snow-covered, its blankness broken by black, tumbled rock and lonely patches of pine. Halla veered from the shore toward a line of islands as steep as spear-points, dotted with white birds. Seals basked on sheets of ice while the fins of porpoises sliced through the channels between them. As the sun rose higher, it caught on a point at the far side of the bay and dazzled it.

When they flew closer, this point of light grew until it resembled a ball of fire, brilliant orange and white against the black pine woods behind it.

"Is it burning?" asked Arrow.

"It is Gnoze. Wait and see."

They flew closer still, and the ball of fire swelled into a swarm of burnished surfaces, all catching the light and throwing it off each other in an intricate, flickering dance. The city shed its light on the harbor below, tinting its ice with glassy fire.

They flew closer still, and now Arrow could see it: a palace of gleaming amber, dotted with pointed domes swirled red and gold. Bronze walls shielded it from land and sea. But no banner flew in its towers. Instead, a bronze spire rose from the center of the palace, twice as high as the city itself. The point of this spire seemed to gather the sunlight to itself, sucking it out of the air in golden ribbons like lightning that didn't flash but streamed inward. Then Arrow realized the city was not merely reflecting the sun's light; it was capturing it, lighting Gnoze's amber stones from within.

"We come from stars," the Wizard of Two explained. "We're rather partial to light."

Halla, seeing the palace's golden domes, gave a shriek of joy that tumbled out over the cold waters, announcing their arrival. A deep, rasping bell raised its ancient voice in reply. The vine-carved bronze doors of the city wall clanged open, and Halla swept through them.

As they slid down Halla's flank onto the floor's polished amber stones, a fat, short Wizard of Five waddled toward them, his white beard flowing nearly to his feet. He wore blue robes and short, red boots with pointed toes.

"Ah, Dan old fellow!" he cried. "Just in time. Cimarrin has taught us a new game: someone draws a picture and we must guess the word before the sand runs through the minute-glass. I'm losing badly. You might be able to guess at my drawings as you're no more of an artist than I am."

The Wizard of Five stopped short, his mouth falling open. "A human! A female no less! Remember how that went over the last time. They're more demanding than gorgons and far less entertaining. No, Gnoze can't stomach another human for a few centuries at least. We'll have to call a debate to decide whether you can keep her."

Arrow glanced at Dan in alarm, but the Wizard of Two remained nonplussed.

"First, I'm not looking to keep her. I'm merely her conveyance. Second, excellent. Call a debate, Nozzi. That's exactly what I want you to do. Invite everybody. Spread the word that it will be controversial. Get everyone riled."

"Oh, not to worry," Nozzi replied, glaring at Arrow as if she gave off a stench. "Everyone will be riled."

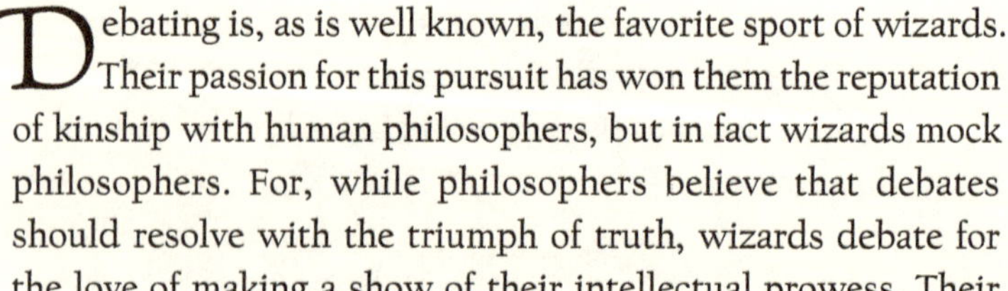

Debating is, as is well known, the favorite sport of wizards. Their passion for this pursuit has won them the reputation of kinship with human philosophers, but in fact wizards mock philosophers. For, while philosophers believe that debates should resolve with the triumph of truth, wizards debate for the love of making a show of their intellectual prowess. Their debates conclude, most often, with wounded pride leading to magical duels.

Dan stressed this potential outcome as he prepared Arrow to enter the Debating Hall that evening. "The most important thing is to speak as little as possible," he warned. "If you annoy them they'll encase you in a block of ice, or something equally as uncomfortable, to shut you up. Just *listen*. I'll listen too. I'm entirely confident we'll discover all we need to know about the Wizard of Seven, if he exists. Then we'll make our exit when the sparks start to fly. It's as simple as that, if only you read my signals and follow my lead."

"I'll try," said Arrow.

As they walked through a set of bronze doors mosaiced in gold, amber, and lapis lazuli, the roar of a crowd greeted them. Some fifty wizards gathered in the hall, arranged in benches that arced in rows around the central platform upon which Dan and Arrow emerged. The platform was raised several steps from the closest row of benches. In this row were three seats like thrones, each crowned with a gemstone the size of an orange. The wizards who sat in these seats were dressed in finer robes than the rest and wore medallions around their necks matching the gemstones on their chairs. More notably, all three were Wizards of Six.

"Well met, well met!" voices cried.

"No humans," cried others. "Throw her out. Why do we need a debate?"

Arrow tripped as she followed Dan to the center of the platform, and the jeers grew louder. Her heart rammed at her sore ribcage.

"Is the Wizard Merkum here?" she whispered.

"No," Dan whispered back. "Merkum never comes to Gnoze. Now hush."

The Wizard Nozzi hobbled up the platform steps and raised his arms to quiet the crowd. "My distinguished brethren, worthy Councilors of Gnoze," he paused and bowed to the Wizards of Six with the medallions, "I have summoned you here due to the arrival of the Wizard of Two with this untidy, vapid-looking human. Though our dignity may naturally take offense at her baseness, I remind you that the laws of our noble city do not allow us to expel a guest without debate, if that guest has done us no harm. I therefore call upon the Wizard Dan to make a case for his charge, that we may debate it."

Arrow stood as tall as she could and tried to keep from bunching her skirt in her nervous hands. Suddenly she imagined Brother Agostin watching her with his big, quiet eyes. *You know your task, Arrow*, he seemed to say. And his eyes shone with pride. She drew a deep breath and let it out slowly.

Nozzi and Dan bowed to each other, and the other wizards drummed their fingers on the arms of their benches in what Arrow took to be a kind of applause as Nozzi sat and Dan stepped forward.

"My worthy Starborn brethren," Dan began, raking back his hair with calm assurance, "when I chanced upon this human in Gallia, she claimed that a wizard had sent an assassin to kill her. This claim did not engage my interest. But she went on to insist that the wizard who desired to kill her was a Wizard of Seven."

"Absurd!" came a shout.

"What was his name, then?"

Some wizards who wore rings began to tap them loudly on the arms of their benches, a sign of annoyance.

"That's exactly what I asked her." Dan remained calm. "She replied that the Wizard of Seven had removed his name, and was for this reason not shown on the Map of Wizards."

The room erupted in shouts. Arrow couldn't distinguish a word. This lasted until the Councilor in the center of the three stood and raised a hand, at which the room fell silent. This High Councilor, whose skin was a rich dark brown and who had only a short, forked beard, stood and addressed Dan.

"How came the human to make this unusual claim?"

Using only the most necessary details, Dan explained how Arrow had first met the Wizard of Seven in the Kingdom of the Giants, how the wizard had taken Wick, and how Arrow had come to the Sorry Islands, where Brother Agostin showed her the Map of Wizards.

The wizards again exploded into arguments, all shouting over each other. Despite the cacophony, it didn't take them long to conclude that removing one's name was an impossible task. Therefore, accomplishing it would make a Wizard of Six into a Wizard of Seven.

"But who is it? What Wizard of Six would do such a thing?"

"And why destroy himself to gain a rank? It would be like turning yourself into a lump of coal to grill your meat."

"Falcius! The old salamander. He'd do it just to see what it felt like."

"But Falcius died."

"Who saw the body? He disappeared!"

Dan raised his two-fingered hands and pleaded until they shushed each other enough to turn back to him.

"That's not all. The monk of Lipa wrote to the Wizard Merkum—"

"A fool," muttered several.

"I hear he's learned to dance." This caused shudders of disgust.

"—and Merkum wrote to the monk. Though the Wizard Merkum is unfortunately not present at this debate, the human girl is prepared to recite his answering letter, if you desire Merkum's evidence for this debate."

"Merkum's evidence for what?" snapped a wizard who was partially invisible. Parts of him were opaque, others translucent, and others completely hidden; as he spoke, the visible and invisible parts of him shifted so that now his arm, now his hip, now his face, would be concealed or revealed. "What are we even debating? Whether to throw out the human, or whether Merkum's a fool? Set some parameters or get off the platform."

But others drummed their fingers on their benches, crying, "Hear it! Let's hear the letter!"

Dan gestured to the High Councilor, who nodded his approval. Arrow stepped forward and began to speak. To her great relief, the wizards listened to the entire letter, though they interjected with many jeers, epithets, and blurts of doubt and surprise. When she finished, the debate began in earnest.

"A Wizard of Eight is a logical absurdity. The rank of seven is the final degree of power."

"What about the limitation of power? Have you read Bodi's Treatise on whether the limitation is truly insurmountable or merely impossible to surpass?"

"Bodi's Treatise is a monument to the inconsistent application of terms."

"There are several myths suggesting the possibility of an additional rank."

"Oh, myths! That all contradict each other. Stick to the Manual."

"The myths agree there is only one impossible thing that could make a Wizard of Eight."

"Which is?"

"No one knows."

"Then my argument stands."

"Could Falcius have found out?"

The Second Councilor stood, a broad-shouldered wizard with a full, frothy yellow beard and a round, red face. "There is one question I must have answered before we proceed." He turned to Arrow. "You claim that the Wizard of Seven sent an assassin to kill you. What basis do you have for that claim? And what was his motive?"

"The assassin said a wizard sent him," Arrow replied. "But he also knew my name. The only wizard who knows my name is the Wizard of Seven."

"Wrong!" cried the partially invisible wizard, leaping to his unseen feet. "Merkum knows your name."

Arrow's mouth dropped open. "Yes, but why would Merkum want to kill me?"

"Well that's obvious," the invisible wizard continued. "Because you're part of the Wizard of Seven's scheme to become a Wizard of Eight, and Merkum wants to prevent it."

"That's absurd!" Arrow cried.

"Agreed," said Dan with a nervous laugh, clutching Arrow's elbow and yanking her behind him. "More likely, the Wizard of Seven didn't want her trotting off to Gnoze to alert us all to his existence, for which we should thank her."

"Starborn brethren," boomed a voice from the back of the room. A tall, pale, black-haired Wizard of Five stood. "I have a piece of evidence for this debate."

"With regard to motive, Ardian?" asked the Second Councilor.

"Yes."

"Proceed with the evidence."

The bickering died away as the Wizard Ardian strode forward and mounted the platform. A pale yellow mist hung around his feet, moving with him as he walked. Arrow stepped to the side as he took his place, keeping well clear of the mist. He did not look at her.

"In his letter," said Ardian, "Merkum speaks of others who have encountered the Wizard Who Changes Things into Other Things. I am one of those others."

"What!"

"Where?"

"Why didn't you say so from the start?"

"How long have you been sitting on this egg, you old hen?"

Ardian waited in silence until the questions died away. Then he continued. "For many years, I have probed the Virgin Shores beyond the Far Deeps. In my travels, rumors came to me from the Kingdom of the Giants, which, investigating, I found to be true. What I now relay are facts. I beg you hear my entire tale without interruption."

"Get on with it then, Ardian," called a red-bearded wizard with smoke curling from the ends of his fingers. "It's too hot in this hall and your wind is feeding my flames."

"Less than a score of years ago, a nameless Wizard of Seven arrived in the Land of the Giants. He brought with him two infant humans, a boy and a girl. Where he acquired the infants is unknown, but one was an African of the Far South, the other a Norseman of the Far North. These he sold to the Queen of the Giants, who kept them in a private collection. Though the Wizard feigned disinterest in the children, it became known that he watched their progress with the greatest concern, for through them he hoped to become a Wizard of Eight."

All Arrow's strength drained from her body, flooding away into the ground. A ringing grew in her ears as a white fog began to settle over her vision.

"Arrow," hissed Dan in her ear, "don't cave now." Despite his hatred of touch, he grasped her hand and wrung it to the point of pain, clearing back the fog. "Stay. Listen. This is why you came."

Ardian continued, "I sought further into the Wizard of Seven's schemes, but his namelessness made him difficult to track. At last, in the vast and treacherous Centaur Forests of the Great Wilde, I uncovered the root of his pursuits.

"In that land fresh rumor cried that a clan of centaurs had been completely wiped out except for infants and a few elders feeble with age. I found one of these elders, who claimed the Wizard of Seven had destroyed his clan because they were possessed of knowledge which laid bare his plans. He proceeded to tell me of an ancient order of wizards that once dwelt in that part of the Wilde, hiding themselves by removing their names. All were Wizards of Seven whose aim was to overthrow the limitation of power and surpass the final degree—that is, to become Wizards of Eight. The Order of the Nameless consulted sorcerers, demons, and planets; they made studies and recorded the results. At last, they discovered the only means by which the limitation of power could be surpassed."

Murmurs swelled through the hall. The High Councilor stood, once more silencing the room, and said, "Surely this Order of the Nameless must have seen their folly! For the limitation of power is precisely this: that a wizard cannot destroy the will of a rational creature. If any one of these wizards were to overcome the limitation, he could immediately reduce the others to thralls."

"Hear, hear!" others roared, clanging their rings against the arms of their benches. "Utter folly!"

"Remember Merkum's letter," said the partially invisible wizard. "In all the legends, the Wizard of Eight destroys the Race of Wizards. If Falcius succeeds, the first thing he will do is make us his appendages!"

"Verily," said Ardian. "Evidence shows that this Order of the Nameless ultimately killed each other, one by one, because of their fear of one reaching his goal first and enslaving the others."

"What have the human children got to do with it?" the red-haired, smoking wizard hollered. "Get to the point, Ardian, before I'm tempted to speed you up!" To make his point, he shot a ball of fire from his middle finger that landed at the edge of Ardian's mist, illuminating it like a torch.

Ardian continued unfazed, "The Order of the Nameless discovered, as I said, one means by which the limitation of power could be overthrown. They recorded this means in a document, a copy of which was preserved by the aforementioned centaurs, and which is now in my possession."

The wizard withdrew from his sleeve a small roll of parchment, opened it, and began to read.

PART III · CHAPTER 11

The Concise Findings of the Nameless
or, Field Notes for Enlightened Wizards

Though the Starborn have always considered the perfection of free will to consist in the unlimited exercise of power, earthborn species do not all share this view. Analyses of their legends, songs, and treatises show that the noblest earthborn beings—centaurs, fairies, sorcerers, and the like—consider the highest freedom to consist not in acts of power, but in acts of love.

Further study and experimentation have revealed the will's capacity to love (still rightly understood by wizards as a practical weakness) as not merely the crown of volition but its very root. Thus, to overcome the limitation of power—that is, to destroy the free will of a rational creature—one must perform an impossible task which strikes at this root: one must break an unbreakable love.

A Caveat

An unbreakable love is so rare in the postlapsarian world, a wizard cannot expect to come across it more than once in his lifetime. Because this bond is entirely dependent on freedom of will, it cannot be manufactured by magical means, but its formation may be encouraged through conditions which foster it.

If an unbreakable love can be found, the most effective method for weakening this bond (though the feat of breaking it has yet to be achieved) is to exert influence on the mind of one party (referred to in our findings as the Select), while leaving the other party (referred to as the Left) free. Killing both parties is futile, for this only preserves their bond unbreakable in the Unreachable Realm. Killing the Left is nearly as disastrous. In addition to preserving this party in the Unreachable Realm, it unleashes the force of grief in the Select, softening the memory of faults and exaggerating perfections. No, the Left should remain free. For the enemy of love is jealousy, and the free acts of the Left are the best means of fostering this enemy in the Select.

For the first time in the history of Gnoze, utter silence filled the Debating Hall.

Then Arrow spoke, her voice trembling at first but quickly growing strong. "It wasn't the Wizard of Seven who sent the assassin. Nor was it Merkum."

"No," said Ardian. He looked down at Arrow, his eyes glowing the same pale yellow as the mist which hung about him.

"It was you, sir."

He nodded once and looked away. "It was."

Half the wizards in the room leapt to their feet, while the rest turned to each other in frantic bickering.

"Ardian's got it right! Kill the human pawn. Thwart his chances as best we can."

"But she's done nothing worthy of death. It goes against the first degree of power and the nature of rational existence, which humans share with us."

"Well let's kill the Wizard of Seven then."

"Kill him later—kill her now!"

"What if we put her in the dungeon?"

"But the other one—the Select. Isn't he the one who really matters?"

"Yes, where is he? Where is the nameless wizard now?"

"I know where he is!" Ardian shouted above the din, silencing it.

Arrow's heart beat so loud it filled all that silence. Dan was hissing something frantic in her ear but she couldn't hear it.

"However," said Ardian, "we cannot assault him without years of cunning strategy, and that may be too late. The Wizard of Seven keeps the Select on the Buried Isle beneath the Far Deeps."

She knew where Wick was.

She knew where Wick was.

He was buried beneath the sea in the Far Deeps.

She knew where Wick was.

Ardian continued, "But hear this: the Nameless grows anxious. He has failed to break the human boy. I learned this from deep-sea witches; I swear on my fingers it is true. He begins to doubt his choice of the Select and thinks of seeking the Left. Clearly," he gestured to Arrow, "this human lacks the strength and wit needed for such a trial. We must kill her now, before it is too late. I beg the Council to agree, and if you will not see reason, I beg my Starborn brethren to take the matter into their own hands as I have done. Though this human may be innocent now, she will not remain so if the Nameless finds her."

The same black shadow swept over Arrow as when the Wizard Dan unveiled the darkness of her dreams, flooding her with horror of herself. Then—

"Mother of tripe!" exploded Dan, leaping forward with such rage Arrow thought he might strike his peer. Ardian raised his hand in warning; Dan skidded to a halt.

"For shame, Ardian!" cried the High Councilor.

"What is this?" fumed the Second Councilor. "A call for anarchy and treason in our own Debating Hall?" Raising his left hand, he twisted his wrist; iron shackles clamped around Ardian's wrists and ankles, and an iron band covered his mouth. Then the Second Councilor raised his right hand. Flying through the air, Ardian crashed against a marble column from which marble vines shot out, binding him fast to the stone.

But the Third Councilor said, "Ardian is right. Prudence must take precedence over principle. The human must be sacrificed for the good of us all. I cast my vote." Half the wizards cheered and drummed their fingers, while the other half protested, clanging their rings.

The Wizard Dan raised his arms and began to holler until his face turned nearly purple, "Wait! Wait, listen to me! I have more to add to my case."

The High Councilor raised his hand, but the clamor barely dimmed.

"Listen to the Wizard of Two?" jeered the flame-throwing wizard. "Who has as much at stake as a blind cyclops!"

Dan's cheeks reddened, but he called out, "Hear me, all of you. There is something you haven't considered. I've observed this human (her name is Arrow), and I do believe she shares a remarkable bond with the other human (his name is Wick). If an unbreakable love is so potent it can thwart the limitation of power, shouldn't we learn what other qualities it possesses? Perhaps... perhaps we can gain some insight from Arrow if we—"

"Spoken like a human!" sneered a wizard whose beard appeared to be made of root vegetables. "About what I'd expect from the likes of you."

But another said, "The Wizard of Two is right. We should bring her to the laboratory and study her properties. What if we can use Falcius's own weapon against him?"

"No, you don't understand," Dan spluttered, running his hand through his hair until it bristled like a lion's mane. "That's not what I—"

"You there," called the Third Councilor, "human girl, have you any powers?"

Arrow raised her chin. "I can read and write in three languages. And I can run very fast. When I dance, it always draws a crowd. If you would like, I will show you."

Dan let out a low groan as the hall erupted in mocking laughter.

"But the boy," demanded the Second Councilor. "Surely he has powers, to cause the Nameless to guard him so jealously?"

"Oh yes," said Arrow. "So many powers."

“What can he do?” the wizards demanded in an overlapping chorus. “Can he wield a mighty weapon?” “Can he speak a word of destruction?” “Does he read omens?” “Tame fell beasts?” “Raise the dead?”

“No, none of that. But he sees things no one else can see. Dear, precious, wonderful things. Please, won’t you help me rescue him? If he were to be lost—oh, nothing on earth could make up for the loss of him. You will understand once you meet him.”

“Kill her,” said a voice.

Several wizards rushed forward, but the High Councilor restrained them. Leaping in front of Arrow, the Wizard Dan splayed his long arms and legs like a windmill. Sweat poured down his face and soaked his shirt.

“They have a language,” Dan shouted, his voice cracking from the strain. “These two humans, they speak a language that is unlike anything I’ve ever heard. There is power in it, I tell you! It is more striking than a comet, more intricate than a web of silk. When you hear it, it... it changes you. And if that is the power of an unbreakable love, we must all hearken to it.”

Arrow’s mouth fell open in astonishment, for her companion’s voice altered as he spoke until it trembled with an earnestness she had thought him—and all wizards—incapable of.

Howls of laughter broke out. “Listen to him! He’s gone utterly soft!”

“He’s probably in love with her himself.”

“That’s ridiculous,” Dan fumed.

“Yes, that’s it! The only impossible feat he could ever accomplish. Wouldn’t be surprised if he grew *balls* instead of fingers!”

Dan’s face burned deep crimson as the laughter rose into a storm. “I’m speaking objectively!”

“Get him off the platform,” roared the flame-throwing wizard. Raising his right hand, he shot a fireball from each finger. Dan dodged them all but the last one, which caught him in the shin. The fur trimming his boot burst into flames, but he crushed the fire out against the marble floor.

Another wizard whirled on the flame-throwing wizard, conjuring a dark, sticky ooze which slapped over him in a sheet and hardened like clay. A third wizard retaliated on the ooze-thrower by sending a pack of snapping wolves' jaws—not whole wolves, just jaws—after him.

"Order, I must have order!" demanded the High Councilor.

No one heeded him, so he hastily threw up a shield of what appeared to be liquid glass between the platform and the crowd. Just in time—grappling hooks, swarms of bees, and several varieties of enchanted darts bounced off of it. As the three Councilors sprang in front of the shield, a staff of radiant amber appeared in the hand of each, sizzling with red and gold light. They fought to deflect the onslaught of enchantments and weapons hurled at Dan and Arrow, but the mob was beyond their control.

A glowing missile with spikes like a mace smashed into the shield, tearing a hole in it. Then came another. This one shot precisely at Arrow's head. Dan rushed forward, plowing her out of its path. Catching him in the shoulder, the missile hurled him against the back wall. He crashed to the ground, gasping.

"Dan!" Arrow sprang to his side.

His shoulder was a mangled mass of blood; his arm hung limply from it. His green eyes shut and opened rapidly from the shock.

"Oh, Dan. This is my fault."

"Not remotely," said Dan, clenching his teeth against the pain. "But you have to flee, Arrow. Take the bloodstone. Call for Halla. She'll take you away."

"But what about you? I'm not leaving you here!"

"I'll hold them off as long as I can." He struggled to his feet. "Just go. Quick!"

With his good arm, he pulled the whistle from around his neck and thrust it into Arrow's hands. As Arrow looked down, she gasped. "Dan—your hands!"

Dan looked. Each of his hands had three fingers. His mouth dropped open in amazement. "W-what did I do? What impossible thing could I possibly have done?"

"You saved my life. You kept saying it was impossible for a wizard to act unselfishly. But you just did."

"I did," he whispered. "Arrow, when the wizards were mocking me just now, they were right, and I knew it. Not that I'm in love with you. But—you're my task. I'm not sure how it happened, but you are." He started laughing uncontrollably. "That's my impossible thing? I'm the first wizard to have a friend."

A mass of blue light struck his side, exploding into shards of ice that pierced him in a dozen places. He screamed.

"Dan!" Arrow caught him as he fell. He shoved her back.

"Go, Arrow. You're my friend; you must do as I ask. Now run."

Arrow ran. Bursting through the doors at the back of the platform, she streaked down the corridor. As she ran, she brought the bloodstone to her lips and blew, tapping the whistle's holes as she had watched Dan do. Then she stumbled to a halt. The city gates were shut. Shouts sounded from the corridor. Sparks skittered off the flagstones as magical weapons clattered and exploded around her.

The griffin Halla bounded over the city wall. With one glance at Arrow and the horde of wizards barreling toward her, she snatched the girl up in her talons and soared into the air, spiraling along the palace's central spire, then wheeling off across the Bay of Teeth as the last rays of sun slipped behind its icy waters.

"Oh Halla," cried Arrow, "Dan is terribly wounded. We must find a way to rescue him."

A black, winged shape drove straight into the griffin's side. Halla tumbled sideways, pitching Arrow off her back. With a scream that seemed to die as it left her mouth, Arrow hurtled downward. A swirl of black water, white ice, and jagged rock rushed toward her. A second winged shape snagged her shoulder with its scaly claw, jerking her upward moments before she would have hit the surface.

Halla's shrieks pierced the air as she shook off her foe, which resembled a bat the size of a horse with blood-red eyes and claws. She surged toward Arrow, but a dozen of the monsters erupted from the darkness, battering her wings, biting her sides, clawing her face.

Halla fought tooth and talon. The monster carrying Arrow flew out of sight. Then, as suddenly as they had come, the host vanished. The griffin was left torn, bleeding, alone.

Long did she search for Arrow, in all directions.

But no track, nor scent, nor trace of the human girl or her abductors was to be found.

PART IV

THE REMEDY

"And they said: in the innocence of girlish ignorance,
she knows not what she says.
They began to sport with her in a great chorus
until the fiery burden fell upon her."

—Hildegard of Bingen

12

Selected Excerpts from the Private Writings of Grell, Sorceress of Glen Droighinn

17 September

The flea has come crawling back. At last he admits that his scheme is on the brink of failure, though he could not look me in the eye as he said it. I feigned surprise as he begged my assistance. I am still considering the terms. Or perhaps I have made up my mind. What of it? It does him well to wait on me.

9 October

I have decided. I will help the flea, but only if he agrees to my price. I doubt he will refuse. The payment I ask is so small, to him it may seem nothing. Far less than what it cost him to remove his name.

12 October

All is settled after my meeting with the flea this morning. In itself, the thing is ignoble; the terms make light of my art as if I were a mere ruffian for hire. If I succeed, my victory is not properly my own but attributable to him, since it was he who laid the board and moved its pieces into position, he who commissioned me to deal the final blow. To make it indisputable that I act only at his bidding, he demanded that the terms of payment be written out in the solemn way.

I merely shrugged at the terms. He may have his victory, so long as I have my reward.

We wrote out the terms in the blood of a fairy newly taken from its mother's cradle. Then, at my insistence, we drank what remained; thus shall the blood pact dissolve our innards should either of us break it. The more power the flea gains, the less he is to be trusted.

The terms, in simple language, are as follows:

I will break the girl for him.

He will leave me free when he overcomes the limitation of power.

He will give me the youth for my own.

13 October

As token of his promise, the flea has given me a little glass in which I may gaze on the youth whenever I please. I keep it in an ivory case in my divining chamber, in the same chest where I secret these writings. No one knows I have it, not even my good apprentice Coira nor any of my ministers.

Of course my lover does not know I have it, for I killed him last night. Great was his surprise, for we had hardly time to tire of each other. Poor fool; he had not yet learnt the signs that I had grown inwardly cold, though my body still burned.

From the moment the wizard told me of this Wick, of his unbreakable love which gnaws him with insatiable longing, my heart moved toward him as it has never moved toward any creature. I did not sleep that night. For the first time, it seemed to me that somewhere on this cold crust of earth, a heart was beating with a passion that could match mine.

Some say the Sorceress Grell is fickle. That I burn through lovers like matchsticks because my moods flicker and change. They are wrong. Others say I am a monster who feeds off my lovers, that I must consume them to sustain my own life. They are less wrong. The truth is nearer to this: I destroy my lovers because I seek something they cannot give. Once I have taken all and they reveal themselves as empty shells, what else is there to do with this hull but discard it?

But this youth, he is different. He loves with an unbreakable love. Once he is made to feel the loss of it, his inner fire will burn as dark and hot as my own.

I yearn for him.

Today I watched him rise and clothe himself. He took food and ate it as he rode his horse at a steady pace through the city. At last he reached the Isle's perimeter, where the rounded dome of air meets the water that encloses it like a wall of warm ice that cannot melt or shatter. Putting his hand on that wall, he held it there. He whispered words I could not understand. Then he walked. All that day, he walked the perimeter of the Buried Isle. His eyes were sometimes like that of a wolf who has not eaten through a cold winter, and sometimes like a mother gazing on an infant.

My desire for him is so different from what I have felt toward my former lovers, it is as if I am kindled for the first time.

14 October

Now, to my task. The way is clear and needs only to be followed. I will never tell the flea my method, and he will never guess. He may claim the victory, but he will always wonder why he could not succeed without me.

Here is why:

Wizards are born from the cold, clear light of stars; sorcerers are born from the liquid fire which surges from the belly of the earth. We *are* our loves. We consume all in our path and become it. Wizards consume nothing, become nothing, are wholly contained in themselves. They cannot understand love the way a stone cannot understand what it means to absorb water.

The wizard has failed because he tried to make the boy hate the girl, or replace her with another. In this, he followed the advice of other nameless wizards who had failed before him. But there is a much easier way to destroy love, a quicker and truer way which would never occur to a wizard. Sorcerers know it because it is thus, whether we wish it or no, that we destroy our own loves.

This will be my way: to make the girl hate herself.

17 October

The first step is to learn about Arrow all I can. She dwells in Lipa of the Sorry Islands. There is, on Lipa, a petty sorcerer named Marzak. Summoning him in his sleep, I commanded this Marzak to open a shadow-gate in a secret place on the island. Awed by my beauty, he had no thought of refusing me. Tomorrow I will pass through the gate into Lipa, commencing my study.

While I am away, I have instructed Coira to use all her art to change the appearance of Glen Droighinn to such as is desirable for a young woman. To make roses bloom from its brambles, to clothe its archways in festive ivy, to beckon graceful, sportive animals to its hollows and hills, to brighten its waters until their reflection dazzles the walls of our fortress in blue and white. Coira's eyes brightened at this task. She has not yet tired of beauty and craves it always. I do not mock her, for such I once was, and I was happier thus.

13 December

I am returned from Lipa at last. Though my errand was not what I expected, it has borne much fruit.

When I traveled through the shadow-gate, I found the island in great distress. Not five days before, in a fit of madness the very girl I sought had burnt a new-built ship to the ground. Its black carcass still loomed in the harbor, smoking like wreckage of war. Arrow herself had disappeared.

This news pleased me greatly, for it showed how right I had been in my choice of her. When the flea asked me to find an infant girl for his scheme, I went to the Norsemen. Their warriors are known to fall into a blind battle-fury in which they destroy all in their path, afterward scarce remembering what they have done. I chose this girl for two reasons: the rage of her father and the shame of her mother. The flea chose the boy. His father was a softspoken king, a seer of sad visions whose people overthrew him soon after. So Wick and Arrow are perfectly matched, for we who have no lineage understand this best: humans cannot escape their blood, no matter how they try.

In Lipa, I first took the shape of a young peasant girl from the hills, in this guise plying many people of the town until they led me to Arrow's three foster-sisters. These sisters taught me a great deal, especially the youngest and the eldest.

From there, I took the shape of a pious youth desiring to enter Lipa's monastery. The porter, Brother Agostin, took me under his wing and unhesitatingly answered each of my questions. Gradually I brought him round to speak of his friendship with Arrow. I discovered that the girl was learned—could read and write several languages, and had a great capacity for study. In general, I gained far more insight into Arrow's character and habits from this monk than from her own sisters.

I then sought a youth by the name of Tomás de Rueda, meeting him in the shape of a lovely young woman. This got me nowhere; he hardly looked at me but with sadness and a kind of dumb pity. Next I met him in the shape of a jovial, kind-hearted sailor newly arrived in Lipa. He spoke scarcely more to me in this new guise, and with no amount of coaxing could I convince him to take wine or strong drink. Yet his wariness taught me something: he knew where Arrow was and would not allow himself the chance to slip and betray her.

At last I met him in the shape of a fisherman's child, not yet four years old. I was there on the beach, heaping shells in a pile, as he paced along it looking anywhere but at the ruined ship. Rushing out and grasping his hand, I pulled him down to sit beside my pile. I began to pass him shells, one by one, without a word.

Then he told me all. Everything I needed to know. Once he began, his misery came pouring out of him like a cask split with an axe. I said nothing in reply. All the while, I kept handing him shells. When his grief was spent I left him there, aimlessly plowing the sand with his fingers.

He is a noble man, this Tomás de Rueda. He would never have knowingly betrayed her. But we all must speak our sorrows to someone. It is why I write these pages, though none shall read them until I am dead.

Before I returned through the shadow-gate, I did one other thing. No one shall know of it—I dare not even write it—until such time as I choose to reveal it.

14 December

I have sent three faithful birds to find Arrow: a crow, a gull, and a hawk. The flea tells me she is somewhere in Gallia, traveling north in search of the Wizard Merkum. It should not take my birds long to find her, for there are few good roads which lead that way.

Today I looked into my glass which shows me the youth. I have long yearned to see him, for I dared not bring the treasure with me to Lipa.

In my thoughts I have begun to call him my True Love. I use the term with fearful and tender awe, as if I were a shy young bride. I have never called any of my lovers thus.

Again I watched my True Love rise and clothe himself. His body is strong and lean, his skin dark as aged bronze. He wears his black hair very short and has no beard. His eyes are keen and deep, his gaze sometimes soft and sometimes hard. This gaze, betimes both soft and hard, pleases me greatly. His lips are full but frequently pressed together. Here, in his lips, he carries his burden.

Because he cannot escape the Buried Isle, and because the flea is wearied of him, my True Love is free to roam the golden city as he pleases. Today he went to a hovel (apparently there are hovels even amid the city's matchless splendor) and talked to an old woman for a long time. She was not a witch or a sybil, just an ordinary woman. He asked nothing of her. They laughed a great deal. Once, it seemed they were singing. Then he departed. I put away the glass and went about my work.

3 January

My good hawk has returned. He found Arrow, but there are several complications. Cursed be all wizardkind with their endless tangle of schemes! I immediately sent my winged ministers to retrieve her. If they are too late and the wizards have killed her, I shall not receive my reward. Fly, my ministers, fly!

14 January

She is here. My ministers brought her just as the sun was rising. I went to meet her in a dress the color of primroses, my hair braided with ribbons. Coira does not know how to laugh and I have rarely seen her smile, but when she saw this dulcet dress a corner of her mouth hooked sideways. Let her smirk as she pleases; I know how to play the game.

My ministers had not been gentle and Arrow's shoulders were badly torn by their claws. She stood there, shivering with fear and weariness as blood ran down her arms and dripped on the floor. Recalling her warrior father and her burning of the ship, I felt a bit disappointed at how small and fragile she looked.

"Where am I?" she demanded in the Wizardish tongue. "Is the Wizard of Seven here? Has he sent you to capture me?"

She was not awed by my beauty. Seemed hardly to notice it at all. For a moment I doubted myself; could it be the radiance of my body was fading? Perhaps the primrose dress—but no, I reasoned, the less intimidating she found me the better.

"Quite the opposite, my poor one. I and my winged ministers have been sent to rescue you, though I am afraid they have been crude in their haste. We must take you to the infirmary at once and tend to your wounds."

Arrow only noticed her shoulders now that I mentioned them. Looking at her torn flesh revived her sense of pain, but she did not stagger or shrink. I perceived that this was not by any means the first time she had been injured. Her struggle for self-mastery reminded me of a seasoned warrior who, though wounded, keeps his head in the battle and fights unhindered. My previous impression of her fragility vanished.

"Rescue me! Who sent you to rescue me? Who are you? I was already rescued by a valiant griffin, whom your monsters fought and injured."

Here I laid my first trap. All subsequent lies would be determined by this one, and I half held my breath.

"I am the Sorceress Grell. The Wizard Merkum sent me. He has been seeking news of you for months. When he discovered that the Wizard of Seven plotted to capture you—while other wizards plotted to kill you!—he knew he must save you from both perils. He asked me to bring you here, to my fortress in Glen Droighinn, until a plan can be made for your further aid. A heavy enchantment protects this forest from any penetration. You are safe."

"Safe," she murmured. "But what of Dan!"

Despite her strength of will, her body was fading. Coira came quietly forward to support her. Arrow did not notice Coira's beauty either; this consoled me.

Even as she passed into semi-consciousness, Arrow grasped at her wits, demanding, "Where is Merkum, then? Why is he not here, if he sent you?"

"He has gone to Gnoze. He means to reason with the Council and sway them to your cause if he can."

"You might well be lying. I do not trust you. I must see him."

"He will come soon. Once his task in Gnoze is complete, he will come straight here. I am sorry he could not greet your arrival, but he is seeking your welfare at this moment."

"I must see him," she repeated. "I must... see..."

Her speech began to slur. Coira passed a hand over the girl's eyes, and she fell into slumber.

15 January

I have been tending to Arrow's wounds with great care and gentleness. In addition to the gashes on her shoulders, she has several broken ribs. These, too, I am healing by my art. She mends quickly and tomorrow will be out of bed.

As I leaned over her this afternoon, refreshing the poultice on her shoulder, she reached out and placed her hand in the center of my chest.

I was prepared for this; it was the one thing nearly everyone in Lipa told me about her. The townspeople had thought it an odd form of greeting, but after her burning of the ship they began to suspect the gesture had magical power. No one agreed what kind of power it was, except that she seemed to be reading something in their very souls.

I can now say there is no magic in it. It is as simple as this: one body touching another, and the body speaking what it speaks.

As for me, I do not think my body has much capacity for speech left in it, for she said, "I cannot hear your heart at all. Why is it so silent?"

Answering her not, I finished replacing the poultice. Her eyes showed confusion; she still does not trust me.

16 January

This morning Arrow woke and dressed in one of Coira's gowns which I had left out for her. She was standing by the window when I entered her room. My good apprentice had frilled the room with lush draperies and candles. Light poured in the window. Outside, Coira's roses bloomed relentlessly despite a fresh dusting of snow.

"What is this place?"

"You stand in the castle of Glen Droighinn. The glen is there before you. The forest around it is vast and thick. More than that, it is protected by an enchantment such that if anyone walking through it approaches my glen, he will lose his way and never set foot on my lands."

I did not tell her that this enchantment worked both ways and no one inside may find his way out unless he have wings to fly above the trees' trickery. By the time she discovers that she is a captive, I hope to have gained her trust.

"When will the Wizard Merkum come?"

"It may be several weeks or even months before he returns from Gnoze. The Cold Seas are treacherous with ice and he will need to journey by land. Besides, he may spend much time in the Debating Hall before he wins any allies to our cause."

She shook her head. "I thank you and Merkum for your kindness, but I cannot wait that long. I must go in search of Wick."

"Do you know where he is?"

She paused. "Perhaps. I have heard some things."

Her thoughts are not difficult to read. She knew, but did not trust me with the knowledge. She must have learned it in Gnoze. This was unexpected, for the flea believes his location is unknown to all but me.

"Would it not be best to wait for Merkum's help and advice? You do not seem to realize the terrible power that the Wizard of Seven possesses. Even if you knew where Wick was, much preparation and strategy would be needed to spring him from the wizard's own lair."

She frowned. "If Merkum would come sooner, I could wait. As it is, I must make my own way."

I made my voice very soft. "Arrow, do you know why the Wizard of Seven seeks you?"

Her eyes met mine. The blue of them is not clouded but clear and sharp, with rays of gold fanning in a ring from her pupils. "Yes."

My voice grew softer still. "And if he should find you, do you think your love is strong enough to withstand his attempts to break it?"

Her eyes fell as her gaze went inward. There it was: the great fear. Much greater than I had even hoped. Answering me not, she played with a comb that was there on the table.

Then she said, "Can you send a message to Merkum, asking him to come here as soon as possible?"

"I can attempt it. I will send my good hawk; he is the swiftest of my messengers."

"Thank you."

"In the meantime, if you are up to the task, I wish to prepare you to meet the Wizard of Seven in whatever way I can. I have a library with many books and manuscripts. I can have Coira, my apprentice, read to you all those pertaining to wizardry, so you may begin to understand the foe you face."

Her face rose and a keen light kindled in her eyes. "Oh, yes! I would like that very much. Can we begin now, this moment? I am quite recovered, thanks to your physic. If the texts are in Greek or Latin, I can read them myself."

"You read?" I feigned surprise.

She nodded, already heading toward the door.

I have bought myself a little time to work.

22 February

She has read the Manual of Wizards and, with Coira's help, every commentary I possess in all languages. Now Arrow combs the library for other texts mentioned in the Manual and the commentaries. (She is a great one for reading the footnotes.) She quickly learned the runes of Wizardish script and loves to trace them with her fingers; I have seen her trace them on the table during meals.

More than that, Arrow paces the library up and down, feeling the leather spines of all the books as if they were a herd of cattle to be inspected. The knowledge, the words—they call to her. She hungers to know *all*, though she tries to keep to her task.

Any book of poetry, especially, she cannot resist if it be in a language she knows. I have taken to leaving volumes sitting on tables, lying open. The very sight of them draws her; she feels the pages before she reads them.

Because Coira is so often with her, and because they are nearer in age, Arrow trusts Coira more readily than me. This fact I have decided to use rather than dissuade. I instruct Coira on the things she must say, and by my art I have set up eyes and ears in the rooms they frequent most, so I may perceive how the conversations run.

Here is an important one which occurred today:

"Have you ever been in love, Coira?" Arrow asked.

"Yes, but that is long ended."

"How did it end?"

"I was unfaithful to him and this broke his heart. He killed himself."

There was never one for bluntness such as Coira. But I believe her lack of subtlety served her well here.

"Oh." There was a long silence. Then, "Why were you unfaithful?"

"I did not mean to be. I still loved him. But the heart is large and wild. It can love many things at once."

Arrow nodded slowly. "Yes. That is so. I have thought... at times I have thought it can love *everything* at once. Have you ever thought that?"

"No."

"And yet... don't you think that if some one thing—some precious thing—is large enough in the heart, all the other things can fit inside it?"

"Two lovers cannot fit," was Coira's intelligent reply. "One will always chase the other out."

"No, of course, you are right." Arrow was troubled. "You are right, Coira. There can only be one. I didn't mean... I don't know what I meant."

Coira looked her dead in the eyes and said as I taught her, "I have heard that you have an unbreakable love. Perhaps your heart is different from mine. From all other hearts. Perhaps this unbreakable love so shields your heart that other loves cannot chase it out."

Arrow bit her lip. She shook her head. I watched the fear fill her as she turned toward the window. "I am not different. Not at all."

Then Coira repeated, "The heart is large and wild," and left the room.

I left an intricate golden brooch, inlaid with emerald and pearl, lying on Coira's pillow. She has done well this day.

18 March

A felicitous thing happened today, quite by accident. Coira and Arrow were tending the roses in the garden (for Coira has made a garden now, a thing of dazzling beauty, where the ruins of the west courtyard were) when Arrow stood abruptly, her hands full of pruned shrubbery, and asked, "Coira, have you ever killed anyone?"

My apprentice merely looked at her, prompting Arrow to add, "Not even on purpose, just... by chance, or to defend yourself?"

"Yes."

I laughed out loud as I spied from the privacy of my divining chamber. Coira has killed more people than she could count on both hands, and I do not believe a single one was unintentional.

Arrow dropped her prunings in a pail and picked up her shears. "And... did it change you?"

"Yes," said Coira. "Especially the first one. After that, not as much."

They continued in silence. The beauty of this conversation is that Coira was simply answering in truth; I had not taught her what to say.

3 April

Today a great ruse has played out. I could avoid it no longer. I took the shape of the Wizard Merkum and visited my own castle. Coira took my shape; she is not yet skilled enough to have played Merkum. It is not that her physical form lacks anything in shapeshifting, but she has no art of invention. She stands there dull as a stick and can think of nothing to say. Luckily, Arrow did not notice how quiet Pseudo-Grell was, for all her attention was focused on the wizard.

It was to my advantage that Arrow has never met Merkum. Having only met him once myself, I approximated his shape as best I could and imitated his silly, hobbling gait as I met Pseudo-Grell in the Hall. She summoned Arrow.

"Well, well!" I cried. "Here is the hapless human mite causing such a ruckus in the wizarding world."

She curtsied with grace, then stared intently at me. "I've been seeking you for such a long time, sir."

"And I you, hoping to prevent just such a maelstrom as occurred when you decided to trounce the Debating Hall of our great city."

She flinched. "Forgive me. I never meant... Sir, have you news of the Wizard Dan? Please, I must know what has happened to him."

I waved my hands impatiently. "We'll speak of him in good time. First, I must relay more pressing matters. My journey to Gnoze has been nothing short of a flop; the entire Race of Wizards is determined against you. Good old Grell and her trusty (yet admittedly horrid-looking) ministers rescued you in the nick of time. The wizards are furious at your disappearance and have gone on the hunt, combing the land for any trace of you."

This is one of the only things I told her that was actually true. Her face fell as I said it. I added a second blow.

"At the same time, the Wizard of Seven is also rumored to seek you like a vengeful dragon. His knowledge and reach cannot be underestimated. If you were to step outside this glen, it would be only a matter of days before he sniffed you out."

She nodded. A storm of frustration rose in her. "I understand, sir. But I can't just stay here. There must be some way, some powerful enchantment that can cloak me." She turned and looked pleadingly at Pseudo-Grell. "I must find Wick. He needs me. I need him. If the nameless wizard's hope lies in breaking the bond between me and Wick, surely the best way to strengthen that bond is for us to be together again—to see each other, to talk, to laugh, to weep—after so many years."

She stopped abruptly. I perceived that she had not meant to say this; the thought was striking her for the first time, with great power, as she spoke it. I pounced on the strength of this revelation.

"My dear girl, I hate to be a wet blanket, but I'm afraid the opposite is true. Considering the matter scientifically, the chances of your bond breaking is at least ten times greater—nay, perhaps more!—if you're reunited with this Wick fellow. For the bond was formed when your hearts were pure and innocent and you had no chance of love but in each other. Now that you are past the age of innocence, it's extremely unlikely that you will find each other's love as fair or desirable as it once seemed. You're likelier to be disappointed in a reunion, and it will all be an uphill battle after that."

Her face blanched, then burned deep scarlet.

I pressed further, "Think of your own life since you left the Kingdom of the Giants. Not that I know anything of it, but I know the general way of humans. When you look at your own heart, does it appear the same tasty little dumpling it once was? Or has it moldered and rolled in the dirt a few times since your love last beheld it?"

In profound confusion, she could not speak or lift her eyes. At last she whispered, "But Wick—he can't have changed. He will understand everything."

I thought it best not to reply but to give my face a highly skeptical expression.

Then Pseudo-Grell said, as I had taught her, "Perhaps you are right, Merkum, but perhaps you are wrong. We sorcerers understand the movements of the heart much better than wizards. We must take time to examine the matter."

"But why?" Arrow burst. "Why time, why always time and delay? When we *know* where Wick is!"

Here great delicacy was needed. Arrow had still never told me where she thought Wick was, and I had never mentioned the Buried Isle for fear of giving away this vital secret. But if she had indeed learned the truth in Gnoze, then the Wizard Merkum would also have learned it had he journeyed there. The way she looked at me implied that she thought this the case.

"To be sure," said I, "but I haven't the slightest clue how to find the place or to reach him."

"Can't you find out?" All her confusion was turning to anger. I saw a hint of what I recalled in her father. "Someone must know where it is, or else how did the Wizard of Seven find it?"

I shrugged and waved my hands. "The place is more myth than reality! Why, our own Council, nay all the wizards in Gnoze, have no idea how to find it or they would storm it without delay. Why do you think the Nameless chose it, except that no one knows where it lies?"

"Then let me go," she shouted, striding forward with a clenched fist. "I will find the Buried Isle on my own, if wizards who seem so powerful are utterly useless. Or—take me to the Wizard Dan. He will help me."

I took a single step toward her, so we stood no more than a foot apart.

"Oh yes, I forgot to tell you. The Wizard Dan is dead. He perished in the uproar you caused in the Debating Hall at Gnoze."

She froze. Her face was like that of my lovers as I killed them. Then she fled the hall. I have not seen her since, even after I departed the glen and returned in my proper shape.

19 April

Since the day of my ruse, Arrow has spoken little to me or Coira. She paces the length of Glen Droighinn, up and down the river. The river's trick is that once you reach the edge of my domain, it turns on itself imperceptibly in a circle, and one suddenly realizes one is walking downstream without knowing how. She must have discovered, then, that she cannot leave the glen. But it does not seem to matter to her. She is deeply shaken.

1 May

Arrow reads poetry now, in addition to wandering the glen. This is well, for most of what the poets speak of love is to my advantage. But I discovered her favoring Hildegard, whom I thought less safe. I removed the volume from the library and rearranged the books so she might most easily find those verses which tell of the heart's wrack and ruin.

11 May

Today Arrow came to me as I worked in the room where my herbs are stored.

"My lady, I've been considering all the Wizard Merkum said. It has been very hard. When Wick was taken from me, I promised I would find him. Then, for a long time, I hid that promise from myself. I hid Wick—I put him away from me entirely. I'm ashamed to tell you."

Choking back strong feelings, she continued.

"Then something happened to help me realize what I had done. I renewed my promise to Wick with the feeling that nothing on earth could dissuade me from finding him. But I didn't know that all along, the whole time, we had been part of this wizard's scheme. That we were his toys—his weapons. So that the more the space was taken away between me and Wick, the more dangerous we became. Not just to each other, but to others who were unwittingly caught up in the game."

Setting her jaw, she spoke the rest with a deadness of countenance meant to pass for confidence.

"The caveat which the Wizard Ardian discovered says it's nearly impossible to break a love when one party has gone to the Unreachable Realm. I understand now why this is so. Because in that realm, we don't change. We can cause no future hurt to the other, and all their memories of us grow sweeter and nobler—as if we'd been saints leaded in colored glass, with the sun shining through us.

"I had thought that, if Wick was my task, the best thing I could do would be to find him. To be at his side, no matter what happened to us. But now I see that it would be best for Wick if I could ensure that his love for me remained forever sure, forever as it is now. That there could never arise any change so great it put the space back between us."

She stopped and looked at me as if everything had been said. "What are you asking, child?"

"I am asking you to send me to the Unreachable Realm."

"You are asking me to kill you."

"Yes. Please, if you would."

I put my hand softly on her cheek. "This is a noble thought, Arrow, but a grave one. I will give the matter consideration. I do well perceive the danger that is here, especially the calamity which would befall so many if you ever did anything unworthy of this youth's pure and steadfast love. But I am not wholly agreed with the Wizard Merkum that it is not best for you to find Wick and remain by his side. You may be right, that you are less likely to injure him if you know he can see and judge all your actions."

She winced, then spoke quickly, "It's not only that. It's that others have lost their lives because of me and Wick. Not only the Wizard Dan, but the Gallian Marc who was forced to seek my life. He was not really to blame. He had a wife and three children whom he loved. If I am gone, no others need perish because of me. It's only right. Wick would think the same. I know he would understand, if he could see it the way I see it."

"Let me ponder it, child. I will consult texts of wisdom and ply my art to see if it reveals anything of what this course portends."

"Thank you." She departed. Until the day's end, she walked the river.

"Oh, I know not what to do or where to flee!
Woe is me, for I cannot fit into
this garment with which I have been clothed.
Indeed, I would rather cast it from me."

—Hildegard of Bingen

13

19 May

Today I watched my True Love rise and walk about the city. I believe the flea has entirely given up working with him, for I have sent word that my victory with Arrow is imminent.

My True Love came upon a very young girl dancing in the street. This delighted him. As he began to dance with her, her crowd of little friends gathered round them. Then he taught her a new dance. I assume it is one of those he invented in the Kingdom of the Giants, for it is unlike any other I have seen and has a childish abandon in its steps.

The girl loved this dance. Her friends all learned it too, shrieking with joy.

My True Love laughed as he danced. He laughed and laughed. Then tears began to stream down his face, tears I knew were for Arrow. Yet still he laughed, still danced.

This action—this laughing and crying together—is the one thing I have seen in him that I did not love. It is not as it should have been. When he thought of her, he should have fallen silent and grave, wandered off and wept in secret. His countenance should have become more like that which I first saw in him, of a wolf in midwinter. Thus would he have acted in a manner worthier of my love. Yet he will be grave enough in time.

I see how badly the flea has failed with him. I do not wonder he has sought my help.

20 May

As I left my glass yesterday, my heart seething with desire for my True Love, it occurred to me that Coira has not taken another lover, though she has been without one for longer than I and has no vision of future bliss to keep her thus chaste.

I met my good apprentice alone in her garden, for Arrow has deserted it since she decided to seek an end to all such.

"Coira, why have you not found a new lover since your last disappointment? Surely you cannot still be grieving over one who meant so little to you from start to end."

She answered me not, feigning trouble with an unruly vine.

"You will tell me now," I commanded, my voice growing in strength.

"How can I tell what I do not know myself?" The inwardness of her voice was a foil to mine, as if she kept back the whole of her meaning but a tiny gleam.

This reply, innocuous enough, stung me with alarm. For I perceived anew Coira's flush of youthful radiance, her fierce hunger for all forms of loveliness, and a certain, melancholy clinging to the memory of innocence that has not yet hardened into bitter wisdom. Then the impression struck me with full force that the look I had seen of late in Coira's eyes was just the look I liked best in my True Love: that of a wolf in midwinter.

"Coira," I said, my voice now as quiet as hers, "can it be that you mean to take my True Love from me?"

"No." But she replied too quickly, too decisively.

Gripping her jaw in my hand, I forced her face upward.

"Look into my eyes and swear it is not so."

"I swear."

Though fear streamed from her like the scent of fire, there was no lie in her eyes.

"Why not?" I tightened my grip on her face, pressing my nails into her flesh. "He is nearer your age than mine, and perhaps nearer your disposition. Often has Arrow spoken to you of his perfections, real or imagined. Tell me now and tell me truly. Why do you not desire him for your own?"

Flinching against the pain, she gazed full steadily into my eyes.

"Because," she said in a voice stripped of artifice, "I should fear to touch him."

This answer pleased me greatly, and I let her go.

24 May

Today I called Arrow into my divining chamber. I was dressed in an impressive manner, my black hair streaming loose and my golden torc gleaming around my neck. She looked around the chamber with fearful awe as I stood at the window, sunlight streaming over me. Her hands shook though she tried to hide it; she thought I had summoned her there to strike her dead.

"Arrow, I have pondered the matter you proposed some days ago, consulting secret arts which reveal the true meaning of men's actions. What I have learned is this: though it seemed to you a noble act to sacrifice your own life to spare others, in fact your motives are not pure. In your secret heart, you merely lack the courage to face Wick again—not just to face the Wizard of Seven, but your beloved himself. You are afraid your love for him is not strong enough, and you seek in cowardice to avoid the difficulty of having it tested. For shame, Arrow! Will you flee at the first hint of battle when Wick has been enduring the constant test of his love for years without flagging?"

Shame poured over her. She nodded, red-faced, lips quivering. I let her sit in this wretchedness a while before I continued.

"I beg you to take command of yourself and act less like a humbled child. A great burden is upon you which you must bear more worthily. For after my study, divining, and meditation, I have determined that the Wizard Merkum is wrong. I believe it would be best for you to find Wick and be reunited with him, despite the danger. You are too weak and changeable on your own, but he may strengthen you so you will fail less readily."

She looked up. Hope was kindled in her eyes, a reckless, grasping hope that would do anything I asked.

Smiling, I stroked her cheek. "I have written to the Wizard Merkum and asked him to bend all his power toward seeking the location of the Buried Isle and a way to enter it."

Her heartbeat quickened and her hope burned brighter.

"Yet," said I, "you are not ready to meet Wick. You have changed too much; you have done too many things that are an affront and mockery to the steadfast love he has for you. If you are not to repulse him with the sight of your altered state, you must purify yourself as Crusaders do before battle."

"Yes, yes," she said eagerly. "I wish to purify myself. I have long wished to do so. But how can it be done?"

"We must examine each of the shameful things you have done and assess how badly they have changed you. Then you must cut that change out of your heart."

"You mean—I must unchange?"

"Yes."

"But that is impossible."

"Am I not a sorceress of great power?" As I said this, I cast a blue light to illumine my beauty. All my streaming hair shone blue in it. The stone in the center of my torc glowed with red fire. "What shameful deeds you cannot undo, my magic can remedy."

If she had known how thin were the walls of my deceits. If she had known that in the next room I kept an enchanted glass showing his sweet face. If she could have seen him dance and laugh and weep for her as he laughed, she would have leapt on me and wrapped her hands around my throat, cursing my lies.

But he was as far away as if he had been in the Unreachable Realm, and she in the palm of my hand.

27 May

I have told Coira we are very near to victory, sending her on an errand.

She is to find a man and bring him here. We will need him when I have nudged Arrow to the brink.

1 June

Today Arrow began her remedy. I brought her to my divining chamber because her senses are so alive to the magic that hangs in the air there. She will readily believe I am performing some enchantment if only I wave my hands impressively.

We sat at a table which had nothing on it except a black stone, the purpose of which is so obscure I forgot it ages ago.

"After you left Wick," I began, "what is the first thing you can remember doing that was unworthy of him?"

She thought. Then she told me of how she lied to her foster-sisters and Tomás de Rueda, telling them Wick was only a doll.

When she finished, I looked at her for a few moments as if stricken dumb. Setting my hand on her arm, I said, "Arrow, whatever happens you must never, ever tell Wick you have done this thing."

She squirmed. "But he will understand. I've always thought... he knows just why I did it, and when I tell him he will explain it so well that I will understand too."

"You are quite wrong. It would wound him irrevocably if you told him what you have done. Indeed, I have never heard of anyone doing a more hurtful thing. And you still thought him your brother!"

"Well unchange it, then!" she cried. "Didn't you say you could?"

"Yes, but I did not know you had done something so heartless as that. I will try to unchange it, but you must still keep it carefully hidden from him, should you ever meet him again."

"I will."

"Put your hand on the black stone."

She did. I waved my hands and said some ridiculous thing. Looking at her, I sighed and said, "Well, I have done my best for today. But the effort has tired me. We will try again tomorrow."

22 June

Arrow's remedy continues much in the same vein it began.

Today was significant, for she at last told me of her love for Tomás de Rueda. I stopped her at several points. The first was this:

"But Arrow, do you mean to say that you *knew* Tomás had slept with your foster-sister, and you fell in love with him anyway?"

"Yes. Noemi told me. I think she meant to dissuade me. But... can one keep oneself from falling in love? Isn't that how it works? You fall, and then you realize you've fallen."

I pursed my lips prudishly. "Perhaps. I simply thought that things might be different for *you*. That *you* might not have raised your eyes to the man who seduced your sister, because your heart would have belonged so faithfully and completely to Wick."

I have raised her blush many times but this one made the others look like chalk.

"I never thought of it like that... that Tomás seduced her. It wasn't like that between them."

"Well, continue. I have hindered your tale."

I did not interrupt again until she arrived at the day she burned the ship.

Just before she came to the burning, I asked, "Tell me more of this Eloi Fernandes, the shipbuilder. You knew him well?"

"Yes. He called me his lady-apprentice. He taught me so many things: the properties of a hull, the function of a bowsprit, the mechanics of a rudder."

"He was your friend?"

"Oh yes, my dear friend."

"Had he family?"

"His wife died more than twenty years before while giving birth to a child, their only child. His little daughter died three days later."

"Ah, what a tragic tale! So he had nothing left but joy in his craft. He must have loved this ship almost as if it had been the daughter he lost, since he brought it to being."

"Yes." She fell silent.

"But go on, Arrow. What happened next?"

"I... perhaps we should stop for today."

I sat up straighter. "Are you playing the coward again?"

She clenched her jaw. Then she told me all. I did not interrupt again.

At the end I said, "This is grave indeed. I will need to summon all my magic to remedy the shameful things you have brought forward this day. But even then... I simply did not know, Arrow, that someone who seemed so devoted could have done such things. If I had, I might have counseled you differently."

Her eyes flashed; there was still enough defiance in her to thrash against the web I wove. "But didn't I give him up? Didn't I choose Wick over Tomás in the end? Does that mean nothing? Doesn't it mean *everything*? To me, it meant everything. More than everything."

"Ah, but did it mean too much? The truth lies in that, Arrow. There is only one more thing I will ask you. Your answer will determine all. My question is this: when Tomás kissed you, did you ever wish afterward that you had not stopped him?"

She stood so fast her chair fell over with a bang. Her lips pressed white together, her forehead tautened. "I will never tell you that." She ran from the room.

So today she did not put her hand on the black stone. I performed no absurd incantations over her. All she brought forward throbs in her mind not merely unchanged but blazoned anew, like a fresh brand on the skin of a slave.

25 June

I am concerned that Coira has not returned from her errand, for we are getting close to the end now. It cannot be that hard to find a man. He need not be handsome or possess any wit or charm. He need only be a lecherous brute who knows how to do the thing quickly. In fact, the more loathsome the better, for the greater will be Arrow's shame when she realizes what she has done.

I know just how it will be when I bring her to the brink: a storm of Norse rage, utter wrath and hatred of the whole human race and her own participation in it, just as when she burned the ship. Then I will send the man in to her. In the moment, she will devour his very brutishness as if thirsting for her own damnation. Yet even this may not be enough to break her. It is the shame that will come after; this is what will turn her away from Wick for good and all, dissolving her solace in him to bitter wreckage and despair.

And then, oh then! I shall be to my True Love the solace he has lost.

I will be so good to him.

10 July

Today I summoned Coira, but she did not respond to the summons. Has something happened to her? Could she be ill?

I do not know what will prompt me to spring the final blow on Arrow, but she is ready. It could happen at any time. I am near to searching out a man myself, but I dare not leave the girl alone for any length of time.

Or I could change my shape and do the deed myself. The thought is distasteful to me, especially when I am so near to possessing my own True Love. I would rather keep myself for him.

Tomorrow I will try summoning Coira again.

14 July

Today a difficulty arose.

Arrow sat on a rock near a large bend in the river. The sun over the hills shone warm and golden on her face. High summer has come and all the lushness my good apprentice conjured has swollen into fecund beauty, though it grows wild and haphazard in her absence. Glen Droighinn has never seen so many birds.

Arrow was singing, unthinking, scraping at the rock's crust of lichen with a stick.

This boded ill, for the song was strange and I felt sure it belonged to her and Wick. What filled my mind was the memory of my True Love dancing and laughing. What if Arrow should laugh? Much ground would be lost.

I walked down to meet her. She did not stop singing until I stood beside her as she sat on the rock. When her song faded to silence, she did not look at me.

Then she said, "You don't know Wick. That's all I can say, my lady. I know you've meant well, but you don't know him. He's not like you think he is."

"Perhaps... he *was* different. But then he was a child. Now—"

Her face snapped toward mine, eyes keenly narrowed. "And yet, all this time you've told me he is unchanged. That I alone have been altered by the things I've done, while he loves me in just the same way he always has."

"Ah," said I. "You misunderstand my meaning."

"I misunderstand nothing." She slid off the rock so it stood between us, facing me with her fists clenched at her sides. "It is you, Grell, and the Wizard Merkum, who don't understand what it means when the space is taken away between two people. If I'm the one who knows what it's like, then I must act as my knowledge shows me to act, not as you would have me."

"Yet my remedy has revealed that you rarely act in accord with that love, that at each opportunity you come within a hair's breadth of breaking—"

"Stop, stop!" She pressed her hands over her ears. "You know nothing about it." Then she began to hum the song she had been singing.

So the ground was already lost. I took it in stride, did not fight to regain it.

A critical moment has come. Swift action will now be needed. I can wait for Coira no longer. Tomorrow I will play my hand.

A Song of Wick and Arrow
in their own language

Show me it, your little hurt;
Your big hurt, show me.

Here is one kiss
And here are three more
And here is a joke we both know well.

Where's the sting now? Where has it gone?
Here is a joke we both know well.

15 July

This morning I left sitting on a table in the library an account of the Battle of the Firebirds, in which every able-bodied seaman of the Sorry Islands was killed. The battle took place three weeks ago; I had the account sent to me from Iberia. This is the official governor's report which was copied and distributed to all the western port cities, containing not only the details of the battle but also a full list of the dead. I did not go near the library all morning, but left her to discover it alone.

When she had been in the library several hours, I went in. Arrow knelt unmoving where she had slid from her chair to the floor, bent forward with her hands braced on the ground in front of her. The governor's report was near her but cast to one side, crumpled, smoothed, partially torn, wet with tears.

"Such a tragedy," I said. "I am so sorry for your kin and countrymen, child. The news came this morning."

She replied not a word nor moved a hair. Scarcely seemed she to breathe.

I continued, "I could not bring myself to read through the list of the dead. Was... he... on it?"

The tips of her fingers turned white as they pressed against the floor. That was all.

"By he I mean the one who saved your life after you committed your crime. Tomás de Rueda."

She gave the tiniest nod, as if her head and neck were encased in plaster which she had to crack in order to move at all.

I sighed deeply, compassionately. "Poor child. This news must be unspeakably difficult for you. What a bewildering tangle of the heartstrings. With the hope to prevent Wick from perishing, you left Tomás behind. Yet if you had not left Tomás behind, he would not have perished in the battle. It is as if you made a great wager, and you lost."

"Silence!" she seethed, springing to her feet and whirling to face me. "You shall not make me, *cannot* make me feel I am to blame for his death."

"Arrow, Arrow!" I rushed forward to embrace her quivering shoulders. She wrenched free and stumbled backward. "Oh dear child, how pitiable you are."

Sobs broke from her. Again I moved to embrace her; with greater violence she fled me.

"Don't touch me! I will kill you if you touch me." Her tone grew hysterical and shrill. The rage was falling on her, just as I hoped. "I can see it in your eyes. You're glad I am wretched. You want me to hate myself."

She broke off, gasping as one who receives a blow to the stomach. "Is that it?" she whispered. "Do you wish me to kill myself? Is that your aim in all this?"

"My aim has been to protect you from yourself. To protect others from you. Have a care, Arrow! Your countenance just now—if you could only see it! How it frightens me."

Inch by inch, her body coiled as she spoke. Each muscle, each tendon, each nerve. "Yes, you should fear me, Grell. I hate you. I hate you!"

"Blame me not for what you have done. I have only held up a mirror to your pitiful face."

She flew at me, snarling. I drew forth my dark fire to burn her as she touched me, but she felt nothing. Because it was not my aim that she should destroy herself in hatred for me, I sent forth ropes of twisted steel to bind her fast. She cut all her flesh straining against them but could not free herself. Still she raged toward me, screaming with wrath, snapping her foaming jaws like an animal. Truly, the warriors' fury was a sight to behold as her blood fully rose.

I stood there still as a Madonna, allowing her to spend herself. Then, when she was so exhausted as to be scarce able to stand: "Arrow, you are not yourself. This news, I fear, has driven you close to madness. You must allow me to heal you by my art. Remember that much is at stake. You approach a dangerous threshold. Do not cross it!"

"Yes," she whispered, spittle dripping from her mouth. "Yes, I know. Oh, I know." Her eyes flashed pitiably up at me; frailty and fear replaced all her foment. "Help me."

Releasing her from her bonds, I lifted her in my arms and carried her to her chamber, laying her limp body in her bed.

"Where is Coira?" she murmured.

"She will return soon."

I touched each of her injuries, soothing her burns and sealing her cuts.

The calm of utter exhaustion held her in stillness. Her listlessness was like that of a child after a near-fatal fever. I saw that my work could not be completed while she remained in this frail state. Kissing her forehead, I stood and turned to leave the room.

"Coira was not there," she called softly after me. "When Merkum came. She should have been; I saw her just after he left."

"Hush, child. Let nothing trouble your thoughts."

"He never came." She said it with no emotion at all, no strength or accusation, looking not at me but at the painted canopy which hung over the bed. "Coira was Merkum. No—you were Merkum, Coira was you. His voice and your voice: they are the same."

"The scent of madness hangs about you yet, Arrow. Recall the danger if it be kindled afresh."

She looked at me, dead in my eyes. "Merkum did not send you. The Wizard of Seven sent you. I've known it such a long time—for weeks—but any time I came near to seeing it, you trapped me again."

"The madness returns, Arrow. Have a care!"

She struggled to sit up. "You will never break me now. I will escape you. I will find Wick and tell him everything, *everything* I have done since we were parted."

"Then you will destroy him," I said simply, "just as you destroyed Tomás de Rueda."

"I did not destroy him!"

I strode forward, leaning over the bed. My black hair fell rippling across her breast. I whispered close in her ear, "It was I who convinced Governor de la Concha to attack the Isle of the Firebirds. I did it because of you, because it suited my purpose to injure those whom you loved. Tomás died because of you. Mundo Albares and Eloi Fernandes died because of you. A fleet of innocent men, some of them African slaves, died because of you. The Gallian Marc, the Wizard Dan—all because of you. Wherever you flee I will follow, churning up death in your wake. When you meet Wick again, my hand will be on your shoulder. I will be the poison, but you the knife whose tip drives it home."

I straightened.

There, in her clear blue eyes, swelled the fruit of my labor: her hatred turned inward. The warriors' rage rushed back upon her, but her body could not support it. She fell back in a faint.

Now hangs she from the brink. Tomorrow I will cut her loose.

16 July

There has been an upheaval.

Arrow has escaped.

I know not how. I only know that Coira has done it. For the glass through which I gazed on my True Love is missing from the ivory case in my divining chamber. In its place, an intricate golden brooch inlaid with emerald and pearl.

17 July

It is worse, so unspeakably much worse than I feared.

The shadow-gate leading to the Buried Isle has been destroyed. Coira must have done this. The flea, it seems, is trapped there. I have not been able to find any evidence that Coira returned through the gate, so either the flea killed her or she remains buried beneath the sea.

But someone else came through the shadow-gate before it was destroyed.

I can smell his scent; I know it is him. All my heart screams the truth of it.

Wick himself rescued Arrow.

They escaped with the help of the Wizard Dan, eluding my forest's enchantment on the back of the griffin Halla. My ministers gave chase but could not overtake them.

Without my glass, I have lost the best means of descrying them and must ply other arts to discover where they have fled. For the moment, one passion consumes all others in my breast: hatred of Coira. I pray that the flea does not kill her. I wish to deal with her myself.

Still, I cling to a fragile hope. In Arrow's chamber were signs of a struggle. Her reunion with Wick was not the thing of bliss for which she—and he—long hoped. I also smelled an herb which Coira grows to cause a drugged sleep. Only thus subdued could the youth bring her from captivity. If her mind remains my captive, I may yet win the game.

A Letter to Arrow
From Coira, Apprentice Sorceress

Dear Arrow,

If you are reading this letter it means you are far from Glen Droighinn.

You will not understand why I have done this. I do not fully understand it myself. But it has to do with a question you once asked me: Have you ever thought that the heart can love everything at once?

No, I have never thought that. Nothing I have known would lead me to such a thought. But day by day I saw the reason for that thought shining out of you—and you unaware of it, as one clothed in diamonds who thinks them dewdrops.

Then, as I watched the light in you grow dim, I realized I would rather die than see it destroyed. I pray I am not too late.

—Coira

PART V

THE GAME

"From my mother's womb he gave me my name."

—Isaiah

14

"She must be viciously hungry," said a voice.

"Will she wake on her own?" said another.

"The real question is," replied the first voice, "what will she do when she wakes? And can we put her back to sleep if things go badly?"

"We've used up all the herb Coira gave us," said the second voice. "But even if we hadn't—we're here now, we're safe. No matter what she does, it's time to face her. To let her face us."

"Right then. Let's feed her straight off. No matter how much a person's mind has been twisted, it could never be brought to such extremity that it failed to be heartened by a good hunk of ripe cheese."

A strong smell filled Arrow's nostrils. Her mouth watered violently. Or, at least, it tried to, but her tongue lay so thick and dry it filled all her mouth.

"Water," she croaked.

"Aha!" said the first voice. "You see?"

A skin of water was held to Arrow's mouth; she drank deeply. As she did, she noticed a rumbling all around her. The deep tremor was not like waves or a rockslide, but like thunder drawn out into a languid melody. A warmth emanated from the tremor, soft yet relentless. Putting out a hand, she tested the warmth to see if it was liquid or solid. The tremor grew, the warmth strengthened around her, and Arrow perceived that she was resting against the belly of a purring griffin, its tail wrapped around her.

"Halla." Arrow put her arms around the thick, shaggy tail and hugged it, though the griffin twitched her tail's tasseled tip in mild annoyance.

"Yes. Halla and cheese," said the first voice, holding out the pungent substance once more. "What more could any rescued damsel want?"

The second voice said nothing.

Arrow devoured the cheese. Her hunger reminded her of when the Tailcatcher had found her in the Far Deeps. When she finished the cheese, someone handed her a piece of bread which she ate in like manner.

"That's the last of it," said the first voice, "except a rather tatty piece of dried venison I've been using to plug a hole in my boot. I don't suppose—"

"Yes," said Arrow.

A sigh. "I hope you don't regret it later."

She knew by then whose the first voice was. The second voice—she couldn't think about that one. Perhaps there was no second voice. Perhaps it had been part of the same dream she was always dreaming, clinging to her mind as she wakened. Of course it was.

Still, she wasn't ready to open her eyes. Instead, she caught the hand that handed her the scrap of meat. Though the hand tensed, trying to pull away, she held it fast. Then she felt its fingers: one, two, three—

"Four!"

Arrow opened her eyes.

The glittering green eyes of the Wizard Dan blinked down at her as he wriggled his hand free of her grasp. He grinned.

"Would you believe it, I'm a Wizard of Four now. Turns out it's not that hard to do impossible things once you get a running start."

Dan held up his hand and wiggled his fingers admiringly.

"But," Arrow whispered, "how are you alive?"

"Alive! You don't think that skirmish in the Debating Hall could have done me in? It takes more than that to kill a wizard. What would mean death to a human merely sends us to the infirmary for a few weeks."

It was too much to take in: how alive he was, after she had believed him dead for so long. Staring at Dan also gave Arrow a reason not to look around to make sure the second voice had been a dream. She began to work at the venison with her teeth. "How did you become a Wizard of Four?"

"Well, you may notice you are no longer in the bonny glen of the Sorceress Grell. Halla flew over the forest's enchanted barrier to fish you out, but she wouldn't have had an easy job battling the giant bat horde if someone hadn't drawn them off to the other side of the valley."

Flopping on the ground beside Arrow, his long legs stretched out, Dan propped himself on one hand while using the other to gesture with affected nonchalance.

"At first, I tried taunting the monsters in their own language. Though I offered the most vivid insults I could muster, the effect failed to impress coming from my comparatively small larynx. Then I tried banging on rocks with sticks, shaking bushes, and any number of other such feeble actions. Not a single fiend came to investigate my existence. The time grew critical, as I knew Halla was too impatient to hold her cover much longer."

Arrow once again put her arms around Halla's tail. There was never anything in the world so comforting as that tail. Her arms didn't know how to let it go, despite some nudges from the griffin's hind paw suggesting the embrace was beneath her dignity.

"In the place where I was," Dan continued, "just outside the ensorcelled trees that turn you around so you can't go further in, there was an old wall of tumbled stone, the ruins of an older castle. Well, I was kicking these stones, knocking them together, hollering, trying to get the filthy beasts to fly at me, when all of a sudden, a thought came to me. It wasn't even so much a thought. I started doing it before I thought of it. In fact, I didn't even know what I was doing until I'd done it."

Halla tried to pull her tail away, but Arrow caught a different part, near the tip, and held it fast, running her fingers through the thick red-golden fur. "An impossible thing?"

"An impossible thing. I put my hand on the rocks of the ruined castle, and they started talking."

"Talking rocks?"

"No, not 'talking rocks'. Mother of tripe! That sounds so elementary. I gave the rocks a tongue, Arrow. A language of their own. A new language, perfectly suited to these ruins of this particular castle and no other thing under the sun. Unfortunately I think I'm the only one who can understand it. But the sound itself was *terrifying*, as the ruins were not pleased to be ruins and it was clearly Grell who had ruined them. The flying beasts sped over in a fury, and they were so fussed they didn't notice me creeping off into the darkness. It wasn't until we'd fully made our escape that I noticed I had another set of fingers."

Dan beamed, once again admiring his hands. The sight made Arrow's heart ache and throb. She just wanted to look at him and cling to Halla's tail, unmoving, unthinking, for a long, long time.

"Turns out," the wizard continued, "now it's one of my powers—my very first power, aside from moderate friendliness—to give tongues to mute things. I tried it out first on an earthworm two days ago. Sure enough, the little chap had plenty to say in the wormiest voice you can imagine. Then I patted an old stump, and it started spewing out its whole history from seed to sapling to tree. They were both so relieved to have someone to tell."

"It's like our language," said Arrow. "Me and..."

She stopped.

All this time, she'd been trying not to think about the second voice and doing nothing but thinking about it. All this time, she'd known it wasn't a dream. She knew that the speaker, though he made no sound or movement, stood some ten feet off, past Halla's front talons. She knew, though she didn't look at him, that he'd been watching her this whole time.

Arrow burrowed further into the warm down of Halla's underwing. Though the griffin allowed this, she whisked her tail away for good. Arrow shivered.

"Where am I?" she asked Dan.

"These are the Highest Mountains, the domain of the griffins. Unreachable except by wing. This cave is the home of Halla's family. Mother, father, one of her brothers. The other brother has a mate and a cave of his own, close by. You'll see their three cub-chicks when they return from the morning's hunt; they visit their grandsires every day."

"Why is it so cold? Isn't it summer?"

"We're very high up on the mountain. There's snow here most of the year. It only just finished melting, and the air is still quite cool."

"How did I get here?"

"Halla brought you, of course. You were asleep. We had to give you something. It was the only way to keep you on her back. You've been... unwell, Arrow."

She didn't want to think about it. She didn't want to think about anything.

"Do you want to know how we found you?"

She made no response. Her body felt numb, her mind blank.

"It was the sorceress's apprentice, Coira. She found me and Halla and told us we must rescue you before it was too late. So we sped to Glen Droighinn. Halla and I waited in the forest while Coira passed into the glen; its enchantments are designed to let her through.

"In Grell's fortress, there's something called a shadow-gate. Coira explained that this shadow-gate can lead to any other shadow-gate a sorcerer has opened, no matter where it is. The Buried Isle has a shadow-gate, for there was once a sorcerer there. It was because of him, in punishment of his ancient sin, that the isle was first buried.

"Coira went through the shadow-gate to the Buried Isle. She found Wick and took his shape so the Wizard of Seven wouldn't notice his absence. Then she sent Wick back through the shadow-gate. He found you in the fortress and carried you to Halla, who bore you from Glen Droighinn."

When Dan spoke of Wick, he turned and made a careless gesture toward the place, just past Halla's front talons, where the second person was standing. But Arrow didn't look. Instead, she squeezed her eyes shut.

"And Coira?" Arrow's voice trembled so she could hardly speak.

"We don't know what happened to her. But... she wanted to destroy the wizard. She planned to fight him, with the intention to kill him. An apprentice sorceress fighting a Wizard of Seven? I doubt it ended well."

"Tell me one thing more," said Arrow. "How much time do we have?"

"Time?"

"Before they find us. The wizard and the... the..." The room began to swirl around Arrow.

"My dear Arrow," Dan continued, shaking his head and sighing, "there you go again demanding to know things that will strain your manifestly fragile grasp on sanity. What you should be asking is how we're supposed to acquire any cheese here in the Highest Mountains, and how—"

Arrow reached out, grabbed Dan's collar, and pulled him down. "Tell me how long I have until she finds me."

Then she let the wizard go because suddenly she couldn't breathe. She was gasping, everything was swimming around her. Halla whined, nudging her face. When Arrow tried to rise, she couldn't find which direction was up.

Then she felt a hand on her head, stroking her hair.

"Hush, Arrow," said the second voice. He spoke her name in a language no one knew but him. "It's alright. I'm here. I'm here. Shhh."

She grabbed Wick's hand. She didn't think she could ever let it go.

Wick was very tall. Long arms and legs, narrow hips. He wore his hair short, cropped close to his head. His mouth was large and his teeth white. What shocked Arrow most was his sharpness; his jaw was angular and hard, his shoulders sharply squared. When he sat on the ground, his knees and elbows jutted like a heron's. Yet, in contrast to the Wizard Dan, whose limbs seemed to be little more than bones loosely roped together with skin, Wick's frame was tightly knitted and he moved with graceful strength.

Arrow didn't observe all this right away. It was too hard to look at Wick at all. Once the blunt shock of his presence passed, an excruciating shyness washed over her. After that first, raw clinging to his hand, she abruptly thrust him away and they did not touch again. When they spoke, it was in Wizardish.

Wick caught her shyness like a fever. But it was he, that same evening, who answered Arrow's question about how much time they had until they were discovered.

"We have several good reasons to hope." Wick's voice was low, resonant, and melodically smooth. A singer's voice. "The Wizard of Seven's primary means of tracking our whereabouts has been two magic mirrors—one that showed each of us, wherever we went. Coira obtained both mirrors and destroyed them."

"The wizard knew where I was, all this time? He watched me?"

Wick nodded without looking at her. Arrow felt sick. Lowering her head, she let her hair fall like a curtain to hide her face.

"Another reason to hope," Wick continued, trying to smooth out a strained note in his voice, "is that Coira planned to destroy the shadow-gate in the Buried Isle after she sent me through it. The Wizard of Seven will have to devise some other magical way to leave the isle. That will take time, even for him."

"What of the sorceress?"

The Wizard Dan, who had been listening at a distance, strode over. "Her winged beasts gave chase as we fled, but none could come close to Halla's speed. We soon left them behind."

"She has spies," said Arrow. "She will never stop seeking us."

"We've alerted all the griffins to be on the watch for enemies who seek to harm Halla and her kin. Griffins are loyal to the death. As long as no spy returns to Grell, she can keep sending as many as she pleases."

Arrow shook her head. "You don't know her power."

"But we have some time, at least," said Wick. "Time for you to recover. Time to make a plan."

"A plan for what?" Arrow flung the words through her curtain of hair. "A plan to spend the rest of our lives fleeing, waiting for the noose to pull tight and the ground to drop out from beneath us? I'd rather be dead."

Wick said nothing.

Arrow stood and moved to a different part of the cave, where Halla was.

From then on, Arrow built a very thin wall to stand between her and Wick. Any time he spoke to her, looked at her, simply passed nearby, this wall throbbed up inside her, pounding outward to push against him, holding him back. The more Wick felt the wall, the less he dared even to glance at her. When he walked from one place in the cave to another, he took a long path to avoid coming within two arms' lengths of her.

The Wizard Dan watched it all in complete bafflement.

"After all this desperate fuss to find each other," he whispered to Wick when he thought Arrow couldn't hear, "you're as shy as two minnows."

"If we said anything, we'd have to say everything."

"Then why don't you? Say everything? It would put the whole cave at ease. Mother of tripe! The griffins' fur starts to bristle whenever you come within ten feet of each other."

Wick did not reply.

The griffins' cave opened on a sheer and treacherous face of the mountain, impossible to reach save by flying. It was a bare place, all dark rock, jutting above the tree line. Nearby, snowfields still blanketed grooves the sun rarely reached. The mountain stretched upward from the cave to a peak encased in blue ice. Similar peaks rose as far as the eye could see. Every so often a griffin flew in or out of a cave on a distant peak, hardly more than a speck.

The mouth of the cave was too small for dragons, though its interior opened into a vast and complex cavern of many rooms. Most of the rooms were filled with gold; the booty was not merely dumped in piles but sorted by size and quality, arranged into intricate sculptures. The hoard reminded Arrow of a glittering beach where children have built cities out of sand.

Each of the griffins had a nest in the main body of the cavern, near the entrance. Upon their visitors' arrival, Halla and her family built new, smaller nests: one each for Dan, Wick, and Arrow. Though lined with down, the nests were not comfortable to sleep in, as they were made of sharp sticks and designed with the intention that the sleeper remain curled in a ball.

"Don't drop any hints that you'd rather not sleep in a nest," Dan warned the humans. "Griffins are proud of their hospitality and prone to take offense at a guest's displeasure. You'd rather not find out what happens when they take offense."

Every morning, the griffins hunted in the valley below. They took either Dan or Wick to procure such food as creatures their size preferred to eat. Only Halla allowed them to ride on her back; when necessary, the other griffins carried them with their talons wrapped gingerly around their waists so as not to crush them.

Dan was a surprisingly good hunter."It's not entirely sportsmanlike," the wizard confessed. "I simply call the creature I'm in the mood to eat and it comes bounding along. That's the end of it, for I've always been a good shot with my bow."

In the first few days, Wick made himself a yew bow with a string of boarhide; this seemed to be a craft he knew well. Sometimes Wick also fished in a valley stream, and Dan taught him to forage for mushrooms, berries, and wholesome plants.

One day, a week or so after their arrival, Arrow announced that she wished to join the hunting party. "Not to hunt. I'm just sick of this cave. I'd like to go for a walk in the valley."

"Excellent!" Dan thumped her on the back. "Glad to see you getting your strength back. You might think about bathing while you're at it. You probably can't smell yourself as well as we can, but—"

"Yes. I will bathe in the stream. It might take me awhile. See that none of you disturb me."

Wick glanced at her. She shook the curtain of hair deeper over her face.

When Arrow reached the stream, she walked a good distance down into the warm, wooded valley. The sound of the stream was loud in her ears after the quiet heights of the griffins' cave. Her polished calfskin boots—once Coira's—sank deep in vivid green moss that smelled both fresh and dank.

At last, removing her boots and her thin stockings, Arrow sat on a rock and plunged both feet into the stream. The cold made her gasp, but she kept her feet submerged until they went numb. Then she slowly undid her wide, woven belt, embroidered with roses, and pulled off the blue linen dress—also Coira's—she had been wearing the day she left Glen Droighinn.

Though the cold stung deeply as she lowered her body into the water, soon her limbs felt as numb as her feet. The rushing water pulled away her body's filth with little aid. She closed her eyes.

All at once, the numbness gave way to a throbbing ache, her body begging release from the frigid cascade. Shivering, Arrow sloshed back to the bank. A shaft of sun fell on one of the rocks and she crawled into its warmth, naked and dripping. She felt no fear at being so exposed in the wilderness, only a quiet alertness. The forest's sounds came to her one at a time. Droplets of water on her pale arms glistened like pearls. A myriad of pungent scents swirled from the rocks, the water, the bracken, the trees, and the mountain itself.

This is the world, Arrow told herself. This is my world. I must learn it.

Then she stood, yanked her fingers several times through her wet hair, slipped on her dress, and tightened her belt. With her boots in one hand, she waded back into the stream and picked her way across to the far side. Donning her stockings and boots, Arrow left the stream and strode into the forest. The stony earth beneath the trees was thick-strewn with pine needles, allowing her to move quickly without a path. Hurrying forward, she kept her eyes focused on the ground to avoid roots, holes, and rocks. She began to run.

Before she'd gone half a mile, a twig snapped a short distance ahead. Arrow glanced up.

Wick stood in front of her, his bow slung across his back.

With a sharp intake of breath, Arrow stumbled to a halt.

"It's alright," said Wick in Wizardish. "It's just me."

Blood rushed to her cheeks. Her damp hair was pushed back from her face and she felt exposed without her curtain. "What are you doing here?" Her mouth tightened small and hard, her eyebrows drew down. "Did you watch me bathe?"

She knew he hadn't. The question was thrown down like a gauntlet.

"I was hunting. I heard you running."

"No you weren't. You were waiting for me. Go back, Wick." Veering to the left, she increased her pace.

Wick strode quickly forward and stood in her path. "Where are you going, Arrow?"

"Get out of my way."

He didn't move. "Tell me where you're going."

"Go away, Wick!" she yelled.

When he made no response, she bent down and snatched up a rock. "Get out of my way."

"No."

Arrow hurled the rock. It struck Wick square in the center of his chest. Though he flinched, he didn't move.

"I will hurt you, Wick." Arrow bent down to pick up another rock. "I will kill you. I have already killed a man. His name was Marc and he had a wife and three children."

"I'm not letting you leave, Arrow. Not alone."

Arrow threw the second rock, but her aim was poor and it struck a tree. She put her hands on her hips.

"I burned a ship. I burned it because I was angry. I should have been hanged but a man hid me for a bribe."

Wick took a step toward her.

Arrow picked up another rock. "I fell in love with a man who belonged to my sister. I let him hold me and kiss me. I wish I had let him lie with me, and I wish I had borne his child so I had to stay with him and marry him and never come looking for you, because then he might still be alive." Her voice rose to a shriek. "I wish I had never tried to find you, Wick. Do you hear me?"

Wick took another step forward.

Arrow threw her rock and did not miss. Wick put up an arm to shield himself. The rock struck his forearm, tearing his shirt and cutting a gash that began to bleed.

"Wick," she demanded through clenched teeth, "why are you smiling?"

Wick was, in fact, not smiling, but one corner of his mouth had risen slightly higher than the other. "Because you're acting so much like Arrow."

An angry tear burned down her cheek. "I have to go. Don't you understand? The sorceress—she will kill Halla. She will kill the cub-chicks, all the griffins, the Wizard Dan. Anyone who helps me. Anyone whom I love."

"I know. At least, I don't know the sorceress, but I know the Wizard of Seven."

"So why are you trying to stop me?"

"You can't leave like this. You have no cloak, no weapons, nothing to make a fire even. You'll not last three days."

"But that won't be my fault. If wolves seize me or I fall faint from hunger. If I stumble into a crevasse. It won't be my fault, and no one else will die because of me."

"At least let me come with you."

Arrow's face fell blank and hard. "What if I don't want you, Wick? What then?"

He dipped his chin, looking down at his bleeding arm and twisting his shirtsleeve tighter around the gash. Arrow felt a vague, dizzying triumph at his confusion. But a moment later he raised his head.

"If you don't want me, I will leave you and never come back. But only if it's really you sending me away. This, right now—this isn't you. It's who Grell has tried to make you."

Arrow shook her head. She realized her fingernails were digging into her palms like thorns. When she tried to release her clenched hands, she couldn't.

"It's no use, Wick," she said. Then her hands released; her arms hung slack. "Don't you understand? I've changed and you haven't. I can never cross back over to where you are."

Wick's silence throbbed out from him, a living, lashing thing.

"Is that...?" His lips twitched, groping for words. "Is that what she told you about me? That I hadn't changed?"

They dared to look into each other's eyes. Each found the truth written there like markings chiseled on a gravestone.

"What's the point, then?" whispered Arrow. "What's the point of anything, if we can't go back?"

"I don't know." Wick clipped the words short and clamped his jaw once they were said. He turned away, staring off through the trees. Lost, small, scared.

I could walk past him, thought Arrow. I could walk off into the wild, and he wouldn't stop me now.

But she didn't. She watched his tight jaw, the rigid lump of muscle at the back of his cheek. She watched it swell, crest like a wave, and dissolve. Wick took a deep breath.

"Maybe we can go forward, Arrow. Maybe we can face it together—whatever comes."

For a long time, Arrow was silent. Wick twisted his shirt-sleeve tighter around his bleeding forearm, clumsily using his other hand. She reached out to help him cinch the cloth over the wound, but the bleeding didn't stop. The gash was long and deep; it needed a needle and thread.

"I hurt you."

"Actually, the one you threw at my chest hurt worse."

"I will always hurt you."

"Not always. Sometimes. And I'll hurt you, too. Probably not with rocks."

She shook her head. "I'm not ready, Wick. Not yet."

He nodded. "Then let's go back to the cave. When you're ready, when we have a plan, we'll leave together. Please, Arrow?"

She didn't respond. But when Wick started walking back in the direction of the stream, Arrow followed. They walked side by side, in silence, until they returned to the place where Halla and Dan were waiting.

The wizard's face lit up at the sight of them. "Well! Having a good chat, I see! I knew you couldn't go on like mincing turtles much longer. All is well? Just like old times? Mother of tripe, Wick, you're bleeding like a fountain. Can you sit in front so you don't stain my breeches? Even if we are in the wilderness, I'd rather not look like a gladiator coming from the ring."

As the three of them sat lumped in a row on Halla's back, first Dan, then Arrow, then Wick, waiting for the griffin to spring, Arrow leaned forward and whispered, "I'm sorry, Wick."

And he whispered, "I know."

When Wick said *I know*, it was different than when other people said it. Because when Wick said it, it was true.

The three cub-chicks were the size of large dogs. Their fur was less reddish than mature griffins, more of a buttery yellow, soft as a kitten's. Their eagle heads were gawky, with too-large beaks and long, unmuscular necks. Having learned to fly only recently, they were prone to misjudgments and collisions. Yet they also crashed into each other simply for the fun of it, to feel their bodies go flying and the joy of catching their balance midair.

The cub-chicks loved Wick most of all. When they came to visit they often greeted him first, even before their grandsires, swarming him until they knocked him down. He laughed, petting their necks, smoothing their wings, combing out the tangled tassels of their tails. Then he wrestled with them. At first all together, but, the young griffins having no sense of their own strength, Halla soon made a stern rule that only one could fight the male human at a time.

Three or four days after the incident by the stream, Wick was examining a cut on one of the cub-chicks' hind paws. He played with the young griffin, teased it, coddled it, to distract its notice as he gripped the paw and spread back its fur to expose the wound.

As Arrow sat cross-legged in her nest, watching them through her curtain of hair, Wick looked up at her. It was so sudden and unexpected she had no time to throw up her wall. Despite the curtain of hair, their eyes met and locked. Arrow drew a sharp breath. But she didn't raise the wall. The cub-chick squirmed away, limping off to the other side of the cave.

Wick and Arrow looked at each other.

Wick smiled. His smile said, *I'm so afraid you'll be afraid of this smile, but I'm smiling anyway.*

Arrow did not smile. Her face said, *I am afraid, but I'm still looking at you.*

Wick's foot twitched a little. His hands tensed. His body said, *Can I come and sit beside you?*

Arrow remained still as a statue. Her body said, *Not yet.*

Then two baby griffins, the two without injured paws, crashed into Wick, knocking him flat on his back.

Arrow laughed.

Gasping, she clapped her hand over her mouth. All the griffins and the Wizard Dan snapped their heads to stare in amazement. She hadn't laughed since they brought her to the Highest Mountains.

Though Wick didn't look at her, his whole countenance changed. It was as if he grew larger at the sound, his face warmer, his eyes brighter. He lay still, staring up at the ceiling of the cave, while the cub-chicks swarmed over him, pouncing him repeatedly.

This was too much for Arrow. She hung her head, closing the curtain of hair; the wall swelled around her. But for the first time, she felt a reluctance at its return.

The next morning Arrow woke with a stick poking into her left side. Grunting, she shifted until she could peer over the edge of her nest. Through the cave's open mouth, pinky-purple light blushed between the mountain peaks, tinting their edges.

Wick stood on the ledge of rock jutting out from the cave's entrance, hands clasped behind his back. Arrow could only see his silhouette. He was so much taller than her. The shape of his jaw was so square. But his chin tilted in the old way, reaching out toward the things he saw.

She knew what she was going to say.

She knew what would happen if she said it.

She knew what it would mean if that happened.

"Wick," she called softly, "what do you see?"

She called it in their language. Wick made no motion, but she knew he heard.

The sun reached the tip of a low peak, casting ropes of yellow light across the valley and into the cave. As it did, the sky washed from purple to blue.

"I see... the mountains, covered with ice, taking a deep breath." Wick hesitated, swallowing. "Breathing in the sun, breathing it in."

Arrow stood. Not bothering to put on her boots, she padded barefoot across the cave's floor to stand beside him. As the sun rose higher, they both looked out.

"I see the lungs of the mountains swelling." Wick's voice was so low and resonant that, next to him, Arrow felt it buzz inside her own chest. "Cracking the ice around them. Breathing in the sun. They're getting ready to shout."

"I see it too."

He looked at her. The sun lit up the tangles in her hair.

I'm ready, said her eyes.

"Arrow," he whispered.

This was the thing about Wick. If they had lost everything else, if they had no idea how to begin, still they had this: Wick was the only person who knew her real name.

"Wick," she said. His real name.

Then she lifted her hand, palm outward. Wick raised his opposite hers, a few inches away. But he stopped. Shaking his head, he slowly lowered his hand.

"Not yet, Arrow."

"How do you know? Can't we try?"

"First we need to say everything. All the things we're most afraid to say. Then—come what may."

That morning, when Dan and the griffins left for their hunt, Wick and Arrow stayed behind. They climbed into Halla's nest; their own nests weren't large enough to hold them both at once. The sides of it scooped around them like a bowl, providing a sense of privacy. They sat with their backs along the sides of the nest, knees pulled up to their chests. Arrow caught at a piece of straw and began to twist it in her hands, tying it in knots and loops, then untying them. Wick sat still, his eyes never leaving her face.

"I'll go first," said Arrow, because she always did.

She told him how Prince Cob set her free and how she was rescued by the Tailcatcher in the Far Deeps. She told him about Mundo and Ona and her three foster-sisters. Somehow she kept forgetting to mention Tomás. Her stories all featured Noemi, Loida, and Irma. It wasn't that she left Tomás out on purpose, but her memory hurried her onward any time she was about to realize there had been another child there, a boy.

Arrow twisted and untwisted the piece of straw more rapidly as she reached the day they showed her the watchtower on South Hill. (Again, somehow it was only her three sisters urging her up the tower steps.) She felt it would be easiest if she rammed right into the worst of it, blurting it without stopping to think, as when one jumps into the sea on a cold day.

"When we reached the top, I said, 'This reminds me of the table where Wick and I used to dance.' And… and Noemi—she's the oldest—Noemi… then they didn't understand… so Noemi said…"

Arrow, whatever happens you must never, ever tell Wick you have done this thing.

"What, Arrow?" His voice was soft. "What did Noemi say?"

Arrow realized she had left off twisting the piece of straw and begun bunching her skirt in her hands until it barely covered her knees. Her face reddened as she smoothed it back down.

"She said… she said bad things. About you. Sad things. So then…"

Above all, this was the part where Arrow needed to ram ahead. She repeated the words *so then* five times, each time trying to leap beyond them. But it was no use. She buried her face in her hands.

"Arrow, I already know. What you said."

She shook her head, not looking up. "No, Wick. You can't imagine it. You've never heard of anyone doing a more hurtful thing."

"You told them I was a doll."

Arrow looked up. "What?"

"That there was never anyone with you, only a doll you pretended was your brother."

"But—how do you know?" Then she remembered. "The wizard's mirror! Did you... did you spy on me, Wick? How could you?"

She sprang to her feet. Her whole body seemed to melt up through her neck until she was nothing but a pair of burning ears.

Wick rose also, fumbling with his hands. "Arrow, I never thought... we shared everything, all our lives. Every time you breathed, I knew it. How could it be wrong for me to want to see you, to know how you were and what you were doing?"

"What else did he show you?" she demanded.

"Lots of things. He tried to make me jealous. Mostly he showed me when you were happy. On the shore with your friends, or... But even if I was jealous, I still loved to see you. You could *run*. I loved watching you run. There was no cage around you, no wizard near you."

"But Wick, he didn't show you..."

All at once, she realized she hadn't mentioned him. Had left him out of every single story.

"Tomás de Rueda? Yes, he did."

Whipping around so her back was to Wick, Arrow pressed her hand down on her heart. Then she leaned forward, clutching at the side of the nest.

"Arrow," came Wick's voice from behind her, "if I've wronged you, I'm so terribly, terribly sorry. Never until now, this moment, did it occur to me that—"

"He's dead. Tomás de Rueda. He's dead because of me."

"I know."

Arrow pressed her eyes shut but couldn't stop the tears streaming down her face. "How do you know? Did the wizard show you that, too?"

"No. You... you yelled it at me, when we were in the woods. When you threw the rocks."

"I forgot about that. I was trying to make you hate me. Or at least, to be relieved to let me go."

"I know."

Arrow's tears started to come thicker and faster. "He's dead. Tomás is dead. He loved me, and I left him, and he's dead."

Wick took Arrow's hand. She felt the bright pain course through him. Part sorrow, part anger, part shame at still being alive. In essence, Arrow's same pain. His rose to match hers, making a river that rushed both ways at once through their joined hands.

When a river rushes both ways at once, it forms a whirlpool. Tomás had taught her this. The water sucks down in a hollow funnel, unstoppable. Though a whirlpool of pain may sound like an agonizing thing, Arrow found that it wasn't. It sucked away some of the brightness of her grief; in the eddy's hollow center, a stillness opened that felt clean and simple, almost sweet. It was the opposite of aloneness. It might have been peace.

After a long time of that, Wick said, "Arrow, maybe I should go first this time. I think it would help you tell your tale if you knew mine."

So he did.

15

Wick's Tale

When the Wizard first took me away, I became very ill. It seemed to me that I was cold, cold enough to die. As if my body could make no heat of its own, and you had been the only thing keeping me warm. Without you, all was ice. Food he tried to feed me, blankets he put on me—all ice. Most of all, the Wizard himself froze me. He soon learned not to touch me, but his presence was enough to set me shivering until I lost consciousness.

Eventually the Wizard realized I was going to die and his power couldn't save me. He brought me to a clan of centaurs deep in a forest, offering them seeds from a rare and magical tree if they would take me in and heal me. They readily agreed.

The Wizard went away, then, for a time.

A centaur-wife named Kemawi tended me in her home. Her hair was silver and her eyes were gold. Her coat and tail were soft gray, like morning fog in a valley. She was strong, even fierce, but there was warmth in her touch. She forced me to eat, to wake when I wanted only to sleep, to look around and see trees and sunlight and the antics of centaur children. She saved my life.

Kemawi had a son named Kobi. He, too, had golden eyes and gray fur, but his hair and tail were black and long and braided with feathers. Though a year or two younger than I, Kobi was much stronger and braver. He taught me to hunt with bow and spear, to hide from enemies, and to make fires for warmth. He tried to teach me to fight, but he was too strong and his hooves bruised me badly. Kobi was amazed how little I knew. I was amazed how much he thought it possible to know.

I like him, Wick. I like Kobi. I wish I could meet him.

I wish that, too, Arrow.

When I could speak the centaur's language well enough, I tried to tell Kobi about you. He didn't understand. "A girl?" he snorted. "No wonder you're so soft. You're better off without her."

Maybe I don't like him after all.

But Kemawi understood. "This girl needs you, Wick. She will die without you, as you nearly died without her. Or worse. She needs you more than you know."

"Please," I begged, "will you help me get back to the Kingdom of the Giants? I will rescue Arrow, and if I can't, I'll give myself up to the Queen and ask to be put back in the cage with her."

"But what of the Wizard Who Changes Things into Other Things? He will be displeased if you return to the girl. In his wrath, what will he do to you both?"

I could see fear in Kemawi's eyes, but at that time I knew so little of the Wizard's ways.

"What else can I do?" I replied. "I can't just let her die."

So the centaurs called a council. All their clan attended, except young children and the infirm. They bade me speak of you, asked countless questions about 'the human girl'. They asked even more questions about the Wizard of Seven, but I didn't know the answers. At the Wizard's mention, their fur bristled and they stamped their feet impatiently.

Then the chieftain said, "Human boy, do you know that you are a being of great power?"

"No sir." My heart beat fast. "And Kobi will gladly tell you otherwise."

He laughed. "Your strength is of another kind than Kobi's. Thus would the Wizard of Seven flick Kobi aside like an insect, whereas he would give a king's ransom to keep you alive and within his grasp. Yea, human boy, wars may be fought over you, before the end."

"Why, sir?" I cried in distress. "Is it because Arrow and I really are the only humans left in the world? But why did the Wizard leave Arrow behind? I'm nothing without her. Surely he must see that—you all must see it! You must!"

The centaurs were silent.

"There are millions of your kind, human boy," said the chieftain, "stumbling over the face of the earth. The Wizard wants you."

I began to cry. I couldn't help it. Over and over I whispered, "I don't understand."

I don't understand either, Wick. What power did they think you had? In Gnoze, the wizards only scoffed when I tried to tell them you were important.

They meant us, Arrow. Our unbreakable love. But I didn't understand this until many years later.

So not a real power. Not magic. Just an unbreakable love.

Just an unbreakable love.

The centaurs watched me weep. Kobi shook his head, embarrassed by my weakness.

Then Kemawi said, "We are allied with a dragon who hates the giants. If we offer this dragon a tribute of gold, he will fly to the Kingdom of the Giants and rescue Arrow."

Hands clasped, I fell to my knees and begged the centaurs to pay the tribute of gold. I think I may have sworn to repay it. I don't remember. I would have sworn anything.

Kemawi raised her hand to hush me. "The dragon will take you with him, clasped in his claw. He will carry you and Arrow far away, setting you down in a place where the Wizard will not find you—for awhile. Meanwhile, we will deceive the Wizard and make him think we hold you captive from him. Thus will his attention be turned from the dragon until it is too late."

"But if you deceive the Wizard..."

The chieftain's voice thundered in reply, "We will go to war. This is the first war that will be fought for you, human boy. The centaurs against the Wizard of Seven."

"And—you will win? You wouldn't go to war if there was a chance you would lose."

As if he hadn't heard my question, the chieftain continued, "You must make us one promise, human boy. If we do this for you, if you are reunited with Arrow, you must never leave her again. Never, in all your lifetime. And if the dragon's attempt should fail, and you are not reunited with her, you must spend the rest of your life seeking her."

I stood tall, clenching my fist. "I should do that, sir, even if I had made you no promise."

"It is well spoken," said the chieftain.

All the centaurs reared up, striking the air with their hooves and shouting in assent.

But before their hooves returned to the ground, the centaurs began to change, one by one. Some became withered branches, others shapeless stones. The chieftain shrank into a mushroom. Kemawi strove to protect Kobi, until she curled into leaves and blew away.

Kobi was one of the last centaurs remaining. He saw the Wizard emerge from the trees, contorting his seven-fingered hands as he worked his magic. Streaking forward, Kobi reared up behind the Wizard to strike a blow with his powerful hooves.

The Wizard didn't turn around or take any notice of him, but before Kobi's hooves could crash upon the Wizard's head, they sifted into a shower of gently falling snowflakes. I watched my friend's body dissolve into snow, melting as it touched the ground. The last part of him to go was his long, black tail, braided with feathers.

Oh, Wick. The poor centaurs.

"No!" I screamed. "Why?" I attacked the Wizard, striking him with my fists as Kobi had taught me and wishing they were sharp hooves.

Rather than changing me into anything or hindering my assault, he let me wear myself out, seeming pleased by my fury. Each time I hit the Wizard, his coldness exploded inside me until I curled into a ball on the ground, frozen.

Then the Wizard said, "You are quite cured of your illness, I see. In that case, it is time for us to journey on."

"Please, bring them back," I whispered. "Bring back the centaurs. Even if I never see them again, please let them live."

The Wizard sighed. "The centaurs are not real, Wick. Nothing is real. I tried to teach you that before, but you wouldn't listen. Perhaps you'll be more attentive in the future."

He let me lie there, frozen in a ball on the ground, all that night. You might think I would have become ill again, but I didn't. Instead, a new strength grew inside me—the kind Kobi said I lacked. The cold hardened in me like ice. I clutched this ice, pressed its numbing force to my heart. If I froze myself, the Wizard couldn't freeze me.

I know exactly what you mean, Wick.

When I awoke the next morning, the Wizard of Seven was dressed for travel, scraping his boots on a rock that had formerly been a centaur. "Wick, do you know why I took you from the Queen of the Giants?"

"No, sir. The centaurs said I have some power you seek. But they were wrong. If I had any power at all I would have used it to stop you last night."

He laughed, showing his brown, pointed teeth. "Indeed, the centaurs were quite wrong. I took you from the giants because I felt pity for your enslavement."

"Then why not set Arrow free, too?"

He raised his eyebrows. "My dear boy, when I speak of your enslavement, I do not refer to the Queen's cage. I speak of the slavery of the heart, sometimes called love. Of all forms of bondage, most pitiable. The girl does not exist. I have freed you of her. Now it is time for you to live."

Tears filled my eyes, and I grasped inwardly for the ice to freeze them away.

"That is why I must insist that you never seek to be reunited with that human girl. If you run from me, plot against me, or in any way show signs of desiring to return to your former bondage, I will have no other choice but to teach you another, more intimate philosophical lesson about the nonreality of things. Do you understand, Wick?"

I could hardly breathe. It was as if a giant had flicked me in the stomach.

"Repeat what I just said in your own words, so I can be sure you understand."

I choked out, "You will kill Arrow. You will kill her if I seek her."

Chuckling, he shook his head. "Humans have such a crude way of viewing the end of personal existence. As if it meant something."

Then he turned and began to walk. I followed. We journeyed southward and westward—away from the mountains, away from the sea. I had no thought of escaping. I had no thought of my promise to the centaurs that I would spend my life seeking you. I had no thought of you, alone in a cage in the boudoir of the Queen of the Giants. I had no thought of anything at all.

Thus began my life with the Wizard of Seven.

We traveled all over the world. I saw everything, Arrow. Endless sand deserts with tombs like mountains of brick, three-headed gods, monsters and jungles and palaces hung in trees. The gates of the underworld. The glory of it all thawed me a bit; I couldn't see it clearly if I was frozen, and I wanted to see every speck and shimmer.

Everything I saw, I thought, I'm seeing this for Arrow, because she can't see it. I tried to remember them exactly—the beautiful things, and many of the dangerous things, but none of the terrible things—so that one day, when I saw you again, I could describe them so fully it would be as if you saw them, too.

As soon as I began to thaw, I felt sure I would see you again, despite the Wizard's threat that I must never seek you. I thought he might die, or tire of my company. I thought you might come find me as you had promised, and somehow you would know how to escape the Wizard.

Meanwhile, I saw everything for you. I kept all these things in a special place in my mind, a little shining world where the Wizard could never come.

I called it Arrow's World.

Whenever we saw something particularly wonderful, the Wizard would change it into something else. The more noble or grand the thing, the more he seemed to resent it. Once we saw a tree a thousand years old, the size of a village. A whole tribe of elves lived in it, and they'd carved its living wood into a palace. The Wizard changed it into a stinking fen where none could live but creatures of slime. He changed a clear, shimmering lake into a cow. He changed a lion into a cheese-knife. They were not real, he said: the tree-palace, the lake, the lion.

But still I kept them in Arrow's World, and I dreamed that someday I would help you see them as clearly as if they still existed.

Did you put the centaurs there, in Arrow's World? At least Kemawi and Kobi?

Yes, Arrow. I put all the centaurs there.

Good.

So you don't think it's foolish? That I had this imaginary world so precious to me, though I was a grown boy?

Foolish! Why would that be foolish? We should all have imaginary worlds we build for other people in our minds, if only we were as thoughtful as you.

I'm glad you think so, Arrow. I'm so glad.

The day came when the Wizard changed a mermaid into a fig and ate it. She was a child, perhaps eight years old. She had green-white hair and gray-green eyes, and when I looked at her I knew she would have been your friend, if you ever met her. The Wizard must have guessed my thought—perhaps by how I stared—for he gave a particular laugh as he ate the fig.

"That fig now, that almost tasted real." And he licked his seven fingers.

Something happened in me then, Arrow. I won't be able to explain it, but I'm going to try. A huge, strong feeling swelled up in me. It was part anger and sorrow for the mermaid. It was also part love for you, as if you were beside me watching it happen. And it was part something hardest to explain: that this mermaid was still real, and that she not only should have been your friend but *was* your friend, if the deepest truth of all things could be laid bare.

Oh, I'm explaining it so badly. Do you understand what I mean, Arrow?

No, Wick. I'm trying, but I don't.

That's alright. It still happened, even if I can't explain it.

Then I imagined something so vividly it seemed realer than my own hands and feet. I imagined that I was a being of great power, as the centaurs had said. More powerful than the Wizard of Seven. Any time he tried to change something out of existence, I could steal it away and keep it safe in Arrow's World. I felt this power surging up inside me, pouring out of me, blurring the edges of death and the space between worlds.

I brought the mermaid to Arrow's World, where she could swim and laugh and grow and be your friend, and where the Wizard could never find her.

I half-believed I had really done it.

Next, I brought all twenty-seven of our children into Arrow's World, to keep the mermaid girl company. You remember, that game we used to play? Lanky and Spanky teasing Rina until she bit them with her wolf-sharp teeth. Remmy who wasn't afraid of anything. Bluebella Rainbow who had blue hair and rainbow eyes.

No, Wick, her name was Rainbow Sky. Bluebella Rainbow is a stupid name.

That's right. Rainbow Sky, who could fly and play the bagpipes. They were so happy there, Arrow. They belonged. As if the whole place had been built for them.

Of course they were. Of course it was.

For awhile, I was happy, too. The more I lived in Arrow's World, the more it seemed truly real, and my life with the Wizard nothing but a dream.

All this time, I thought you were still back in our cage, alone. I felt guilty any time the Wizard gave me anything you didn't have. So I tried to hush my heart when he brought me Frida the Otter and declared she was to be my pet.

At first I told myself: I will not love Frida, because Arrow has no otter to love.

Then I told myself: I will not love Frida too much, because Arrow has no otter to love.

Then I told myself, I will love Frida for Arrow, because she has no otter to love.

Frida was the best otter in all the world. She had a white tip on her tail and very long whiskers. Her body was long and slippery and thumpy. Thumpy because she was always running too fast and tripping over her own feet.

At that time, we lived in a forest where there was lots of dark magic, many trolls and witches and imps. Frida would hide in hollow logs until the imps gathered for tea, then burst out, scattering them and eating their dainties. I laughed and laughed.

She always put her paw on my knee when she wanted me to watch her do something funny. She loved to fall off benches on purpose. She especially loved to play in rivers, to slide down banks and scare frogs and fight lily pads as if they were monsters.

One day, the Wizard looked at Frida, looked at me, and said, "This otter has become a philosophical danger to you, my boy. You're beginning to think of this creature as if it existed."

And he changed Frida into a rusted nail.

It happened so fast I didn't have time to say anything, to say goodbye or tell her she was the very best of otters.

She was all I had to love, Arrow. At least, all I had to hold. I tried to bring Frida to Arrow's World, to keep her safe, but my heart was screaming in such pain I couldn't see Arrow's World at all.

Oh, Wick. Your poor otter. Poor Frida.

The Wizard watched me for some time. Then he said, "I recall another such creature you once thought was real. You may have imagined her pining away in her cage, but I'm happy to report she has left the Kingdom of the Giants. She has a family now and has quite forgotten you. Would you like to see her?"

It was then that he showed me the enchanted glass for the first time.

In the mirror, you were sleeping under a table with a three-legged dog. You had your arms around him. He woke you by having a dream where he was running very fast. (In his dream he must've had four legs.) You laughed until the dog woke up and licked your face.

I felt so many things at once, Arrow.

I was so glad you were free of the giants. Free of the cage. Free of the Wizard. I was glad you had a dog you loved as much as I loved my otter. But in that moment, it felt as if you had everything and I had nothing, when I had imagined it to be the opposite. My greatest joy, aside from Frida, had been to store up everything I saw in Arrow's World so that one day I could give it all to you. But you didn't need my shabby dream-world; you had a real world of your own, and I was not part of it.

After that I had no one, for a long time. The Wizard went days and weeks without talking to me. He didn't allow me to see anyone else. When I tried to escape into Arrow's World, the comfort had gone out of it.

Then the Wizard showed me the glass again. I saw your foster-family: mother, father, and sisters. I saw how you swam in the sea with your friends, how you ran through the town asking questions, and everyone—all the shopkeepers and grooms and smiths—laughed and answered you. Everyone in Lipa was your friend. I saw Tomás de Rueda giving you a little piece of sea glass in the shape of an arrow. Then I saw you telling your friends I was nothing but a doll.

Wick, that's terrible. It wasn't like that.

The thing was, it didn't work the way the Wizard planned. I could see it in your face. I knew why you said it, about the doll.

Why did I say it? I've been waiting to ask you for such a long time.

It's like our language, when that giant from the Highborn Ladies Concerned for Culture asked us to speak it, jotting notes in her little book. Suddenly we realized—it's not for her to hear. And we couldn't tell her any more.

Yes. It was like that. Oh Wick, it was just like that.

So after that, I knew you still missed me no matter how many friends you had. I felt less lonely for awhile. The Wizard realized his mistake; he didn't show me the glass again for a long time.

As the next three or so years passed, I began to wonder why the Wizard was so determined to keep me captive. The reason he had originally given me—that he pitied me and wanted to set me free—was clearly a lie. I'd learned by then that all wizards are wholly selfish, incapable of seeking anyone's good but their own. The Wizard of Seven was surely no exception.

Yet if he was carting me across land and sea from a selfish motive, I was at a loss to perceive it. Reluctantly, I considered what the centaurs had told me: that I had some kind of power the Wizard sought. Since he had shown only distaste at my singing, I couldn't imagine what this power might be. Pondering further, I remembered how many questions the centaurs had asked me about you, that they had been willing to start a war to reunite me with you, and that they made me promise never to leave you once I found you.

I had a thought—maybe more than a thought, maybe a hope—that my power had something to do with Arrow's World. That if we were ever reunited, some sort of magic would kindle that would allow us to escape to Arrow's World, and to bring other creatures there to keep them safe from the Wizard.

Oh, how I wanted it to be true!

What had always prevented my running away before was the Wizard's threat on the night he destroyed the centaurs: that he would destroy you, too, if ever I sought you. Now I wondered, was that just another lie?

I lay awake a whole night, hearing this dialogue endlessly repeated:

You must make us one promise, human boy. If we do this for you, you must spend the rest of your life seeking her.

I should do that, sir, even if I had made you no promise.

It is well spoken.

Then I lay awake the next night, hearing this:

If you run from me, I will have no other choice but to teach you another, more intimate lesson about the nonreality of things. Do you understand, Wick?

You will kill Arrow. You will kill her if I seek her.

On the third night I tossed and turned, torn between the two, until suddenly I saw you, standing beside my bed with your hands on your hips. It was half a dream, half the creation of uneasy thought.

"Wick, you goose," you said, tossing your hair, "you've got every part of it wrong. If the Wizard meant to kill me, he would have done it straight off and spared himself the headache. You'd better come find me at once before you believe something even stupider than that. No wonder the centaurs thought you needed me."

So the next morning, I ran away.

The Wizard found me a matter of hours after I'd made my escape. He didn't renew his threat against you, didn't mention you at all, only vented his fury on my body. I was elated; all this time, I'd been bound by a lie that meant so little to the Wizard he didn't even remember it. As soon as I recovered from the punishment, I ran away again.

When it got to the point where I was running away several times a week, the Wizard took me to the Buried Isle. I think I was about fifteen. I didn't know how he got me there; he put me to sleep during the journey. I woke up not knowing where I was. The first thing I did was run away.

The Buried Isle isn't so full of gold and jewels as the legends say. There aren't piles of treasure lying about. But all the palaces and buildings are gilded, and the streets are rose-colored marble. Despite my determination to escape, I found myself gaping, turning in slow circles. I'd never seen such beauty. Fighting my awe, I continued to flee, wondering why the Wizard didn't come after me.

Then I reached the edge of the isle.

All around it is a barrier like glass. Neither liquid nor solid—it moves like water, but it is impenetrable as ice. Outside churns miles and miles of dark ocean. There is no way out.

Desperation filled me. Though it had been years since the Wizard showed me his enchanted glass, I broke into his chamber and found it.

I saw you run to meet Tomás de Rueda. It was night and the sky was full of stars. Pointing up, you began to name all the constellations and planets. Tomás beamed; you must have learned it all in his absence. His eyes shone as he taught you the names of more stars you hadn't yet learned. And I knew, though he still saw you as a child, that one day you would fall in love.

It's not really fair that you knew it then, when I didn't know it until such a long time after.

Beside myself with despair, I tore the Wizard's chamber apart. Ripped and burnt books of enchantment, smashed magical tools, scattered herbs and powders.

The Wizard punished me very cruelly. I can't tell you about it yet, Arrow. Someday I will, but not now. For many weeks afterward, I lay staring at the wall. I was frozen again, clutching the ice against my heart to keep it numbed.

As Arrow listened to Wick's tale, she was sitting in Halla's nest facing Wick, who sat opposite her with the entrance to the cave behind him making a bright frame around his face. Suddenly, the bright frame darkened. Arrow looked up, thinking that the griffins had returned from their morning hunt.

A bat-winged monster of Glen Droighinn swooped down, gripped Wick by the shoulders, and tried to snatch him up. He cried out in pain and terror, clutching at the side of the nest.

Springing to her feet, Arrow pulled a sharp stick from Halla's nest. As Wick lost his grasp, Arrow leapt up and drove the stick into the ankle of the bat's claw. Twitching, the claw opened as the bat shrieked with rage. It shook Wick like a rag doll in its other claw, but Arrow hurled the stick at its face, striking its open mouth. Furious, the bat dropped Wick and sped toward Arrow, knocking her flat on her back.

Kicking, Arrow fought the scaly claws, but the monster seized hold of one of her feet and lunged into the air, dragging her upward. Arrow pawed at the nest, but the sticks gave way in her hands. She dangled upside down, writhing but unable to free herself, as the bat sped toward the mouth of the cave.

Suddenly it dropped her, screeching. Arrow crashed facedown onto the cave's stone floor. Blood streamed from her forehead. When she looked up, wiping red out of her eyes, she saw one of Wick's arrows sticking out of the monster's breast. As it reeled back toward the mouth of the cave, Wick whipped a second arrow from his quiver and fired it straight into the bat's throat. Its cry cut short, the bat dropped onto the ledge of the entrance.

Wick ran forward to examine it. "Dead." He pushed the hideous carcass with his boot until it slid off the ledge and crashed into the valley below. Then he rushed back to Arrow. "Are you alright?"

"I think so," she gasped, pressing her sleeve against the cut on her forehead. "Are you?"

"My shoulder is torn, but I can still use my bow."

The entrance to the cave darkened again, and Wick and Arrow staggered backward. Wick whipped another arrow to his bowstring.

But it was Halla's brother, Thellan. His yellow eyes blazed with such wrath Arrow fell to her knees, and she and Wick threw their hands over their ears as the griffin let out a piercing war cry. After determining with a quick glance that the humans were alive, Thellan positioned himself at the entrance to the cave, his massive body crouched to spring, his wings arched.

Wick and Arrow looked out. The sky was darkened with black shapes. There must have been fifty winged beasts wheeling above the valley. Halla's father and mother were fighting them, tearing bats to pieces with their talons, snapping their necks with their bright beaks. Soon Halla's other brother and his mate came speeding from their cave to join the fray. More griffins swooped in from further mountains, until there were ten flurries of golden fur and white wings amidst the dark cloud of invaders.

Rushing alongside Thellan, Wick knelt and fired his arrow at the first bat that wheeled toward the cave. But his shot went wild as he gasped in pain, clutching his bloodied shoulder. With a half-growl, half-shriek, Thellan lunged forward and drove the point of his beak into the monster's breast, then pulled his beak out and snapped the scaly neck.

As the griffin returned to his post, Halla sped into the cave with the Wizard Dan on her back.

"Mother of tripe, you're alive!" shouted Dan. "What are you doing out in the open, you idiots? Go hide in the back of the cave. Bury yourselves in gold or something."

Sliding off Halla's back, the wizard shoved Wick aside and took his place at the entrance to the cave. Dan fired three arrows in rapid succession, and three black shapes dropped out of the sky.

"We can't just hide while you fight!" cried Arrow.

"Weapons," said Wick. "At least we can find more weapons."

Wick raced back toward the gold hoard. Shaking free a golden-handled battleaxe from a sculpture composed of golden armor, he slung its strap across his back. Arrow pulled a gilded dagger from a pile of ancient coins. They rushed back to the front of the cave.

"I'm out of arrows," muttered Dan, cursing.

Halla was guarding the cave's entrance now while Thellan swooped outside it, battling four bats at once. His white breast was stained pink with blood.

"Dan," said Arrow, "Wick and I must leave. If we flee, they'll follow us."

"Yes, which is exactly what we don't want them to do."

"You said Halla was faster than these monsters."

"She'll have to get past them first. Remember what happened at Gnoze. They swarmed her and she couldn't defend you. There are many more here."

"We've got to risk it. For the griffins' sake."

"Hang on!" Dan jumped to his feet. "I've got a better idea. We'll trick the bastards."

Rushing back toward the griffin hoard, he began tearing through piles of gold. "Here!" he cried, holding up a gold-studded saddle. Then he gathered several large pieces of armor. "We'll put this saddle on Halla's back, pile it with armor and such, and cover it with my cloak. Then I'll fly off, but it will look like three of us escaping together. We'll draw off the whole lot, and Thellan can sneak off with you two in the opposite direction. It's brilliant! I astonish myself."

"What happens when you get caught?" protested Arrow. "When they realize they've been tricked?"

"Oh, I suppose they'll shred me to bits. But if all goes well, that will happen somewhere over the pyramids of Egypt, and you and Wick will be sitting by a fire in some remote village in Byzantium, eating cheese. I do hope it's cheese."

As he spoke, Dan tossed the saddle up the mountain of Halla's back and began to clamber up after it with his piles of armor.

"You can't do this, Dan," said Arrow. "I won't let you risk your life for me again."

"Perhaps you haven't noticed, but wizards don't do things because you *let* them. Nor do griffins. We do them because it damn well pleases us."

Arrow opened her mouth in hot protest, but felt a hand on her shoulder.

"His plan is the best we have," said Wick. "We've got to hide until he and Halla are gone, then make our escape in secret."

"I can't bear it, Wick. I can't bear that anyone more would die so I can go on living."

"I felt that way when the wizard changed the centaurs into leaf and stone. But the centaurs knew they were choosing war and death. They chose it anyway, because it was right. Now their choices stand behind us. All who chose the right and the good stand behind us now. We didn't ask for wars to be fought over us, but we can stand with those who fight."

"Wick, how is it you've always been able to see so many things I can't? About what's right and good and all that?"

He looked at her so seriously with his old-man eyes. "Because I've always been looking at you, Arrow."

Meanwhile Dan had gotten Halla and Thellan to agree to his plan. "Please do hurry and hide yourselves," he urged the humans. The bundled shapes beneath his cloak looked remarkably like two figures crouched on Halla's back. "The moment you're out of sight, we'll take flight. If all goes well, Thellan will come get you when the skies are clear."

Wick ran to his nest, grabbing his leather pack and his cloak; Arrow also took her cloak. They ran as deep into the cave as they could go without being completely deprived of light, casting themselves into a trench in a pile of gold coinage. At first their breathing was so loud it echoed off the walls, but as they calmed they could hear the battle outside. A screeching went up from the bat horde; a flurry of scaly wings snapped against the wind as they changed direction. Then it all faded, except for the squeals of a few enemies still locked in griffin talons.

"I think it worked," whispered Wick, wincing as he gingerly shouldered his pack.

A few minutes later, Thellan swooped in. Wick and Arrow crawled out of the trench. Without a sound, the griffin picked each of them up in one of his talons. Gliding to the cave's entrance, he looked out. Not an enemy was in sight. Several griffins, including Halla's parents and her other brother and his mate, were still circling the nearby peaks. The three cub-chicks peeked out of their cave.

Thellan plummeted into the valley forest. Hovering only a few feet above the ground, he wound between trees and skimmed along streambeds in areas so thickly wooded Arrow could hardly see the sun through the tree canopy. They flew all day and into night, but Thellan made no sign of stopping. When the sun rose the next morning, they had come out the eastern side of the Highest Mountains, a bare and lonely place littered in dun-brown rock and scree. The air was hot and dry; brown dust blanketed the landscape, and the vegetation that grew was such as can survive months without water.

One small yet determined river cut through a ravine, beside which Thellan let the humans down. Then he bent toward the water, drinking deeply and noisily. The humans followed suit. Arrow washed the blood off her face while Wick attended to his wounded shoulder. His thirst slaked, Thellan sat and began to preen his feathers.

Without Dan to translate, Wick and Arrow couldn't thank the griffin. So Arrow strode forward until she stood between his front talons. Raising her hand, she pressed it into the white down of Thellan's chest, still matted with blood, and felt the steady, resolute boom of his heartbeat beneath her palm.

"Thank you, Thellan," she whispered. "You are worthy of your heart."

With no reply save an enigmatic blink, the griffin leapt into the air and vanished over the ridge of the ravine.

Arrow and Wick began their journey down the river.

16

Aside from their weapons and cloaks, Wick and Arrow had brought nothing except the contents of Wick's pack, which were:

A leather bottle to hold water.

A hook and line to fish.

A flintstone.

A needle and thread.

A book of poetry, slightly smaller than Arrow's hand, written in Wizardish runes.

Their only clothing was what they'd each been wearing when they escaped captivity, now bloodstained and torn. Wick was better attired than Arrow, having wool breeches and a leather jerkin over his shirt. Arrow had nothing but her blue linen dress. Her polished calfskin boots were less suited to walking than Wick's sturdy riding boots; he caught her arm whenever she slipped on smooth stones.

Because of Wick's torn shoulder, Arrow had to carry the pack, but he insisted on bearing his own weapons. Wick looked so funny with the gleaming, golden battleaxe strapped across his back. Like a poet costumed as a warrior in a play. Still, it made Arrow feel shy.

As they walked, Arrow told her full tale, all the way through her captivity in Glen Droighinn. Wick listened in the way he always listened, which is to say that he seemed to understand and feel everything as deeply as if he had experienced it himself. Nothing perplexed him, even the things that perplexed Arrow.

After three days' journey, they reached a bend in the river that created a sheltered place in the ravine, overhung by scrubby, leaning trees and trailing lichens. Large rocks made the river easy to cross and slowed its current into pools for bathing.

They looked about them.

"Here, do you think?" said Arrow.

"Yes," said Wick.

"Our first hideout."

"Our first home. Can it be a home, Arrow, even if we don't stay long?"

"It can be a home."

They built a one-room hut. Its posts and walls were driftwood, secured in a base of stones. The ceiling they thatched with bark and moss. The door was made of saplings lashed close together with green bark. Unable to fashion any sort of hinges, they kept the door inside the hut and set it over the doorway each night, securing it with two large stakes and a pile of rocks. Any large creature, even a wolf, could have forced it open. But it was the best they could manage.

After the shelter was built, they dragged stones from the river to make a fire ring in the silt and sand along the shore. Sitting before the fire with a supper of roasted fish, they surveyed their handiwork. Wick's battleaxe still leaned against the hut amongst a carnage of woodchips.

"Wick," said Arrow, "you never finished your tale. You had just reached the part where the wizard brought you to the Buried Isle. Can you finish it now?"

But Wick didn't begin right away. Though he wasn't quite scowling, his face grew very serious. He twisted a piece of dried grass in his fingers and threw it in the fire.

"I told you all my hard things," said Arrow.

"You did."

With a deep breath, he began.

Wick's Tale, Continued

After I had been in the Buried Isle a little over a month, the Wizard brought me a tutor-guardian, a young man only four or five years older than I was.

"This wondrous city," said the Wizard, "provides an opportunity for you to spend time amongst other humans without suffering from the temptations that plagued you previously. The Buried Isle prizes education above other pursuits, since they have no wars to fight or lands to conquer. This human is to see that you are taught whatever it is you most wish to learn."

I wished to learn poetry, the great sagas and histories of ancient peoples.

I wished to learn the names, classifications, and habits of flora and fauna.

I wished to learn mathematics, to a point.

I wished to learn sword-fighting and hand-fighting, as well as racing on horseback.

I wished to learn singing and all the musical instruments used to accompany it.

I wished to learn animal husbandry, especially the care of horses.

Under the watchful eye of my tutor-guardian, who reported all my actions to the Wizard, I was allowed free range of the city. Its citizens found me fascinating, for I was the only new inhabitant to arrive in the Buried Isle since it sank beneath the sea centuries before. Though the Wizard of Seven had come and gone by some unknown means as long as anyone living could remember, he had never before brought anyone with him.

The islanders dogged me with questions about my past, but the Wizard forbade my answer, concocting instead this story for me to repeat: he had found me unconscious amid the wreckage of war, and I remembered nothing of what came before. This tragic tale made me an object of pity as well as fascination.

At first I was terribly shy, having spent so little time with humans. Though I scrutinized the behavior of other boys, I felt foolish imitating their easy banter, playful scrapping, and loud, frequent declarations of superiority over one another. For a year or two I hardly spoke. The boys called me "Rabbit," but they were rarely cruel to me. Often, when an argument broke out, someone would raise his hand and say, "Shut up, all of you! What does Rabbit say?" I would speak what I saw, and they would accept it, grudgingly or no, as if I had been a priest.

In that city, men and women are educated just the same. Knowledge and craft are taught by masters in golden halls of learning. Because it frequently happens that a man marries a woman he met in the learning halls, discourse between the sexes is an art that, though no master teaches it, young students are most eager to learn. As I observed this art, I was astonished to see that most men, as they talked to a woman, failed to listen to her at all: failed to hear the telling catches in her voice, failed to notice the small changes in her face which belied her words, failed to see the questions shining out from her eyes. As a consequence, the men either made utter fools of themselves or pained the women. Or both.

This was difficult to watch, so I began coming to the aid of my friends. "What she means to say is thus-and-so," or, "But that isn't really what you want him to do, is it?" The unintended result was that women began to turn their shining eyes away from my friends and toward me. This happened increasingly as I grew to manhood.

In short, Arrow, I must tell you that I became an object of special fascination to the women of the Buried Isle. They all told me the same thing: "Wick, no one has ever understood me the way you do." And in most cases, that was true. I could just *see* them—who they really were—without making any particular effort. I don't know why other men couldn't. They sought my favor. Invited me to sing at banquets, dropped their books so I would pick them up, sent amorous letters.

How many women did this, Wick?

I never counted.

Five? Ten?

I never counted, Arrow.

Were any of them beautiful?

Yes, many of them were quite beautiful.

More beautiful than me?

Please, you must be quiet now. This is the part where you can't say anything until I'm done. Or I'll stop.

Sorry.

Thank you.

Just one more thing, Wick—were you in love with any of them?

I was in love with all of them. Every single one. Some more than others. It was so bewildering. A woman would do no more than look at me, and my heart seemed to pour out of my chest into her little hands. Especially the ones who were sad. I wrote them poems and took them on garden walks. I kissed some of them. Each time, it felt utterly sincere.

Naturally, the women talked to each other, and each began to realize she was not the only one to receive my affections. They became upset, confronted me for my duplicity, and wept in my arms, which only caused me to want to kiss them more.

The Wizard was delighted by my new turn of character. He made no more speeches about the slavery of love and the non-reality of things. Instead, he hired a courier to handle all the love letters and furnished me a private apartment in a style that lent itself to entertaining women.

I didn't think of you.

Not often, anyway, and not outright. If I did, it was as I had last seen you with Tomás de Rueda, laughing and looking at the stars—stars I would never see again.

Please don't think I was jealous, seducing these women to nurse my spite. It wasn't like that. It was as if I were a wine cask brimful of love, and any woman who shot a hole in me could drink herself sick. No matter how many holes they made, I never seemed to run dry.

In Lipa, we had many names for a man like that. A ladies' man, a Don Juan, and worse. None of them were nice names.

Yet that's not how I saw myself. I felt like a hero, not a conqueror but some kind of savior.

But you can see now? That you were a worse fool than your friends who couldn't peer into women's secret souls but still had sense enough to love only one at a time?

Yes. I can see that now.

You'd better skip to the part where you learned it.

There was one woman, Iliana, who was very wise. We met in the bard's hall studying music. She was somewhat older than I, perhaps twenty-four. Unmarried. Her eyes were dark and keen. I may have loved her more than the others, but it's difficult to say.

One evening, when I began to kiss her, Iliana put her hand over my mouth.

"Wick," she said so quietly, "you need to stop this. You are devastating our city with your sweet voice and your endless, unquenchable sadness. Is that why the Wizard brought you here, to prevent your thirst from draining the whole world dry?"

"My thirst, Iliana? I only want—"

She laughed bitterly. "Do you think you love us? Your embrace is the desperation of a drowning man who pulls down his would-be rescuers in his fight to live. We can't save you, Wick. Perhaps no one can. But you must stop before you become something I know you don't wish to be: a monster, an eater of hearts."

With that, she left. Pain seared through me as from a blinding light. Now I saw no wine cask brimful, pouring out benevolently, but a cask from which the bottom has been torn, unable to hold even a drop. I thought I would die of shame.

I tried to stop, as Iliana had begged me.

But I couldn't. In fact, I got worse. I had a vague sense of the Wizard watching me greedily, even gleefully, but my burden crushed me too much to allow me to wonder why.

One day the Wizard came to me after an encounter of which I was particularly ashamed. "As you have clearly lost the trivial emotion you once felt for the human girl with whom you were enslaved, I don't suppose it will interest you to know she has done the same."

I was silent a few moments. Then I asked, "Tomás de Rueda?"

"I haven't the slightest idea. Do you think I concern myself with the vagaries of human concupiscence? But you can look for yourself, since such things clearly interest you."

And he showed me the enchanted glass.

I saw you running down to the shore, barefoot. Your dress was rough wool, your hair free and tangled by the wind. Your smile flooded your whole face; your eyes danced. You tripped over your feet because they couldn't carry you fast enough, like my otter Frida.

You ran to Tomás de Rueda as he disembarked his ship. Then you put your hand on his chest. Both your faces changed. He pulled your hand angrily away, but his anger was love. Too much love, unconsidered and unbidden. As I watched him fight against it, shame washed over me anew. Tomás deserved you; I did not.

Then the glass changed. I saw you and Tomás in a barn, terrified of each other, with a donkey thrust between you as a barrier. I saw you walking together in a shipyard. I saw you on a watchtower, exchanging a kiss.

The glass fell from my hands, clattering to the floor.

"Careful, fool!" said the Wizard. "This is worth more than your life." Retrieving the glass, he left me to my own black thoughts.

That night I went to Iliana.

"I want to stop," I told her. Tears streamed down my face, but she knew better than to take me in her arms. "Why can't I stop?"

She didn't answer, only waited for me to calm myself. Then she lifted her dark, keen eyes toward mine and said, "Wick, what would happen if you told even one person of your sorrow?"

It was as if she had pulled back her arm and fired an arrow into my chest at short range. I staggered back until I hit the wall. My breath started coming in gasps; my hands shook. I slid to the floor.

"I can't." I meant to whisper it, but it came out in a grinding kind of scream. "If I tell you, the Wizard will kill you."

Iliana knelt facing me, very still and composed though her face was pale. "I didn't ask you to tell me. I asked, what would happen if you did?"

"If I told you... if I told you..." And the answer burst out of me like a swollen sore split open. "I wouldn't be alone anymore."

She nodded. "Yes."

Taking my hands, she pulled me to my feet and led me into a passageway. Then she opened a door and began to climb a stair, leading me by the hand. When we reached the top she brought me out on the roof of the house, closing the door behind us.

"Now," she said, "you *are* going to tell me."

"I... I don't remember. The Wizard found me unconscious amid the wreckage of war—"

"Tell me what happened to you, Wick. Tell me what the Wizard did."

"The last person I told was a centaur. A whole clan of centaurs. My friend. His mother who saved my life. The Wizard killed them all."

She let out her breath in a rush. "I knew you remembered."

"You think you can escape him, Iliana, by hiding out on this roof? He can climb the air, can walk through walls. I'm not so naïve as I once was, thinking I could ever be free of him. I can never tell you what he's done to me."

"You already did. You told me he killed a clan of centaurs to punish you. So you see, it's too late for me to escape. If he kills me, he kills me. Until that happens, you might as well tell me the rest. Quick, then—the time may be short."

It took me all night to tell her everything. When I finished, Iliana said nothing. Taking me in her arms, she rocked me as if I had been a child. We waited for the Wizard to come. Fell asleep waiting for him to come. When we woke, the city's dome was growing light.

Iliana squeezed both my hands and kissed them. "Thank you, Wick." Then she led me out through the courtyard.

The Wizard never knew.

From that day I was different.

Not all at once but more and more, like someone recovering from a fever. I rode my horse again, spent my days in the stables shoveling out stalls and caring for injured animals. I began to meet the city's street children. I proved a matchless teller of tales, a just arbiter of games, and a heroic rescuer of lost and broken toys. The children introduced me to everyone else worthwhile to know: chatty widows, toothless old men, bluntly observant beggars.

The Wizard was furious at my shift in character. Then, for the first time, he seemed to lose all interest in me. He didn't seem to notice or care what I did. Never spoke to me, spent his time locked away in his wizarding chamber. I felt like I could breathe for the first time in eight years.

Since the night I told Iliana, I avoided seeing her so the Wizard wouldn't suspect us. But when more than half a year had passed, she approached me on horseback as I went for my daily ride and asked me to race her to the top of the hill. We raced. I won. The hill was a grassy sward used for pasture, dotted by a few lone trees but without roads or houses. We were quite alone.

"Wick," she said bluntly, "I know why the Wizard took you from Arrow."

My reaction was so strong it startled my horse. "Who told you this, Iliana?"

"You did. The centaurs believed you had some kind of power, but it all had to do with her. The wizard has done everything to keep you from her. Not only that: to make you forget or forswear her. Your power is your love for Arrow. He's afraid of it.

Or he wants it. Wants to break it. I don't know why, but can't you see it?"

The memory flashed through my mind of the day the Wizard first came, how he tried to teach you the paradox about the space between all things, and how his eyes glinted when you said, *But not between me and Wick. All the space is gone. Someone must have taken it away.*

"Wick," Iliana continued, "you have to find her. Whatever the consequence, it must be terribly important, or the centaurs wouldn't have been willing to die for it."

"If there was any way to leave the Buried Isle, don't you think someone would have discovered it in the last twelve hundred years?"

"But the Wizard brought you here. That means he can bring you out."

"Yes, if he chose! He's told me a dozen times I will never leave, alive or dead."

Iliana scowled, pressing her lips together. "Then we must make him choose it. We will force the Wizard to take you away."

"How could you possibly—?"

"I will tell everyone what he did to you. When the Buried Isle rings with the tale of the Wizard's malice, how can his plan succeed as long as you remain here? He needs you alone and afraid, Wick. But when they learn the truth, everyone in this city will come to your aid. Everyone who loves you, everyone who has seen your sorrow or heard it in the way you sing. Every mother and father and sister and brother, every husband and wife and son and daughter who understands what it is to love. We may be mere humans, but we are seven hundred thousand strong. The Wizard will have to take you away, because everywhere you go you will hear us say: we are with you, Wick. We won't let him break you."

I whispered, "He will kill you. He will kill everyone who opposes him, but especially you, Iliana, if he finds out you began it. He will change you into a.... a grain of sand."

She stared at me hard. "The centaurs warned that many wars might be fought for you. This is my war. Iliana's War."

As she spurred her horse down the hill, she called over her shoulder, "If the Wizard takes me, bring me to Arrow's World."

That was the last time I ever saw her.

The next day, a new ballad spread through the streets of the city, sung first by beggars and minstrels, then students and bards, then nobles and princes. It was called *The Ballad of Wick and Arrow*, and within three days there was no one living in the Buried Isle who had not heard it. Such an outcry arose against the Wizard that an army was raised. Not by the king, but by many small, loyal bands who joined together: my friends who used to called me Rabbit, the students in the halls of learning, the farmers and their sons, the drapers, the smiths, the poets, and the priests.

Because the Wizard was so much absorbed in his chambers, he didn't hear the clamor until it was too late. By the time he realized his deeds had been trumpeted through the Buried Isle, all he could do was lock me in my room and busy himself with magical fortifications of our dwelling against the impending onslaught.

But his shrewd perception pierced my secret hopes. "Did you think I would flee back to the surface like a startled fish?" he sneered. "Perhaps I will depart the way I came, being wearied of this noisome city, but I will not take you with me. Oh, no. You have utterly disappointed me, Wick, and nothing will please me more than leaving you behind. My philosophic pursuits have taken up a new subject. A human, yes, but a female this time, with all the weakness of her sex and some peculiar faults of her own. A malleable eagerness, a rash temper, and a terrible guilt in the knowledge that she never searched for you, though she promised she would."

"Don't you touch Arrow!" I shouted. "I will kill you if you touch her. I will find you and I will kill you!"

He locked me in my room without food or water and did not return. I thought he had retreated to the surface and left me to die. But his own cruelty thwarted him. He wanted to punish the city before he left it; he especially wanted to find the person who had written *The Ballad of Wick and Arrow* and punish him.

So the Wizard's attention was fixed elsewhere when Coira came through the shadow-gate, when she found me locked away and revealed her plan to take my place, and when she led me out to you.

Thus hangs the thread of my tale, Arrow. Now it rejoins with yours, and our tales weave together. The pattern is ours to make.

Let's begin then, Wick.

Let's begin.

That first night, as they crept into their hut, Arrow paused at the door.

"Wick, we're brother and sister, aren't we?"

"Of course we are." He blushed furiously.

"Just making sure."

They talked endlessly, every morning and every night, around the fire. Arrow told Wick everything she'd learned in Lipa—from Brother Agostin, Mundo, Ona, Tomás, Eloi Fernandes, and all the others. He told her of the things he'd learned in the Buried Isle. They compared the books they'd read: history, science, poetry. Wick recited some of the poems from his little book, most of which he had written himself, and Arrow declared them extremely wonderful. He sang the songs he'd learned on his many travels. Then he and Arrow sang their own songs and danced their dances.

Each morning, Arrow caught fish in the stream while Wick made a fire. After breakfast, Wick went hunting. He mostly shot the large, scrawny hares that haunted the ravine, nibbling at the vegetation along the banks.

Arrow sewed the hare-skins together with the needle and thread from Wick's pack, making herself a very unsightly jerkin. She had long been jealous of Wick's sturdy jacket, and Coira's linen dress was beginning to wear through in places.

When she first put on the jerkin, Wick laughed so hard she took it off.

He pleaded with her to put it back on. "I'm sorry, Arrow. It doesn't matter what it looks like. I want you to be warm."

"It does matter. A little."

"Why? Why out here in the wilderness?"

"I can't explain. Men never understand. You should've just told me it looked nice."

"Put it on again; this time I will."

"But I'll know you're lying."

"You would have known it anyway."

With a sigh of defeat, Arrow put the jerkin back on.

One night, as they were lying in their hut waiting for sleep to come, Arrow said, "I need to ask you a question."

"Right now?" he muttered sleepily.

They had just spent several hours talking by the fire.

"Please, Wick."

"Alright, what is it?"

"In the Buried Isle, when you were in love with all those women—"

Wick shifted so violently the walls of the hut quaked. "We need to discuss this now?"

"Well, yes. Otherwise I'll lie awake all night wanting to ask you and be cross in the morning. And *you* might lie awake wondering what I was going to ask—"

"Alright. Ask."

"How many did you kiss?"

"That's what you want to ask me? Right now?"

"I actually want to ask you something else. This is a way of easing into it."

A pause.

"I don't know how many I kissed. Maybe... a dozen? Fifteen?"

"And how many did you—?"

"Three."

"You don't know what I was going to ask."

"Yes I do. The answer is three. Now can we go to sleep?"

They both lay awake, staring at the ceiling.

After some twenty or so minutes, Arrow said, "When I kissed Tomás, I wondered if it would take away the space between us. But it didn't. It tried to, but it didn't. So sometimes I wonder... if we had gone further, would that have taken away the space? And I wondered if you might know."

Wick was silent for so long Arrow thought he must have gone to sleep. Her own eyelids got heavier and heavier. Finally, with a sigh, she rolled toward the wall and closed her eyes.

"It doesn't take away the space," he said. "It just sets it all on fire."

"I thought so. That's what Noemi said too. In her own way." Now that Arrow had closed her eyes, drowsiness fell heavily upon her. "I think that—the setting on fire—is why I was afraid to let Tomás... I was afraid I'd be too much for him. Poor Tomás. I was afraid..."

"You were afraid you'd burn him up. As you burned the ship."

"Yes." She was almost asleep as she murmured, "That's the best thing about you, Wick. You understand everything before I say it."

Either Wick made no reply, or she fell asleep before it came.

One thing puzzled Arrow, though.

In his tale, Wick had spoken of Arrow's World, how he built it all in his mind in order to show her someday. She kept expecting him to show her, then, to describe Arrow's World the same way he described all the other places he'd seen: its towns and castles and seas and rivers. The adventures had by its inhabitants, the kind of feasts they held, that sort of thing.

But he never mentioned Arrow's World again. Not for months.

So one day she came right out and said, "Wick, when are you going to show me Arrow's World? I've been waiting a long time."

His face went slack.

Arrow threw up her hands in confusion. "I thought you wanted to show me! I thought that was the whole point."

"I did. I do. I just... I can't, Arrow. Not yet. I can't explain why." And he hurried away.

Arrow was deeply shaken. Clearly, there was something in this hidden world Wick was afraid to show her. What could it possibly be?

Days passed, and Wick said nothing of the incident. Arrow hoped that if he forgot to stand guard over his secret for a moment, it might come tumbling out. If, for example, she brushed against his arm in just the right way when she reached for something, maybe she could dislodge his secret. But her attempts had the opposite effect; Wick began to stiffen whenever she touched him. At last she had to admit to herself, Arrow, you fool, you'll never get him to burst out with something. He's not like you. You've just got to wait.

Waiting didn't stop her from guessing. Indeed, if Wick had known how many shameful deeds she'd tried on him like clothing, he would have bared his soul at once to put a stop to this mental exercise.

He might have killed someone, and the dead person now haunted Arrow's World.

Or he might still be in love with all those twelve or fifteen beautiful women he'd kissed, and have built each of them a palace in Arrow's World.

He might even have fathered a child, but it was impossible to believe that Wick would leave a son or daughter behind in the Buried Isle. He wouldn't have lasted three days before regret drove him stark mad. Other men could do such a thing, but Wick never could.

What baffled Arrow most was that no matter how many grave sins she imputed to Wick, she couldn't think of a single one that seemed too hideous to confess. Not to her, anyway—she was just Arrow. What was he so afraid of?

As the days grew shorter, the ravine grew cooler. Arrow began to shiver in her sleep.

Once, in the middle of the night, Wick touched her shoulder. "Do you want me to put my arm around you, Arrow?"

"I don't think so." She curled into a tighter ball beneath her cloak. "We'd better not. We're not really brother and sister, Wick."

Even in the dark, she knew he was blushing.

The next day, he shot a fox. Cleaning the pelt, he gave it to her as a blanket. Then he shot a goat and made a warm, shaggy rug to cover the dried rushes of her bed.

"Don't you need a pelt, Wick? It's not fair if I have both a rug and a blanket, and you have neither."

"The next one is for me."

A week or so later, Wick found Arrow as she cleaned a fish for their breakfast. It was the first day they could see their breath in the air when they woke.

"Arrow, you know we can't stay here for the winter. It's too wild of a place, and we're too ill-prepared. We need to follow the birds south to a warmer home."

"I know we need to go." Arrow rinsed her hands in the river and dried them on her skirt. "But we've been so safe here, even if we have nothing."

He laid his hand on her shoulder. "Soon, though."

His hand felt heavier than usual, or warmer, or larger. Something about it was different. Arrow looked up at him, curious. When their eyes met, something about that was different, too. Wick pulled his hand away, clasping it behind his back.

"I'll put the fish on the fire." He hurried off.

Arrow's shoulder felt cold in the place his warm hand had been.

That night, as they were laughing by the fire, sitting close together for warmth, Arrow turned suddenly toward Wick, eyes sparkling, and asked, "Boy or girl?"

She only meant to play their old game, just to remember how nice it was. She certainly didn't mean they should no longer be brother and sister. Not imminently, at least. But a storm gathered over Wick's brow, and he pulled away.

"It's just a game," Arrow laughed, putting her hand on his arm.

Jerking his arm away, Wick snapped, "It's a childish game. We're grown now."

Arrow started back as if he'd slapped her. Then her temper rushed in like a swarm of hornets. "No more childish than making an imaginary world and putting all our imaginary children into it."

Springing to his feet, Wick stalked off into the dark ravine without a word.

Arrow rose, astonished. She heard Wick trip over a root, curse, and keep walking. His footsteps crunched the dead leaves, fading until she couldn't hear them anymore.

Leaning forward, hands on her hips, Arrow shouted into the dark, "I don't want to marry you either."

Marry you either, *marry you either*, echoed off the walls of the ravine. An owl hooted in indignation and flapped noisily away. Arrow groaned, burying her head in her hands. Maybe he'd been too far away to hear.

The fire burned out. Wick did not return. When Arrow crawled into their hut, she placed the door over the doorway without fastening it shut. She lay awake, waiting and shivering. But he didn't come. The night had never been so cold.

When they lived in a cage, Wick could never leave.

The next morning, Wick shook her roughly awake. "Arrow, you need to get up right now."

It was barely light out.

Arrow smushed her eyes with her hands to clear her vision. "You were bad last night, Wick. Did you come home at all?"

"No, I slept in the woods. You need to get up. We don't have a moment to lose. I saw footprints in the woods."

Arrow continued to blink awake, trying to understand whether Wick was still cross with her. "What kind of footprints? A wolf?"

"No. Human footprints. But larger."

At this, she shot upright. "A wizard?"

"It's possible. We need to flee, Arrow. We need to run."

Without another word, Arrow tied the fox pelt around her shoulders and Wick lashed the goatskin around his waist with his belt. The rest of their things they bundled into Wick's pack. Then, as silently as they could, they stole from the hut and began to run along the goat track that wove along the brown, leaf-choked river. Arrow carried the pack while Wick carried his weapons. He ran with his bow strung, prepared to meet enemies.

Neither spoke. From time to time, Arrow glanced over at Wick. He kept his eyes on the path ahead. Every so often he glanced back over his shoulder, but he never looked at her.

I'm sorry, Arrow.

That's all he needed to say. Three words, or even two.

Maybe that wasn't all. Maybe he needed to tell her why he had stalked off into the night and left her alone. Maybe he needed to tell her his terrible secret that guarded the door to Arrow's World. And maybe he couldn't say *I'm sorry, Arrow*, because he couldn't say those other things.

As Arrow ran, she felt as if it were not Wick running beside her, but his secret. His secret pounded the ground with heavy footsteps, his secret breathed its soldier-like staccato march. Wick was somewhere on the other side of that secret, hiding shamefully, hiding not like a boy or a man but like a scared rabbit.

And she had hidden nothing from him.

Arrow ran faster and faster until Wick couldn't keep up. Good. Let him fall behind, if that's what he wanted. Let him see how wide the space between them had grown.

The walls of the ravine cramped in, crowned with ghoulish lumps of rock. The river dwindled into chalky rivulets threading through a cracked, brown bed. When the goat path veered away from the river, rising to a grassy ridge above the ravine, Arrow ran up it, skidding and scrambling as scree gave way beneath her feet. She heard Wick calling something behind her; blood pounded in her ears and she ran faster. At last she reached the top. A vast, barren plain came into view, stretching to the horizon. Arrow ran along the ridge, aided by the wind at her back. Though she didn't look back, she heard Wick following.

Faster and faster she ran toward the brown blanket of the plain, endless as the sea. Then she screeched to a halt as the ridge dropped away into a sheer cliff. Some thirty feet below lay a tumble of rocks with jagged points lifted like spear tips. The path had ended in a point jutting out into the plain like the prow of a ship; there was no way down except to turn back the way she came.

Wick puffed up behind her, gasping for air. Arrow felt a mean twist of triumph at the sound of his fatigue. Standing pole-straight at the edge of the cliff, hands clasped behind her back, she gazed out over the plain while her hair thrashed around her.

At last Wick flung some words at her, clipped short from lack of breath: "Arrow, don't you think I want to tell you? Don't you think I would if I could?"

But these weren't the words she wanted to hear. Putting her hands on her hips, Arrow whirled around to face him.

Then she cried out.

The Wizard Ardian stood on the path behind Wick, blocking their only way down from the point.

17

Whether Arrow rushed back or Wick rushed forward, somehow they found themselves side by side, facing the sallow-skinned wizard.

"You!" she gasped. "Ardian!"

"How did you find us, sir?" said Wick, striving to speak calmly. "It's a long way from any road, and we've sought secrecy for reasons well known to you."

"Indeed." The Wizard of Five smoothed down his sleek, black hair as the wind ruffled it. "You've done well to have thus far avoided detection by the Nameless. But you overlooked a potentially disastrous detail, which I have had the good fortune to discover before our mutual enemy."

"What, sir?" said Arrow. "There's no need to gloat; just tell us where we erred."

Reaching into his coat, the wizard pulled out a roll of parchment Arrow recognized at once. She gasped.

"The Map of Wizards!"

"It is an aberration well-known in the wizarding world that the Wizard of Two never appeared on the chart from which no Starborn can hide. Yet I seem to be the first to have conjectured that, upon the Wizard Dan's ignominious achievement of the Rank of Three, the Map of Wizards might begin to show him.

Imagine my surprise to find our hapless mutual acquaintance labeled on said map as a Wizard of Four! Having little doubt as to how he gained the first degree of power so quickly, I simply followed his position past the Highest Mountains. From there, discovering your exact location wasn't difficult."

"But Dan isn't—" Arrow stopped as Wick made a quick gesture. Why did the map show the Wizard Dan near the Highest Mountains if they hadn't seen him since the summer? Could its charting somehow be delayed? Changing the direction of her speech, she demanded, "How did you get the map? Did you harm Brother Agostin?"

The wizard laughed. Pale yellow mist began to ooze out from beneath his robes. "No indeed. I merely told him you were in danger and it was imperative I find you before your enemies did; this was no lie. The benevolent fool handed over the map at once." He nodded toward Arrow. "He even sent you a letter, but we've no time for that now. I'd like to do my duty as soon as possible. I've never liked killing; there's a reason I hired an assassin for my last attempt."

"But we're innocent, you coward!" Arrow stepped forward, fist clenched.

Wick grabbed her elbow. "Arrow, please!" The childlike tremble in his plea brought her back to the moment when he had realized, in the Kingdom of the Giants, that the Wizard of Seven was about to take one of them away.

Ardian shrugged. "You should thank me, really. All I'm doing is preserving your love safe in the Unreachable Realm, unbroken for all eternity. Could you ever wish for anything more noble, more desirable than that?"

"Yes," said Arrow. "We wish to get married and have twenty-seven children. Perhaps we'll name one after you, if you can prove yourself less despicable."

As she said this, Wick whipped an arrow from his quiver and fired it straight at the wizard's chest. He couldn't miss at such short range.

Ardian caught the arrow in midair. His hand closed around its shaft when the point was an inch from his breast. Then he stared at it. So did Wick and Arrow. Cold sweat poured over them.

Ardian smiled unkindly. "Didn't anyone ever teach you the paradox of Zeno? If everything occupying an equal space is at rest, the flying arrow is therefore motionless."

He turned the shaft over and over in his hands as he spoke. With each turn, it fanned out from itself, multiplying until it was at least a dozen arrows. The wizard breathed on their tips; they glowed red hot.

Wick turned toward Arrow.

"I'm sorry," he said in their language. "For not coming home last night. For not telling you why. For everything."

"I forgive you—I'm sorry, too. But Wick, now we're going to die with space between us. And... and it makes me so angry. That's all."

At this, something broke open inside Wick. Wrath poured out, not so bright and searing as Arrow's anger but deeper and stronger, like an erupting fire mountain. Turning back toward the wizard, he hefted the golden axe from his back. Arrow drew her dagger.

Gathering the arrows in two fistfuls, Ardian raised them above his head, preparing to hurl them like javelins.

Wick and Arrow rushed at him, raising their weapons with loud cries. As if in answer, a piercing shriek filled the air. Its strength flung the humans headlong and staggered the wizard backward. Halla bore down from the sky, her red tongue blazing from her open beak. Ardian fired a handful of arrows at her. One of them pierced her wing as she swooped down and bit off his head.

The Wizard Ardian's body thudded to the ground in a pool of yellow mist. Dark blood gushed over the tips of the remaining arrows, causing them to sizzle and reek.

As Halla landed, the Wizard Dan slid off her back.

"Oh, hello," he said. "You two look like something out of *The Iliad*."

Casting aside his axe, Wick flung his arms around Arrow. "Arrow, oh Arrow. Arrow, forgive me. Forgive me."

Arrow couldn't respond because Wick's right hand was pressing her face against his chest as if he was staunching a wound. His left arm crushed her so tight it hurt, but Arrow didn't want him to stop. The hurt of it was right, healing the hurt of his absence in the night. Fury still poured out of him in volleys and cataracts; she had never felt anything like this coming from him before. It was terrifying because it was Wick. It was beautiful because it was Wick. As she clung to him, a lightning's knife of sweetness rived her from head to foot, demanding that she kiss him. Reaching up, she put her hand around his neck and pulled his face toward hers. Their mouths were both open, still gasping out their fear of death in shuddering waves.

"You might start by thanking me, you know," came the Wizard Dan's voice. "Is this the third time I've saved your neck, Arrow? Ah, pardon, it's the fourth."

As if startled from a dream, Wick wrenched his face away.

Arrow drew a sharp breath; her eyes filled with tears.

"Dan, w-what are you doing here?" Dizzy with confusion, she laid her head on Wick's throbbing chest. "How did you find us?"

Dan examined the wound in the griffin's wing as she made a noisy meal of what remained of the Wizard Ardian.

"It's an unexpected effect of my powers. Now that I can give anything a language, most things are so grateful they answer my questions quite readily. The ravine told me where you were. Didn't you hear it rumbling earlier?"

"But when did you come?" Wick let Arrow go so abruptly she stumbled.

"Halla and I reached the Highest Mountains several weeks ago. Then we waited to ensure we hadn't been followed before we set out to search for you. But it seems we were followed after all. Yes, I overheard that unfortunate bit about the Map of Wizards. Halla and I glided up through the ravine when we saw you—and Ardian—on the ridge. Then we waited for the most gratifying moment to make our entrance."

His fury not yet wholly spent, Wick choked out, "You... you waited? You almost let us die? You let us believe—"

"Yes, naturally. The stakes were much higher that way. It was a splendid thrill. Why, whatever is the matter?"

Wick was striding toward Dan with clenched fists. Arrow darted between them, putting her hand on Wick's chest.

"Dan," said Arrow, "there are some things you don't yet understand about friendship. A human friend would have rushed in the moment he saw his friend in danger. To prevent him from feeling distress."

"Oh." Dan scratched his ear in confusion. "But doesn't the value of a friendly deed correspond to the recipient's degree of distress? The greater the distress, therefore, the greater the friend?"

Arrow opened her mouth to say no, then shut it, trying to remember if there was anything in Plato that debated the question.

"No," said Wick decisively. "It does not."

Dan sighed. "I suppose that's why Halla was so keen to rush in from the first. I could scarcely restrain her."

Her meal complete, Halla sat and began to lick her torn wing.

"Well, sorry and all that." Dan waved a four-fingered hand. "I suppose I'm still an apprentice friend. I'll make it up to you by telling you my plan."

"What plan?" Wick's voice was still hard but softening in the face of Dan's frankness.

"The one I've been hatching for the last six months. Actually, I have two plans; you can pick which you prefer. Clearly you don't have a better one."

The previous summer, when Dan and Halla sped from the Highest Mountains with a host of enemies in pursuit, they led the winged beasts as far from Wick and Arrow as they could. For weeks, Halla managed to remain far enough ahead that her pursuers never discovered the ruse, yet she took care not to lose them completely. Somewhere in the salt wastes of Persia, the griffin and her rider decided their false trail had been well enough laid, and they vanished from enemy eyes for good.

Well pleased with themselves, they took a holiday in the Mediterranean.

On this holiday, whom should they meet but another wizard on holiday—none other than the Wizard Merkum, bored of piracy and preparing to join a harpooning expedition advertised under the title, "Monsters of the Ancient Deep: Guts, Gills, and Thrills." Merkum had, of course, heard about the now-famous debate in which Dan had at last become a Wizard of Three. After peppering him with questions about the mechanics of friendship (to which Dan gave highly confident, dubiously accurate answers), Merkum's interests turned to the source of the debate: the nameless wizard's quest to overthrow the limitation of power and become a Wizard of Eight.

The mention of the Caveat propelled Dan and Merkum into a rigorous debate that lasted several months, at the end of which Dan at last convinced his colleague that Wick and Arrow should not be killed. Rather, the humans should be aided, in hopes that a means of defeating the Dreadful Duo might arise through a systematic examination of their treatment of Wick and Arrow. The two wizards then set about making such an examination, aided by the consumption of much cheese.

They drew an important conclusion which led to the formulation of Dan's first plan.

"It boils down to this," Dan explained to Wick and Arrow. "The Wizard of Seven could never have removed his name without help. It would be like performing a surgery to remove one's own heart. Who better for such a task than the heartless harpy herself?"

Arrow's eyes widened. "You think Grell helped him?"

"It seems quite likely, since he trusts her with other precious schemes. In any case, the wizard's name hasn't been destroyed—if it had been, he wouldn't have survived—so she must have locked it away somewhere. If it's found and released, that'll be the end of him, for a wizard can't betray his name without it betraying him. And if Grell has made a blood pact to guard it, that'll be the end of her too."

"Is that likely?" wondered Wick. "A… a blood pact, whatever that is."

"You don't want to know what it is. And it's not only likely, it's nearly certain. That being the case, I will now relate a very important piece of information I've been withholding. I suppose I've been withholding it to produce the greatest possible effect at its revelation, which I'm now learning may not entirely be in accord with the principles of friendship. Nonetheless, here it is: When I did my second impossible thing, making the ruins outside Glen Droighinn speak, the stones threatened Grell: *We know where you've hidden it. We will ruin you as you ruined us. We will ruin you both.*"

"Ruin who?" said Arrow.

"Her, of course!"

"But who is you *both*?"

"Well, possibly the sorceress and the Wizard of Seven... if the 'it' she's hidden is the wizard's name! The conjecture answers to reason as easily as a cat to cream: she could have imprisoned his name in some sort of linguistic tomb, perhaps even within those silently watching stones. If the name is discovered and released, she's doomed and so is he. So you see, my plan is quite simple. All I have to do is sneak back to Glen Droighinn, get that pile of stones to tell me where Grell has hidden the nameless wizard's name, and set it free. *Voilà!* Instant death for your enemies and a new set of fingers for me, if setting a nameless wizard's name free is an impossible thing. Which it almost certainly is."

Wick and Arrow looked at each other.

"What's your other plan?" asked Wick.

Dan sighed. "To hide. So jejune. My other plan is to hide in a place where they can never find us."

"Where?" the humans cried together.

"Well, I've not actually been there, but I learned of it off the coast of Anatolia from a very decrepit, foul-smelling seagull. She, in turn, learned it of a goat, who learned it of a fairy, who had actually been there. It's called The Refuge, located somewhere in the ancient forests of Anatolia. The troublesome thing is that you can't actually find it unless its guardian (who is called The Guardian) wants you to find it."

"Who is this guardian?" asked Wick. "What sort of creature is he?"

"He is a she," Dan replied. "Her species is debatable but certainly of the magical variety. As far as whom she lets in, there's some kind of test and only those deemed worthy can enter. A fairly common bit in those parts. Nothing we can't handle between the four of us."

"It depends on her idea of worthiness," Arrow said. "Wizards have very different ideas of worth than humans, or giants for that matter."

"Too true, yet by all accounts you and The Guardian weigh worthiness similarly."

"What do you mean?" asked Wick.

"Well, the tale passed from the fairy to the goat to the gull is that The Guardian has known an unbreakable love. This refuge is a monument to her lost love, and though she has a reputation for savagery, star-crossed lovers are her tender spot."

So it was that Wick, Arrow, Dan, and Halla decided to chance their fate in Anatolia.

Later that evening, Dan approached Arrow with a folded, sealed paper in his hand. "I found this in the Wizard Ardian's pack. Unfortunately the Map of Wizards must have been in his coat, which is now making its way through Halla's bowels. I hope it doesn't disagree with her. In any case, this is for you."

Arrow opened it.

To Arrow
From Brother Agostin

My precious child,

In this season of profound sorrow, our hearts so heavy we can scarce pry them from the mud, this news of you has come like a stone rolled away from my tomb. I can wake another day, chant my hours in the chapel, sweep dust from the doorstep, because you are alive somewhere, being Arrow, seeking what you must seek.

One other shard of hope gleams among the ashes here in Lipa. You may not have heard that several days before he embarked to the Battle of the Firebirds, Tomás de Rueda married your foster-sister, Noemi Albares. Noemi now believes herself to be with child.

New things rise, you see. Ecce ego facio nova, et nunc orientur, utique cognoscetis ea. *They break over us without our choosing, demanding us to look up—for their sake, if not our own. Whether you have found Wick or not, I beg you: take heart. Take heart for Tomás. Take heart for Noemi and her child. Take heart for this foolish monk who weeps any time he reads Plato because he misses you so much. Take heart for singing and laughter that must come; no evil can hold it back forever. Open the door to it.*

ἐρρῶσθαί σε εὔχομαι
B.A.

"I'm happy for you, Noemi," Arrow whispered so quietly no one could hear. "I'm happy for you, my sister."

The strangest thing was, it was true, despite the tears that poured down her face.

Even in winter, Anatolia had such a wild, deep, aching beauty it made Arrow want to both laugh and weep. Blue mountains wore skirts of green and gold, somehow both stiff with age and rioting with growth. Masses of white rock veined in red-gold slept under heavy blankets of lichen. Waterfalls shimmered quietly into pools thick with yellow leaves. Here and there, in open patches, the pale, broken stones of ruins cried out tales thousands of years old. Anatolia was old. Its trees were old. Its moss-rimed rocks were old upon old. Its air was old; Arrow could breathe in its weight of years.

And it was wet. Rain fell in soft, fine sheets every few days. Even when the skies were dry, wetness hung in the air, clinging to them like sweat. They had to stop frequently and build fires to dry their cloaks, for the cold only bothered them when these soaked through. Except at night, the wind brought no chill bite, only a stinging freshness and a smell like crushed herbs.

They flew like this: Dan in back, talking incessantly, then Wick, then Arrow, both of them silent. Arrow was aware of Wick at every moment. To be always touching him was sometimes wonderful and sometimes unbearable, but never a matter of course. When Halla lurched and swooped, she let the weight of him press against her in whatever way it wanted to. Sometimes he encircled her protectively though she was in no danger of falling. Sometimes he pointed ahead at something lovely, his arm sliding along the length of hers. There was no question whether he felt as unbrotherly toward her as she felt unsisterly toward him. Their bodies spoke all day, though they each feigned deafness and the Wizard Dan remained as oblivious as a child whose parents speak above it in coded words meant to shield from alarm.

Each day, Dan called to the various high-flying birds—eagles, hawks, kites—to ask if they knew where The Refuge was. Most didn't know what he was talking about. Some asked if he meant this or that landmark or ruin or ancient wonder which didn't match the original gull's description at all. But every now and then, a bird would say: The Refuge is that way.

The further they went, the more creatures had heard of The Refuge. "It is by the mountains," they said. "It is by the sea." And Arrow's heart lifted, because she loved the sea best of all.

One day they met a jackal in the woods. It laughed when Dan asked about The Refuge.

"Whose refuge?" the jackal jeered. "It's not for the likes of you. You she'll feed to her lions."

"Ah," Dan replied. "Her lions, of course. Whose lions, exactly?"

"The Mother of the Mountain," called the jackal as it slipped into the bracken.

But the next day, when they reached the far edge of Anatolia and the ancient sea's shock of blue burst through their vision, a young seal fat with fish told a different tale.

"Whatever threat you flee, the Mother will protect you. All except the griffin."

"Why won't she admit the griffin?" asked Dan.

"Her lions. Her lions will protest a griffin." And the seal shuddered, hiding its face in its flipper.

"Oh dear," Dan muttered. "Lions again. Halla never could meet a lion without picking a fight."

At last they reached the foothills of a mountain where everyone said The Refuge was, though no one knew exactly where.

"If you seek her," explained a salamander, "she'll find you. Then she'll either help you or eat you."

Dan sighed, flicking back his hair. "I thought it was her lions that ate people."

"Was it the lions? I was never clear on that point. No one who finds her ever returns to set the record straight."

"Presumably," said Dan, "they fail to return not because they've been eaten but because they're lazing snug and happy in The Refuge."

"Still," said the salamander, "they fail to return. Isn't that fearful enough?"

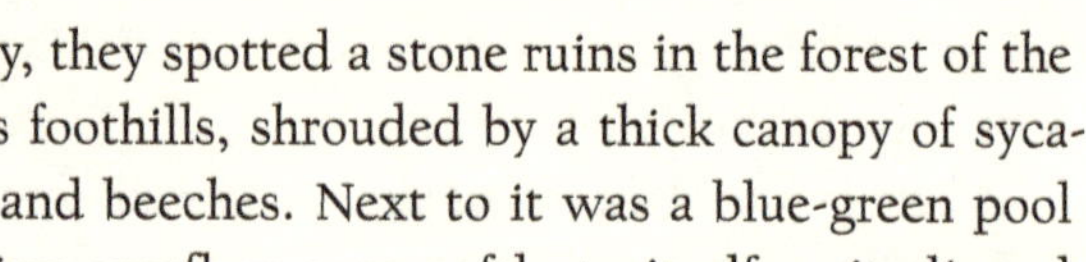

The next day, they spotted a stone ruins in the forest of the mountain's foothills, shrouded by a thick canopy of sycamores, pines, and beeches. Next to it was a blue-green pool whose cascading overflow sang softly to itself as it slipped down the hill; when Arrow dipped her hands in the pool to drink, she gasped, for the water was as warm as the south shore of Lipa on a summer's day.

"Hot spring," said Dan after he felt the water. "Excellent for bathing, which I might suggest is something we all need, you humans rather desperately. We might as well make camp here for awhile. It's a wonderfully hidden place and there's a kind of reassurance in knowing that rational creatures once chose to build here, even if several of the world's ages have passed since then."

Following the pattern marked out by the ruins' age-eaten foundations, they ventured to construct a fort of several rooms around a courtyard. It was like solving a puzzle, reading someone's millennia-old plans in the broken lines of stone. Stacking fallen stones to rebuild the walls, they patched the cracks with mud and left gaps near the top as small windows to let in light but not much rain. The roof they thatched with thick layers of branches and ferns. Then they smothered the whole with a mess of living vines; when it was done they could scarcely make out their own fort at a distance greater than ten yards.

"Was it a temple?" wondered Wick as they surveyed their work.

"Let's hope not," said Dan. "The more ancient the god the more fearful its disturbance, in my experience."

Putting his hand on one of the stones, the wizard closed his eyes. A yawning rumble issued from the ruins. Halla yowled, lunging into the tree canopy. Wick and Arrow stumbled as the earth shook beneath their feet. The rumble faded into silence.

Dan patted the stones good-naturedly. "They say they're a tomb. But the princely bones they housed decayed into dust several thousand years ago. And he wasn't a jealous prince. They're more than happy to provide a home for the living."

At that moment, two female lions burst from the forest. Crashing straight into the group, they knocked Wick and Dan flat on their backs. Arrow raised her dagger and lunged after the lion that stood over Wick, while Halla gave a furious snarl and reared up toward Dan's assailant.

So quickly Arrow scarcely saw it happen, the lion whirled around and flicked her wrist with its front paw; the dagger whizzed out of her hand. A second blow sent her sprawling, and a heavy paw crushed down on the center of her chest. Gasping for breath, Arrow clawed at the paw with her fingers. Wick scrambled up from the ground, but the lion leapt into the air and, with a lightning-quick flip of its agile body, knocked him down beside Arrow. Then the lion held them side by side with a paw pressed so firmly on each of their chests that, no matter how they writhed, they couldn't wrench free.

"Be still," came a woman's voice. "All will be easier if you hold still."

Wick and Arrow froze. Not because the voice told them to. Because the voice had spoken their language.

18

"Who are you?" Wick whispered hoarsely. He whispered it in their language, just to make sure he hadn't dreamt the voice.

Arrow's horror was too great to make a sound. No one, not even Grell, had ever spoken their language. She felt as if the voice had stripped her naked.

"Some call me The Guardian," said the voice. "Others call me The Terror. Others call me the Mother of the Mountain."

What could have possibly happened to Halla? She was three times the size of the lions, and she had wings. Why wasn't she tearing them to pieces? Arrow craned her neck to look, but the lion thrust its muzzle inches from her face and growled. Its teeth gleamed like jewels in a crown. Saliva dripped onto Arrow's nose and lips and ran down the side of her face in a sticky line.

"We've come seeking your aid," Wick gasped, struggling for breath under the lion's heavy paw. "Please. Will you hear our tale?"

A soft laugh, rippling like a mountain stream. "I know the tale of Wick and Arrow. I know it as well as my own."

"How can you speak our language?" breathed Arrow. "How *dare* you speak it? What do you want from us?"

"Mysteries cannot be explained," said the voice. "They must be received. Will you receive me?"

Wick said *yes* and Arrow said *no* at the same time. Then they each switched and said the opposite. They glanced at each other in despair, which caused the lions to growl.

The voice laughed again. "It is enough. Come, my beasts."

The lion withdrew immediately, loping off in the direction of the voice. Arrow and Wick scrambled to their feet, reaching for each other's hands and gripping them tight. When they looked toward the voice, they saw not only the two lions but also Halla circling a woman and purring. The griffin's purr was so loud the stones quaked; her eyes burned with a fierce gleam of honor and delight.

"Halla?" squeaked Dan, who had apparently just been released from a similar hold by the other lion.

"Yes," said the woman, this time in Wizardish. "Halla, too, is mine, though I have never met her until today."

The Guardian was not tall. Not nearly as tall as a wizard, and scarcely taller than Arrow herself. Though her snow-white hair hung in two long, thick braids, she might have seemed no more than a child except for the quiet force that emanated from her as ancient as the mountain itself. Her skin was brown and smooth, her eyes clear amber. She wore a garment of moss and ivy that seemed to grow on her. Bare feet and head; a necklace of smooth pink shells; long pendants of bone and pearl hanging from her ears. The lions flanked her, and Halla planted her majestic form behind the woman, wings arched like the canopy of a throne.

Was she beautiful? Not like Grell. Her radiance was more like Halla's fierce majesty, making her unbearable to look at for more than a few moments. Arrow dropped to her knees. The memory flashed through her of when she had first seen the sun setting across the sea and its golden path led straight to her.

The Mother of the Mountain walked forward. Approaching Arrow, she put her hands on her shoulders and raised her to her feet. Then she gently lifted Arrow's chin with her fingertips and gazed into her eyes.

Up close, the woman's eyes were not amber but a swirl of many colors, orange and green and purple. It reminded Arrow of the flickering aurora in the night sky of the Kingdom of the Giants.

"Do what you wish to do," said the woman.

With a trembling hand, Arrow reached out and put her hand on the heart of the Mother of the Mountain. She listened. Their gazes remained locked. But a look of confusion spread over Arrow's face until she pulled her hand away.

"What is it?" asked the woman.

"They're the same. Your heart and... my heart."

"Of course they are."

"How can that be? What does it mean?"

"It means you are a being of great power."

"I don't understand."

"Mysteries cannot be explained. They must be received."

"Oh, please!" Arrow cried. "Please tell me what it means."

But The Guardian looked at her so sharply she quailed.

Then the woman turned to Wick. As with Arrow, she turned his face toward hers and made him look into her eyes. A tear slid down the woman's cheek.

"Will you let me see it?" she asked.

"No," said Wick.

"I can restore it."

"No." His jaw tightened until it shook. "It will hurt too much."

"Only if you are alone."

Wick made no reply.

So the woman addressed them both. A shaft of sunlight fell on her and the green of her raiment glowed. Her hair dazzled brilliant white. "Who took away the space? When you were children? Who took away the space between you?"

"Was it you, Mother?" whispered Arrow.

"Or was it us?" whispered Wick.

She only smiled.

Then she turned to the Wizard Dan, whose face flushed red as a flag. When he tried to speak, a few high-pitched squeaks came out. When he tried to look at her, he blinked and squinted as if looking into the sun.

"You are not outside this unbreakable love," said the woman in Wizardish. "You are bound up with it. Do you understand?"

"N-no," stammered Dan. "That is, I understand each of your words, including their full etymology, the syntax of your speech and its inflections. As to the meaning—"

"When you hear Wick and Arrow's language, you hear it not from the outside but from the inside. From the moment you heard it, it woke the impossible in you. Now you can't unhear it, though you do not speak it. It is inside you."

"I understand," said Dan. He gave a kind of hiccup that was a laugh and also a sob. "I understand."

"Good," said the woman, and she returned to her lions and Halla.

"This is The Refuge," she said. "No evil can enter it. You will be safe here as long as you choose to remain. My beasts guard the threshold; you will see them only if you pass out again into the Striving World."

They dared not ask her any questions.

She put a hand on each of the lion's heads. They let out such a roar that the wizard and the humans had to bury their heads in their hands. When they looked up, she was gone. Only Halla remained, placidly blinking as if nothing had happened.

While the Mother of the Mountain was with them, it was easy to believe anything. It was easy to believe the ruined tomb was an enchanted refuge protected by mythical lions. It was easy to believe the Wizard of Seven couldn't change the whole fort to liquid fire as they slept. It was easy to believe the sorceress couldn't send her spies to claw and snatch. It was easy to believe Wick and Arrow could set their fears aside like winter cloaks once the storms are past.

But after The Guardian departed, her appearance felt like a dream. They couldn't find any visible markings to show the boundary of The Refuge, and even when Arrow walked all the way to a cliff overlooking the sea, the lions did not reappear. Neither did Halla, flying to the top of the mountain, ever spot the guard-beasts. Rabbits, deer, and other game were plentiful, and animals came and went as freely as they pleased, with no sense of containment or hiddenness. The Guardian had spoken of *mystery*, yet everything felt so ordinary.

Until one night, not long after that, when fairies came.

Arrow was asleep when she heard Wick calling in a whisper, "Arrow, come quickly. But hush!" His voice was eager, not afraid.

Slipping on her tattered boots and tying the fox pelt around her shoulders, she crept into the courtyard. Dan was fast asleep, sprawled against Halla's side with her hind paw as his pillow.

Wick put a hand on Arrow's back, wordlessly guiding her to the low wall, about three feet high, that flanked the fort's hidden doorway. Brushing aside the curtain of vines veiling the open space between the roof and the wall, he revealed the forest beyond. All around, soft lights flickered, reflected in the warm pool.

A stone path of sorts, mushroomed with growth, marked the entrance to the ancient ruins. Graceful olives and laurel stood sentry on each side. Ribbons of ivy trailed from low-hanging branches along the path. Amongst it all—swinging from the laurel, dashing over the moss, winding through the ivy—were fairies.

Each was as tall as Wick's hand was long. Their light was warm and inconstant, like candles that breathed. In flight, their wings appeared a blur; wings at rest displayed dragonfly iridescence, blue and green and purple.

Though they had the appearance of adults, the fairies frolicked like children. Some danced. Some kissed each other, laughing. Some chased each other.

"Oh, Wick," breathed Arrow.

"Shall I wake Dan?"

"No, don't! He's seen them before, many times. It's not the same for him as it is for us."

As silently as they could, Wick and Arrow crept on top of the low wall, shrouding themselves in vines, so their legs dangled down outside the fort.

For the longest time, they didn't want to speak, only watch.

Then Arrow whispered, "Remember what we used to say—"

"—about your eyes."

"The fairy grace."

"The nurse took me away because I cried, so I missed the whole thing."

"Not this time, though."

And Arrow took Wick's hand. Because there was no other way to find out what would happen.

He didn't pull it away. He swallowed a few times, so loudly Arrow was surprised the fairies didn't hear. She laid her head on his shoulder. After awhile, he put his arm around her, pulling her close.

It always should have been this way.

It always was, only they had finally changed enough to become it.

Her heart hammered, but the hammering brought a hazy calm as it drowned out everything else. Wick's heart hammered too, louder than hers.

"Arrow," he whispered.

Sliding off the wall, he faced her and gripped the wall on either side of her. If the fairies noticed, they didn't seem to care. His face was just at the level of hers. Lifting one hand, he brushed away the vines that hid her from view. He looked and looked.

"The fairy grace," he said. "I see it in your eyes."

Then he kissed her eyes. First one, then the other, with his hand cupped around the side of her face. His other hand slid around her waist, and he drew in close.

Reaching up, Arrow touched his face. She traced his jaw and eyes and nose and lips. If he hadn't been so close, she would have fallen off the wall when she leaned forward to wrap her arms around his neck.

At the same moment, they decided to kiss each other.

It was everything it should have been.

It was everything.

Then the fairies noticed them. With little gasps and shrieks like rain tinkling on glass, they darted in furtive swarms through the grove. They weren't alarmed; they were delighted. As they gathered to watch, their light washed over Wick and Arrow in ever-swelling waves.

Putting both arms around Arrow's waist, Wick pulled her

down from the wall and whirled her around. The fairies cheered. They whooshed in clouds, wings fluttering against the humans' hair and clothing, as he set her on the flagstones of the ruined path and kissed her again.

They kissed and laughed, hugged and laughed. Laughed and laughed. The fairies never tired of it. At last, Wick held Arrow close to his chest. They breathed with each other until, breath by breath, Arrow felt something crack open inside Wick.

What poured out of him was fear.

Deep, echoing fear. The unexpectedness of it caught Arrow and held her there, listening, letting it pour over her until it filled them both, causing them to look up.

"Arrow," he said, "I need to tell you what happened to Arrow's World."

Wick's Tale, the Missing Part

The Wizard of Seven cannot read minds. At least, I don't think so. I've tested this many times. But it's true what Dan says, that the intelligence of wizards is much greater than ours. The Wizard could guess many things I never told him, things most precious and hidden. Though he couldn't see these things, he could feel them in the dark.

Somehow he guessed about Arrow's World. Of course he didn't know I called it that. He couldn't see its landscapes or its peoples. He couldn't enter it; it was like this refuge. But he knew it was all for you. And he knew, or sensed, or felt in the dark, that I had brought all our children there. So he knew how to punish me when, after he imprisoned me on the Buried Isle and I saw you and Tomás in the enchanted glass looking at the stars, I destroyed his chambers in rebellion.

Arrow, he took away my children.

What do you mean? Do you mean our *children? How could he possibly do that?*

No, I mean my children. My real children. Something that never was, that might have been, but never will now.

Speak very plainly, Wick. Say it straight out, so I don't misunderstand.

I can't have children, Arrow. The Wizard took that power from me. Not my manhood—he wanted me to keep that. But he knew how I pictured our children sometimes, when I was most in despair of finding you. That I dreamed of them and spoke their names and made them a home. So he took that away. That's how he punished me. I couldn't tell you before.

Wick, Wick, how can you not have shown me such a big hurt? How can you not have let me comfort you? Here, let me hold you. Hush, now. Oh Wick, let me hold you.

There's more, Arrow. Listen. But keep hold of my hand, if you can.

In my bitterness, I did something terrible.

I did it. The Wizard didn't do it to me. I did it. The most terrible thing I've ever done. The thing I've been too afraid to tell you, all this time. I decided to do it, and then I did it.

I froze Arrow's World.

I buried it under ice and snow, buried it a hundred miles deep. I buried the tree-palace and the shimmering lake. I buried the mermaid girl and the centaurs. I buried Frida the Otter and all the other animals. I buried our children. I froze them all, Arrow. I froze the sun itself, the moon and the stars. There's nothing there now, no one. Only windswept blank white cold dark nothing.

That is why I couldn't show you Arrow's World. Because I destroyed it.

They were sitting side by side in the doorway of the ruined tomb, on the step of the threshold. Clinging to each other, they wept.

"I'm sorry, Arrow," Wick sobbed. "I'm so sorry."

"I forgive you. But oh, my poor Wick, you were hurt, and you didn't tell me. How can you not have told me? What's the point of me, except for that?"

"Arrow," he said, "hold me tight." And he clung to her.

The fairies looked on, whispering in confusion. Turning away, they tried to cheer each other with silly jokes and dances.

When Arrow awoke, it was the deepest part of the night. She had fallen asleep on Wick's chest in the doorway of the fort. One of his arms rested heavily across her body; the other sprawled on the ground. Snails had made shimmering trails across his wrist. Having worn themselves out, the fairies lay in contented piles on the mossy stones at the edge of the pool, dozing and chattering. The moon was high, small, and bright.

Eventually Wick shifted a little and clasped his hands together, holding her, so she knew he was awake. They looked out into the night. Their hearts hung limp and ragged, empty of tears. A warm, sweet wind began to blow.

Arrow said, "When the Mother of the Mountain spoke to you, she was speaking of Arrow's World."

"Yes."

"She said she could restore it."

Wick drew a deep breath. "I've tried to go back, Arrow. Especially in these last few months. The night I went off and didn't come home—all that night, I tried to go back to Arrow's World. But it's so cold there. If I try to enter, even the handle of the door freezes me solid."

"But she said: only if you're alone. I will come with you, Wick. I want to come with you. I know I can, if you let me."

"We can't unchange, Arrow. It's the one thing we can't do."

"But we can keep changing, until we become who we always were."

Putting her hand on his heart, she closed her eyes.

She listened.

Oh, the sound of him was all longing and tenderness. All quiet vision and strong shelter and a soft place to rest. All songs of clear, stinging beauty. The ache of the distance between stars, the laughter of the new day. A hugeness and a home. She loved him, she loved him, she loved him.

As Arrow listened, she began to see. In her mind's eye, Wick's heart took shape around her like a red, pulsing room with many corridors which she followed deeper and deeper in. Nothing stood in her way until she reached the very center. Here was a door frozen shut. Arrow pulled at the latch, pulled and pulled, but it would not budge. Ice bulged and sagged through the cracks of the door frame. She breathed on the ice, pressed her hands against it, but it would not melt.

"Do you see the door, Wick?" she asked.

His eyes were also closed. "Yes. I see you trying to open it. Your hands are blue with cold and there are cuts all over them. Will you please stop now, before it freezes you? You can see it's hopeless."

"We need something very warm. To melt the ice. What's the warmest thing you have?"

He didn't answer right away. Arrow was afraid he'd given up. But at last he said, "Our birthday. The toy reindeer you made for me. But it's lost."

"No it isn't. See, it's here in my hands."

And it was. That precious bundle of twisted rags, its mouth smudged off from being kissed so many times, its tail that was a braided loop of her own hair. Arrow danced the reindeer all across the doorway, as Wick used to dance it across the floor of their cage.

"Do you see what I'm doing, Wick?"

"I see you dancing the reindeer over the door."

"Good. Now you try."

Suddenly Wick stood beside her in front of the frozen door. He didn't look quite the same as the real Wick; he was more like the boy-man from her imaginings. The boy-man Wick took the reindeer and danced it across the door until all the ice melted. Arrow pulled the door open. A blast of frigid air threw her backward. Shrinking away, Wick shivered until his teeth rattled. The light from the doorway glimmered on a wall of white snow. Beyond that, all was blackness.

"We'd better send in the reindeer first," said Arrow. "Reindeer like snow."

So Wick set down the reindeer in front of the door. With a happy neigh, it galloped into Arrow's World. Everywhere it stepped, a trench began to melt through the ice and snow. Taking Wick's hand, Arrow pulled him through the door and they began to follow along the trench, which protected them from the bitter winds. Once they had stepped in, it seemed less dark. Perhaps they brought the light with them.

"We should sing," she said. "Let's sing my birthday song."

Turn my pockets inside out
Hang me from a star
Burrow me beneath the hedges
Where the rabbits are...

Wick was shivering too hard to sing, so Arrow sang loud enough for both of them. As she sang, the sun rose high in the sky, yellow and hot like the sun over the Sorry Islands. Everywhere they looked the snow began to melt.

"It's working!" whispered Wick. He sang with her, and they danced.

Call, then call, now call me out me—
Echo-shout the hill.
I'll scurry out and shimmy down
And up my pockets fill.

"Look!" cried Arrow. "A mountain! It's the top of a mountain."

Wick laughed. "It's the mountain where the centaurs live."

"Let's run."

By the time they reached the mountain, it had fully emerged and the snow was receding from the valleys, revealing rivers and villages and the thousand-year-old tree carved into an elf-palace. Kobi the Centaur came to meet them, his long black tail braided with feathers.

"Kobi," said Wick, "I'm sorry I froze you."

The centaur laughed, tossing back his proud head. "I don't know what you're talking about. I just woke up from a glorious dream. A beautiful woman with shining white hair taught me to climb a height on the mountain I've never been able to reach before. I'm off to find it!"

And he raced away.

"Wick," said Arrow, "I want to meet the mermaid girl."

Taking her hand, Wick led her to the sea.

"Hello," said the mermaid girl. "Are you Arrow?"

Her dark blue tail swished through the water as she spoke. Her green-white hair was tangled in front of her eyes, and she tugged it back to get a better look. She wore little earrings of coral and nothing else.

"Yes," said Arrow. "What's your name?"

"I forgot," said the mermaid girl. "I've been asleep such a long time. Will you give me a new one?"

Arrow drew back in surprise. "Can I do that? Just give someone a name? Aren't names very powerful things?"

"*You* can. This is your world, Arrow. We are your task. But you'd better give me a good one."

Arrow looked at Wick. Happiness was bursting out of every part of him like fireworks.

"Niora," said Arrow. "Is that a good name for a mermaid?"

"Oh, yes!" shouted Niora, flipping through the water with delight. "It's a very good name. It's *my* name." And she dove down deep, feeling the cool water slide over her, tasting the joy of being a mermaid named Niora.

Wick gave a cry of joy. Turning to look, Arrow saw Frida the Otter quivering with excitement, crawling all over him and poking him with her nose. The otter smelled overwhelmingly of fish. Wick made Frida do her best tricks for Arrow, who laughed as much and more than they merited, thus winning Frida's devotion forever.

Then Arrow looked around. Everything was exactly right. Wick had arranged everything just the way she would have chosen. Green hills and red-gold cliffs strewed the sea's rim like a garland, with blue mountains massed behind that didn't loom or threaten but opened up and up endlessly until they kissed the sky. Toward the south, jungles danced with raucous flashes of chartreuse and crimson, begging Arrow to join them. Everything was wild, tumbling out from itself in an excess of eagerness to be the thing it was, yet there was room enough for all and more. There was only one city, built of sunrise-colored stone, and that was more like a garden than a palace. In its highest tower waved a banner of blue with a golden arrow.

"Oh Wick," whispered Arrow, "it is good. It is so very good."

"Yes. And it is yours."

"Ours."

"Ours."

When they opened their eyes, Arrow looked up at Wick. He was himself again, a man, but the boy-Wick shone out through his eyes. She touched his face.

"Are we magic, Wick? Did we just do magic?"

"I think we did."

And he kissed her.

"It must be true, then," Arrow continued when he'd finished, "that we are beings of great power."

"I think we are."

And he kissed her again. The fairies started to wake up, pointing and giggling.

Wick smoothed back her hair. "What do we do now?"

Arrow sat up straight. "Let's get married."

"What—now, Arrow?"

"Yes. Right now. Why not?"

"But who will marry us? The Wizard Dan?"

"Oh, no! Not him." Arrow grimaced and Wick laughed out loud. More of the fairies woke.

"Why not?"

"Because it's a holy thing. He's not holy. No, we need to find a priest somewhere."

"Do you think the fairies have a priest?"

Arrow's eyes lit up. "Dan can ask them. That's one thing he can do."

The wizard was not pleased about being awakened. "You need to get married *now*? Why now, in the middle of a mercifully dry, blessedly uneventful night's sleep?"

"Because fairies are here, and they might have a priest. We need you to ask them. Please, Dan, they might never come back!"

"Mother of tripe." He staggered to his feet, muttering and kneading his face.

"Shall I wake Halla?"

"Lord, no. She eats fairies like bats eat bugs. Come on."

The fairies swarmed around the wizard as he began to speak their tongue. After several minutes of chirping and tinkling, Dan turned to Wick and Arrow. "The fairies do have a priest. But they want you to give them a gift in exchange for his service."

"A gift! Should I give them my fox pelt?"

"What in heaven's name would they do with that? They couldn't carry it from the grove."

"Maybe if they all carried it together—"

"No, Arrow, they don't want your tatty old fox. I'll tell you what they want. Once you told me you knew how to dance, that you used to draw a fair crowd. There's nothing fairies like more than a good caper."

Arrow looked at Wick. They burst out laughing.

"Of course," said Wick. "Of course." He held out his hand to Arrow. "Our wedding dance."

They both knew which it would be.

They danced *Little Lady Linden* for a fairy horde and a disgruntled wizard and a sleeping griffin, on the threshold of a tomb in the heart of a forest in Anatolia, in the middle of a winter's night. Somehow it seemed the stars were dancing too, and all the trees, and the earth beneath their whirling feet. Or maybe that was only the echo of Arrow's World, bleeding through into their own.

Then Wick put out his hand thus, palm facing hers. Arrow brought her hand up to travel half the distance toward his, and again half, and half again, and so on, until her palm met his palm and her fingers bent his slightly back. She pushed each of her fingertips—one, two, three, four, five—against Wick's. Her hand was hot; so was his.

Wick held out his other hand with his palm facing up and his fingers cupped like a bowl. Arrow cupped her hand in his, palm facing up. The fairy-priest flew and landed in the bowl of their hands. He looked very holy and solemn, with long robes and a chestnut headpiece, though the rest of the fairies kept laughing and turning somersaults in the air.

The fairy-priest chirped in his tiny voice.

"He's asking you," said Dan, "if you intend to belong to no one but each other all the days of your lives, until death do you part."

"Yes," said Wick.

"Yes," said Arrow.

"He's asking you to make your vows to each other."

"I don't know the words," said Arrow.

"Yes you do," said Wick. "Like this: I, Wick, take you, Arrow, to be my wife."

"I, Arrow, take you, Wick, to be my husband."

"I will love you always, whatever the cost, until the end, however it comes."

"I will love you always, whatever the cost, until the end, however it comes."

"I think that's it. Have I forgotten anything?"

"Have we forgotten anything, Dan?"

Dan twittered a bit, and the priest replied.

"He says no, you haven't forgotten anything. But do you have rings?"

"Rings, Wick! We need rings!"

"Of course!" Wick's laugh brimmed over the edges of him as he felt in all his empty pockets. "We're so poor, Arrow." Then he sang, "*We haven't got a silver thread. We haven't got a flare.*"

"Here," said Arrow. Pulling forward some strands of her hair, she cut them with her dagger. Quickly, she braided two loops. She and Wick tied them around each other's fingers and trimmed the extra.

The fairy priest chirped solemnly.

Dan translated: "He pronounces you man and wife."

All the fairies clapped and cheered. They tore off bits of moss and fern and threw them in Wick and Arrow's hair as they kissed.

Dawn was breaking. With parting cries of joy, the fairies swept away to their nests. The Wizard Dan flopped back down against the sleeping Halla, muttering. Wick took Arrow to his room, whispering, "Our bridal chamber."

They laughed until they fell over.

A Song of Wick and Arrow
from Anatolia

If I could choose again
Choose it all, all days, all ways,
I would choose this.
I would choose again—this.
Nothing less.

Tomb's Song

Well, here is something new.
My old bones creak—the heft of it
Not heavy but weighty,
Not a burden but a yoke.

Is it a death?
I cannot tell.
For death is weightiest of all things that are.
Thus did I color my stones in it
Until death on death drabbed me.

But here is something new.
I cannot enclose it.

"He made of me a sharp-edged sword
and concealed me in the shadow of his arm.
He made me a polished arrow,
in his quiver he hid me."

—Isaiah

19

Not three weeks after the wedding, the Wizard Dan shouldered his pack, donned his wide-brimmed hat, and announced, "Well, Halla and I are off. We'll come round again in the spring to make sure you haven't kissed each other to death."

"You're leaving?" cried Arrow. "Why, Dan?"

He flicked back his hair. "Because wizards are meant to seek impossible things, not to skulk in magical fortresses with lovesick humans. The two of you no longer require my protective services, at least at present, and Halla's as restless as a sea-serpent in a pond. We need some danger, frankly. More danger, less kissing."

"Where will you go?" asked Wick.

Dan gave a secretive, self-satisfied smile. "Nowhere of particular interest. Somewhere I can catch a whiff of impossibilities."

"You're going to Glen Droighinn," said Wick, alarmed. "Dan, if you're caught and tortured—"

"Let us recall that I've lived nearly five times as long as you, and in all that time I've been neither caught nor tortured. Not significantly, that is. Please don't insult my competence by comparing it with your own."

With that, the Wizard Dan scrambled on Halla's back. The griffin indeed looked happier than she'd been since their arrival in The Refuge. Crouching to spring, Halla suddenly halted, stretched out her neck toward a nearby rock formation, and let out a joyful chirr.

They all looked. Perched on an outcropping of rock, two female lions sat side by side. Their long tails were wrapped around their feet, twitching rhythmically; other than that, the lions made no movement. Their eyes were fixed on Dan and Halla.

"My gratitude for your diligence, ladies," Dan called to the lions. "We've been stiflingly safe here, thanks. We leave these two humans in your capable paws. Look for our return when the mountain's in bloom."

With a piercing farewell cry, Halla soared up through the tree canopy and out of sight. The lions watched them go, then departed as silently as they had appeared.

Arrow stared into the blank sky, hands on her hips. "It is, a bit."

"A bit what?"

"Stiflingly safe."

"I wish I had my horse, now that Halla's gone."

"I wish we could go with them. I wish we could—just live, Wick. With other humans, in a little village by the sea."

"At least we're not in a cage."

"Aren't we, though?"

"At least we're married."

"At least that."

Nearly every day, they went to Arrow's World. They didn't go together, not in a magical way as on the night of their wedding. Either that experience had been a grace from the fairies, or it was a magic that only sprang to life in a moment of extremity. In any case, they still loved to go to Arrow's World in the ordinary way: through telling and listening until they saw the same thing, each in their own mind.

Through this game, they learned a great deal about their twenty-seven children, who had grown, naturally, since Wick and Arrow were children. Their eldest daughter Rina (the one who had originally been a wolf) was discovered to have a blunt, reserved manner very similar to Coira's. Remmy the brave, who killed giants by tripping them into crevasses, could have been the twin brother of Iliana of the Buried Isle.

But no new children were born in Arrow's World. Wick and Arrow never discussed it, for it would have required them to voice something too bitter to speak aloud. Yet one day the bitter thing had to be voiced anyway, as bitter things generally do.

"Arrow, we said we would never have any secrets from each other, ever again."

"Oh, don't ask me, Wick! It's not fair. It's not really a secret, it's just..."

"Something you don't want to tell me, because you don't want to hurt me. But remember when I did that? It hurt you worse because I hid it."

"No, I know. I didn't mean to hide it. I didn't realize I was, until you asked me just now. Alright, I'll tell you then."

As Arrow tried to matter-of-factly recount the contents of Brother Agostin's letter—that before his death Tomás had married Noemi, who was to give birth to their child in a few short months—she found that instead of speaking she dissolved in tears and had to sit down on the front step, clutching her knees to her chest.

Wick sat beside her until she reached out and gripped his hand. Then she told him everything.

"I'm happy for her, Wick," she sobbed. "I'm happy, do you hear me?"

"I hear you," he said. "Shh, Arrow. I hear you."

And he sang to her until she grew quiet and still.

In early spring, Dan and Halla returned. Though the wizard still had only four fingers on each hand, his look of absolute smugness caused Arrow to demand, "Tell us at once what you've been doing and why you're so pleased with yourself."

"Oh, no reason in particular," said Dan as he sat and eased off one of his battered boots. "Except that I've discovered a means of destroying the two most powerful villains in the world."

Halla began polishing her talons with her beak.

"Well, tell us!" said Wick. "Does it have to do with your theory about Grell helping the Wizard of Seven to remove his name?"

"That, *and* I was correct in assuming she's made a blood pact to protect it. If the wizard's name is ever released, she'll die that same instant." Dan dumped a handful of dirt, pine needles, and feathers from his boot.

"What do you mean *released*?" asked Arrow.

"Well, the only way the wizard could have removed it was by separating and imprisoning it, somehow—in a jar, say, some kind of gruesome and magical jar. Since wizards are always on the move and the sorceress lives in an impenetrable fortress, naturally he left the jar under her protection in exchange for some service I'm sure we'd rather not know about."

"And you believe," said Wick, "that the Wizard of Seven will die if his name is released from this jar?"

"Die is one word for it. His name will consume him in flames, I imagine. Or pulverize him into dust. Or implode him out of existence. In any case, that'll be the end of him."

"How did you find this out?" wondered Arrow.

"Asked the ruins outside of Glen Droighinn, of course. I explained that I was happy to thwart the sorceress for them if they would tell me how, as quietly and inconspicuously as possible. At first I thought they made no reply. Then I realized they were muffling their voices in the moss that covered them, as we might put our hands over our mouths. So I pressed my ear against the moss. They told me the whole tale, including where she's hidden the wizard's name."

"Where?" gasped Wick and Arrow together.

Dan swelled with such feline self-satisfaction Arrow wouldn't have been surprised to hear him purr. He looked at her keenly. "Have you ever seen Grell wear a golden torc?"

"What's a torc?"

"A kind of collar made of gold, worn around her neck. An ancient symbol of power and conquest, full of sorcery."

"Do you mean something like a rope of gold, thick as a man's finger? With a large ruby in the center?"

"It's not a ruby. It's some kind of gruesome and magical jar. The wizard's name is trapped inside it."

Arrow shivered. "Yes, I've seen her wear that. Coira says it's the source of Grell's greatest powers. She conjures ghosts with it, even brings the dead back to life."

"Fascinating," said Dan. "That must be what Grell got out of the bargain. Through the harnessing of the wizard's name, she has wedded the power of the Starborn to her own eldritch devices."

Arrow continued, "I only saw it once, when she wanted to make a great show of power. She caused the jewel to flame like red fire. But Coira told me Grell always wears it; most of the time it's invisible, but she never takes it from around her neck."

"Hmm," said Dan, "that makes destroying it both more straightforward and more delicate."

"How can it be destroyed?" asked Wick.

"It can't be. That's the thrilling part. The jewel is impossible to break, burn, or otherwise harm. Well, then! If it's written into my name to be a Friend of Lovesick Humans, don't you think it would be my task to do the impossible thing that frees my friends from a life of wretchedness and hiding?"

Wick and Arrow only looked at him with doubt-shadowed faces. Dan bristled with umbrage.

"Please you to remember," he continued, "what the Mother of the Mountain said to me on this very spot. It may have meant nothing to the two of you, but it meant a great deal to me."

"Dan," said Wick softly, "your friendship means a great deal to us. But other friends have lost their lives trying to help us. You attempting to destroy an unbreakable jewel that the Sorceress Grell wears in an invisible torc around her neck is about as futile as Coira attempting to kill the Wizard of Seven. We can't stop you from trying, but we can beg you not to."

"And we do," added Arrow. "We do beg you not to, dear, ridiculous Dan."

"Oh," said Dan, waving a skinny-fingered hand. "I wasn't thinking of going alone."

"You mean—?"

"The only way to detect the jewel's weakness (if it has one) is to set Grell talking about it. One can only set her talking about it if she's interested in talking to one at all. She'd as soon make me into a pair of slippers. But she's very interested in talking to the two of you."

Arrow shook her head, her lips pressed white together. "You don't know what you're saying. You don't know Grell."

"No, but I know you. You're more like wizards than you think. You'll never be satisfied hiding here for the rest of your lives. You were made to do impossible things."

"The wizards in Gnoze didn't think so," said Arrow.

"But the centaurs did," said Wick, almost to himself. "So did Iliana."

Arrow narrowed her eyes at Dan. "What happens if we fail?"

"By fail," said Dan, "you mean—?"

"I mean the sorceress or the wizard or both succeeds in breaking our unbreakable love, if we leave this refuge."

"Ah. In that case, the Wizard of Seven will become a Wizard of Eight and overcome the limitation of power. Which is to say, he will have power not only to change us into chestnuts, but to alter our very wills to desire and choose whatever he desires and chooses. I suppose he'll make us exquisitely evil, but we won't suffer much because he'll cause us to enjoy it. At least we're none of us possessed of much power that can be used for ill—except Halla, oh dear. It will be much worse when he gets his hands on the rest of the wizards."

"We can't, then!" cried Arrow. "The risk is too great. For the good of all the world, we must stay hidden here."

"It won't do any good, though," said Wick quietly. "If the Wizard of Seven fails to find us, he'll take two other children and put them in a cage. Then he will test them to see if their love is unbreakable. If it is, he will have learned from the mistakes he made with us. If it isn't, he will discard them and find others."

"How do you know that?" said Arrow.

"Because he had a jar of pebbles in his wizarding chamber. Smooth, dull, gray pebbles, all the same. The label said, *Trials According to the Caveat: The Ones Who Broke*."

A red wave rose towering up and crashed over Arrow. It was like when she burned the ship: she wanted to burn down the whole world.

The Wizard Dan cleared his throat. "Funny—ahem—funny you should mention that."

They turned to face him. His rusty-red brows were furrowed with what seemed one part reluctance, one part bewilderment. One of his hands was thrust in his coat pocket, fidgeting with something.

"I stopped in Paris, you see, on my way back from Caledonia. Was dying for a good meal. I love Paris. So much cheese. I didn't take Halla of course. Walked through the city. Blended right in, except I suppose my hair and, well, that I'm a wizard. Pickpockets everywhere, urchins crowding against me. I caught someone trying to take my purse. During the scuffle, someone else must've slipped this into my other pocket. I never saw who did it. But of course... I can guess."

He pulled out a neatly folded note.

Esteemed Sir,

When you return to your human friends, please inform them they have nothing more to fear from the Wizard Who Changes Things into Other Things or the Sorceress Grell. Because of recent difficulties, this indomitable pair has determined on a new course of action. The sorceress herself will adopt two human children from birth, rearing them with a mother's watchfulness in her fortress of Glen Droighinn.

Since the girl Arrow failed to meet the sorceress's aims, it seems fitting that her replacement should be taken from amongst those she holds dear. Please assure her that the child of Tomás and Noemi de Rueda will be brought up for a truly noble purpose.

Best wishes for a speedy journey.

As they journeyed toward Lipa, they made a plan. Arriving at night, they would land atop the old watchtower on South Hill. Halla would hide there, ready to be called by the bloodstone whistle if the need arose. Covered in their cloaks, the wizard and the two humans would go to the monastery to find Brother Agostin. There, Wick and Arrow would wait out of sight while Dan accompanied Brother Agostin to the house of Noemi Albares de Rueda and convinced her to flee with them back to The Refuge. It was too risky for Arrow to meet Noemi herself, since she was a wanted criminal in Lipa.

The night was perfectly still when they reached the island, the sea's sigh barely perceptible. The streets were silent except for a few servants scurrying with torches on urgent errands. Arrow, Wick, and Dan kept to the shadows as they crept toward Lipa Monastery.

When they reached it, Wick said, "I'll knock, in case it's not Brother Agostin who answers."

Arrow and Dan hid around the corner of the gatehouse.

Silence followed Wick's knock. He knocked again, louder, and a third time.

The door's iron grate screeched aside, revealing the flare of a torch within. "Who are you?" whispered a fearful, familiar voice. "Throw back your cloak and show yourself."

Arrow burst around the corner. "It's me, Brother Agostin. It's Arrow. I've come."

Silence.

Then, trembling wildly, the voice said, "Prove yourself. Tell me something only Arrow could know."

"Brother, what has happened? I swear, I'm Arrow! But here—you sent me a letter telling me to take heart."

"You could've stolen that letter. Tell me something more."

"Your favorite poet is Ephrem the Syrian, and you fast from his verses during Lent as a mortification of the senses."

"Oh, child! My child!"

"Wait," said Dan. "Prove you're Brother Agostin."

"I understand. Arrow will know me when I remind her that she once spared me great embarrassment by informing me that the backside of my robe had worn through before we walked together through the city."

"It's you, it's you!"

"But hush."

The lock slid in the gate and Brother Agostin eased it silently open.

"My child, my child. How is it you are here?" He took Arrow's face in his hands, kissing it and weeping. "Tonight of all nights, how are you here?"

"What has happened, Brother? Something has happened. Tell me!"

"How can I speak it?" Groaning, the monk bent forward and cradled his head in his hands.

Arrow gripped him by the shoulders, forcing his face upward. "Is it Noemi?"

His eyes widened. "You know?"

"No! I know nothing. Tell me!"

"She's dead. Whether in childbirth or by the hand of another I know not. It may all be the same, for some foul witch was her midwife."

Arrow was falling, falling, falling into a sea of nothingness.

"I was there, praying with the family for a safe delivery, when the old woman came out holding an infant girl. The baby cried loudly; we all shouted for joy. Then the midwife dropped her wizened shape, growing tall and terrifyingly beautiful, with black hair and milk-white skin. Straight at me she looked, and laughed. She wore a golden collar around her neck, with a jewel in the center that burned like fire. Then—she disappeared. When we went in to your sister, she was dead."

"But the child?" cried Wick.

Brother Agostin shrugged in a gesture of despair. "Gone! Taken! Oh, we are cursed here in Lipa! Cursed for our crimes with sorrow upon sorrow."

Arrow reeled, pawing to grasp Wick's arm as he caught her.

Then a furious shriek, wild and fearsome, filled the air. Brother Agostin shrank into a corner, terrified, but the others sprang to attention.

"Halla!" Dan pulled the bloodstone whistle from beneath his shirt and sounded the griffin's call.

A few moments later Halla swooped down, knocking a stone from one of the pillars of the monastery gatehouse in her haste. Chirring and snapping, she related her news to Dan. Brother Agostin's legs gave out at the sight of her.

"She says the sorceress is here," said Dan. "On top of the old watchtower on South Hill. She has the infant. She is waiting for us."

"It's a trap," said Wick. "This is just what she meant to happen."

"Yes," said Arrow, "and we're going to walk straight into it. At least we're going to get the baby out, if we can't free ourselves."

"Excellent," said Dan. "It sounds absolutely impossible."

"Please," gasped Brother Agostin, recovering from his faint, "let me come with you. Let me help."

"No," said Arrow. "This is our fight now, me and Wick's. No one else is going to die because of us."

"Yet I claim it as my fight also, because I claim you, Arrow, as a father claims his child. There's a sword in my cell, though I haven't used it in twenty years. If you don't take me with you,

I'll run all the way to South Hill and up the tower stairs, sword in hand."

Tears filled Arrow's eyes. Throwing her arms around Brother Agostin's neck, she hugged him fiercely. He wept as he embraced her in return.

"Might as well bring a biscuit as a sword," said Dan, "so let's not waste time fetching it. Good luck keeping yourself on Halla's back. A bookish monk, an apprentice wizard, two love-sick humans, and a loyal griffin, off to fight the most powerful magicians in the world."

PART V · CHAPTER 19

A Song of Wick and Arrow
from Anatolia

This is a love song.
This is not a sad song.
I will be with you
All the way from here to there, until the end.
Until the end, all the way from here to there,
I will be with you.
This is not a sad song.
This is a love song.

Halla brought them to the top of the tower so quickly they had no time to think. Sliding off her back, they landed in a cloud of dust amidst the broken stones, spluttering, coughing, and waving the dust from their eyes until they could see.

There in the center of the tower stood the Sorceress Grell. Her gown of silver threads cast a cold gleam over her white skin. Her thick black hair, crowned by a band of silver, cascaded over her shoulders and down her back. There was no sign of the golden torc around her neck. As her gaze fell on Wick, the sorceress's black eyes burned. Her lips were blood red.

At her feet lay a basket with a bundle of blankets inside.

"Naturally," said Grell, "if the griffin makes even the slightest threatening movement toward my person, the infant will die the same instant."

"Naturally," said Dan with a short laugh meant to be nonchalant that came out rather shrill. He hastily translated the sorceress's greeting for Halla, whose rumbling snarls sounded like a rockslide burying a wolfpack.

A voice came from behind them. "Such bandying is tiresome now that the birds are in the snare."

They whirled around. The Wizard of Seven emerged from behind a shadowed crevasse in the parapet.

Having received no prohibition against the assault of wizards, Halla launched herself at him, snarling. Her bronze talons stretched wide; her beak opened; her fur bristled.

The next instant, she was gone.

Her sinewed body with its spread wings, its black shadow on the ground, blinked out of the air before any of them had time to understand what it meant. Except Wick, who shuddered and looked away. Where the griffin had been, a single white feather floated down.

Striding forward, the wizard lifted his seven-fingered hand and let the feather drift into his palm.

"Halla?" whispered Arrow.

The Wizard of Seven turned the feather over in his hand. As he did, it crumbled into white ash. He flicked it away. "Halla does not exist."

Halla, Halla, Halla, Halla.

Oh Halla, Halla, Halla.

Arrow's eyes squeezed shut. She pictured Halla's wings and imagined them spread on either side of her as she soared on the griffin's back. She pictured Halla's tail and imagined catching and pressing it as the griffin tried to twitch it away. She pictured Halla's plumy breast and imagined placing her hand on it, listening to the boom of her magnificent heart.

Dan stared, still unable to believe what he saw. He called out a few words in Halla's tongue. Then, for the first time in his ninety-four years of life, tears began to stream down the wizard's face.

Brother Agostin appeared to be murmuring an inaudible prayer.

Wick remained motionless, a hard, cold statue of himself.

"Did you forget," said Grell with annoyance, "that you promised me the griffin?"

"Ah," said the Wizard of Seven. "I did. My apologies."

"I trust you will not forget who else you promised me."

"There is no fear of that."

"Unharmed."

"In body, yes."

Frowning until his eyes were fully hidden beneath his ponderous eyebrows, the wizard began to walk in a slow circle around Wick. No one else dared to move.

"I hope you will take no offense, my dear boy, when I tell you that I sincerely hoped never to have to see you again in my life."

"Nor I you, sir." Wick's jaw scarcely moved as he spoke.

"That was quite a trick you played, leaving me stranded in the Buried Isle with an army of fools throwing rubbish through my windows. Needless to say, those responsible have been made an example of."

Gripping one of Wick's wrists, the wizard lifted his hand and dropped a small object into his palm: a chestnut. Wick closed his eyes as he closed his fist around the chestnut, trying to prevent emotion from contorting his face.

Then the wizard turned to Arrow. "And one for you." He dropped a second chestnut into her hand. "Although the sorceress was displeased by it. She demanded that I return her apprentice for proper punishment, but magic has its rules. What I change is changed forever."

Arrow stared at the chestnut. The pitch of her grief rose too high for her heart to hear. She was hardly aware of the wizard, or the sorceress, or the infant in the basket. Hardly aware of Wick, until he reached out and took her hand, so the two smooth nuts were pressed between their palms. A river of anguish surged out through her hand, pouring into him. His own pain answered.

When a river flows both ways at once, it forms a whirlpool. The stronger and swifter the river, the more powerful the whirlpool and the larger its hollow center. In the clean stillness of that center, Arrow heard something.

She heard a voice. Two voices. Coira and Iliana, calling out in Wick and Arrow's language.

Name us, the voices said.

Gasping, Arrow sprang back as if lightning had shot between her and Wick. The chestnuts rattled to the ground and rolled away. Arrow looked up at Wick. His eyes were wide, his heart hammering, his breath short.

He had heard the voices, too.

A thrill sliced through them both. Whatever had just happened, it was akin to the magic of that night they went together to Arrow's World. Was that where the voices had called from? They certainly hadn't come from the chestnuts.

Zinging with the thrill of it, Arrow took a deep breath. She turned toward the Wizard of Seven and searched his face. It was bitter and hard like a shriveled orange peel. The last time she had seen him she was a child, awestruck by his aura of learning and greatness. He had called himself a philosopher, and she hadn't even known what the word meant.

"Sir," she said, raising her chin, "we know your aim. Very well, we have come. But let these others go. Send the baby away with this monk, and Wick and I will do whatever you ask of us."

He snorted. "I knew you were simpler than most humans, but not so simple as to think you could make any semblance of parley. You are entirely in our hands."

"That may be so, but I have read Aristotle since we spoke last. If you coerce us through terror, our actions may not be completely voluntary. How can our love break if we don't choose freely against it?"

After an astonished pause, the wizard let out a trumpet-sneer of laughter. "This mouse thinks herself a philosopher!"

"The human speaks the wisdom of her kind," said the sorceress, her silver gown rustling drily as she glided forward, "which is founded on the fragility of the human mind. May I remind you your crude excess of terror is how you first failed with the boy?"

The wizard's lip curled. "You may remind me of anything you like, so long as you remind yourself that I am the master of this task and you my faithful assistant."

"Oh, how could I forget?"

Pretending not to hear the mockery in Grell's voice, the Wizard of Seven turned back to Arrow. "Do you think I brought you here for a symposium, mouse?"

"You didn't answer my question, sir."

"Nor do I mean to."

"Is that because you are afraid of philosophy, or afraid of mice?"

A roar of laughter from Brother Agostin echoed off the stones of the tower. Clapping his hands, the monk shouted, "Right on the mark, Arrow! True to your name! *Sicut sagittam electam*—"

The next moment, Dan shrieked in terror and shrank away from Brother Agostin. In a black-and-red frenzy, hundreds of spiders swelled from the dust at the monk's feet and swarmed up his legs, enveloping his body in a shroud of gray webs as they went. Brother Agostin staggered, unable to put out a hand to break his fall as the spiders' silk pinioned his arms to his sides. He tried to shout something, but spiders swarmed into his mouth, packing it full with webs as with balls of wool. Then the loathsome creatures vanished as quickly as they had come.

Wick and Arrow sprang to help the enshrouded monk. Before they had gone three steps their feet froze to the paving stones. They fell forward, then struggled to their feet, striving in vain to free themselves.

The Wizard of Seven looked at Grell. "Was that dainty enough for your delicate sensibilities?"

"I will concede," she said without looking at him, "that whatever you lack in subtlety you make up in ingenuity."

Laughing, the Wizard of Seven lifted his hands and spread his fingers. The broken stones on the floor of the tower began to rattle and leap like water droplets in a pan of hot oil. Higher and higher the stones leapt, until they grew into long, thin strands that stretched above Wick and Arrow's heads and changed from gray rock to bars of black iron.

They were in cages. Dan and Brother Agostin in one, Wick and Arrow in another.

As the humans looked about them, their hearts sank. Their cage was the exact size and shape of the one in the boudoir of the Queen of the Giants. The giant pincushion bed sat in one corner. There was the teacup bathtub, the clothes chest, the thimble chamber-pot. All just as they remembered it, with one notable difference: this cage had no door.

With a broad wave of his hand toward Grell, the wizard said, "They are all yours, my faithful assistant."

The sorceress nodded curtly, then turned toward Wick and Arrow's cage. She fixed her eyes on Wick. Her head tilted to one side as her gaze traveled over every part of him. Pursing her lips, she drew a deep breath and slowly let it out. She continued to stare until shame and confusion flooded him. Then she smiled.

"I was afraid," she said, "that you had been tamed beyond remedy. That the unquenchable thirst I so admired in you had been slaked at last. Now I see that it cannot be so. You are a stallion yet. Your passion is far too great to be harnessed to this pony cart."

Arrow kicked the thimble chamber-pot, which clattered against the far wall of the cage. Wick put his hand on her shoulder.

"We know your whole game," he said, forcing the words out through clenched teeth. "What you have to win—and what you have to lose. Alright, then, we'll play. But not until you return the infant to her family. We demand that you send her away with Brother Agostin."

Grell shook her head as at a silly child. "We have nothing to lose and you know it. You could as soon bargain with us as with that giant pincushion."

"We know about the torc," said Wick.

Dan, still mastering his horror of the spiders and his grief over Halla, looked up and drew a sharp breath. He clutched the bloodstone around his neck as his memory grasped at the wreckage of his original hope for an encounter with the sorceress.

"The torc?" said Grell after a pause.

"The torc where you've hidden the Wizard of Seven's name," said Arrow. "The invisible one around your neck. The one that has the power to destroy you both."

Grell said nothing, only stared with blinks as fierce as Halla's.

The Wizard of Seven turned on her in fury. "You told this human my secret? Then you're either a fool or a traitor!"

On his final word, a speck of saliva flew from the wizard's contorted lips and landed on the sorceress's cheek, which turned whiter than the moon. Reaching into the fold of her sleeve, she brought forth a white handkerchief, wiped away the offending speck, and incinerated the handkerchief in a flash of blue flame.

"Silence," she seethed in a whisper Wick and Arrow both heard. "The human made a felicitous guess. You have told your own secret, and I bear no responsibility for the consequences."

Grell looked back at the humans with a mirthless smile. As she smiled, the torc appeared around her neck. It was over an inch thick, a rope of solid gold hammered with intricate patterns. Curving from the back toward the front of her neck, it swelled into two golden talons with an uncut stone the size of a quail's egg clutched between them. The jewel had more of an orange cast than a ruby: fire, not blood.

"Is *this* what you hoped to bargain for?" she laughed with an expression of mock surprise. "Did you plan to destroy my favorite jewel? By all means, try."

Reaching up, she pulled the torc open as if its metal turned soft as wet clay in her hands. Removing it from around her neck, she tossed it through the cage's bars to Wick, who caught it. He gripped the torc like a bull's ring and, crouching, smashed its jewel against the floor of the cage. It did not break. He tried again, harder, crying out as the clash of gold-on-iron stung his hand. His strike rang like a bell from the tower, but the red stone remained unscathed.

"If you dropped the entire weight of this island on it as from a fulcrum," said Grell, "you could not so much as scratch it. That stone was born from the deepest pit of a fire-mountain, hardened in the white-hot heart of a dying star. No force on earth can break it. But here," she looked at Arrow, "it suits you so much better than me."

Wick gasped as the torc disappeared from his hand and reappeared around Arrow's neck. She tried to pull it open as Grell had, to no avail; the golden rope was now hard as steel.

"Oh dear," said Grell, "it is too loose."

The torc shrank tight, wrapping so tightly around Arrow's throat that each breath pressed it into her windpipe, threatening to choke without quite doing so. She pawed frantically at it. "Help me, Wick!"

Bending down toward her neck, Wick examined the torc. Though his own fingers were shaking, he whispered, "Shhh, stay calm. Breathe slowly. Feel it, learn it, find its weakness."

Arrow reached up and felt the torc. She ran her fingers over the rough, uncut stone that imprisoned the Wizard of Seven's name. To her surprise, she felt no sense of evil or cruelty. Rather, the wizard's name was full of light. A light that could burn as hot as a star, if it were kindled. She felt a surge of longing, a howl of injury. The name had been silenced. It longed to be spoken.

"You will need to remove your head if you desire to remove that neckband," said Grell. "As I have no doubt you will desire to do before the night's end."

"Don't listen to her," said Wick. "Listen to me. What am I humming?"

Arrow absorbed the deep rumble of his voice. It was a song they made in the Kingdom of the Giants. As she tried to hum it with him, Arrow realized he was humming one phrase over and over:

This is a flame song. Speak me your name song.

He was trying to tell her something. About the torc? She gave the tiniest shake of her head to show she didn't understand.

He shortened the phrase. *Speak me your name song.*

Arrow's gaze flicked toward Dan, who scowled with concentration as he trained his eyes on the torc. Arrow began to sing the phrase Wick was humming. Dan's eyes narrowed further.

"What a hideous language," said Grell.

"It's Giantish," Arrow replied. "A song we used to sing about our fireplace. We were asking the flames to tell us something."

"As if they knew a secret," said Wick. "But flames are mute, of course. They have no way to let their secret out, if they held one."

Grell's face grew hard and suspicious. She looked from Arrow to Wick and back. "We are wasting time," she said.

The baby began to cry.

20

"Ah, there, little one," said the sorceress as she reached into the basket and lifted its occupant.

Wick and Arrow rushed forward, gripping the bars of their cage.

The newborn girl was wrapped in a soft woolen blanket that Ona, her grandmother, had woven. Black fuzz haloed her pink face. Arrow could see her tiny nose poking upward as her head squirmed, searching for comfort.

The sorceress straightened, and suddenly it was Noemi standing there in a plain linen frock and wool skirt, barefoot, with the full figure of a mother just after childbirth. Arrow's hands flew over her mouth to stifle a scream.

"Hush, hush," said Noemi. Loosening the strings of her bodice, she exposed her breast and began to nurse her child.

"How dare you," whispered Arrow hoarsely.

Noemi looked up. Arrow had forgotten how long and thick her lashes were. Her voice was sweet and high. "How dare I? What have I ever done to you, Arrow? Oh, I remember. I used to play tricks on you, as most children do. Once I made fun of your precious Wick. Is that why you've been so cruel to me? Is it because in your secret heart you've always hated me for that? You never quite forgave me, did you?"

"I... I..."

"Don't speak to her, Arrow!" cried Wick. "Don't listen to her! It's not your sister, it's the sorceress."

Pursing her full lips, Noemi smiled at Wick and shook her head. "She knows it's true. Don't you, Arrow?"

"No." But Arrow had hardly breath to speak the word. The torc pressed heavy and hot and close around her neck.

"It's alright." Noemi shrugged. "I forgive *you*, Arrow. For stealing Tomás from me—twice. First his love, then his life."

"I never meant it to happen. I never meant to fall in love with him. I never sought his love."

"Ha! Didn't you?" And Noemi mimicked Arrow putting her hand on Tomás's chest.

"Shut up!" Wick shouted. "Be silent, you hag."

Pausing to smooth and kiss its hair, Noemi tenderly moved the child to her other breast. "I'm happy for you, sister, that you got what you wanted in the end. I see you've found your true love. If only my love hadn't had to die because of him."

Arrow felt as if she were lying paralyzed at the bottom of a grave, unable to move or speak to prevent the gravediggers from covering her over.

Wick thrust his face in front of hers, between her and Noemi. Taking her face in his hands, he forced her to look into his eyes. "It's all lies, Arrow. Don't speak to Grell. Speak to Noemi."

Then, pressing close behind her so she could feel his heart pounding against the back of her head, Wick put his hands over Arrow's ears.

Noemi stood there scowling, holding the child upright against her shoulder with her hand cupping its fuzzy head.

"I didn't realize you really loved Tomás," said Arrow. "Your way of loving is so different from mine. But it was still real, and you depended on his love. I'm sorry, Noemi. I'm sorry he died.

I'm sorry you died. I'm sorry for all the ways I wasn't a good sister to you."

And it was Grell standing there, scowling, coddling the infant against her gown of silver.

The Wizard of Seven let his breath out impatiently. "I hope I made it clear that I desire the task completed tonight, not ten weeks hence."

"Whose scheme was it to put them in the same cage? You have once again proven your ignorance in these matters."

Suddenly Arrow was standing next to Grell near the baby's basket. Wick remained inside the cage, which seemed to shrink back into the shadows as if it were part of some other, distant world.

"If you attack or displease me in any way," said the sorceress, "I will strangle you with that torc. Do you understand?"

Arrow nodded, swallowing.

"Ah, look," said Grell, holding out the bundled blanket, "the infant sleeps."

Arrow looked at the baby. Its eyelids were translucent, like wet vellum. Parting its pink lips, it heaved a tiny sigh. Grell set the baby back in its basket, arranging its blanket. Straightening, she turned to Arrow.

Loida stood in her place. "I want my sister back. You were never really my sister. That's why we made you sleep with the dog."

Arrow pressed her hands over her ears, turning away. As Grell paced around her, her voice sounded inside Arrow's head, clearer than before.

Now it was little Irma circling her. "You're so ugly. You're not a real human girl at all, are you? Not like us."

Now it was Ona. "I let you into my family. Now my husband is dead, my daughter is dead, her husband is dead."

Arrow wrenched away. She tried not to listen or see, tried to hum, to sing, to look at Wick. But Wick was wrapped in shadow and she was in a howling storm of dread.

Now it was Mundo. "I should never have brought you home with me. I should have let the sea keep you. You should have died, Arrow. Not all of us. All of us."

And now it was Tomás.

Arrow was lying at the bottom of the grave. Dirt poured over her, covering her. And she couldn't move.

"I waited for you, Arrow. I waited, but you never came back."

A lock of his dark hair fell over his forehead; the rest was blown back as if by sea winds. He wore new black boots because he was a second pilot now. Everything around Tomás faded as he grew brighter and realer. His cheeks flushed deep red.

She whispered, "I told you not to wait. I told you, Tomás."

"I couldn't help it. It was because you tried to kiss me, back on the ship when I first found you. I wish you hadn't done that. It changed me, Arrow."

Hot tears that she couldn't wipe away ran down Arrow's face. "I'm sorry."

He stepped closer until his hips almost touched hers. "I never loved Noemi like I loved you."

"Hush, Tomás, don't." She tried to step back, but she couldn't.

With a start of surprise, Tomás noticed the basket. Approaching it, he picked up the sleeping infant. She looked so much smaller in his arms than she had in Noemi's. For what seemed an eternity—it wasn't longer than a few minutes—Tomás watched his daughter sleep. Arrow could hear the baby's little lungs learning to push air in and out, learning to be a human girl.

Then Tomás looked up at Arrow. "I wish she had been your child."

"Stop!" Though Arrow tried to scream the word, it came out such a tiny sound not even she could hear it.

He lifted the baby to his face, kissed her, smelled her hair. A single tear slid down his cheek. "I miss her already. But you'll take care of her, won't you, Arrow?"

"Yes. I will take care of her for you. She is my task, Tomás." Arrow stepped closer, reaching for the child.

But he pulled back. His mouth hardened into a scowl. "No, Arrow. You can only have one task. Isn't that what you taught me? You had to choose between me and Wick."

"That was before I found him," Arrow insisted. "But now—"

"No!" His harsh tone startled the infant awake; she began to fuss. Tomás did nothing to soothe her. Keeping his eyes on Arrow, he curled his upper lip. "I know you, Arrow. You can't give her what she needs."

"I will give her everything, Tomás."

"You won't. There is only room in your heart for one person. You will always choose him, no matter who suffers because of it. I know you now."

Arrow could make no response. All thoughts fled out of her mind, replaced with a kind of red, wordless fog.

"I'm sorry," Tomás continued. "I must take her where someone can look after her."

As he spoke, a shape loomed up behind him, blacker than the darkness of the night. Narrow and tall, framed by a ghostly arch gleaming pale silver, the black shape seemed to open into a void, as if a rent had been torn in the fabric of time and space. Though Arrow had never seen its like, she knew it at once: a sorcerer's shadow-gate. The child began to cry.

"Please, Tomás," she gasped. "Please don't. I beg you!"

He shook his head sadly. "You've left me no choice. The sorceress has promised to care for my little girl, to teach her how to love with an unbreakable love. What more could I desire for her than that?"

"I will teach her how to love. I will teach her so much better. Give her to me. Please."

Tomás looked down at the wailing child with an impassive, measured gaze. Then he shrugged, stepped forward, and placed her in Arrow's arms.

"Hush," said Arrow. "Hush, hush." But her voice shook, her arms shook, and the infant screamed louder.

Shaking his head in disgust, Tomás wrenched the child back from Arrow. "Look what you've done now. My poor little girl. She will be much better off in Glen Droighinn." Turning, he strode toward the shadow-gate.

"Wait," cried Arrow, rushing after him. Stumbling, she fell to the ground and clutched at one of his boots. Tomás kicked her in the face.

"Arrow!" shouted Wick. His voice sounded far away, as if it came from beneath deep water. But it caught Tomás's attention. He looked at Wick, then back at Arrow as she struggled to her feet, wiping blood from her mouth.

"Unless..." murmured Tomás. "There is one way for you to prove yourself, Arrow. Only one way."

"Anything, Tomás. I will do anything."

He paused, passing his hand over the baby's face; its cries ceased at once, and it fell into a deep sleep. As Tomás returned the infant to its basket, the shadow-gate faded behind him. Arrow's heart hammered with wild hope and wilder dread.

His dark eyes narrowed. "Anything?"

Reaching into his boot, Tomás drew out a knife. It was the same knife he had given her when she left Lipa, that had been lost in the river when she killed Marc. He placed it in her right hand. Then, gripping her shoulders, he turned her around until she faced Wick.

Watching at a short distance, the Wizard of Seven's eyes burned with anticipation; his hands clenched into fists as he strove to restrain his desire.

"Never," said Arrow.

"Then," said Tomás, "you are as selfish a bitch as I thought you were."

"It doesn't matter what you say; I cannot do that."

"You need not fear for your beloved. The sorceress will not allow him to remain dead for long. Before he even reaches the Unreachable Realm, she will bring him back to life. Alas, he will no longer be yours. But what a noble thing, Arrow, to sacrifice your selfish love for a selfless one. I'm sure Wick would gladly give you up to spare the infant if he were in your place; he was always a nobler soul than you."

Arrow looked at Wick, looked hard into his eyes. To her surprise, he seemed to be beckoning her forward. She took a step toward him, then another. Though the distance seemed interminable, in an instant she stood before him. All the while, she kept her eyes locked on his face. Then she realized he was humming the same song as before, so low that only she could hear. Arrow gave a tiny nod; he nodded in return.

She drew a deep breath. Then she raised the knife.

"End it," commanded the Wizard of Seven. "End the game now. We've all played long enough."

Suddenly Arrow dropped her hand. "I can't."

"Then I will kill you all!" he shrieked, no longer concealing his impatience. "And nurse the infant with your blood."

"Wait." Arrow was amazed at the command in her own voice as she stepped back, still holding the knife.

"I can't kill Wick, but I can end it all the same." She looked at the Wizard Dan, who was watching her intensely. "Let me kill the Wizard of Four instead."

Wick sprang back. "What! Arrow, how could you even think such a thing? For shame!"

Dan also staggered back. His face slackened in a look of shock and disbelief. Brother Agostin, still bound and gagged in webs, gave a muffled yelp.

Tomás frowned in confusion. "What?"

"I want to kill Dan," she repeated. "The effect will be the same."

"But Arrow," whispered Dan, "I saved your life. Four times."

"Arrow," shouted Wick. "I beg you not to do this. Kill me! Please, don't kill our friend. It would destroy us. How could I ever love you again?"

Arrow's eyes narrowed as she stared at Tomás. "You see?"

Tomás and the Wizard of Seven looked at each other. They looked at Wick. They looked back at Arrow.

"Yes," said Tomás. "You may kill the Wizard of Four."

"No, Arrow, please!" Wick yelled.

Dan stumbled backward, pleading in terrified gibberish.

Lifting his hand with a summoning gesture, the Wizard of Seven dragged Dan's body to the front of the cage and thrust it up against the bars. Arrow strode forward until she stood a few steps from her friend. Their eyes locked. All the while, Wick called out desperate protests.

"This is the only way," said Arrow. Her hand trembled so violently she almost lost her grip on the knife.

"The only way," hissed the Wizard of Seven in her ear, "or the infant is lost forever. Go, now!"

Arrow rushed up to the Wizard Dan, brandishing her knife. "Go, now!"

Dropping his show of fear, Dan reached through the bars of his cage and put his hand on the torc, his face blazing with triumph.

In the same moment, the Wizard of Seven and the sorceress realized their peril. Their hands shot out simultaneously. Arrow felt herself yanked back by the neck. The torc tightened. Hard, hot metal squeezed around her throat until it cut off her breath completely. Her hands flailed, clawing her neck, clawing the air her lungs couldn't reach. She dropped to the ground as her vision went red and her mind swam.

At the same time, the two iron bars between which Dan reached burst free of the cage, thrust him backward, and began to beat him as if wielded by invisible trolls. He crumpled, curling in a ball to shield himself, until a blow knocked him senseless. Then the iron bars returned to shore up the walls of his prison.

Arrow's chokehold released. Gasping, shuddering, she reached up a hand to beg for mercy. Wick hurled himself against the bars of his cage, beside himself with anguish and helplessness.

"Fools!" spat the Wizard of Seven, his mouth foaming in fury. "Clowns! You will pay for every such trick. When I have overcome the limitation of power, I will make you punish each other—and make you relish it!"

"Truly, sir," said Grell, who had dropped Tomás's shape in her alarm and blazed with fell beauty once more, "they deserve some commendation. All three sang their parts in such harmony they had us swaying to their tune. The gambit was well laid and well played. Nevertheless, it has failed."

Grasping Arrow by the hair and dragging her to her feet, the sorceress removed the torc from around Arrow's neck and secured it around her own.

"You were right, Arrow," she said. "That was the only way. You have risked all, and you have lost."

As she said this, the moon and stars seemed to blink out and vanish, leaving the tower in utter blackness except for a dull flicker from the torc's jewel and a dingy light quavering from Wick's cage. Wick froze, shrinking as if some great horror had fallen on him. Then he began to shiver. He closed his eyes.

"Wick?" whispered Arrow. She ran, stumbling with weariness, toward the cage. "Wick, what is it?"

But he seemed not to hear. One by one, faces appeared in the dull light surrounding him, gray figures trapped inside the cage with him. Marc, a knife sticking out of his bloody abdomen, groped through the bars calling the names of his children. Mundo pleaded for mercy as a firebird swooped down on him. Noemi cried out in deadly childbirth. Stone-faced Coira held up an arm to shield herself from the Wizard of Seven. Eloi Fernandes wept over his destroyed ship. A beautiful, dark-eyed woman who she knew was Iliana reached toward Wick, caressing his hair with hands like cold mist. Above them, Halla beat her wings bloody against the dome of her prison. Tomás staggered, battle-torn. Behind him were several hundred others: all the sailors who died in the Battle of the Firebirds, all the centaurs, all the citizens of the Buried Isle who died in Iliana's War. Those Arrow didn't recognize, she somehow knew. They were not a nameless crowd. Each person stood out as if he or she were the only ghost. Arrow could see their histories, their loves, their ruined hopes. Each of them, it seemed, had realized in the moment of death that they died in vain. Each of them blamed her, cursing her as they pressed close around Wick, hissing with hatred.

Wick shrank against the bars of the cage. The ghosts pawed at him as if they could steal handfuls of life from his warm flesh, grasping at his face and arms, pulling his clothing until it tore.

The stone around Grell's neck now flickered and spat with an angry glare as it strove in the summoning of this host greater than any the sorceress had yet conjured.

Stepping close behind Arrow, Grell whispered, "Are you worth it, Arrow?"

"No," she said.

"Is *he* worth it?"

Each time a ghost touched Wick, it seemed to sponge away a little of his color and his aliveness until he, too, seemed gray and faded, like a papery husk that has dropped its seed. He looked at her, but his eyes were empty.

"No," she said.

A burning sensation seized her left hand. Arrow looked down. Her wedding ring, braided of her own hair, scorched black and fell away. The smell of burning hair singed her nostrils. Wick clutched at his hand as his ring did the same. Any color that remained in him faded to gray; Arrow could almost see through him. His body trembled as if from bitter cold. Still, he kept his eyes on her face.

"Good," said Grell. A tongue of orange light snaked out from the gem, kindling the sorceress's black eyes. "Then end it. You always knew it would come to this."

Once more, the knife was in Arrow's hand.

The ghosts hushed to utter silence. Clinging to the bars of the cage and straining outward, they shut their mouths and stared at her. Wick didn't flee as she stepped up to the cage. He pressed against its bars, his mouth forming words she couldn't hear. Arrow lowered her face. "I'm sorry," she whispered. "I told you I would hurt you." Then she put her hand on his chest to find the place where his heart was. His chest was so cold it numbed her fingers. She could hardly find his heartbeat. The ghosts crowded close around him, breathless, hopeful.

But a shudder went through Wick at her touch. Closing his eyes, he lifted one of his hands and began to make strange motions in the air—sometimes slow, sometimes quick, first high, then low. The movement puzzled Arrow and she paused, her hand still on his heart. It wasn't any dance she knew. The ghosts, too, were puzzled, backing away from the motion as if threatened, though Wick took no notice of them. The slightest bit of color returned to his face. His movements grew larger, stronger.

Suddenly Arrow gasped. She knew what Wick was doing. He was taking his toy reindeer and dancing it through the cage, because it was the warmest thing he had. At the thought, a rush of warmth gushed out from her own heart. Now she could feel Wick's heartbeat, sure and true, against her palm. He opened his eyes.

They looked at each other.

Then they turned to the ghosts, who shrank back, hissing and spitting. Arrow searched their gray, hollow faces. Her eyes locked with the ghost that was Coira.

Name us, the voices had said.

"Rina," she said in a loud, firm voice. "I name you Rina."

It was like the way the Wizard Dan described doing his first impossible thing. She started doing it before she thought of it. She didn't even know what she was doing until she'd done it.

Though Coira-Rina didn't grow furry, pointed ears, a silver plume of a tail, or wolf-sharp teeth, something else happened. Color flooded her face as she drew a deep breath. This color grew brighter and brighter until it was light itself, so vivid and warm its rays poured out through the bars of the cage and lit up every flagstone of the battlement. She smiled.

Arrow turned to the ghost of Mundo. "Lanky."

She turned to the ghost of Eloi Fernandes. "Spanky."

They, too, flooded with color as they breathed deeply; the two men started laughing and clapped each other on the back the way sailors do. Light dazzled and sparked from them like a show of fireworks.

"What are you doing?" seethed Grell. "Stop this at once!" Gripping Arrow by the back of her neck, she wrenched her away from Wick and hurled her backward. Arrow dropped the knife.

But Wick took up what she'd begun. "Manky," he called, pointing at Marc. "Windy," he named Kobi. "Sunny," he named Kemawi. "Greenie. Pellow. Nika."

Each time he gave a ghost one of their children's names, it flooded with color and light.

Grell gave a shriek of alarm, releasing her hold on Arrow. Turning, Arrow saw that the stone in the center of the torc around Grell's neck had grown dazzlingly bright. Rays of orange light burst from it. Whenever Wick named a ghost, a new ray shot out from the gem, all of them aimed at the Wizard of Seven like spears of light. The blaze staggered Grell backward and she clutched at the kindled jewel as if to shield herself from it. Her own summoning spell was turning against her.

As the stone's rays pierced the wizard, a fathomless black shadow spread out from him, not just behind but all around him. It was dark in the way the shadow-gate was dark: a hollow opening into a void, a nothingness. A namelessness. This shadow swallowed him until he could hardly be seen in the midst of it. Though he contorted his seven-fingered hands toward the light-ghosts, their radiance repelled his darkness as oilcloth sheds water. His magic had no effect. Cursing, the wizard glanced from the radiant cage to the blazing torc.

"What have you done?" he raged at the sorceress. "Remove these phantoms at once—unsummon them!"

But Grell paid him no heed. Convulsing, she bit her red lip until it streamed redder blood. Though she clawed frantically at the torc, it remained solid metal; she no longer had power over it. "Take it off!" she gasped. "Help me, you fool. It burns me!"

Arrow turned back toward the cage.

"Flicker," she named Tomás.

"Jewel," Wick named Noemi.

As Noemi and Tomás blazed to life, they seized each other in a joyous embrace. Then they beamed at Arrow as they took each other's hands.

"Remmy," called Wick, putting his hand on Iliana's gray face and watching radiance stream through it.

"Rainbow Sky," called Arrow up at Halla, whose wings burst into fountains of many-colored light that flowed from the sides of the tower and streamed down the hill.

With a strangled cry, Grell dropped to her knees. The jewel in the torc swirled with a hurricane of rainbow-colored light. Smoke rose from it. Red scorch marks spread across Grell's milk-white skin.

As if groping his way through the thick shadow that enveloped him, the Wizard of Seven stretched out his hand toward Arrow, but she pressed close to the bars of the cage. The ghosts swarmed behind her with their hands on her head and shoulders, forming a shield of light.

The Wizard Dan groaned softly as he regained consciousness, blinking against the brightness that rushed over him. Brother Agostin's net of webs melted away and he crawled to Dan's aid as the Wizard of Four began dragging himself toward the edge of his cage.

All of Wick's cage now glowed as if a star had landed atop the old watchtower. As Arrow's eyes became accustomed to its light, she saw that the space behind the brilliant ghosts was vast and wild, a tumult of mountains and sea and forest. Niora the mermaid waved at her from the distance. The blue banner with the golden arrow danced above the sunrise palace. If only Arrow could get through the cage's iron bars, she could escape where her enemies could never follow.

"Wick," she cried. "Let me in! How can I get in? And how can I bring the others?"

"No, Arrow," he shouted back as sparks rained and sizzled about him. "Not let you in—let them out!"

The wizard and the sorceress looked at each other. Fear flashed between their gazes. Then, fighting her agony, Grell began to summon the shadow-gate. The Wizard of Seven sprang forward and picked up the infant in its basket.

For the first time, Noemi and Tomás saw their daughter. All the light in them turned to blazing wrath. Opening his mouth, Tomás-Flicker roared a stream of dragon-fire. In the furnace of his breath, the iron bars of the cage grew red-hot, then white.

"Hurry, witch!" the Wizard of Seven shrieked at Grell, for the shadow-gate was only half-formed, the shadow of a shadow. In his rage, he struck her. She turned on him, claws to his face. At the same time, fingers of fire shot out from the torc's stone and wrapped around his throat. To shield himself, the wizard dropped the basket with the infant still inside.

Tomás's dragon flame surged brighter. The bars of the cage melted away, forming a door.

Wick and Arrow's children rushed out in a stream of brightness. Halla and the centaurs flew at the Wizard of Seven, who gathered the darkness around him into missiles of shadow and hurled these at the light-ghosts. Tomás and Coira went straight for the sorceress. The others swarmed behind. Noemi sped to her baby, but alas! She had no flesh that could lift a living child and carry it to safety.

Her eyes filled with glimmering tears, Noemi turned to Arrow. "Help her, please."

Darting forward, Arrow snatched up the infant, dodging the rain of shadow-stones that were crashing in every direction. Wick raced after her, throwing his arm around her as a shield. Many missiles struck them; they staggered.

The Wizard of Seven managed to form a dark barricade around himself. Seeming to think that if he could destroy the humans, the ghosts might lose their power, he trained his attention on Wick and Arrow. Under the onslaught, he couldn't focus his strength enough to turn them into chestnuts, but he managed to lift a fallen stone pillar that lay near him and hurtle it at their heads. Noemi sprang in the pillar's path and put up her hand; a bolt of lightning shot out from her palm and the pillar shattered.

But a chunk of stone struck Wick's head. He dropped to the ground, unmoving.

"Wick!" screamed Arrow.

Iliana ran forward, throwing herself over Wick's body. A host of others formed a burning wall around the humans as debris rained down.

Meanwhile, Coira stood in front of her former mistress. Grell writhed in pain, clawing at the tortuous brightness around her neck. The look in Coira's eyes was almost one of pity, but not quite.

"Now you understand," said Coira, "why I said I should fear to touch him."

And she put her hand on Grell's heart.

A strangled cry ripped from the sorceress's throat as the jewel around her neck burst into white flame. Everyone froze in horror, even the Wizard of Seven. Wick groaned and opened his eyes.

"Take it away!" Grell screamed. "Take it away! Set me free!"

And she began to run.

"Stop!" bellowed the Wizard of Seven. He tried to run after her, but the ghosts throbbed in a pulsing mass behind her, goading her onward. Frida the Otter snapped at her heels with fiery teeth. Halla spread her rainbow wings to block the wizard's path while Tomás breathed a stream of fire to thrust him backward.

The sorceress rushed up to the cage where Brother Agostin was lifting the Wizard Dan to his feet. Clasping the bars of the cage, she pressed her face close.

"Please," she gasped. "Take it away."

So Dan put his hand on the burning stone in the center of the golden torc.

"Speak me your name," he said.

The stone spoke in the new tongue Dan had given it, blinding them all with arrows of red light. Escaping its prison, the Wizard of Seven's name sang from the tower, clear and warm as a horn on a mountain.

The Wizard of Seven gave one shrill shriek, then dissolved into a heap of ash.

"Thank you," whispered Grell, bowing her head. And she was no longer a sorceress but a shriveled corpse, and then she was nothing but a heap of dried thorns.

As Wick struggled to his feet, the cages melted away. Brother Agostin rushed to Arrow, half-carrying the Wizard Dan. Though he couldn't stand, Dan held up his hands with a huge grin, wiggling all ten fingers.

Then the crowd of ghosts looked, suddenly, toward the east. Wick and Arrow looked, too, but they saw nothing. A soft, sighing wind swept over the tower. One by one, the light-ghosts shivered and disappeared like candles blown out.

Heaving a deeply drawn yet diminutive sigh, the baby went to sleep.

"What will we call her?" said Arrow.

"How about... Fairy Eyes."

"Or... Apple Dumpling."

"Or Cub-Chick."

"Or Little Lady Linden."

They were in the porter's cottage at the monastery, the baby bundled in her blanket on Arrow's fox pelt before the fireplace. Wick and Arrow sat one on each side of her. Wick's head was bandaged. The Wizard Dan lay in a bed in the corner as Brother Agostin tended to his many wounds.

Arrow stuck out her pinky; the baby curled its fingers around it. "Look at her fingernails, Wick. How are we supposed to cut them?"

"Look at the dip in her upper lip."

"Could we call her... Halla?"

"Halla! Name her after a griffin?"

"A griffin with a magnificent heart. Loyal and brave and free. Always seeking."

"Alright," laughed Wick. Then he gasped. "Oh no, Arrow!"

"What?"

"We don't have last names. What will her last name be?"

"I didn't think of that! What about... Dan."

"Dan?"

"What's wrong with Dan?"

"The Dan Family."

"Wick Dan, Arrow Dan, Halla Dan, and the Wizard Dan."

They watched Halla sleep.

"Will we tell her, Wick?"

"Someday. When she's old enough. We'll have to tell it in just the right way."

"In a song, maybe."

"We'll sing her so many songs, Arrow."

"Where will we live?"

"What about Anatolia?"

"I was thinking that. But not on the mountain. In that little village by the sea, with the mountain standing guard behind."

"We'll take her to The Refuge once a year to see the fairies."

"On her birthday."

They muffled their laughs, trying not to wake her.

Then Arrow took Wick's hand. "You know it's only pretend, Wick?" she said softly. "She's not ours; we must return her to her family—what family she has left."

He nodded, swallowing. "I know. Unless... they let us keep her? Once they see how much we love her."

She put her hand to his lips. "Don't even say it. There are so many *ifs*. If Ona agrees. If Tomás's family agrees. If my deed of saving her can win pardon for my crime of burning the ship. If we can make a real home. If we can teach her how to be human, when there's so much we never learned."

Halla opened her eyes.

Dropping onto their stomachs, Wick and Arrow put their faces together right above the baby's. She had Tomás's dark, serious eyes and Noemi's long lashes. She looked and looked.

"No matter what happens," said Wick, "she's still ours. In Arrow's World, she belongs to us and always will. In our language, her name will always be Halla."

"Wick," said Arrow, "have you ever thought that the heart can love everything at once?"

"Oh Arrow," he whispered, "see how beautiful we are when we grow up."

Many thanks to everyone who walked with me along the slowly unfolding path of Arrow's journey, especially my family, Erika, Fr. Jon, Rose, Katy, Sam V., Sam P., Olivia, Bernadette O., and Hannah W. Thank you to the Passionist Nuns of Whitesville for taking such good care of me in your guest house while I wrote Part I. Thank you to Hannah R., Meg, and Danny for the beautiful book design, as well as your enthusiasm. Thank you to Sarah for all your publishing wisdom.

I am also indebted to Jacques Maritain for his book Creative Intuition in Art and Poetry. I encountered Maritain's philosophy of the artist just as this story was conceived. "Poetry," he says, "...proceeds from the totality of man, sense, imagination, intellect, love, desire, instinct, blood and spirit together. And the first obligation imposed on the poet is to consent to be brought back to the hidden place, near the center of the soul, where this totality exists in a state of creative source." In writing Wick and Arrow's story, I have striven to be faithful to this obligation—to consent to be brought back to the hidden source—first for my own sake, then for theirs.

—Mary Shaffer

www.ingramcontent.com/pod-product-compliance
Lightning Source LLC
Chambersburg PA
CBHW020911310726
48980CB00011B/840/J

* 9 7 9 8 9 9 8 6 1 3 6 2 3 *